Praise for The Emperor's Son

"Vamba Sherif's, *The Emperor's Son* is a captivating [illegible] about tumultuous wars and doomed alliances that is as rich in fervor as it is imaginative in reconstructing the adventurous life and times of the fabled Mande emperor, Samori Touré. In this beautifully wrought book, Sherif creates characters—imbued with the full range of human strengths and failings—who inhabit and take us along on heart-stopping journeys of life and death."

– **Momoh Sekou Dudu**, author of *Harrowing December: Recounting a Journey of Sorrows and Triumphs*

"*The Emperor's Son* is a bold, richly imagined and ambitious piece of historical fiction, drawing on a number of fascinating factual events to produce an evocative portrayal of a vibrant, prosperous West African empire in the nineteenth century at the cusp of the French and English colonial invasions. The region's cultures, traditions and their economic and political civilizations are powerfully rendered through clear themes of war, love, loss, family, identity, abandonment and sacrifice, while the life and exploits of the protagonist provide a compelling central focus for the plot. The women, particularly Ma-Sona, Massah, Sarankenyi and Naminata were a strong force and they, along with Demba and Talata were memorable characters amongst a diverse and colorful cast.

– **Vimbai Shire**, Editor

THE EMPEROR'S SON

THE EMPEROR'S SON

VAMBA SHERIF

ISKANCHI
PRESS AND MAG

Published in 2023 by Iskanchi Press
info@iskanchi.com
https://iskanchi.com/

ISBN: 978-1-957810-10-2

Cover art: Olajide Ajayi (@LA_Draws)
Cover design: Akeem Ibrahim

Printed in the United States of America

I have come out of that landscape, that forest, that mud, that silence, to roam, to go singing through the world.

Pablo Neruda

For my brother Vamadu Sherif who showed
me the depth of his humanity.
You are my inspiration!
For the historian and Samorian scholar
Yves Person who lit the fire.
For Sembene Ousmane, the novelist and father
of African cinema, who kept the fire burning.
For Isaac Bashevis Singer who showed me the way.
And for Liberian novelist Wilton Sankawulo
who gave me Zaiwulo.

The Haidarah Household

Talata	Scholar, teacher, and head of the Haidarah household
Zaiwulo	Protagonist, Talata's student
Demba	Talata's assistant and friend
Soko Kenneh	Talata's best friend
Sona	Talata's wife
Osman	Talata's eldest son and Samori's envoy to the English in Freetown, Sierra Leone, and England
Karamo	Talata's second son
Massah	Talata's best friend's daughter
Foningama	Talata's father-in-law (Sona's father)
Naminata	Foningama's youngest wife
Benjamin Anderson	Americo-Liberian, visitor to Musadu in 1865, and author of *Narrative of the Journey to Musardu* (1870)

Samori's World

Samori	Trader, king, conqueror, emperor
Sarankenyi	Samori's favorite wife
Morifin-Djan Diabate	Samori's griot (Djeli) and childhood best friend
Kemeh-Brimah	Samori's favorite brother

Kemoko-Bilali	Samori's friend and one of his generals
Porokerrie	Samori's friend and one of his generals
Sarankenyi-Mori	Samori's son by his favorite wife, Sarankenyi
Jawulen-Karamoko	Samori's favorite son and envoy to the French
Jawulen-N'nagbe	Samori's daughter, married to Karamo-Sidikie
Karamo-Sidikie	Talata's brother, Samori's son-in-law
Prempeh the First	Samori's ally, king of the Ashanti people
Sere-Brimah	Samori's adversary who enslaved his mother
Gbanguno Saaye	Samori's adversary, Saaye of the Gbanguno Mountain
Tieba of Sikasso	Samori's adversary, builder of the famous Tata (wall)
Marie Étienne Peroz	French commander and Samori's adversary
Louis Archinard	French commander and Samori's adversary
George Garrett	British envoy to Samori
Queen Victoria	Queen of the United Kingdom of Great Britain and Ireland
Jules Grévy	President of the French Third Republic

Samori's Empire

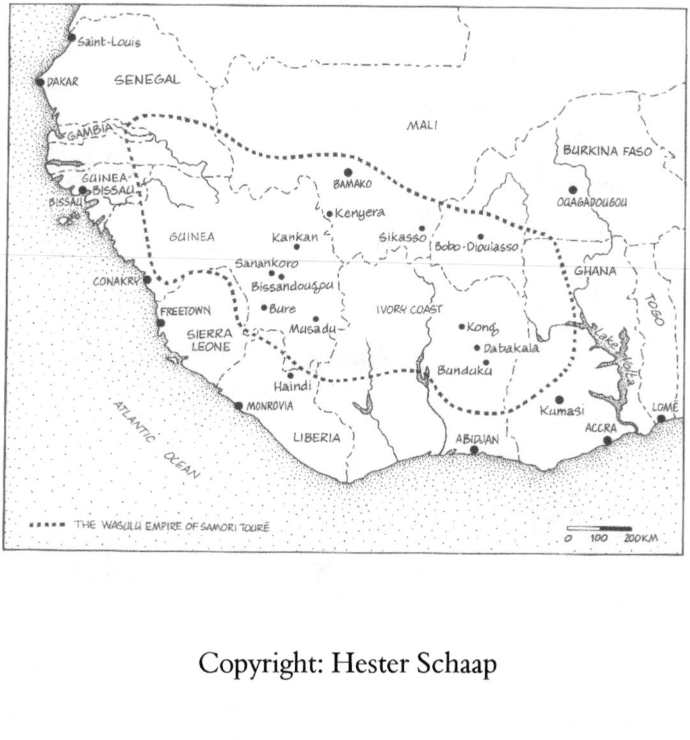

Part One

BELONGING

1875

1

There was nothing remarkable about Zaiwulo to suggest the kind of man he would become. The boy, who would turn thirteen that year, was carrying a tree sapling with him when he arrived Musadu in Koniyan. He was wearing a short tunic and amulets around his neck and biceps. His hair was closely cropped, and at his tender age, he walked with a stoop.

Though the dry season had ended, a wave of heat swept over him as he made his way down the hill to catch up with his father who was walking ahead and had almost reached the river. The land around Zaiwulo was a lush green and yellow grass dotted with anthills and tree stumps. The verdant grass was bare of the trees and huge mountains of the land of his birth. From where he was on the hill, he could see Musadu beyond the river, shielded by walls unlike any he had ever seen before.

The earthy, sharp smell of the savannah filled his nose, and as he watched from the hilltop, a horse appeared in the distance, then came the sound of jangling bells alongside hoofbeats. The animal looked to be without a rider, but as it bore down on Zaiwulo, closer and closer, as if intent on running him over, the boy noticed a man astride the horse. Except for a few tufts of hair, the rider was bald and rode barefoot on the steed which was adorned with bells.

The horseman spurred his ride toward Zaiwulo, and the horse, teeth bared, snatched the tree sapling from the youth who screamed so loud that the animal let go of the sapling and reared back in agitation. The rider tugged sharply at the reigns and strained to calm the horse.

Zaiwulo picked up his treasure and hugged it tightly to his chest, as though it were a living being. It was a flame tree sapling yet to blossom into full orange-red leaves.

The rider looked down at Zaiwulo, surprised at the boy's courage, for he was a man used to people fleeing at the mere sight of him.

"What does the tree mean to you, child?" he asked in Mandé.

The language was a variation of Kpelle, Zaiwulo's native language. For reasons unknown to him, his father had insisted that he learn to speak Mandé since childhood.

By then, Zaiwulo's father had run back to join them. He angrily shoved his son aside and faced the horseman with a broad smile.

"We are not from this part of the world," he said in a quavering voice. "We are from the forest. And my son —"

"My mother was one of your people," the horseman said, his eyes still fixed on Zaiwulo, as if appraising him. After a few moments, as though it were an afterthought, the horseman added: "For many years now, I've been fighting in Samori's army."

On hearing Samori's name, Zaiwulo's father threw himself before the horse and rider. Zaiwulo had never seen his father prostrate before any man, not even a king. To conceal his confusion and his inability to explain the gesture, he did the same.

The horse nuzzled against Zaiwulo's neck; its tongue moved across his skin in a sustained caress that made the horseman laugh.

"You are a peculiar child," he said, and with a click of his tongue, he prodded his ride down the road, toward the river and was gone.

Father and son did not move, not even after the sound of hoofbeats faded in the distance. They only rose to their feet when they were sure they were alone. As though imparting a terrible secret to his son, the father said, "that one is a sofa—a horse father. They are warriors who regard their horses as human beings and consider themselves their guardians. Beware of them."

Before they departed from his home in the forest, Zaiwulo could sense the tears his mother and sisters were concealing as they hugged him. Their effusiveness bothered him, but his father's behavior had been even more troubling. The man had thrown a sack of their belongings onto his back and beckoned for Zaiwulo to follow him. And that was how they left Haindi. The father's protracted silences and his refusal to take his son into his confidence had marked their journey. It unnerved Zaiwulo.

Now, Zaiwulo bundled up his courage. "Why are we here, Father?" he asked.

"Come," the man said, ignoring the boy's question and walking on towards the river.

The boy did not move.

The father finally replied, his back still to his son, "To see the greatest scholar in this part of the world. People come from far and near to seek his counsel."

They were at the Jon River, a tributary of the great Niger River flowing alongside the walls of Musadu. The river had recently burst its banks and had spread across the main road like a hasty conqueror, swallowing up a huge swath of land.

Zaiwulo leaned over and cupped palmfuls of water to quench his thirst. He soaked the tree sapling in the water as he had done every time they had stopped along the way. Zaiwulo could not swim, so he watched as his father waded through the river with astonishing ease.

Once the older man was on the other side, he called to his son and said, "What awaits you across the river will prove much more daunting than your fear of swimming. So swim."

Zaiwulo inched forward, deeper into the river. Water rose to his neck, but for fear of his father's outburst, he stifled his anxiety. The current tugged harder as the water invaded his mouth, his throat, and nose. In panic, he began to beat against the current with his feet and right hand, a forlorn attempt since he refused to let go of the tree sapling in his left hand. Just as he was about to go under, a wall of mist emerged from the depths of the river and then parted slowly to reveal a woman. His mother. The apparition held her hand out to him and Zaiwulo grabbed the hand in desperation. Slowly, she led him—sapling and all—to safety before vanishing.

Zaiwulo stood for a while to consider what had just happened, and when the tears came, he let them flow, his body rocking in gratitude to his mother. Suddenly, the ochre earth upon which he stood, the butterflies, and the green-yellow hues of the savannah grass looked more radiant than ever. He was alive.

As he rushed after his father, it occurred to him that perhaps he had imagined it all, that it was his efforts that had saved him. For how could a mother he had left behind a few weeks ago materialize and rescue him from drowning?

He was breathing hard when he caught up with his father at the fortified gate that formed part of the great walls of the city.

•×•

One of the sentries clad in baggy trousers and a short tunic pointed his Dane rifle at Zaiwulo's father and said, "What brings you here?"

"We are guests of the great Talata Haidarah," the father said.

"Show me your belongings," the sentry said.

Zaiwulo's father set the sack with their belongings before the sentry.

"I hope for your sake that you are not carrying weapons," the sentry said as he searched the bag. He pulled out a small, sharp machete. "What is this?" he asked, hefting the knife and wielding it around.

"I use it to peel fruits and cut my way through difficult paths in the bush," the boy's father replied.

The sentry weighed the words and nodded. "Please forgive us," he said. "These are uncertain times. A while ago, a sofa came along claiming that he was a guest of Talata Haidarah. We still took all his weapons before allowing him in. Anyone who comes to visit our great scholar is welcome in Musadu."

Zaiwulo regarded the huge walls. They were constructed from long poles, mud, and grass. Buzzards were perched on their parapets, as though waiting for a moment that would send them into a frenzy. Enthralled by the edifice in front of him, he did not move for a while.

"Come," his father said.

Father and son walked through the gate.

Musadu overwhelmed Zaiwulo with the noise of its marketplace, a crowded jumble of shacks and stalls that stretched along both sides of the main road. The boy and his father moved past stalls, behind which stood men in fine embroidered gowns with gold and silver jewelry spread on red fabric. The customers were trying on bangles and necklaces with leaf-shaped pendants. The gold earrings were round like cowries and so heavy that they were held onto the ears by red threads that the women tied around their heads. A girl with a large bowl of *monnie* on her head praised the delicate sweetness of the rice porridge as she hurried past Zaiwulo. Other women called out to passersby about wares that consisted of dried cassava, vegetables, and greens. The boy followed his father with a slack pace through a narrow path with stalls displaying fine clothes he would learn later were imported from Kankan, Fouta Djallon, and the Toucouleur kingdoms. His heart swelled when he saw a group of women selling kola nuts, the most treasured goods from his part of the world. These were stimulants believed to restore youth to the aged, but which, he would come to know, were primarily used in the savannah to dye clothes into indigo or scarlet colors. At the edge of the market, after pushing their way through a throng of people, Zaiwulo and his father emerged into a large square teeming with men trading in the most precious commodity of all: arms and ammunition.

This must be the city center, the boy thought. He could see students and scholars gathered around hearths before homes around the square, chanting solemnly in a language unfamiliar to him. He followed his father along the largest thoroughfare, and although the pungent smell of cow and horse manure pervaded the city air, the homes were neat and the stables studded with spirited horses that reminded

Zaiwulo of the horse and rider he had encountered at the river. The boy was fascinated by the build, elegance, and beauty of those animals. He dreamed that he would ride and own a horse one day. Perhaps, he thought, he would even become a horse father.

Father and son veered off the main road and took a small path that led to the entrance of a walled compound. The wall covered the length of the road, suggesting the influence and wealth of those who lived within its confines. Zaiwulo saw a group of men sitting outside the wall, all attired in scarlet as well as black-and-white tunics.

"We are here to see Haidarah," his father said.

"You will find him in the smallest house beyond the hearths," said one of the men.

Zaiwulo's father thanked the men and led the way through the wall. The homes stood around a large courtyard with a set of three hearths, beyond which was Talata's study.

The boy rested his tree sapling against the wall and followed his father into a room crowded with manuscripts and wooden slates.

Tall and slender with a light-brown complexion, Talata Haidarah exuded a rare grandeur in his white brocaded gown and red cap bordered by a white band of cloth. Zaiwulo would learn later that the band was the symbol of Haidarah's importance as a scholar. The host's gestures, even the slightest ones, had a cultivated and refined air about them. He seemed the exact opposite of the rugged man sitting next to him, a man who looked familiar. It was the horseman Zaiwulo and his father had met earlier. The boy could not see his father's face, but he noticed how his father stiffened.

"Haidarah, I came as promised," Zaiwulo's father said, after exchanging a lengthy greeting with the two other men in the room.

"I met the child near the river, Haidarah," said the horseman. "He was so brave."

Talata Haidarah did not respond. His pursed lips and furrowed brow made Zaiwulo wonder whether he was upset.

"The child will make a fine sofa," the horseman said and stood. On his way out, he said, "Please consider what we discussed, Haidarah." Then he winked at Zaiwulo. "One day, I will return for you."

Zaiwulo turned his attention to the manuscripts piled to the ceiling. The wooden writing slates were arranged in corners of the study. Beyond the manuscripts and writing slates was a black curtain, from behind which wafted the scent of incense. The mysterious fragrance, the unfamiliar setting, and the infectious stare of his host, which shifted from his father and settled on him, heightened Zaiwulo's unease.

Zaiwulo's father leaned forward, eyes lowered. "Here is the child, Haidarah," he said, his voice trailing off into a whisper.

Talata nodded, thanked Zaiwulo's father, and stood up. He moved to the door, and in answer to his call, a boy appeared. "This is my oldest son Osman," the scholar said. "Osman, these are our guests from the forest. Please take them to their lodgings."

Zaiwulo and his father followed Osman. He was the spitting image of his father: they shared the same earth-brown skin, the same build, and height. Zaiwulo, inclined to make friends, smiled at him, but Osman either did not notice the gesture or chose to ignore it. He merely turned now and then to glance at the tree in Zaiwulo's hand.

On reaching the lodgings, Zaiwulo opened his mouth to say something to Osman, but the latter sucked his teeth and strutted away. As he watched Osman turn a bend, disappearing behind one of the houses, Zaiwulo felt a deep dislike for him.

2

The lodgings were at the far end of the courtyard, close to the back wall of the Haidarah compound. An old rainwater container made from clay stood to the right side of the house. The house's roof had been mended with fresh thatch.

The bed where Zaiwulo's father would sleep was a rectangular-shaped structure molded from mud. The boy shivered as he turned to the ceiling decorated with amulets; even in that secluded space, he was careful not to do or say anything that could offend his host, for stories abounded regarding the power of men like Talata. Men like him were believed to perform inexplicable miracles. Mountains disappeared at their whim, rain fell at their behest, enemies were vanquished, and barren women conceived by the power of their prayer beads.

Zaiwulo placed the tree sapling on the floor next to his sleeping mat, near the spot where his head would rest. Not for a while had the child felt as close to something as he did to the tree at that moment. Now that its leaves had withered, it could have been any tree, but it seemed to bear the loss with a dignity that touched Zaiwulo. He caressed the tree trunk and its branches.

It was cool in the house. The thatched roof offered protection from the heat. Through the spaces between the roof and the wall, sunlight poured in, creating intricate patterns on the floor from which Zaiwulo tried to discern a message regarding what he had experienced at the river. Had he really seen his mother, or had he dreamed it all?

His father's continued silence unsettled him, and prompted by his unease about his mother he made up his mind to speak.

"Father," he began, "I saw Mother today."

"Where?"

"At the river. She saved me from drowning."

Zaiwulo felt his father's burning eyes on him; and fearing that the man would pounce on him, he lowered his head.

"I can't remember you ever lying to me, Zaiwulo, so don't try to do so now. Tell me exactly what happened."

Breathless and stuttering, Zaiwulo recounted his experience at the river. As he spoke, his father's face contorted, and then the man began to cry. "Your mother," was all his father could say as he sobbed, "your mother!"

Zaiwulo's father left the house shortly after.

3

As Zaiwulo sat on the bed waiting for his father, his mind conjured scenarios to explain his father's strange behavior. The tears baffled him. He had never seen his father so vulnerable. Had something happened to his mother, or was his own life in grave danger? The house felt small, unable to contain his fear, so he rushed to the door to escape the stifling silence and the growing sense of displacement. However, fearing his father's reaction, he retreated and returned to the bed but immediately stood up again. As he paced around the room, it occurred to him that his father might have abandoned him.

He was in the throes of terrible anguish when, after what seemed like an eternity, his father returned. His face was cal nowm, without the terror and sadness he'd left with.

"I went to see Haidarah," his father explained. "I thought your mother had passed on, and that it was her spirit that had rescued you from the river. But don't worry, Haidarah looked into the matter and assured me that she's alive."

Zaiwulo moved to hug his father, but his father turned away and laid on the bed. The boy waited until his father was snoring away his weariness before sneaking out of the house to acquaint himself with the compound.

It was sizzling with activity. Around him, people were splitting firewood, weaving cloth, and shelling groundnuts. Others swept the compound with huge brooms. Zaiwulo came upon a heap of pots and pans piled to dry on wooden crates. In one of the courtyards, in front of the largest house in the compound, which he presumed belonged to his host, were three huge hearths still burning. Dozens of writing slates covered with strange symbols rested against rocks encircling the hearths.

Zaiwulo thought he heard the pounding of pestles in mortars, so he walked in the direction of the sound. It was somewhere in the compound. After some minutes of meandering under alcoves and through pockets of activity, the child stumbled on more than two dozen women pounding dried cassava the same way his mother and sisters pounded food in Haindi.

"Come here," one of them said.

She was heavy with child and had pronounced features, especially her nose, which sat proudly atop her plump well-formed lips. She wore a loose black-and-white head-tie that revealed parts of her intricately plaited hair. A mischievous smile danced across her sweaty face. Around her, chickens pecked at crumbs on the ground. Her arms were covered with white powder from the cassava she was pounding. Even before she introduced herself, Zaiwulo knew that she was his hostess.

He stuttered as he greeted her.

She burst into hearty laughter. "I cannot understand why men lose their tongues in our presence!"

Her words were meant to cheer him up, but they only added to his embarrassment. It did not help that the other women burst into laughter. The women were all young, including his hostess who could not have been older than his own mother. In their laughter, he discerned mockery. Perhaps, he reasoned, it was their way of making him feel at ease.

The faint but persistent smell of incense filled the air, and with it came a familiar voice. "Sona, don't tease our guest."

Zaiwulo turned to see Talata. The warmth he exuded seemed to enfold everyone around him, including Zaiwulo who relaxed in his presence.

"Guest or no guest, that's not how a man is supposed to look at a woman, Haidarah," Sona said. "Those eyes!"

"He will learn," Talata said.

"I hope so. If not, he will get into trouble soon."

The women laughed. Sona went back to pounding with such vehemence that her husband pleaded, "Think of the child, Sona!"

She ignored him.

Her mercurial behavior during this pregnancy confounded and worried Talata. The good news had come as a pleasant surprise to both of them many years after the birth of their second child. During their marriage, Talata had hoped his home would be filled with at least a dozen of his own children, but as his two sons grew and Sona did not get pregnant, such a possibility grew increasingly remote. The situation could perhaps have been bearable had he been left alone, but Talata had learned that no one was ever left alone in this world.

Proposals had continued to pour in from reputable scholars willing to give one of their daughters to him as a wife. It was argued that a man of his stature should not confine himself to a single woman but must fill his household with dozens of them. To them, it was not a matter of satisfying those women—carnal or otherwise—but of prestige: the larger the household, the more impressive the scholar's reputation. Talata had reminded them that his household was the largest in Musadu, except for the king's. It included his many students and their families, his wife's apprentices and servants, and their other relatives and their families. The household had grown so large that many feared that sooner or later, his ambition might exceed his role as a mere scholar and he might entertain the idea of taking the king's place as Musadu's ruler.

•×•

Until her latest pregnancy, Sona had run the household with an efficiency bordering on despotic. She was up before everyone and was at ease with most, but she could be ruthless when required. Now, she was often at odds with her husband. One moment she was at her most amiable. The next moment, she was hurling harsh comments at him, sometimes, even in the presence of his followers.

Talata attempted to say something appropriate now, a remark to smooth over their differences and calm her, as he was used to doing, but once again he retreated in the face of her temper and left the courtyard.

Zaiwulo used that moment to escape to a less crowded part of the compound, a place at the edge of a slope.

A boy was sitting under a tree's shade reading a manuscript. He was as dark as Zaiwulo's hostess, Sona, and had the same broad face, build, and height.

"You must be new here," the boy said.

Zaiwulo nodded and told the boy his name.

"Come, sit down," the boy said, patting a space beside him. "What brings you here?"

Zaiwulo was silent. He did not know.

"Are you here for the ceremony?"

"What ceremony?" Zaiwulo asked.

"The biggest of them all," the boy replied. "I am not prepared for it at all. While everyone is looking forward to it, I want to escape it."

Zaiwulo didn't know what to say.

"Here I am burdening you with my problems. Tell me about yourself. Where are you from?"

"Karamo, why are you talking to this idiot?" a voice hissed before Zaiwulo could answer. Osman, the boy who had sucked his teeth at Zaiwulo earlier, had come up behind them. He spat on the ground. "Don't you know where he comes from?"

"What do you mean, elder brother?" asked Karamo.

"Those forest people," sneered Osman. "They don't even read or write. They live in absolute darkness. Did you know they are also cannibals?"

Zaiwulo jumped up, aghast at Osman's words.

"Elder brother, don't judge a person before getting to know him. He might turn out to be better than you are," Karamo said.

"Are you joking?" Osman retorted. "We are going to deliver him out of the darkness. We will even give him a new name because his name is as backward as where he comes from."

Zaiwulo rushed towards Osman, ready to fight, for he would not allow anyone to insult him. Not now and not ever.

"No, Zaiwulo," a familiar voice interrupted. It was Talata, again. "Osman, your behavior towards our guest is unworthy of this house."

The scholar had come to his rescue for the second time that day, which left Zaiwulo wondering what it all meant.

"Where's your father?" Talata asked.

"He's resting, Haidarah."

"Come with me. I have some business to attend to before the ceremony."

4

On the way to the city center, Talata was showered with praises at every turn. The young and the old celebrated his deeds. Zaiwulo saw people bowing and greeting his host.

"Haidarah, we can't wait to attend your great lectures during the ceremony," an old man said.

Soon, a crowd assembled around Talata. The admirers' intrusive presence bothered Zaiwulo, especially as they shoved him aside. Each person was anxious to come closer to Talata so that they could touch him or the hem of his gown.

"You will, once again, astound us with your knowledge," another man said. "Koniyan is fortunate to have you. The world is fortunate."

"The ceremony will once and for all establish your reputation as the greatest scholar in all of Koniyan and beyond," another man said.

Talata tried to wave them off. "I'm in a hurry. I have to prepare for the ceremony." But they ignored him.

One of them, a man in a long scarlet garment, pursued Talata. "You are a Haidarah," the man sang. "Son of Saleyah, son of Ayouba, son of Sekou, son of Vamadu." He went on naming Talata's ancestors from different centuries in a long chain, each one more illustrious than the one before. The crowd echoed the names over and over, chanting them like a hymn, their voices rising in pitch every time an ancestor was named.

The man attributed Musadu and Koniyan's prosperity to the power of Talata's prayer beads. "You are the truest scholar in all the lands of the black-skinned people, the one worthy of bearing the mantle of knowledge bequeathed to you by your ancestors. So, be proud."

The spectacle made Zaiwulo think of kings believed to live in the forest, who breathed fire, slept on beds of human skulls, danced at night with spirits, and copulated with them, often producing children who were not of this world or the next and so never died.

Only when the man in scarlet turned to face him did Zaiwulo realize that he was blind. The boy was struck by the agility with which the blind man carried himself. His handsome face, which poured with sweat, seemed to overshadow his dead eyes.

"Demba, that's enough," Talata said. "Go home and take care of things in my stead. I'm on my way to see my father-in-law."

"Your time has come, Haidarah," the blind man said, and left.

•×•

In a walled compound within the vicinity of the city center, Zaiwulo saw someone whom, at first, he thought was a ghost. Gray hair was strewn all over the man's body, including parts of his face; his white gown billowed around him like an ethereal cloud. He was chewing on a tiny stick, which people in the savannah as well as in the forest used to clean their teeth. When the old man saw Talata, his eyes hardened and his forehead crumpled into a frown. He turned around and walked toward the bolon, a thatched roof erected on long poles, where he received people.

Zaiwulo followed his host to the bolon and sat on the mat behind him. Now and then, he could hear voices emerging from the homes. They were faint, lethargic, tempered by the midday sun. Granaries towered above the compound; from what he had seen of the city, Zaiwulo knew they were the tallest buildings in Musadu.

Zaiwulo could not keep his eyes off the ghost.

"What is it this time numo, my son-in-law?" the ghost asked.

Talata sighed and went straight to the point. "You know my crops failed last year, so I want to use the supply in the granaries," he said.

"It's Musadu's property," said the ghost, his frown becoming more pronounced.

"I will inform the king and the elders later. But because you have the king's ears, I wanted to talk to you first. If everything goes well next year, I'll return double of what I've taken."

"Are you sure? I don't want to have to defend you."

"Defend me?" Talata realized he should not have come to see his father-in-law.

The old man turned to Zaiwulo. "Child, why are you staring at me like that?"

"He's a newcomer," Talata said, by way of apology.

"But he should not stare at the world as if it will disappear at any moment," he said. "It will bring him much suffering." He gestured to Zaiwulo to approach.

Zaiwulo knelt before him, and the old man held his face in his hands. "You are from the forest," he said. "From a people who once held great sway over this area. What brought you here? It's been years since someone from your people set foot here."

Zaiwulo was silent and tried to avoid the old man's gaze.

"Don't be afraid, child," he said. "Understand this before it's too late: knowledge of people is the most important of all knowledge, although your host here might disagree with me. He buries his head in books and expects us all to treat him like a monarch beyond reproach."

The old man's name was Foningama, he told Zaiwulo, but everyone in Musadu had ceased calling him by that name since Talata married his daughter, Sona. Now he was only known as Talata's father-in-law.

"That's what happens when you come close to the Haidarahs, child. You end up becoming someone else," Foningama said.

Zaiwulo caught Talata fighting his growing irritation by folding the hem of his gown between his legs. But the old man was not done. "How's my daughter faring?"

"I'm worried about Sona," Talata replied.

"She shouldn't be shouldered with the responsibility of organizing such a ceremony. Sometimes I think you are impervious to her condition. She's with child, Talata!"

Once again, Zaiwulo noticed Talata shift in his seat. Unable to conceal his growing irritation any longer, Talata said, "the pregnancy has affected your daughter in ways that worry me. She seems unlike her usual self these days."

"I suggest she come to rest here for a while," Foningama said, "far from that crowded and noisy place that is your household."

Once again, Talata did not respond. This led the old man to guess that something else was on his son-in-law's mind. "What is it, Talata?"

"Samori sent one of his sofas to see me."

"What does he want?"

"He wants my help."

"What did you tell his sofa?"

"I told him that I'm a scholar who is only interested in dispensing knowledge to others. I told him the truth."

Foningama heaved a weary sigh. Waving a warning finger at Talata, he said, "Samori is already a household name in Koniyan which he wants to conquer. You should be wary of that man and his capabilities. Don't court his friendship no matter what happens."

"I don't want to befriend him."

"Samori could persuade or even force you to join him, which could mean more trouble for me and my daughter. You were not my first choice to marry her—no, Talata, our great scholar. But the people believed that you saved Musadu with the power of your prayers."

"That's all past," Talata insisted. No longer able to contain his irritation, he stood up to leave, but a young woman blocked him. She was holding a calabash of water. During their discussion, she had worn a disinterested look as she peeled cassava roots with a sharp knife under the shade of a tree close to the bolon. Now, she had an amused look on her face, as though she could see through any person whenever she looked into their eyes. There was no hesitation in her walk; instead, she wore a certainty that bordered on arrogance.

Zaiwulo would learn later that she was the old man's youngest wife. As she bowed to serve Talata, her eyes met Zaiwulo's. She held his gaze without flinching. "Haidarah," she said, "who is this stranger?"

Sweat collected under Zaiwulo's armpits. He fidgeted before her gaze, for he'd never met a girl as beautiful and brazen as this one.

They were introduced.

"So you are the boy with the tree. All of Musadu is talking about you. Why do you have the tree? What do you plan to do with it?"

"Naminata, leave him alone," Foningama said.

She passed the calabash to Zaiwulo, who drank his fill.

"If ever you are in trouble—and I am sure you will be—come to me and I will do all I can to help you," she said.

Zaiwulo wondered what she meant by this, and how she could help him, if his stay in Musadu was temporary and he would be returning home in a few days or weeks at most. He could not wait to see his mother and sisters. He returned the calabash and thanked her. Naminata laughed, her voice laced with pride. Zaiwulo stared at her until she entered one of the houses.

When she was gone, Foningama said, "She's one of a kind, isn't she?"

Talata nodded.

5

As he followed Talata through a dusty lane in the direction of the western gate, Zaiwulo was still thinking about Naminata's beauty, her unprompted promise to come to his aid if he got into trouble, and the ease with which she dealt with Talata and Foningama. Despite Naminata's young age—he knew that she couldn't be more than a few years older than him—she spoke to the men with a rare confidence, as though she were their equal. She seemed so sure of herself in a world in which he felt increasingly insecure, even regarding the true intentions of his host.

The houses in this part of the city were cramped close to each other and, unlike the large compounds of the wealthy, most were unwalled. The city, he would later learn, was divided into quarters. Each quarter bore the names of the largest families. This part of the city was named after Talata's best friend, Soko Kenneh. Zaiwulo observed the children wrestling in the dust, and a bevy of women frying termites while huddled around a makeshift hearth near the road.

"What are you thinking about?" Talata asked.

"Nothing," Zaiwulo answered.

"That's impossible."

"Who is Samori, Haidarah?"

Talata had not expected the question, but he answered. "Samori is a man of humble beginnings who has distinguished himself through courage. He is as brave a conqueror as they come. I don't know why he needs my help instead of other rulers and scholars. It intrigues me." Talata reached out to stroke Zaiwulo's hair.

"I have another question," Zaiwulo said. "Why are you taking me everywhere you go?"

Talata laughed. "You will know in due course. We are on our way to see Soko Kenneh, my best friend. He's the richest man in Musadu."

Talata told Zaiwulo that when his ancestor, the first Talata, came from Timbuktu centuries before, he was received and lodged by the ancestor of this wealthy man. "We are a family of sorts," he said.

•×•

The two met Soko at the back of his compound, in the vicinity of the western gate. He was supervising the workers attending to his impressive herd of cattle. Soko Kenneh was small, and the simple, worn-out gown he wore—an affront to his station — swallowed his slight frame.

"I know why you are here, Haidarah," he said.

Talata smiled.

"You came to beg me again. The greatest scholar in the land cannot even afford his own ceremony."

"What can I do without you?"

"That's what I would say, if I were you."

"You know me."

The banter between the two men was easy, and Zaiwulo noticed how Talata's shoulders relaxed in the company of his friend.

"You came at the right moment," Soko Kenneh said to Talata. Gesturing to one of his men, he asked the man to fill a gourd with fresh milk, which he handed to Talata who passed it to Zaiwulo.

"For you and your father," Talata said to Zaiwulo. Zaiwulo had never seen so many cattle gathered in one place. For him, this was the greatest display of prosperity. He had also never had cow's milk before, the forest was not always merciful to the animals. He looked forward to sharing the milk with his father.

Soko smiled at Talata. "My cattle are at your disposal."

"I need only seven cows, and I want to pay for them this time."

"Something must be wrong for my friend to pay for cows that belong to him as much as they do to me. Tell me, Haidarah."

Talata was silent for a while, and then he said, "One of Samori's sofas came to see me."

"That's an honor," Soko said.

"He wants my help."

"You two are similar, Haidarah," Soko said. "Your hunger for knowledge equals Samori's ambition to be the sole master of Koniyan. I met him once in Freetown. He was a trader then, exchanging gold and other goods with the English for arms. In the forest and along the coast of Liberia, he traded cloth and utensils for kola nuts, arms, and other goods. He was as gifted a trader then as he is a warrior now."

"I'm not sure of his intentions."

"Perhaps all he wants are your prayers, or for you to intercede on his behalf. Circumstances have made him the man he is today. His mother was captured and enslaved, as you know. What he did to free her equals only the deeds of the great Sundiata, The Lion King, king of kings. You know the story very well."

Talata knew the story which had been written and kept among the hundreds of manuscripts that filled his study. But his friend's words, though reassuring, were not enough.

"Samori has opted for ways that are not mine," he said.

"What ways?" Soko said

"His conquests, his wars. I'm afraid he will draw me into them."

"He acknowledges your strength and authority."

"My strength and authority? I have none."

"You worry too much, Haidarah." Soko shook his head, as if he disagreed with his friend or was very disappointed in him. Zaiwulo, who followed the exchange closely, realized that even while absent, Samori continued to wield great influence over people as important as his host Talata.

"When can I fetch the cows?"

"Whenever you are ready" Soko said.

On arriving back at the Haidarah compound, Talata turned to Zaiwulo. "You and your father are welcome to dinner."

6

One arm across his face, Zaiwulo's father was sprawled out on the bed, resting. On noticing his son, he sat up and was surprised by the present from Talata. The two drank the milk which tasted surprisingly pleasant, much like the palm wine his father usually drank at the end of each day. Back home, in the forest, he would sip the wine leisurely while resting on a chair in front of their house, the setting sun giving his face a coppery gloss.

Again, the image of his mother at the river rose before him as she pulled him across the water to safety. Zaiwulo blinked to dispel the haunting memory, for it made him uneasy. He traded that image for the ones of Sona and Naminata: the former with her motherly disposition; the latter, daring in her beauty, courage, and youth. Both were smiling at him.

He remembered Talata's request.

"Haidarah has invited us to join him for dinner."

Zaiwulo's father eyed him as though he had said something wrong, and then without responding, he got up and left the house to join Talata for dinner.

Zaiwulo followed him, confused; he had not intended to upset his father. More than ever, he longed for his mother. She often sang songs in which he featured as a hero, as a buffalo who took on lions. She had taken to calling him Buffalo because it had been Zaiwulo's first word. It had taken him long before he learned how to speak, and this had worried his parents. When he finally did, it was to name an animal he had never seen before. His mother then took to singing to him whenever she bathed him at their home in Haindi, saying, "You are a buffalo, son of a buffalo, the strongest of the strong."

This side of his father—with the temper and the secrets—was new to him. The man was usually not this hard on him except when he neglected a responsibility, used the wrong choice of words when addressing an elder, failed to shoo away birds at the rice farm, or forgot to fetch firewood. His punishment was usually a few quick lashes with a cane or a sharp command to right the situation, and then it was all forgotten. That father was absent now. The father who, when Zaiwulo had wronged one of his sisters, had demanded that he bowed and touched the sister's feet to ask for forgiveness; the father who had advised him to respect and honor women, whether they were family or not. What happened to that man whom he had grown to appreciate and had emulated in everything?

•×•

Father and son found Talata and several dozen guests sitting crossed-legged in the bolon where the scholar received his audience. The guests were enveloped in a musky scent. The region around their eyes—including the lashes—was adorned with kohl and a yellowish-white powdery substance. The makeup rendered their eyes bolder, clearer.

Many of them were conversing in subdued voices. On Talata's right sat the blind man Demba. He was calling out the names of the scholars and their retinue who had poured into Musadu to honor Talata. Beside him sat Karamo who whispered a name in his ears for Demba to announce to the public. "The protector of Fouta Djallon, the great scholar Suleiman Bah," Demba announced. The scholar nodded to the audience.

On Talata's left sat Osman, his eldest son, dressed as sumptuously as his father in a white gown and red cap. They seemed, from a distance, like twins or brothers, Zaiwulo thought. The sight of so many people intimidated Zaiwulo, so he fixed his gaze on his father's back as they walked along the space left by the seated guests who flanked the mat. When they got to Talata, they both fell to their knees before him. "The honor to share a meal with you is too much for us, Haidarah," Zaiwulo's father muttered. "We simply cannot accept."

"You are the one honoring me by being here," Talata said.

"I don't deserve it, Haidarah," Zaiwulo's father insisted.

"You would be insulting me by refusing to join us," Talata said.

Zaiwulo's father turned to the blind man and pleaded to him and to the other scholars to unburden him of the weight of such an honor. "You see, we are but humble people and Talata, a great scholar. The greatest," he said, his voice laced with pain. "Don't force us to do this."

No one intervened, which surprised Zaiwulo, for he had thought that those people regarded them as guests who deserved to be treated with the greatest respect. He was horrified when the man he had often looked up to burst into tears.

"He's truly from the bush," Osman muttered.

Talata got up and took Zaiwulo and his father's hands, and led them to the spot where Osman was sitting. "This is your seat," he said.

As Zaiwulo sat, he was suddenly aware that every eye was on him and his father. He wanted to escape it all, but he was pleased that Talata had intervened and forced his son Osman to go sit at the far end of the line.

Dusk was falling, but dinner was yet to be served.

Talata thought that his wife was delaying dinner to get back at him after what had transpired that morning, but he was wrong. Soon, a long line of women approached, each bearing a dish of food on her head. They covered the length of the mat and knelt in turn before him, saying, "Here is the food, Haidarah," and then waited for his comment, which varied from, "Your peanut sauce is incomparable," to "I've never had such well-prepared and delicious *toe* before,'" as he sampled the pounded cassava.

Zaiwulo could not keep his eyes off one of the women. She was, in fact, still a girl. Tall and lean, with bony arms and large eyes, her hair was plaited into three large rows. She moved with the gait of a woman capable of bearing the looks of the men facing her. She was not a beauty, but the way she carried herself, with her back straight and her neck long and proud under the weight of the large earthen bowl of food, compensated for her looks. Unlike the other women, the girl did not wait for Talata's comment. The moment she set the food down, she stood up to leave. Her gesture fell short of the respect accorded to the scholar.

"What are you doing, Massah, disgracing my father?" Osman snapped at her.

"Behave, Massah," Demba said.

The blind man stood, and with Karamo's help, reached to where Massah stood. Holding her by her shoulder, Demba slapped her across her face before leading her out of the courtyard, saying, "You dare insult Haidarah! You dare humiliate my teacher!"

The girl was Soko Kenneh's daughter.

7

Zaiwulo and his father returned to their lodgings late that night. On their way, in the silvery hue of the moonlight, the boy detected an ominous change in his father. The man's mood became like seething hot water that could, at any moment, spill and burn Zaiwulo.

Once inside, Zaiwulo rushed for cover by sitting in a corner of the room, at the head of his mat. He leaned against the wall, not daring to look up. The delayed beating must be imminent, so he braced himself for it.

When his father spoke, it was in a solemn voice: "You must think that I behaved shamefully tonight, but if ever you want to make it here, you must learn to conceal your true feelings from these people. Unlike them with their strange customs and worship of an invisible god, you are rooted to the earth. No matter what happens, you should never turn your back on the ways of your ancestors, my son."

Zaiwulo felt the weight of every word his father spoke, but he did not understand him. His father heaved a heavy sigh and approached him. "A tree changes according to the seasons but remains, in essence, the same: smooth in the rainy season and susceptible to all kinds of influences. Rain, insects, worms and snails—a refuge for everyone and everything. In the dry season, it becomes hard and merciless. Then gorgeous with its vibrant colors, shadows, and beauty. You are the tree that you brought with you, Zaiwulo. So plant it here, for it belongs to this place now, to the earth of this land far away from home."

Why was his father talking in parables, the boy wondered? What did he mean? Zaiwulo wrapped himself in the coarse sheet on the mat and soon fell asleep.

His mother came to him in his dream. Her presence filled the space around him, enfolding him in deep softness. She was wearing a single piece of cloth that covered her body to her knees, her gray hair plaited in simple rows. She had aged considerably, the once slender face was a riot of wrinkles, her owl eyes laced with weariness, as if she were in tears. She bent down towards him on the sleeping mat and said, "You are alone now, namesake of my father. Confront whatever comes your way with courage. Be brave!"

Zaiwulo jolted up in the wake of the silence that trailed her words. Still in the clutches of the dream, he noticed his father's absence and stumbled out in search of him. A thin strip of ochre line bordered the horizon, heralding dawn; mist and smoke coiled up from homes. All around him, life unfolded in a flurry of activities, undeterred by his predicament.

He inquired from a few people he met whether they had seen his father. They hadn't. He continued walking until he met the blind man. "I cannot help you, son of the forest," Demba said. "Haidarah is unavailable now, but you could talk to Sona."

Sona was already up. She sat kneading cassava dough in a small mortar that rested firmly between her legs. Seeing her so large with child—utterly vulnerable in her maternity but still exuding strength—momentarily dissipated Zaiwulo's qualms about his father. Sona's eyes were fixed tenderly on him.

"I was just about to send someone to fetch you," she said.

Women milled around her, and while some stirred the contents of huge brass cauldrons with long wooden ladles, others cleaned rice and millet in mortars or pounded dried cassava into powder.

The women began to tease Sona. "It seems Haidarah has a serious rival, sister Sona," one of them said, laughing.

"He should certainly watch out for this boy," Sona joked.

The women burst into laughter when she entered the house with Zaiwulo.

"Fetch that bowl on your left," she said.

It was a bowl of rice porridge sweetened with honey.

"Go on and eat. I don't want to be accused of neglecting a guest." She suddenly seemed exhausted. It was then that Zaiwulo noticed that her eyes were bleary from lack of sleep. Zaiwulo wondered what it was about her that reminded him of his mother. Perhaps, it was her kind eyes that seemed to follow his every movement.

He dipped his hand in the delicious porridge.

Once he was finished, Sona said, "Now we can talk. Your father left this morning. He couldn't bear to bid you farewell. He said that you are here because of a promise he made to my husband."

His father had abandoned him, Zaiwulo thought. He fought the tears. What promise did his father make? He could only conclude that his father had been preparing to leave him in Musadu all along since the day they left Haindi. He had never felt so alone.

"Tears are useless," Sona said. "Join the other students. Just follow the chanting. Haidarah wants you to learn to read and write."

•×•

The students were crowded around the three hearths located in the main courtyard. The older ones held handwritten pages, and the rest had wooden slates balanced on their laps. The two groups recited words written on their pages and slates. Some students buried cassava in heaps of burning coal, their attention shifting from the slates to the fire. Now and then, they would prick a cassava root with a stick to see if it was done. If it was, they would break it into pieces and dip it in palm oil before devouring it. This was their usual breakfast.

"You there, join the beginners' group," one student said.

Zaiwulo walked to the hearth and sat down. He felt several mocking eyes on him. He was about to leave when someone touched him. It was Talata's second son, Karamo. He was the teacher at this hearth.

Karamo fetched one of the writing slates that had been washed in muddy water and dried above the hearth. He dipped a reed pen in an inkpot that rested on a rock beside him and began to daub letters on the slate. When he finished, he dried the tablet and handed it to Zaiwulo.

"Recite this after me," Karamo said. "*Aa! Ba!*"

Zaiwulo's first attempt at learning the alphabet was greeted with derisive laughter from the other students. "This one is a slow learner," a student on his right said.

Zaiwulo cursed under his breath.

"He will spend years here," another said.

"No, he will grow old and still be stuck to that slate."

"Stop it, all of you," Karamo said. "You are forgetting your beginnings."

But the laughter persisted. Humiliated and angry, Zaiwulo jumped up and raced off to his lodgings. The flame tree stood against the wall in a corner of the room. He approached it, not knowing what to do. Then he remembered his father's words: *You are the tree that you brought with you, Zaiwulo. So plant it here, for it belongs to the earth of this land, far away from home.*

Zaiwulo left the house with the tree.

Ignoring the students—including Osman and Karamo—he searched for a spot in the main courtyard and found one not far from the main hearth. He began to dig a furrow with a sharp stick he had found lying beside one of the hearths. The students, abandoning their lessons, stared at him. His progress was slow, but he went on until the hole was large enough to hold the tree. He covered the roots and closed the furrow with dirt. Finished, he stood up to see what he had done and was satisfied.

It was as though the tree had always stood on that ground.

Only then did Osman leave his hearth. "Bush Boy, do you think that you can plant a tree here without our permission?" he yelled.

Zaiwulo felt no fear, but he was puzzled at the sight of Osman rushing toward him with a wooden slate in one hand, intent on fighting him. Why was Haidarah's eldest son so bent on picking on him?

Sona, who had asked some of the girls and women in the compound to keep an eye on Zaiwulo, intervened just in time. "Get back to your lessons," she said.

She left to see her husband in his study.

"Haidarah, tell your students to leave Zaiwulo alone."

"What happened?" Talata asked as he emerged from the study.

"That foolish son of yours—Osman was about to fight him because he planted a tree in the main courtyard."

"I want to see that tree," Talata said.

"Why is he here, Haidarah?" Sona asked.

"He's here to be my student."

"What did you tell his father? The man seemed sad."

"He was sad because he had to part with his son, Ma-Sona."

She shook her head as if she doubted his words.

Talata went to see the flame tree and took his time to contemplate it. After a while, he turned to his wife and students with a solemn expression on his face. "No one shall ever disturb this tree. It's part of us now."

8

Unable to sleep, Zaiwulo left the lodgings and entered the pale light of dawn in search of water to quench his thirst. The rainwater holder in front of his lodgings was empty. Since planting the tree, he had longed for ways to escape the claws of loneliness ripping him apart. It baffled him how he could feel so alone in a place crawling with people. He stumbled around, hoping that he wouldn't lose his way in the vast compound.

The previous day, Sona had shown him the well. The well was locked now. Crouching near it, he wondered at the futility of his trip. He was still there when he heard someone approach. It was blind Demba with his walking stick.

Zaiwulo rushed to lead him to the well.

"Child of the forest," Demba said, "you didn't sleep, did you? Life can be difficult for a beginner here, but don't give up," he smiled. "I came here with nothing, child, but today, I am the assistant to the greatest scholar in our world. Be patient."

Not completely at ease with the blind man, Zaiwulo could not tell him how much he longed for his mother, for his sisters, for Haindi. "Thank you, Uncle Demba," was all he said.

Demba chuckled before opening the well. After Zaiwulo drank his fill, Demba asked him to wait at the well. He would join a group of men who would arrive to draw water to build new homes for the dozens of people expected to attend the ceremony.

"This well was built by the wife of the first Talata," Demba said. "We guard it carefully because there are not many such wells in the city."

The men soon arrived. They formed a long chain from the well to the building site outside Haidarah's compound. Zaiwulo drew water with a brass bucket and passed it to the man next to him, who handed it to another until it reached the building site. There, women and men used the water to mix dirt and grass with their feet before filling the mixture into spaces in the walls of the new homes. Someone started a song, and Zaiwulo joined in the singing. He relished this moment of reprieve from Osman's constant bullying since he planted the tree a few days earlier. Here, he cannot reach me, Zaiwulo told himself.

He worked for most of the day. Joints aching and longing for sleep, he returned to the lodgings where he found Osman with some newly arrived guests.

"This is no longer your place," Osman barked.

"What do you mean?"

"From now you will sleep in the beginners' house."

"What did I do to you?" Zaiwulo asked.

Osman laughed and ignored him. Again, Zaiwulo wondered why Talata's eldest son was so intent on bullying him. He entered the house to gather his belongings: a cutlass his father had left him, a fishing hook and net, a large sheet of cotton cloth, and ground peanuts wrapped in leaves.

The new guests took over the house, and Zaiwulo followed Osman to a place befitting his station in the Haidarah household.

The beginners' house, a round mud building located close to the entrance of the compound, was already filled. Students were haggling over places to sleep on the floor. The house lit up with the oil lamp Osman was carrying. On seeing Osman, they all cowered.

"Choose a spot to sleep," he told Zaiwulo.

It occurred to Zaiwulo that Osman seemed every bit like his father. Although he was respected and held in equal esteem, Zaiwulo also knew that he had to be wary of him.

When Osman left the room, the house fell into darkness.

"You belong outside, Bush Boy," one of the students said.

When Zaiwulo did not move, a few of them grabbed him and threw him out. He fell in the dust, and his face nearly hit a stone. Knowing that it would be no use to return to the house, he stood, wiped the dirt off his face and tunic, and decided to wait outside until everyone had fallen asleep.

Outside, exposed to a night alive with distant voices and the sound of crickets, he suddenly understood the depth of his mother's experience in Haindi. She was bow-legged; her awkward gait, her looks, and watery owl eyes had been a source of embarrassment to him. She was called The Ugly Woman behind her back. It did not help that she moved as though she was dancing to a song only she could hear. Those peculiar steps often drew derisive remarks from his friends. Zaiwulo, however, didn't perceive his mother through the eyes of others, because what he saw was her ability to heal. She could cure the sick and the wounded with herbs.

Somewhere in the compound came the neighing of horses. He went in search of the animals and found them in a stall. The horses were all smaller than the sofa's horse he had seen on his arrival in Musadu. He adored the animals because of their silence—which he thought was a sign of infinite wisdom, the knowing look in their eyes. It pleased him. They seemed to understand him much better than the people of the savannah.

One of the horses—a spotted pony—drew near to him, as if to seek his approval. Zaiwulo fetched some grass from a pile nearby and began to feed it. The horse's tongue on his hand emboldened him to move his other hand across its muzzle. He wanted to unburden his heart to the animal, to confess his fear that he'd never amount to anything in this new world.

"They can be cruel, you know," a voice said.

It was Naminata, Foningama's youngest wife. Only when the horse withdrew did Zaiwulo turn to face her. She was so dark that the moonlight transformed her face, arms, and slender body into a shade of burnt wood.

The frown on her face suggested she could be harsh when it was required.

She was harsh now when she said, "Once, I saw a horse kill a man. It dragged him along the road until a brave man stopped it."

"How does it feel to ride a horse?" asked Zaiwulo.

"Forget about the horses," she said. "Come, I want to know your story and what brought you here. Tell me about the tree."

Her interest in him, in a world where he felt out of place, led Zaiwulo to tell her about life in Haindi and the journey to Musadu with his father.

"My mother gave me the tree to remind me of her," he said. She is a herbalist."

Naminata then shared her story with him. "I was forced to be with Foningama because my father owed him money and failed to repay. It was done as if one friend was bestowing honor on the other. Since then, it's been a war between me and his wives," she said, staring intently at him. "You and I are very much alike, Zaiwulo," she continued. "We were brought here by people who cared little about us, but I will never give in to that old man–never! You know, I can't keep my eyes off his son-in-law, your teacher," she exclaimed, her eyes searching Zaiwulo's face. After a while, she sighed. "Your eyes," she sighed dreamily. "'My god, they're—"

"What do you mean, Naminata?"

"You won't understand." She shrugged. "The one who will get to gaze into those eyes everyday—forget it. I don't know what I am talking about."

Naminata accompanied Zaiwulo to the beginners' house and waited until he had entered. In a voice even the sleeping students could hear, she said, "Leave Zaiwulo alone, or I will make your lives difficult here."

Once she was gone, someone said, "Bush Boy, if you report us to Naminata or anyone else, it will mean the end for you."

Zaiwulo wedged himself in a spot close to the wall and threw his arms over his head, in preparation for blows he knew were bound to fall. He tucked his legs against his chest, like a worm out in the sun. He was thinking about the spotted pony and how he would ride it through the plains of Musadu when a figure tore away from the mass of bodies and threw himself on Zaiwulo. The blows were swift, powered by a seemingly inexhaustible source. To resist them, Zaiwulo curled more into himself until he felt a blinding pain below his ribs.

Someone had stabbed him.

Zaiwulo decided to leave Musadu that night.

He did not belong there.

9

It was past midnight when Osman retired to the house he shared with his brother, Karamo, and his father's assistant, Demba. He had been up all day. But even at that late hour, guests were still arriving, and it was his task to cater to their needs.

Were it not for Zaiwulo's presence, he would have derived enormous satisfaction from doing what was required of him as heir to House Haidarah. But by planting the flame tree, the Bush Boy was claiming land that belonged to the Haidarahs as his own piece of earth. Such a brazen act! I will never allow it, Osman told himself and sucked his teeth.

Inside the house, he found the blind man still awake.

"Good evening, Uncle Demba," he said.

Demba sat up and rubbed his face to fend off sleep. The oil lamp lit his exhausted face. "Tomorrow will be the most important day in your father's life, Haidarah. We must work hard to make it so," he said.

"Uncle Demba, did you know that Bush Boy planted a tree in the main courtyard the other day?"

"Don't call him Bush Boy. You know nothing about him, Haidarah. And what is wrong with planting a tree?"

"Are you taking his side then?"

"Taking sides, Haidarah? There are more important things than worrying your head over a newcomer who means no harm."

Not even Demba could detect the danger Zaiwulo posed, Osman thought. If no one was willing to see the obvious, he would fight Zaiwulo and not relent until he was gone.

Osman took a quick ablution, changed into a fresh black tunic, and fetched the manuscript he had stolen from his father's impressive collection a few days ago. On entering the study, he had approached the dark curtain with some trepidation. Beyond the curtain was a manuscript around which legends had been spun. Its possessor was certain to attain great powers and gain access to the invisible world. The Haidarah Manuscript, known simply as Tareequ, had, over the ages, brought the family great fortunes. In every generation, a Haidarah was elected as custodian of the manuscript in a chain that stretched back centuries and beyond, into legend.

Osman was sure that one day he—and not his brother Karamo who lacked ambition—would come into possession of the manuscript. He could not resist the urge to lift the curtain and peek. The curtain's weight astounded him. He saw the Haidarah Manuscript lying on a mat of exquisite tapestry, august, terrific, and detached from his reality. It tampered with his resolve. A wall materialized between him and his birthright, so he turned around, angrily grabbed another manuscript, and hurried out of the study.

Written in verse, this manuscript contained his father's ruminations on women, in particular, his wife Sona. Although aware that he had no right to read those intimate details about his parents, he felt that he had to know, because he was the apparent heir and the next custodian of the Haidarah Manuscript. It would prepare him for that role.

Osman read how his parents had always maintained a precarious relationship, belying the image his father had cultivated as a man leading a blissful conjugal life. From the onset, Sona had despised her husband, but Talata had not elaborated on the source of her behavior. The poet had written that on their wedding night, Sona had sworn to poison him. Details were left out, but what followed was a struggle on Talata's part to contain his wife. Osman read on until he came upon the most salient aspect of the manuscript: his father's detailed descriptions of sexual intercourse. The poet seemed to take pleasure in the very act. The vivid and beautiful language with which he described his wife would forever taint Osman's image of his mother and women in general. Soon after that, the image of any person glorying in that act evoked a sense of disgust and humiliation in him.

Osman wondered how a man who inspired such honor and whose fame had reached as far as Timbuktu and beyond, where his writings were read and taught, could relish such a simple, clumsy bodily act. Osman thought of Massah. Being the firstborn, he had the right to wed her. Their union was a promise that their parents had made to each other years ago. He despised her arrogance, her misplaced sense of importance. Osman thought of how once they were married, he would subjugate her during that detestable act and wipe the pride off her face. The fact that she was of privileged background excited him. He would make her his slave.

Satisfied, Osman blew out the lamp and stretched out on his sleeping mat, only to realize that his brother Karamo was not in the house.

"Where is Karamo?" he asked Demba.

"With your father."

"Why wasn't I told about this?"

"Because it's not important. Go to sleep, Haidarah," Demba said. "We have a long day ahead of us tomorrow."

Demba's explanation was unsatisfactory, but an exhausted Osman soon succumbed to sleep. In his dream, he saw a ladder leading up to the heavens. At the top of it, his brother sat gazing mockingly at him. He woke up drenched in sweat. I will never allow it, he told himself, not as long as I live.

Osman got up and went in search of his brother.

10

When the crowd in the main courtyard dispersed that night, it left Talata alone with Karamo. Throughout dinner, Talata had noticed his son's indifference to the bustle around him. Perhaps I could persuade him to confide in me, Talata thought, but his efforts were to no avail.

Karamo seemed uneasy in his father's presence. He was his father's favorite, and although he was tall, well built, and had a broad attractive face like his mother, he was, in behavior, his father's twin, often preferring to avoid trouble instead of confronting it. He was a precocious child, one who had even mastered poems of *The Hanging Odes* from the pre-Islamic era. Karamo often amazed his father by quoting lines by Rumi and other great Sufi masters—present and past—including his father.

But Talata feared for him. It was a fear borne from the conviction that his son might've inherited all his faults. These faults included his inexhaustible love for life, which, in the eyes of many people—his family included—was unbecoming for any scholar of his stature.

Something was festering in his son. I cannot let him go astray, he thought to himself. "Come with me, namesake of my brother."

Talata took Karamo to his study. Standing in a room pervaded by the smell of ancient leather-bound manuscripts, most of which were hand-written on paper, cloth, or starched leaves, Karamo felt inconsequential. On the signal from his father, he picked one of the manuscripts and opened it. The title was etched in pure gold lettering. Karamo browsed through its delicate pages and ran his fingers along its meticulous calligraphy. Countless miracles had been attributed to his father, one of which had been his ability to conjure water to assuage the thirst of his traveling companions during their journey to the far-off and mysterious Timbuktu. His father's weapons lay in those books, some of which had been published in Fez, Cairo, and Damascus. All of them were filled with astonishing secrets and astrological signs. Karamo came across concise formulas which, if recited aloud and properly, conjured genies from the other world. Those invisible creatures could serve on request, enrich a man, or vanquish an enemy. Their breath, which came forth as flames, could turn an enemy to ashes. Some of the genies were multi-headed, and those who invoked them, ignorant of the monstrous effects their appearances had on people, ended up losing their minds.

One secret formula, whispered ninety-nine times, was capable of influencing people.

"Take a seat," his father said.

Talata reached for a tiny clay jar that contained a potion. The potion consisted of words that had come to him in a dream. He had written them on a wooden slate and washed them off with water. Now, Talata poured seven drops of the *nasi* in a bowl and added honey to it. "Drink this," he said.

Karamo gulped down the potion in seven doses, lapping up the rest with his tongue. When his father spoke, it sounded as though his voice came from a dream. "Henceforth, you only have to read a book once to memorize its content. You will be a great scholar."

Thinking the ritual had come to an end, Karamo stood up to leave.

"It is not yet over," Talata said.

He showed his son to a corner of the study concealed behind another veil of cloth, a second secret world.

Karamo stood still with a vacant gaze.

"Don't waver before your destiny," his father said.

Karamo's eyes widened as he realized that his father was about to bestow custodianship of the Haidarah Manuscript on him, when, all the while, he had thought it was his brother Osman who deserved such honor, for Osman had made no secret of his ambition.

Karamo did not move.

"What is wrong?" Talata said. "This is your moment."

But Karamo did not respond, which led his father to conclude that perhaps his son was not ready for the most coveted station in the family.

"Go to bed," he said. "Tomorrow will be a long day."

Karamo left his father's study troubled. The truth behind his hesitation was that his father's request stood in the way of his dreams. I cannot be what he wants me to be, he said to himself. I cannot be what everyone in this house wants me to be.

Falling to his knees, he began to sob.

11

Massah had spent most of the evening with Sona. Together, they had prepared for the ceremony and delegated tasks to the apprentices who had been acquired from cities, towns, and villages in Koniyan and beyond. She had gone through the list of ingredients required for the ceremony. The work involved amazed her. Perched on a mat in the one-roomed house, Massah sat facing Sona who was leaning with her back against the bed. The room smelled of cotton clothes, brass jars, pans, leather pouches, cooking utensils, soap, and musk.

"Sister Sona, how are we going to manage all this?" she asked. "The whole world has poured into Musadu. Will the food be enough?"

"The food will be enough, but we will have no rest. Men often saddle us with responsibilities with no knowledge of the work involved."

Massah nodded, a smile appeared on her face. "Have you seen the tree that the stranger boy planted?"

"There's something about him that I cannot put my finger on," Sona said.

"Yes, he looks so lost. And his eyes—"

"Not that, something else..." The child moved within Sona. All the fatigue of the pregnancy and the responsibility that came with the ceremony suddenly bore down on her. "You will do most of the work tomorrow, Massah."

The girl interpreted Sona's words to mean that she trusted her to do well, and she vowed not to disappoint her. She would do her utmost best. She waited until Sona had fallen asleep to sneak out of the house.

Massah was acutely aware of how the welfare of hundreds depended on her. The compound rippled with subdued laughter and lowered voices. She left the women's quarters and headed toward the men's quarters to see Demba, the man she hoped would be her husband one day. Until recently, she had not bothered to look beyond his dead eyes, but once she had done so, she found a man who was equal to Talata in many aspects, a capable and hard-working man deserving of love.

Demba had reprimanded her at dinner the other night because he was driven by a deep-seated loyalty to Talata. The blind man made no secret of how much he owed to his teacher. Demba often told her that there was only one human being in this world whom he could not refuse a thing, and that human being was Talata.

Basking in the prospect of soon presiding over her own household, Massah walked slowly in the moonlit night with a sense of purpose in every step. She would make sure that the house rivaled or surpassed that of Talata's. She was still making plans when her thoughts were interrupted by Karamo's sobs. She hurried to him.

"Why are you crying?" she asked, squatting beside him.

"I'm not." Karamo quickly wiped his tears.

"You worry too much, Haidarah."

At ease in her presence, Karamo showed a watery smile. Even though she was intended for his brother, he was smitten by her. What he wanted in life, however, stood in the way of being in union with anyone in Musadu.

Karamo dreamed of leaving Musadu. His dream had been ignited by the visit of Benjamin J. K. Anderson some years ago. Anderson had told the people of Musadu that his country Liberia, ruled by black— westerners— from America, had dispatched him to that part of the world because it was rumored to be prosperous in gold. Not only had his government expressed its desire to conduct trade with Musadu and other cities in Koniyan, they had also wanted to form an alliance with its people. Since that visit, Anderson had become a legend in Musadu. The people of Musadu had not only found his attire strange—a tight shirt and uncomfortable-looking trousers—but also his pipe and American pistol. Even stranger was his language which sounded like that of the white men, and so they had taken to calling him Toubabous—Westerner.

Karamo had tried to befriend Anderson, but the man's aloofness and the mystery surrounding him, held him back.

"I feel you have a great longing," Massah said.

Instead of telling her how much he wanted to be part of Anderson's world, he said, "I want to leave Musadu."

"Why?" Massah asked.

Karamo did not respond.

"Your secret is safe with me," she said. "But you can choose to stay here. There are people here who care about you."

Karamo thought that perhaps she meant herself; he wanted to hug her and ask her to choose him as suitor instead of his brother, but unsure of her reaction, he held back.

Meters away, behind the tree, Osman watched the two part ways. He grinded his teeth in dismay. He could only conclude that it was a meeting between two lovers. Hurrying away, he decided that he would keep an eye on them.

The encounter with Karamo confused Massah so much that she aborted her plan to see Demba. She began to doubt what she desired. When it came to making a choice, Karamo was as educated as his brother, but he was young and lacked the experience required to feed the impulses of an ambitious young woman like herself who not only dreamed of becoming a successful trader in her own right, but of being head of her own household. Osman, in contrast, was very ambitious, and Massah could not help but admit that were she to opt for him, his ambition might consume her. She had noticed how he longed to take over from his father, and that made any future with him not only precarious but also fraught with danger. This left her with the blind man as the most viable choice, a man whose love for her was a guarded secret. Only Demba, a man loved and admired by many in Musadu, had the qualities that befitted her ambition. Would he have the courage to ask for her hand, she wondered. And if not, what would her future be in the Haidarah household?

With these questions plaguing her, Massah returned home.

12

Sona awoke to Talata's presence in the house. The mixture of musk, rosewater and soap, lingered on him, and on countless occasions, had prickled her senses into an outburst of overwhelming desire for him. But now, in her pregnant state, the smell made her head spin.

Approaching her, Talata folded the hem of his gown between his legs before easing himself onto the bed beside her. The light from the oil lamp brightened his face; there, she caught a longing that reminded her of their first night of marriage.

Until his name was dropped in her presence, Sona had not considered Talata as a possible candidate for a husband. He had been brought up and educated elsewhere, in Kankan, where a branch of the Haidarahs lived; as a result, he spoke the Mandé language of Koniyan with an accent. But that was not the only critical aspect Sona and some people in Musadu noted in the young scholar. Talata also took himself too seriously. He would confine himself to his study for days and nights at a time, meditating and subsisting only on fruits and water at the end of each day. Sona could not reconcile that ascetic image with the tall, slender man who—clean, well shaven, and often attired in handsome garments—strolled the streets of Musadu as though he were its king. Beside this arrogance was his obvious conceit. For how could he be ascetic and hedonistic at the same time? Sona even believed that the singsong voice he used during his lectures was fake, a ploy used to conceal his shortcomings as a scholar. But it was this singsong voice that aroused the deepest emotions in his audience during his lectures. Some rolled on the ground in tears as he narrated, for example, the trials of Jacob and his sons.

When it was decided that, of all the women in Koniyan, Sona would be Talata's wife, she had waited until the wedding night to say, "I will poison your food one day, Haidarah." Her voice was loud enough to reach the women eavesdropping to make sure the marriage would be consummated.

Instead of a slap to her face or an outburst, Talata had simply said, "Then you will be widowed for the rest of your life, Ma-Sona."

"What do you mean?" she had asked, rolling her eyes.

He had laughed. "No one will ever fill the gap I'll leave in your life because I'm the most educated man in Koniyan. You'll live alone for the rest of your life."

There was a hint of threat in his words. Sona, biting her lip to master the storm welling up within her, countered him by occupying a spot at the foot of the bed. During preparations for his first night with his bride, Talata had been told that if a bride sat at the foot of the bed or away from the groom, it meant the two had begun on the wrong foot. Not only did Sona sit away from him, but she seemed to be in a fighting mood.

Sona threw dagger-sharp glances at Talata as though she were about to explode, which happened when he touched her. Her scream attracted the women who were gathered outside. They rushed in and met a man staring warily at his wife, bereft of any desire. One of the women would later claim that she had caught fear in Talata's eyes. After the women had attended to Sona and were gone, Talata thought of the night before him. How would he produce the white cloth with the bloodstain to prove that the marriage had been consummated? How would he dare face people the next day if he failed to prove that he was a man?

Musadu would never forgive him.

Long after the women were gone, Talata sat on the mat gazing at his wife. After some time, he gathered himself up and approached the bed.

"Don't lay those calloused hands on me!" Sona said.

It was this rage in her voice that fueled his resolve, and he fell on her. The foreplay, meant to show that a woman was not an easy conquest—her refusals and his attempts in light teasing ways to win her over with jokes and caresses—soon turned into a fight. At first, he was delighted with this game. But as it dragged on, the fear that it would exhaust him and he would end up disappointing Musadu crept up on him. Sona grabbed his embroidered garment, purchased especially for the wedding, and tore it off him. She bit him and sank her nails into his chest. The smile that danced across his face even as she fought and resisted him was replaced by a grave puzzlement. He could not believe that anyone could despise him so much, for he was an amicable man and for most of his life women had lauded his looks, his knowledge, and his fame—but not this one.

It was this realization amid the fight, and his attempts to win her over, that compelled him to stop. He held Sona for long, calming her. He did not want to fight her.

As she resisted him, Sona thought that perhaps she could be mistaken about him, that he was not a man only occupied with himself, that she could grow to care for him and bear him children in whose attention she could wallow.

Her body, still in the throes of the fight, gradually began to relax, preparing to receive him.

Now, on the eve of the ceremony, Sona watched her husband toying with the border of his garment like a child afraid of being rejected. She was aware of how important this event was to him and wanted to be generous so that he could go into the ceremony contented. Summoning all her strength, she hoisted herself up in bed and allowed him to undress her.

First, he began to caress her. He was careful with the course his hands took and moved them up and down, from her neck to the small of her back, so that at a certain point, she moaned his name. She lay on her back, revealing her full self to him. She looked big, gracious, and imposing at the same time, even at that vulnerable moment. Her body, smeared with oil and musk after a thorough bath, glowed. Every swell in her body, from her breasts to her stomach and legs, felt as firm as they had on their first night.

In the end, he buried his head at the base of her stomach, deep into the fuzzy triangle, and he felt the child move and heard its heartbeat. He listened, entranced. His joy increased further when she laid her hands on his head, as though to approve his action.

They were unmoving for what seemed like an eternity. Everything outside of that moment seemed trivial to Talata. He wished there was no ceremony the next day; he wished he did not have to go back to his chambers later that night; he wished Sona never had a child and was not pregnant with a third; he wished he was not famous but a simple farmer with few wishes and demands. He wished he could lie with her every night, for the rest of his life.

Then, a fully formed poem appeared in his mind's eye, as if it had been honed and sharpened somewhere else and by someone else. It molded into a shape that could convey his deepest fears and joys. It was a poem about love in its deepest sense, in all its manifestations, and he sang it like a lullaby to his unborn child and its mother.

13

Later that night Talata left his wife and stepped into the light of the full moon on his way to his study to wash and prepare for a night of composition. Sona's compliance was clear a sign as the bright moon, he thought. For whenever things reached their apogee of glory, they began to crumble. It's already happening to me, he told himself. He was on the verge of achieving the highest honor a scholar could ever dream of in his part of the world.

Although he had delighted in this prospect for months, now that the event was almost upon him, he was beset with doubts. What was he trying to prove? Wouldn't he be better off teaching than exhibiting his knowledge in such arrogant ways? He could not remember one of his ancestors ever gathering so many scholars and doing what he was about to do.

Talata could not help but imagine himself standing on a platform. Below him were hundreds of scholars who had come, not only to listen to him but, to test his erudition and mastery of various disciplines including philosophy, linguistics, and esotericism. A single mistake would be enough to question his claim to scholarship. He had to be at his sharpest as he negotiated his way through a maze of Koranic laws, interpretations, and traditions. For forty nights, Musadu would listen to him and celebrate each night with a day of festivities. The world would ring with his name.

Talata was a Sufi of the Qadiriyya order, a way of life which taught that nothing was truly ever lost, that the demise of man was merely the onset of a process that would lead to the disintegration of the body, merging with the earth, fertilizing it. The earth, in turn, would yield products to be consumed by man and animals in an unbroken cycle that would continue forever. In this order, man was not denied life's pleasures, for love was its premise. Once, in his early twenties, Talata had composed a poem in praise of Karamoko-Mori, his teacher in Kankan. *The stupid and the dumb flock hastily to you*, he had written, *and you wash them with the divine soap of your wisdom.* But his teacher was of the Tijaniyyah order which viewed some Qadiriyya practices as heathen because its followers settled among and interacted with animists. Talata's teacher had begun to begrudge Talata's talents, his fame, and to find fault with his views, especially his plea that animists should be respected and that wars should not be waged on them.

This had inevitably led to friction between student and teacher, resulting in Talata leaving Kankan for good.

Talata was thinking about that disagreement with his teacher as he walked toward his study where his manuscripts awaited him. "Oh, Beloved," he addressed God, like a true Sufi. "If anything happens to this city or to me, I entreat you to spare the manuscripts."

It dawned on him that he was within the grasp of something grandiose yet elusive. Karamo's refusal to embrace his heritage bothered him, and Osman's temperament made him an unsuitable successor. He could not explain Osman's open hostility toward Zaiwulo.

Talata wondered how to reprimand Osman and how to make Zaiwulo feel at home. He was keenly aware of the boy's predicament, so far away from home. He would bring Zaiwulo closer and ease his burden of adapting to a new place. He was musing on these thoughts when his attention was drawn to a figure rushing out the compound's entrance. It was Zaiwulo, and he seemed to be running away. Talata followed him.

Zaiwulo took the main road toward the western gate, in the direction of the Jon River, but before he could reach it, Talata caught up to him.

"Why have you decided to leave us so soon? What about your tree? Who will take care of it in your absence?"

Surprised, Zaiwulo stopped and spun around.

"They tried to hurt me and said that I don't belong here."

Only then did Talata notice that the boy's tunic was drenched in blood.

"Come with me," he said and led Zaiwulo to his study where he bound the wound with a piece of cloth. "You will sleep here tonight," he said. "Your fellow students have never interacted with someone from as far away as you. They treat you harshly because they don't know you." Talata showed him to a mat and covered Zaiwulo with a sheet of cloth. "Sleep well," he said.

But Zaiwulo could not sleep, not in a place filled with objects that inspired awe in him: the leather-bound manuscripts, the mounds of papers with strange words written on them, and the long prayer beads sitting amidst the pleasant scent of musk. But most of all, he was wonderstruck by the presence of a man who seemed to contradict everything that this new, strange, and cruel world represented.

Feigning sleep, Zaiwulo watched his teacher sit cross-legged and begin to write. The scholar chanted words as though he were reciting a poem.

Talata was composing his version of the family history, a work meant to be his magnum opus in verse, his legacy to the world. To enrich the story, he often turned to sources other than those in the Haidarah Manuscript. Sometimes, he added a touch of fantasy to create a clear image, especially when it came to aspects of his life that had been ignored by legend.

Talata pored over every word and line before singing the lines aloud to feel how the words sounded and rhymed. Once in a while, he would pause to consider their significance or relevance to the poem.

My ancestor left Timbuktu in response to a call from Foningama, a general of Sundiata Keita, founder of The Malian Empire. This Foningama or Fran Kamara, chosen by Sundiata as the emperor had done with each of his twelve generals, was to travel to the far reaches of his vast empire to settle and expand. Foningama led hundreds of his followers away from the desert, across the savannah until they reached Musadu.

Musadu was at the crossroads where the forest met the savannah. There, Foningama decided to drive out the sorcerer Zoemuza, who was the founder of the town. Bent on protecting his land, Zoemuza employed magic and witchcraft to defeat Foningama, but in the end, the newcomer prevailed. Zoemuza fled to the forest with nothing but a branch from a flame tree that stood close to the river; he promised to return one day and replant the tree. Over the ages, Musadu became the source from which all cities and towns in Koniyan sprang. And my ancestor...

Talata went on with his composition, his singsong voice filling the study with verses sung in a nostalgic, melancholic tone that lulled Zaiwulo to sleep and into a dream about Haindi and in the company of his mother and sisters.

When Zaiwulo awoke, the boy saw his teacher still seated in the same position chanting the verses. It was not long until Demba's voice rose with a call to prayer.

From the neighing of horses in the nearby stalls, Zaiwulo imagined that the animals were beckoning to him. To his delight, he noticed that his stab wound was already beginning to heal, and he could bear the pain.

He left the study and ran toward the stalls.

14

The pinto recognized Zaiwulo when it saw him. Flicking its tail, it edged toward him. The boy rubbed the horse's flank and was about to feed it when Karamo and four boys entered the stables to tend to the animals.

"We are taking them out to graze," Karamo said. Each boy took two or more horses and led them out.

"Do you have horses in the forest?" Karamo asked.

"I saw them for the first time here," Zaiwulo answered.

"You must be afraid of them."

Zaiwulo shook his head. "No, I would like to ride one."

"Watch us do it, and you will soon learn."

But Zaiwulo, impatient and curious, moved to mount the pinto.

"Be careful, or you will hurt yourself," Karamo said.

On his first attempt, Zaiwulo only managed to jump up to the height of the horse and landed on the ground, which made Karamo and the other boys laugh.

The pinto let out a grunt.

"I told you so," Karamo said.

Zaiwulo ignored the laughter. He felt a keen affinity with the pinto and believed that he could ride it with ease, just like the sofa he and his father had met at the river.

"Come, I will help you," Karamo suggested.

But Zaiwulo shook his head. "I can do this."

Just as he had seen the sofa do at the river, he leaped with all his strength onto the horse. The animal, unused to such a clumsy movement, stirred. Zaiwulo held tightly to the rein for fear he might fall, and the pinto, perhaps aware of his insecurity, calmed down. For the first time since his arrival in Musadu, Zaiwulo felt at ease, as if nothing else mattered as long as he was on the back of the horse. He clicked his tongue, and the horse began to move.

"You are lying if you tell me that you haven't ridden a horse before," Karamo said, turning to the other boys. "He's lying."

Zaiwulo rode with the others into the fading darkness of dawn punctuated by flames from hearths along the road. Students were gathered around the embers. Women were preparing breakfast and warming water for their families while the men bathed and traded anecdotes with each other. The morning chill burrowed under Zaiwulo's skin and his wound began to sting. He ignored the discomfort, for the sensation of being on the horse dispelled the cold and his fear of not belonging.

"Musadu's grass is the best for horses in all of Koniyan," Karamo said.

They left the outskirts of the city, the fortified gate, the Jon River, the hamlets, the farms, and reached the fields. The horses were eager to graze which allowed Zaiwulo to take in his surroundings. The grass—a low scattering of light yellow and green colors—was dotted with anthills and dead tree stumps. Egrets sauntered about pecking the ground. Zaiwulo moved closer to them. At first, the birds tolerated his presence, but when he bent over to touch one of them, they all took flight.

Zaiwulo sat on an abandoned anthill to watch the horses feed. Soon, Karamo left the others to join him, and the two were silent for a while, gazing at the horses and the greenish-yellow world around them. Then Karamo spoke, "In distant places such as Kankan, Fouta Djallon, Sikasso, and the Toucouleur, there are warriors who fight with the latest weapons purchased from the whites, warriors who ride brave horses. The English in Sierra Leone and the French on the other side of Niger sell those weapons to the highest bidder. One Benjamin Anderson from Liberia who visited Musadu has the knowledge and weapons of the white men. I want to discover his world."

Zaiwulo did not know why Karamo had chosen to confide in him. Perhaps it was because he was new in Musadu. The world Karamo evoked was alien to Zaiwulo. He had never met a white man before and could not imagine this black man, Anderson, who spoke the white man's language.

Zaiwulo soon lost interest in the conversation, for all he wanted was to feel the back of his horse. "I want to ride again," he said.

"As if you need my permission," Karamo said.

•×•

The horse seemed to be waiting for Zaiwulo, who mounted it with the ease of a seasoned rider. His confidence soaring with every passing moment, Zaiwulo rode in the direction of Beyla and Jacodu, twin cities close to Musadu. As he raced across the plains he had once walked with his father on their journey to Musadu, Zaiwulo felt a sudden surge of longing for home, for the laughter of his sisters whenever they teased him, for his mother's songs when she sat across him, watching him eat, for the pride in his father's voice when he talked about his farm. Zaiwulo was so carried away in that dream of home that he must have given the horse a wrong signal because it gathered speed until, at a point where the road forked into two, it crashed into a thicket of shrub. Headfirst, Zaiwulo was thrown off the horse and landed on his back in the tall grass. Winded, he tried to sit up. It was hard to ignore the searing pain from the wound. He waited to regain his strength.

There is more to horse riding than the mere act of sitting on it and covering distances, he thought. I have to learn to be one with this creature.

The urge to ride was so overwhelming it didn't take long for him to get up. Ignoring the wound, he got on his horse again and rode back to join the others.

"You ride well," Karamo said. "From now you will take care of the horse. Take good care of it. Horses are worth their weight in gold here."

"I will call you Haindi, after my birthplace," Zaiwulo whispered to the horse.

Before the sun had fully broken on the plains, Zaiwulo and the others led the horses back to the stables and returned to the city to prepare for the ceremony.

The group joined Demba who was busy coordinating the ceremony while Talata waited in his study. Karamo and Osman assisted Demba by leading the guests to seats reserved for them in the courtyards. Now and then, silence would descend on the crowd as though the moment for Talata to appear had come.

Fetching a broom leaning against the wall of one of the houses, Zaiwulo joined his fellow students in sweeping the compound. He worked with gusto, moving the broom hard across the ground, gathering up leaves, crumbs as well as masticated chicken and cow bones left from the previous day.

How the blind man detected his presence, Zaiwulo would never know, but as Demba went on dishing out criticisms at the other students, he approached Zaiwulo and said: "Child of the forest, sweep! Sweep so well that you could eat off the ground. Teach this lazy lot how it's done. They take Haidarah's generosity for granted."

Though he had been meeting with her daily for some time, Demba had kept his love for Massah secret. As Talata's right-hand man, he could wed any girl of his choice. But he was reluctant, he feared his disability might make marriage impossible. However, as the ceremony approached, Demba's urge to confide in someone became unbearable. For the second time that day, someone entrusted Zaiwulo with their innermost wish.

"Can you keep a secret, child?" he asked Zaiwulo

"What do you mean, Uncle Demba?"

"I intend to marry Massah."

From where he stood, Zaiwulo could see Massah delegating tasks and moving about as though she oversaw all the women. She was wearing a black-and-white tunic and a wrapper, and her hair was plaited in thick rows. On turning to Zaiwulo, the firm expression she wore while dealing with the other girls dissolved into a smile. His heart fluttered. He realized that she was not much older than he was, but she exuded the confidence of a grown-up, as if she knew her purpose in life and how to achieve it.

"Tell me what you see, child."

Zaiwulo described what Massah was doing, the way she moved about; he did so in such a way that the blind man could see her in his mind's eye and imagine her as she ought to be imagined.

"Don't tell anyone what I just told you."

"You can count on me, Uncle Demba."

15

Zaiwulo finished his chores and went to take a quick shower. One of the students told him that a woman had fetched a bucketful of water from the well for him. The woman, the student told him, didn't want to be known. As he stood in the bathroom—a thatched shed behind the beginners' house surrounded pebbles—he wondered who had surprised him with that act of kindness. Could it have been Massah? But he did not know her well enough to deserve such a gesture. Perhaps it was one of Sona's apprentices. The boy threw water on his sweaty back with one hand, gasping at the touch of the cold water against his skin. Once dry, he rubbed himself all over with shea butter and wore a clean tunic for the ceremony.

By the time Zaiwulo left the house, the crowd had covered the courtyards in the compound. Most of the people were seated on the ground he and his fellow students had swept. Zaiwulo wanted to be closer to the notables, including the king of Musadu who sat at the head of the crowd. Zaiwulo crawled his way through the crowd, bumping into people—some of whom either smiled or frowned at him—until he found a space behind the dignitaries and scholars. From there, he could see the king of Musadu.

The king was tall and lean in his brocaded gown. His sparse goatee framed his pinched face, and he seemed worn out. Zaiwulo supposed that this tired look was the effect of many wars he had been told the king had led.

The ruler's bodyguards, armed with rifles and swords, fussed about him.

Foningama turned to one of the scholars, one of Talata's relatives and said, "Mark my words, Karamo-Kasakoro Musa, my son-in-law will keep us waiting in this heat till noon. He organized all of this for no other purpose than to be worshiped."

"You don't want to admit it, Uncle Foningama," Demba said. "But you owe everything you have and will ever have to your son-in-law."

The scholars laughed.

"I know you, Demba Kamara," Foningama said. "You've become a Haidarah, and in doing so have betrayed me, your uncle."

"If you had another daughter like Sona, Uncle Foningama, I would have married her a long time ago," said Demba.

"I will never allow anyone from this house to marry a daughter of mine again," Foningama said. "Tell me, why is your teacher keeping us waiting?"

In fact, in his study close to the large courtyard, Talata had been waiting for a sign from Demba. To his surprise, the sign did not come from Demba or Karamo but from Osman who was singing a poem he had composed:

Knowledge is a lock and you are the key, Father. To unlock it whenever you desire. You hold the key to the visible and invisible worlds, granted to you at birth. You are the seal of scholars.

On hearing his son, Talata stood and touched the red cap with white band, to better secure it on his head. He stepped out of the study. He was wearing a long, simple scarlet garment. He had washed and rubbed his body with oil bought from traders from Kano and had daubed his face with perfume. Around his neck he wore three slabs of amulets, and in his right hand dangled a long chain of prayer beads.

Osman's voice reminded Talata of the time he praised his teacher in Kankan with a Kasidah—a long and elaborate epic poem that was now being delivered by students at lectures all over the savannah. As Talata stepped out of the study, he expected to meet his sons, Osman and Karamo, and his assistant, Demba. But Karamo was nowhere to be seen. Where was he? Talata searched the crowd for his youngest son.

Your knowledge is as vast as the Gbe Mountains, Father;
and those who claim they are your equals are like hillocks.

Talata stepped up to his firstborn and hugged him. Had he been mistaken? Was Osman much more than his ambitions? Talata and his eldest son walked to the gate and into the street toward the mosque. They were followed by a huge crowd, including the king of Musadu.

Zaiwulo walked behind Talata, Osman, Demba, and the other dignitaries. Never before had he seen such a crowd. The mosque was sparsely adorned. The wood protruding from the walls and holding the edifice in place, gave it an incongruous appearance. Through chinks in the walls, shafts of sunlight usually poured in on the worshipers like gold dust through fingers.

The silence that descended on the crowd was broken by the occasional line from Osman's poems.

If this life was to last for those who had truly honored it,
then you would live on forever, Father.

Osman repeated the line at regular intervals while a man beat a huge drum. A deep silence followed and at its edge lingered the sound of feet and the rustling of clothes.

The crowds, streaming from many directions, converged. The multitude moved as though steered by a single force.

You are our master, master of our time.
You are an effulgent moon crowning our dark nights.

In front of the mosque stood a wooden platform with a huge, colorful canopy. Talata and Osman ascended the platform, and a crowd of scholars surrounded them. Spurred on by the moment, Osman was no longer reciting the poems he had written and rehearsed, he was now improvising. His singular and stentorian voice stirred hearts.

You are our guardian, guardian of our lives.
The brilliant sun lightening our dark days
And filling our lives with contentment.

Osman's gaze swept across the crowd and alighted on his mother. Sona was standing still, as if in trance, her heart swelling with pride. Osman sang:

It is said that heaven is sought by submission to the will of God.
But I seek my heaven beneath your feet, Mother.
My heaven beneath your feet and nowhere else.

Sona burst into tears. She edged forward and towards Osman, but then she thought of her other son, Karamo, who of all people in Musadu should have been there, had to be there, at the forefront of such an event. He should have been here, taking up another poem, dazzling the crowd with his brilliance.

"Where is Karamo?" she asked now, looking around.

Karamo had been present all along, but he had chosen not to draw attention to himself. He had confined himself to the rear of the crowd and would have preferred to be left alone, but his position in the Haidarah household would not allow it. Now, he pushed his way through the people until he reached his mother.

"You are here," Sona said and embraced him.

Talata came down from the platform.

"Namesake of my brother," he said to Karamo.

The scholar expected Karamo to also impress the crowd as he had done on previous occasions, but he caught in Karamo the same lack of interest that had manifested the night he had almost made him the custodian of the Haidarah Manuscript. Talata could feel every eye in the crowd on him; the weight of hundreds bore down on his patience. Despite his apprehension and initial desire not to compel his son into doing anything against his will, Talata heard himself saying, "Recite one of the poems you know by heart."

The crowd was still, watching.

Karamo was mute.

"Don't shame me," Talata insisted.

He reached out to touch his son, to allay his fears.

"*Shame* you, Haidarah?" Sona said, turning to face him.

"Sona, he has done this before," Talata said.

"Perhaps he doesn't want to do it today."

The fact that husband and wife were quarreling in public, at such a moment, left everyone stunned. Karamo did not move. But when he finally spoke in an attempt to please his father, the words and the voice felt as if they belonged to someone else, so he stopped.

"Let him leave if all he does is stand there," a man shouted.

Sona turned to the man. "No one should ever address my son in such a tone," she said, embracing Karamo. "It's all right, my son, don't mind these people."

"Sona, let the boy be," Talata said.

Sona was about to lead Karamo out of the crowd when Talata blocked her. When he touched her, she threw his hands off her.

The king of Musadu spoke for the first time. "Ma-Sona, why are you so bent on disgracing your husband before us all? We came here to honor your house, so please honor us in turn."

Sona let go of Karamo. She wanted to tell the king that although she was married into the Haidarah household, she did not belong to it. Instead, she decided she would show Musadu where she truly belonged. So, she joined the women.

Talata managed to take hold of himself; he led Karamo to the platform.

"Stand there, beside your brother," he said.

The scholar began his lectures by reciting a few lines from one of his poems that summed up his essence:

Homage to those who embrace life in its entirety during the day, and at night meditate in search of answers to life's riddles. Homage to those selected few.

Demba, who stood beside his teacher and sensed the unease and weariness in his voice, picked up the lines, repeated them several times, and then added another line of his own:

To them belonged the here and the hereafter, Haidarah.

Talata chose not to address the incident at all but to turn his attention to the changes that were descending, not only on Koniyan but also on Kankan, Fouta Djallon, and places far beyond the Niger.

"Recently we've heard some scholars preach that we should wage war against animists, against all forms of beliefs except the true one," he said.

A murmur ran through the crowd.

"Good people, hear me out," he continued. "I'm not a warmonger. You only have to look at my slender arms to know that I'm incapable of holding a rifle, let alone of shooting another human. Where is it written that those who differ from us must be forced to accept our way of life or be killed?"

Talata's voice rose as he went on quoting one source after another to emphasize his point that a religion that waged war on the innocents was no religion at all but a violent and divisive doctrine. "Such a religion can claim no right to divinity. No, good people, it is a curse to humanity."

Talata pressed on, but as the day wore on, his voice began to falter. It was soon choked with emotion, compelling him to stop. He was unprepared for the sudden crisis in his life which had left him no room or enough time to prepare for it.

How would he deal with it all?

Shaking his head, Talata turned to his assistant. "Demba, I can't go on any longer. I can't pretend that things are the same."

"Then let's stop for the day, Haidarah."

The king and the scholars concurred.

"We will resume tomorrow," the king said.

But that evening, as hundreds—including households in remote corners of the city —relished the food the women had prepared, Talata, seated on his mat in his study, gave himself over to a deep numbness that took hold of his mind and then his whole body. He managed to convey to the people that Osman should take over from him, a decision the scholars debated but agreed to in the end, to honor their host. Osman did not disappoint. Aided by Demba, he displayed his full range of knowledge.

The lecture went on all night.

"He's the true heir to the house," many concluded.

•×•

At dawn, Zaiwulo felt a deep sense of unease; he retired to bed. He was the first to enter the beginners' house, and he sought a spot from where he could keep an eye on everyone. The fight between his teacher and his hostess had not escaped him. The claws of despair tightened their grip on him, and he felt homesick. But he also knew that he had to prepare himself for his personal war, for those who had hurt him were bound to return and he had to be ready. He had to be tough.

Soon the house was filled.

"If anyone dares to touch me for any reason at all," Zaiwulo said, "I swear on my mother that I will not hesitate to sink my cutlass in his body."

The warning worked. No one bothered him.

Zaiwulo leaned against the wall. I will not fall asleep, he kept repeating to himself, I will not fall asleep. But sleep came.

As Zaiwulo woke to prepare for another day of hearing Osman rub his arrogance in the faces of the people, Demba shared some terrible news with him.

"Child of the forest, Karamo has run away from Musadu."

16

The fish seemed uninterested in the bait. Every time Zaiwulo cast his line, a fish would nibble at the bait and then let it go. They were toying with him. He could see them flashing their tails and smooth bellies, mocking him in the water. His patience was running out. They said that silence was important to fishermen, but he was yet to catch a fish. So he decided not to bother and began to whisper a tune to himself, a song which heralded the appearance of masked beings—guardians of the Poro secret society—in the forest. Would a moment come when his passage to adulthood would be celebrated during a ceremony presided over by those masked beings? He wondered. Or was his life bound forever to the savannah?

Zaiwulo had been sitting on the bank of the Jon all morning. The fish was meant for Sona. He wanted to persuade her to return to Talata. Since the public row with her husband and Karamo's departure, Sona had swapped her conjugal home for her father's house, her *true home*, she had told everyone. All attempts to persuade her to return to her husband had failed. Sona held Talata responsible for their son's disappearance. Although Talata's condition had improved, he had not been able to resume his lectures. The scholars had gradually left Musadu, some promising never to attend any of his lectures again

By midday, Zaiwulo's luck changed.

Fish began to take his bait at every attempt. He left the river with a long rope studded with various fish. Ma-Sona will return once she sees these, he told himself. Zaiwulo's wound had already healed, but sometimes, when he made a sudden move as he did now, he still felt a slight pain in his side.

Hurrying back to the city, he met Foningama squatting beside a smooth stone, against which he was sharpening his spears. "Did Haidarah send you?" the old man said. "Is he using a child now because he's afraid to face me?"

"I went to fish for Ma-Sona," said Zaiwulo.

"That's it! Tell me that your teacher has not washed those fish with nasi?" Foningama said, for the secret powers of Talata's specially prepared holy water were legendary. "We both know that the moment my daughter's lips touch even a drop of it, she will return to him. I will not allow it. Do you hear me? I will not allow it."

Foningama snatched the catch from Zaiwulo and hurried to his daughter. He met her sitting among piles of clothes, utensils, ornaments, and jewelry. Her days of inaction had made her feel restless.

"Ma-Sona, daughter, you need to rest."

"Rest will drive me out of my mind, Father. All I do is think about Karamo. Why has he not been found? Why is no one looking for him?" She turned to Zaiwulo. "Did you notice anything?"

Zaiwulo hesitated, wondering whether to reveal Karamo's secret. Finally, the sorrow in Sona's eyes and voice persuaded him to speak up.

"Karamo once told me about the English in Freetown, the French on the far side of the Niger, and the Liberians beyond the forest. He said that he wanted to be part of their world,"

"You knew this all along and kept it to yourself?" Foningama said.

Zaiwulo didn't know what to say.

"So he wants to become someone else?" Sona said.

"Young people and their foolish dreams. He will return soon," her father said and shifted his attention to the fish. "Talata must have worked his rosaries on these fish. Don't eat them."

"Is that so, Zaiwulo?" Sona asked.

"I caught the fish and hurried straight to you, Ma-Sona."

Without averting her eyes from Zaiwulo, Sona said, "Please leave us alone, Father."

"I will return to fetch you when the child is gone," said Foningama. "You need some shade and some fresh air."

The moment the old man was gone, Zaiwulo said, "Ma-Sona please come back. Haidarah needs you. We all need you."

Sona gave a weary sigh. "You are too young to understand what happens between a man and a woman, Zaiwulo, but your courage has impressed me. Tell your teacher to come see me."

The prospect of succeeding where others had failed sent Zaiwulo rushing toward the gate where he met a peevish Foningama. "My daughter will never return to that house again," the old man said.

On his way home, Zaiwulo met Massah. She walked with the grace that befitted her new station as one who, in Sona's absence, had taken over the affairs of the Haidarah household. Once a day she went to see Sona.

"Ma-Sona wants to see Haidarah," Zaiwulo told her.

"That is a good sign," she said. "I guess all you did was look at her with those eyes, and she was ready to do anything for you."

"I owe my teacher a lot," said Zaiwulo. "I am nothing without him."

"That's nonsense. Believe in yourself and beware of Osman."

"Osman is not my concern, Massah."

"Well, he should be. You have to keep your eyes and ears open here. That way, you have a chance of survival."

Massah's kindness touched Zaiwulo. Before he could stop himself, he blurted out: "Are you the one who's been fetching water for my bath?"

"Me?" she snorted. "You must be dreaming."

When Zaiwulo entered the Haidarah compound, Osman came charging at him.

"Where have you been all day?" he said.

"Your mother sent me to your father."

"Stop intervening in our affairs. You are not a Haidarah. Deliver the message and return to me immediately for your lesson."

Zaiwulo ignored him and walked towards the bolon where Talata sat. Talata's eyes were closed, and he looked like he was reeling from exhaustion. The scholar hardly slept. He spent his nights writing, meditating, and praying for things to be as they were, knowing that such prayers were often left unanswered. Once altered, things were never the same again.

"Haidarah, Ma-Sona wants to see you."

Talata opened his eyes. "That's good news," he said. "Because you brought it, you shall accompany me."

Zaiwulo hoped everyone would see him with Talata and know that he had affected events in that house. Indeed, some people paused to stare and guess the reason they were walking together.

"What are you doing in my house?" Foningama said when the two arrived. "My daughter stays here! Nothing you do will bring her back to you."

Talata ignored him and went straight to his wife. "Wait here, and keep the old man at bay," he told Zaiwulo.

Sona, lying in bed, saw it on his face the moment he entered. It was not grief for their son's departure but a naked longing for her.

"Sona, the boy took off because he wanted to do so," Talata began. "For a while, I felt that he was troubled by something, but he never confided in me. I can assure you that it had nothing to do with the ceremony."

"Haidarah!" she yelled.

"What, Ma-Sona?"

"Why are you not mourning the disappearance of our son?"

He sat beside her on the bed. "I've not slept since he left. I'm as affected as you are."

"I don't believe you. I don't see it in your face." Sona sat up, challenging Talata to contradict her.

"Ma-Sona, come home with me. Together, we will find Karamo."

"I belong here," she said and turned her back to him.

Talata, failing to persuade her, collected himself and left the house.

"Ma-Sona will join us soon," he told Zaiwulo and the boy broke into song in his mother tongue.

17

Foningama was restless, his daughter had not returned from her walk. Despite his protests, Sona had decided to go into the city, and was, perhaps, with her husband. Why trust a woman who has had a child with a Haidarah, even if she happens to be my daughter, he wondered. The prospect of confronting Talata made him more upset, but he had no choice.

Before leaving to see his son-in-law, Foningama went to his chambers to meet Naminata. Women had ceased to interest him for so long that any intimate need for them had often left him cold. It had to do with old age, he had reasoned, with the wisdom that such passion was unsuitable for him.

Naminata, however, had unleashed a craving in him, a need to be with her every moment of the day. But she had refused to sate that need or give in to him in any way. Sometimes, however, she came close to doing so. She would prepare his bed, bath, and even help him into his garments. But, when it came to executing the act itself, she would be distant. As the months went by, it became impossible to share his frustrations with anyone, lest he be mocked by Musadu or the whole of Koniyan. He hoped that one day he would enter his chambers and meet her ready to receive him.

Naminata sat up in bed when he entered. Her body, covered in a single wrapper, was taut like the drum that sounded from the mosque every day. He smiled to break the cold reception, but the hostility on her face bothered him. He wondered what troubled her.

"Have you eaten?" he asked.

She did not answer.

He had an urge to slap her, but he restrained himself. He had learned to ignore her silences, her foibles, and her habit of staying indoors for hours while his other wives worked. It's the price I must pay for how much she means to me, he thought.

Foningama moved to a corner of the room.

"Leave," he hissed.

Naminata wrapped a piece of cloth about her and drifted out of the room as though she'd never been there.

The old man fetched a mask decorated with cowries, feathers, and amulets. He knelt in supplication before it. The family deity had belonged to his ancestor, the first Foningama, that determined, stubborn, and avaricious man. That trailblazer who had moved a whole people from Sundiata's empire, crossing rivers infested with strange creatures, defeating kingdoms until he reached Musadu. "Protector of my people," he prayed, "deliver my daughter to me. You alone can return her to me again."

Finished, he returned the mask to its place and crawled backward to the door.

At that hour, Musadu looked like a deserted city. Most people had gone to their farms or markets in other towns and cities. Usually, as he walked through town, people would throw Foningama a string of greetings that he would catch and throw back. But because the lengthy rituals exhausted him, he decided to avoid them today.

On entering the Haidarah compound, Foningama noticed a peculiar silence. Life seemed to have ceased in that house. He found Talata in his study.

"You are here, numo," Talata said.

"I came to see my daughter."

"As far as I know, Sona is with you."

Foningama was shocked by the dread he caught in Talata's voice.

"Where is she then? What happened to my daughter?"

Talata jumped to his feet. A prayer he rarely said, for it was meant to be invoked only in matters of life and death, moved across his lips.

"Demba!" he called and broke into a run. "Demba!"

On hearing what had transpired, Demba hurried to the mosque and pounded the drum so hard that the whole Musadu realized it was not a call to prayer but to a terrible piece of news.

Within the hour, a huge crowd had gathered on the mosque's premises. Orders were given: "Search every house, every road that leads out of Musadu. Ask the sentinels if they have seen her, and if so, which way she went."

It turned out that the sentinels had seen Sona leave through the eastern gate, but they had paid her no attention, for their work primarily consisted of interrogating people who entered the city, not those who left it.

Tormented by the thought of his wife's disappearance, Talata mounted a horse and charged out of Musadu. It occurred to him that Samori might have captured her.

Talata raced out of the city, down the hill heading toward the twin cities Beyla and Jacodu. When he reached the river, he was amazed at how calm it looked, indifferent to the emotions raging within him.

He dismounted and approached the river, striding forward until the water touched the tips of his Kankan-made sandals, and then he fell to his knees. "Beloved," he addressed God, "I beseech you to protect my family, you who I see in everything, even in the caprices of my wife. Please don't test me, for I'm not strong enough. I might waver. I might break."

From the depths of his being, a desolate cry rose and burst with Sona's name which the silence bore along the banks of the Jon.

18

Zaiwulo heard the cry. He had come to the river that afternoon to fish for Sona again. I will be the one to take her home, he had told himself. It was a prospect that had enabled him endure Osman's insults during the lesson that morning. Shocked by the grief he caught in his teacher's voice, he emerged from the thicket separating them.

"What are you doing here?" Talata asked.

Taken aback by his teacher's recriminating tone, Zaiwulo did not respond.

"Sona is gone, child of the forest. She's left us," Talata said.

This cannot be, Zaiwulo thought, his greatest protector in Musadu cannot leave him.

"I thought she had agreed to return," he said.

Talata shook his head.

Zaiwulo broke into a run. Instead of heading eastward in the direction most people searching for Sona had taken, he raced westward toward the city. He crossed it and ran on until he was out of the western gate. It was said of pregnant women that their behavior was erratic, unpredictable. Zaiwulo knew this. He had seen pregnant women eat clay, swear like drunks, and make their husbands' lives hell. Sona might have chosen another route out of the city to make it difficult to find her.

Hours of searching finally led Zaiwulo to an unfamiliar place. He was off the main road and to his right stood a huge baobab tree, the kind of tree a pregnant woman might choose to rest under.

Nothing prepared him for the sight before him. Sona was sprawled out under the baobab tree, deep in labor. She looked broken. Her face was contorted in pain.

Zaiwulo stood and stared at her, perplexed.

"No one is to know I'm here," she said. "If they do, they will stop me from searching for Karamo. Help me deliver the child." Although she knew that it was forbidden for a man, let alone a child, to be present at a birth, there was no hesitation in her voice. "Do exactly what I tell you," she said.

Zaiwulo reached down and wiped her sweaty face with his palms. Sona, between hard breaths, instructed him. "Be brave; be the man I think you can be,"

Zaiwulo himself was now sweating. His tunic clung to his body.

"No matter what happens," she said, "I want you to remain calm."

Zaiwulo cleared a spot by uprooting the grass. He smoothed over the ground with his feet, creating a space large enough for Sona to lie down on her garment which he had spread out for her. Zaiwulo held her hand. Her fingers tightened around his every time the pain ebbed and flowed in her. He worked with her, her breath becoming his breath until shadows fell on the earth, and the two were part of that nocturnal world.

The night came alive with the sounds of insects and the call of birds. Mosquitoes buzzed about them. The moon emerged from behind a cluster of clouds. Sona was still fighting the soaring waves of labor while Zaiwulo encouraged her. "Ma-Sona, it's almost here," he shouted when he saw the child's silky soft hair. It emboldened him, and he reached out to touch its soft hair. He gasped as he did so, suddenly aware of the child's fragility.

"Now, all you have to do is pull it out," Sona whispered.

Zaiwulo's hands trembled as he held on to the tiny creature. At that moment, he thought of his mother who had gone through this same process. A longing he'd never felt before tore at his heart. He yearned for her buffalo songs, for her owl eyes, her clumsy gait, for those very things that had once embarrassed him.

The moment the child eased out of its mother, at the sight of such vulnerability, Zaiwulo burst into tears. He held on to the child, unwilling to let go, until Sona took it from him.

"Leave now," she said, "I will take over from here."

"But Ma-Sona, you can't be alone," he said.

Sona could hardly stand, but she seemed determined.

"Don't worry, child. I will be fine."

Zaiwulo remembered the pain he had suffered the day he left his mother and sisters. He understood. Mother and child belonged together. He vowed not to tell anyone about them.

He was about to leave when the sound of hoofbeats alerted them to possible danger. While crouching in the grass and shielding mother and child with his body, Zaiwulo saw a group of horsemen heading toward Musadu.

Hard on their heels rode a lone horseman. There was something remarkable about the man, Zaiwulo noted, for he rode his mount as if he owned the world.

The horseman was Samori.

19

The first thing Zaiwulo noticed about Samori when he met him was his hard and piercing gaze. It was a look capable of paralyzing any adversary. There lingered about him an intimidating silence, which, as with everything that formed him, had been cultivated during his days as a slave. The trader-turned slave, then warrior, and now king, had learned that silence bred mystery. It was to this mystery he owed his existence. The dark and glossy skin of his face gleamed in the flickering light of his sofas' torches. His jaw was slender, his chin sharp, and his wrists were marked by vitiligo. Between his brows and around his nose ran two furrows which gave his face an extraordinary intensity.

Outside Musadu's walls and far from the eyes of the sentinels, Samori sat cross-legged on the grass, his back straight as a pole. His posture clearly showed he had come to issue orders and expected to be obeyed. A sword rested on his lap. It was believed that he decapitated his enemies with that sword. Beside him lay his javelin which served as both weapon and staff, for his hands were often restless if there was nothing to hold.

The men surrounding him were the elites of his sofas, most of whom he had selected and trained. They included his brother, Kemeh-Brimah; his favorite son, Jawulen-Karamoko, and the most courageous of his sofas, Kemoko-

Bilali. With him also was a man he regarded as the best of them all, the man he loved and admired more than anyone on earth, the man who made him what he was, his best friend since childhood, his griot, Morifin-Djan Diabate.

Samori smiled when he saw Zaiwulo.

The boy, having left Sona and the child, was on his way back to Musadu when he met Samori and his men. He was surprised to see not just his teacher, Talata, but also Osman, and the blind man Demba with them.

Talata, Zaiwulo noticed, was behaving like he'd known Samori for years. He seemed to be done with his fear and apprehension of the man, which baffled the boy.

"I wish I was the ruler of Musadu to welcome you all, Faama," Talata said, using the title Samori had bestowed upon himself a few years ago. It was a royal title he had not inherited but earned. For years, Samori had borne the title of *Keletigui*—warlord—which he now deemed unsuitable for a man who wanted to unite people.

On noticing Zaiwulo, Talata asked, "Where were you?"

"I went in search of Ma-Sona," Zaiwulo said.

"Did you find her?"

Zaiwulo shook his head.

"Who is the child, Haidarah?" Samori asked.

"He's from the forest, Faama."

"Ah, he is of my mother's people!"

"He's here because of a promise his father and I made to each other, and I intend to keep it. I want him and my son Osman to go with us."

"A promise is a sacred bond," Samori said.

Kemoko-Bilali, whom Zaiwulo recognized as the sofa he had met at the river a few months earlier, said, "The child is brave, Faama."

"Being brave is one thing, being a sofa is another thing." Samori beckoned to Zaiwulo who moved and sat before him. Samori stared at the boy, searched his eyes for traces of the fear that older and battle-tested men often held in his presence. Samori found none. This was new to him. "Yes, a brave child indeed, Kemoko," he said.

Beneath his calm exterior, Zaiwulo was all doubts and fear. He shivered at the thought that he would soon be part of the world of a man whose name was associated with violence and war.

Samori had come to solicit Talata's help.

"Haidarah," Samori said to Talata earlier that evening, "the house to which your wife belongs, the Kamara House, is the same house to which my mother partly belonged. Her father was a Kamara, and her mother was from the forest. You know as well as I do that the first Foningama—the ancestor of the Kamaras—invited your ancestor to Musadu to help protect the city and make him a great ruler. He turned to a Haidarah when he needed help. That's why I'm turning to you for your counsel and invaluable prayers. I need you."

Samori's cunning phrases had made it impossible for Talata to refuse him. Every period had its leader who directed its course, Talata had reasoned, which meant that to survive he had to ally himself with Samori. However, he knew that the consequences of such an alliance could prove costly as he risked incurring the wrath of the king of Musadu who had sided with Saaye of the Gbanguno Mountain, Samori's sworn enemy.

Talata had realized that instead of turning to the other rulers in Koniyan and beyond, whose ambitions were as fiery as his own, Samori had turned to scholars in his attempt to unite and control Koniyan. Real power lay in the hands of those scholars. They were the lawmakers. They helped forge the course of society. Their influence was undeniable.

"Welcome, Faama, my house is yours," Talata had said, in the tone of one left with no other choice. "Where would I be without your protection?"

"You've spoken well, Haidarah," Samori said. "I want you to accompany me to my capital, Sanankoro. We leave tonight."

"You come at a difficult time, Faama," said Talata. "My wife and youngest son have disappeared. I don't know what has become of them."

"Women," Samori said. "When we wrong them, they sometimes retaliate in excess. I will task my sofas with finding your wife and son."

"Your dream has come true, Faama," said the Djeli Morifin-Djan. "Now you have the greatest scholar in our part of the world as an ally. Soon, others will follow suit. Who would dare confront you then?"

Now Samori turned to Osman and Zaiwulo.

"You can bring the boys with you, Haidarah," he said.

Talata glanced at Demba who sat on the grass beside him. The blind man had been silent all the while, not for lack of words, but because of the rapid unfolding of events. It left him confounded.

"You will head the house in my stead, Demba," Talata said.

"But Haidarah, a family without its head, has no chance of survival. You are what makes us who we are in Musadu, in the whole of Koniyan, a great house. You can't leave," said the blind man.

"You underestimate yourself, Demba. Look at your achievements. You are as educated as I am and capable in many ways than I am. If anything happens to me, you are to take care of this house. Don't let me down."

Demba shifted to his knees, as if in supplication, but Talata picked him up and held him in an embrace. They both needed it. "You are dearer to me than my own family, Demba," he said.

Demba knew this to be true. "I will not let you down, Haidarah," he said.

Samori mounted his horse, Kawsu, which had been with him for years. Since the onset of his conquering streak in lower Koniyan, Samori had developed the habit of pausing outside the gates of each conquered town or city, appraising it. He gazed at Musadu which appeared dormant in the distance. Although the city was not yet a part of his possessions, Samori had its greatest scholar as an ally. Musadu was coveted by men like Saaye of the Gbanguno Mountain, another ruler about his age, but his greatest adversary in Koniyan was and remained Sere-Brimah, the man who had captured his mother. Until her capture, his world had evolved around her. He remembered his younger brother Kemeh-Brimah running to him with the news that Masoronah, Samori's mother, had been captured by Sere-Brimah. Though he and Kemeh-Brimah were of different mothers, they were very close. Their brotherhood was cemented by their loyalty to each other. Samori and his brother had decided to consult their father Lafiya. They met him chewing kola nut while lying in a hammock in the shade of a baobab tree.

"Sere-Brimah will let your mother go," he said. "He will not hurt her."

"He could force her to be his wife, Father," Samori protested. "He could deny us ever seeing her again."

Lafiya frowned. "What else can we do?"

Those words of resignation were the onset of the friction between father and son.

"We will free our mother by all means," Samori said.

Together with his brother, Samori rode to Madina, Sere-Brimah's capital. Though he was yet to be king—because his brother, the real king, was still alive— Sere-Brimah was the de facto leader.

Sere-Brimah made the brothers wait for a week before granting them audience, and then, he forced them to prostrate in the dust before him. According to legend, they lay in the dust for a whole day and night, but it must have been a matter of a few hours or more.

"Who are you?" Sere-Brimah had asked.

"I am Samori Touré, and this is my brother, Kemeh-Brimah. We came to you concerning our mother, Masoronah."

"I know no such woman," Sere-Brimah said.

The brothers persisted. "We came to purchase her freedom."

"By what means?"

"By being your slaves in her stead."

Sere-Brimah agreed but refused to let their mother go, even after they had bought her freedom. She was too valuable to him.

Those slave years would make a warrior of Samori first and then a leader.

In servitude, he led campaigns on Sere-Brimah's behalf. He conquered cities and villages in his name. He fought to take control of the kola nut route to the forest and the coast of Liberia. In the end, when it became clear that Sere-Brimah would never let his mother go, Samori fled with her toward the forest, to her people.

"Whenever you are in trouble," his mother often told him, "go to my people. They will never let you down."

During the flight, the cold of the savannah lodged into Masoronah's bones, hampering her movements. Samori covered her with his garment and kindled fires to warm her. Even though the flames could betray them, he wanted her to live. Masoronah gazed at her son through the burning flames.

"Because you've made this fire and exposed yourself to danger," she said, "I swear by the bones of my ancestors that one day, thousands will expose themselves to danger to protect you. And because you've covered me with the only garment you have, one day, people will spread out their garments for you to walk on. So don't fear slavery, my son. One day, you will rise."

Samori thought of his mother's words now, words that had triggered in him the overwhelming desire to fight for his freedom and hers. Her words had ushered in the beginning of his ascendency in Koniyan. This hunger to be the master of his own destiny had led him to Musadu. He vowed to conquer the city, not only because of its strategic location as a trading post connecting the savannah to the forest and the coast of Liberia, but because of its past.

Musadu was the mother of all towns and villages in Koniyan, a place from where people had migrated to populate the savannah. Parts of him were connected to Musadu in the person of his mother whose past was rooted in the forest. The rest of him was steeped in the old empire belonging to Sundiata Keita, the man whose fame had reached the four corners of the world.

Every time Samori thought of his origins—which he often did in those early days of empire building—he was left with the impression that he had the right to everything:

from the vast forests of his mother's country and the endless plains of the savannah to the mysterious desert in the north. They were his birthright. They belonged to him.

The group prepared to leave.

"Can you ride, child?" Kemoko-Bilali asked Zaiwulo.

"Yes, Uncle."

"I've never seen him ride a horse," Osman said, laughing. "He can't ride. Bush Boy, don't pretend to be what you are not."

"Climb up behind me then," Kemoko-Bilali interrupted Zaiwulo who was about to protest. "I will teach you one day."

Zaiwulo held tightly onto Kemoko-Bilali. He was astounded by the ease with which Samori had persuaded his teacher to leave everything of importance behind — including his family and manuscripts— to follow him into the unknown. Was that how the world worked? he wondered. A world in which one was always confronted with a stronger and mightier other?

The boy missed Massah and Naminata who had made his life bearable in Musadu. Would he ever see them again?

20

Under a clear moonlit sky, the men rode along clusters of tall grass in a silence punctuated by the panting of horses. Zaiwulo listened to the animals. Their efforts were endearing to him, and his desire to ride one of them was heightened by their imposing presence around him. He imagined himself returning to Haindi on horseback and the reaction of his mother and sisters at the sight of him mounted on an animal rarely seen in the forest.

The dream was so beguiling that when he snapped out of it at the sound of gunfire behind him, Zaiwulo felt disoriented.

It was an ambush.

Kemoko-Bilali's reaction was swift. He threw Zaiwulo off the horse and raced away to protect Samori. The sofas charged after him.

Zaiwulo dashed for cover in the thicket while the sound of war cries and gunfire filled the air, sowing panic in him. Wishing he could disappear, he grabbed hold of the grass under him. Samorian forces formed a defensive line and fell on the enemy; Zaiwulo saw Samori approach from the back, firing his rifle at the enemy while his horse was in full tilt.

The sofas burst into a single cry: “O, admired one, we follow you. Wherever you go, we go. Whatever you do, we do—to death.”

Their intrepid cries and willingness to die for their leader impressed Zaiwulo as he lay in the grass, waiting for the end of the onslaught. He heard the clashes of swords and spears. Soon, the smell of gunpowder replaced the heady scent of grass. He saw and heard men falling around him, but he did not move.

A voice tore through the gunfire and war cries.

“Samori, I know you can hear me. One day our paths will cross again and then you will know who the true ruler of Koniyan is.”

Samori fired a shot in the direction of the voice.

The man who had threatened Samori withdrew in the darkness from the fierce counter-attack by Samorian forces.

“Packie!” Samori shouted when the battle cries had died down. The word was an exclamation particular to him, which his men associated with those moments when he was extremely angry. “It was Gbanguno Saaye, that bastard,” he said. “Saaye wants Musadu as much as I do. Next time we meet, I will feed him to the vultures.”

Samori dismounted and caressed his horse.

“In gratitude for being so brave, Kawsu,” he said, his head pressed against the beast’s mane, “I will make sure the Djelis sing your praises forever.”

He instructed his men to set up camp. “We need rest,” he said.

Within an hour, in the light of burning twigs, the sofas stitched together some pliant trees, grass, and ropes as shelter for their leader, his best friend, Morifin-Djan, and Talata. When they were done, they sat on the grass in the open expanse and traded anecdotes about Saaye, dreaming of the day they would vanquish his kingdom. The day they would break through the walls of Gbanguno Mountain where he'd barricaded himself.

Zaiwulo was about to join them when Osman approached him.

"I bet you pissed yourself in fear," Osman said, laughing. "Tell me, I saw you lying on the ground, hiding, scared to death. Don't deny it."

"I didn't see you anywhere," Zaiwulo snapped back.

"If you continue to use that tone with me," sneered Osman, "I will make your life impossible here. How dare you? Know your place."

Talata interrupted them. "It's time to rest, boys," he said.

Zaiwulo went to sleep thinking about Samori's bond with the forest, a place to which he, Zaiwulo, also belonged. Was this the reason Samori had taken to him? He thought of his birthplace Haindi and its rivers and animals. He thought of his mother and sisters. He thought of how Samori was related to a people disparaged by so many in the savannah.

21

The horsemen came to a halt atop a hill. Down below the hill nestled a village in the throes of a deep sleep. They had been riding for hours now. From behind Kemoko-Bilali, Zaiwulo gazed at his surroundings. The grass country was draped in moonlight and looked captivating. The undulating hills surrounding it gave such an enthralling sense of continuity that Zaiwulo felt compelled to speak. "Uncle Kemoko, where are we?" he asked.

The sofa laughed. "Faama, the child wants to know where we are."

Samori ignored the question. "You know what to do, Kemoko," he said.

The sofa general rode down the hill to the village while Zaiwulo held tight around his waist. He was terrified and thought of how an astute sentinel might see them coming and let loose a gunshot in their direction, ending their lives then and there. Zaiwulo had the urge to tug at the sofa general's garment and ask him to stop, but, as if he could read his mind, Kemoko-Bilali laughed, clicked his tongue, and his horse burst into a gallop.

Of all the Samorian sofas, the boy would learn later, Kemoko-Bilali was the most battle-tested. Some believed he never married because his way of life did not allow for the stability that marriage demanded. Moreover, no woman could satiate his hunger, and those who risked it were consumed by his avarice. Sometimes, when on a mission, he would drive his horse so hard that the animal simply perished under the pressure of his tenacity.

Kemoko-Bilali dismounted and walked up to the wall. He was so tall that his head almost came level with the top of the edifice. Parts of it crumbled when he slapped it hard with the flat of his hand. "Child of the forest, why do some people set no store for their own lives?" he said and sucked his teeth. "Look at this negligence!"

Kemoko-Bilali helped Zaiwulo scale the wall and jumped over after him. The sofa general walked in front, up to a house close to the wall. When they knocked at the door, a voice, drowsy with sleep, asked, "Who is there?"

"Come out and go tell your chief that his Faama Samori Touré is here."

On hearing the name, a young man bolted out of the house and raced toward the village center, yelling that the man before whom kings trembled was standing at the gates of their village.

"Samori Touré, the Faama of Faamas is here," he cried.

This was a name many in Koniyan associated with absolute power, with the sacking of towns and cities. Rumor had it that during the siege of a town, the bearer of that name had slaughtered so many people that the nearby river had turned red with blood. Not since Sundiata Keita had a name evoked such fear and awe in people as that of Samori Touré.

The elders of the village, including its chief, hurried with oil lamps and torches to where Kemoko-Bilali and Zaiwulo were standing. Zaiwulo noted how the chief's mouth moved constantly. He could not decide if the man was chewing kola nuts or if it was his way of masking his fear.

"Samori, you say?" the village chief asked. "But he's one of us. His family, the Tourés, settled around here when they came down from the empire of Sundiata Keita. It's an honor to address such a great ruler."

"I will take you to meet him," Kemoko-Bilali said. He and Zaiwulo returned to Samori with the village chief and elders in tow.

"Welcome, Faama," the chief said. "Our homes and properties are yours for the asking. Can a father refuse a son who's returned home?"

The Djeli, Morifin-Djan, answered, "No, wise chief, a father cannot, for that would constitute a crime. Your son demands your hospitality."

The village burst into life. Children filled the square and began singing and dancing. Women set pots on the fire to prepare dinner. Men emptied their homes for Samori and his retinue; some offered Samori the gold they kept as dowries for their son.

Zaiwulo and Osman were accorded their lodgings. Seated with Osman before the house, waiting for their food, Zaiwulo saw a group of women escorting a young woman to Samori's chambers. She was clothed in white, with gold bangles around her arms and hair studded with rings of gold.

"Who is that?" he asked Osman.

"The village is offering Samori a bride. In Sanankoro he has a palace the size of Musadu. I heard that it is full of his wives, each with more than ten children. His sons' courage are as legendary as his own, and his daughters wear silk and sandals of pure gold. You will see."

Two girls approached them, each carrying an earthen bowl of steaming food on her head. The girls set the food before them.

"Thank you," Zaiwulo said.

The girls smiled and left silently.

"I am the oldest. I get to eat first," Osman said.

The food was pounded toe with okra sauce and tender meat and fish. Zaiwulo's stomach growled. As he watched Osman eat the pounded cassava, Zaiwulo wished he could stand up to Talata's son. One day, I will fight him, he thought, but what would that mean for my well-being?

What Osman left for him lacked the succulent meat and fish that made it special, but the food did Zaiwulo some good. Later, he went to sleep on the smaller of the two beds.

Osman woke him up at dawn. "My father wants to see us."

Talata led them to the village square where mats had been spread. In the center were large bowls and plates of degue, a gruel that consisted of pounded rice mixed with honey. Samori was surrounded by his retinue and the village elders. Fat bullocks, which the villagers had been keeping for periods of scarcity, had been slaughtered and cooked for the reception.

A Djeli had been summoned from a nearby village. "Welcome, a thousand times welcome, Faama," the griot said. "A son travels across the seas, across the world, but always returns home, to the place where his umbilical cord is buried. You are home, Faama of all Faamas!"

The Djeli cited numerous sources to support his claim that the village chief and Samori shared the same family line.

"We knew it the moment we saw you, Faama," the chief said.

Morifin-Djan spoke on Samori's behalf. "Your Faama demanded that you prepare degue. You've done so. Now, he asks that each of you take a handful of the degue. Before you swallow it, say for all to hear, "With this degue, we pledge our allegiance to our Faama and support his endeavor to unite all our people."

They are all doing it out of fear or deep reverence, Zaiwulo thought as he watched the villagers swear their commitment to Samori.

Later, on their way to Sanankoro, Talata would tell Zaiwulo that the degue represented blood.

"By drinking it, the villagers and their relatives are bound to Samori forever. That's the tactic Samori has been using in many places. It's not always about war," he added, more for himself than for Zaiwulo. "This is how Samori has managed to unite most towns and villages in Koniyan. He can be a man of peace, as you've seen."

22

Sanankoro was a revelation to Zaiwulo.

The city was built as though it had been carefully planned. The whitewashed mud houses and dung-plastered walls were constructed in a straight line and flanked the main road leading to Samori's palace. The main road was as smooth as the mat Zaiwulo had slept on the night before. On the roadside, long queues of people stood, bowing obsequiously to Samori and his men. Musicians hit and plucked at their instruments in a frenzy. The sound of drums, balafon, koras, and xylophones were complemented by the songs of the griots. Each Djeli and his band of singers picked out unique aspects of the Faama's past. They made a heroine of his mother. They sang that long before Samori was born, Masoronah had dreamed of a snake with its length stretching from one end of the earth to the other. They said that the dream had meant that her child would one day conquer the world like Sundiata, alias Mari Jata, The Lion King, had done.

Samori's horse, Kawsu, lifted its head with its polished mane and danced in proud trots. When Zaiwulo saw a throng of exquisitely dressed men, women, and children, he knew they were members of the Samorian household. He gasped at Samori's palace with its thick walls. The sentinels high up on both sides of the encampment stood to attention as Samori approached. Osman, who walked beside Zaiwulo, was just as impressed by the exuberant display of power and splendor.

A sea of people flowed toward the palace.

In the largest courtyard beyond the palace walls, a huge platform and a thatched roof had been erected. A throne covered with cushions sat there.

The people who surrounded the platform must be the other half of the Samorian household, Zaiwulo thought, which, in fact, was true. The sons were in scarlet tunics while the daughters were in indigo wrappers and wooden sandals tied with gold strings. Samori's wives were in black and white with hairdos in the form of pyramids and cylinders. Their polished faces shone with oil.

The sofas dismounted. "Move to the right of the throne," Kemoko-Bilali told Zaiwulo. "You too, Haidarah," he told Osman.

Unsure whether it was wise to come so close to the throne, Zaiwulo hesitated; but just then, Talata laid his hand on the boy's shoulder and led him to a place on the right, below the throne. He was so grateful that he missed seeing Samori ascend the platform and take a seat on his throne.

Samori signaled to a sofa general called Porokerrie to approach him, but a young woman with the smooth skin of a tree bared of its bark beat Porokerrie to the platform. She whispered something to Samori, and when she turned to the crowd, her eyes rested on Zaiwulo. She was struck by the boy's disarming eyes. One day, men and women would weep because of those eyes, she told herself, and the thought excited her. She hoped the child she was carrying, about whom her husband Samori knew nothing, would look like the boy.

The woman then noticed Talata. "So you brought the scholar with you as promised, beloved," she said, and then she turned to Talata. "Haidarah, we hope you succeed in helping our Faama."

The woman's name was Sarankenyi. In fact, her real name was Saran, but she was so beautiful that she had earned the nickname Kenyi–The Beauty.

Sarankenyi leaned toward Samori again. "The moment you left for Musadu, beloved, your uncles began to fuss about how you've taken over their Sanankoro," she said. She had hit on his most sensitive spot: the ongoing silent war with his uncles. It enraged him.

Samori signaled to Porokerrie to approach him.

Sarankenyi did not move.

"What are you still doing here?" Samori growled.

Noting the crowd's unease as a result of her behavior, Sarankenyi's steps were measured and her head held high in defiance as she walked toward her co-wives.

Samori whispered to Porokerrie.

The sofa general turned to the crowd. His furrowed face expressed Samori's anger.

"Our Faama has asked me to remind you all that he brought peace to a city that had not known peace for years. Therefore, Sanankoro belongs to him and him to the city forever."

Samori left the crowd and his family standing outside and headed toward his chambers. He'd had enough of his uncles.

23

Samori met his father Lafiya in his sleeping quarters. Samori's quarters was filled with trophies of his conquests. Sacks of gold and silver with sophisticated leatherwork, English and Liberian coins, French boots, precious swords, and homespun cotton cloth whose value increased with the years. Samori hardly ever paused to appreciate them or consider their value. He would not have cared if the chambers were cleared of everything except for his bed and clothes. The Faama was reeling from exhaustion.

Samori's father had come to warn him about his wife, Sarankenyi. The old man had interpreted the public incident between his son and wife to show that Sarankenyi was losing ground. It was time for him to strike.

Old age had compressed Lafiya's height. Now, he stooped as he walked with a cane, as though bearing a heavy burden. He was fair complexioned, unlike his son with his jet-black skin. They seemed unrelated.

"Sarankenyi is incapable of being a good wife," Lafiya said. "She behaves like she is the only wife and sows discord amongst us."

Samori sat up across from his father. What his father didn't know was that Sarankenyi had prepared the palace, including his chambers in anticipation of his return. She had laid out his clothes and covered his bed with fresh sheets, a task she had not relegated to her domestics but had performed herself. Samori's humiliation of her in public was to conceal the fact that she was his favorite. The world had to believe that he made no exception in his dealings with his people—whether they were family or not.

"Saran was just telling me that my uncles want me out of Sanankoro, Father. Haven't I done enough for them? Didn't I make them rich beyond their dreams and turn their Sanankoro, once a place of no consequence, into the pride of Koniyan? Didn't I do that and more?"

"But we need your uncles. They are family, my son!"

"*Need* them, Father? What have they done for us, except undermine our efforts and cause us much sorrow?"

Lafiya was exhausted by the constant fights between his son and uncles, and between his son and other rulers in Koniyan. It was more out of self-preservation than a genuine concern for his son's well-being. "You could talk to them," he said. "I can arrange it!"

"Talk to them? It's because they are family and have allowed me to be who I am today that I still tolerate them. Otherwise, I would have driven them out of the city a long time ago."

"Don't give up on them, son," Lafiya pleaded.

One of Samori's guards entered to announce that Sarankenyi was waiting to see the Faama.

"Let her in," Samori said.

Lafiya was so annoyed at his son for interrupting their conversation that he stood up and left in silence. On his way out, he met Sarankenyi.

"Good afternoon, Father," she said.

Lafiya sucked his teeth.

Alone with Sarankenyi, Samori leaned back on the bed. Sarankenyi helped him remove his clothes. First his hat around which he had tied a band of cloth, then his tunic, then his baggy trousers. Giddy from the movement of her hands, he let himself go by stretching fully on the bed. Her touch was so calming that it seemed as though she was washing layer after layer of fatigue off his body and mind. It was strange, this feeling she ignited in him. It tripled his sense of his worth as a man. Women were often passive in his presence, intimidated by the hyperbolic stories they had heard about him. But not Sarankenyi, this Koniyan beauty. The one thing they both needed to cement their bond was a child. It was his wish as much as her own.

"What news did your father bring, beloved?"

Samori was uninterested in pursuing the conversation. Sarankenyi did not push him but chose instead to inquire about Zaiwulo.

"You mean the boy from the forest?" Samori said.

"There's something about him."

Samori nodded. "He's of my mother's people. Part of her is connected to the forest. The boy reminds me so much of her."

The moment was right, Sarankenyi thought, to share her secret.

"I am with child, beloved."

Samori could always master his emotions and under any circumstances, but this sudden news affected him. He embraced Saran before summoning his Djeli, Morifin-Djan Diabate. "Tell the world, my best friend, that we are expecting a child." The Djeli left to spread the news, and Samori held Sarankenyi tight in his arms, dreaming of what the two of them would accomplish.

"With this child, the world will fear you, my beloved," Saran said.

At first, Samori did not respond. Instead, he asked one of his guards to fetch Talata. "You have to be careful, Saran," he said at last. He was referring to the fact that his son Jawulen-Karamoko was already the heir apparent. The boy was as ambitious as his father.

"Why should I be? I am married to you."

"Don't go about flaunting your fortune before other members of the household. Be humble and quiet about it."

Although she knew he was right, Sarankenyi was not intimidated by the other wives. Every time she imagined the future, she was alone with him, with no sign of the other women or even other people. She and Samori alone mattered.

Talata was announced.

"Haidarah," Samori said when Talata entered with Osman and Zaiwulo. "You seem to bring good fortune with you everywhere you go. Saran told me that she's with child. You are a scholar to hold onto."

Zaiwulo did not dare look at Sarankenyi.

"It will be a boy, Haidarah," Sarankenyi said and nodded toward Zaiwulo. "One day the two of you will be brothers," she said. "I will make sure of that.'"

"Zaiwulo will be a scholar," Talata said.

"Haidarah, don't compel a person to be what he doesn't want to be," Samori said. "I was born to be a hawker—a *djula*—but look at me today."

"I promised his father that I would teach him," said Talata.

"We will see," Samori replied.

Talata realized that he'd said enough and that if he pushed the subject any further, he might end up incurring

Samori's wrath. "You called me, Faama," he began, bringing attention back to why he was summoned.

"We want you to pray for us, to pray for Saran," Samori said.

Talata approached Sarankenyi and laid his hands on her head.

24

"Haidarah, I want to talk to you alone," Samori said.

Shadows of dusk were creeping over the city. Around the palace, songs spilled out, accompanied by drums and xylophones. Sanankoro was still celebrating the news of Sarankenyi's pregnancy. Samori led Talata to a less crowded part of the palace, a courtyard where he sat on a mat in the shade of a baobab tree.

"Have one of these, please," Samori said, and offered Talata a kola nut, fresh from the forest. The two men chewed in silence.

"I had a dream last night, Haidarah," said Samori. "You scholars are great interpreters of dreams. In my dream, I was standing before a large gate that led out to the sea which was foaming and soaring like my hopes. I was an old man, long past the age of seventy. As I approached the sea, a feeling of being abandoned seized me. So I turned to those who had come to bid me farewell, those I once loved—including Saran—but saw no one. They had all vanished. Out of the depth of my loneliness, a pair of mighty hands reached out and grabbed my neck, tightening their hold on me with such purposeful tenderness that I thought the inevitable had come."

The dream was clearly about his death, Talata thought, but he could not explain the sea and why Samori was walking toward it.

"What do you think, Haidarah?"

"Some dreams are very difficult to interpret, Faama. Sometimes one has to make do with a sacrifice to avert a harmful dream."

"Spell out the sacrifice, and it shall be arranged. If the sea means my death, then let me tell you that it's useless contemplating it. Death is inevitable."

"Seven lambs will do, Faama," Talata said.

Samori nodded. "But I didn't call you here to only interpret dreams."

Talata looked up at Samori.

"There is talk of a very special manuscript belonging to your family. I was told that your elder brother, Karamo-Sidikie, in Kankan had it, but he told me that you were the one entrusted with keeping it. Tell me, is it true what they say about the manuscript?"

"What do they say, Faama?"

"That you can achieve goals with it."

Gripped by fear, the scholar sat upright. What if Samori were to lay hands on the manuscript? What would that mean for him, for the world?

"I'm but the custodian of the manuscript, Faama. I don't perform miracles. You shouldn't always believe what people say."

"But what are the true attributes of that famous book?"

No one outside of the family should know the true attributes of the manuscript, not even Samori, Talata thought. So, he decided to tell him an aspect of the truth.

"The manuscript contains nothing else but the history of our people. It offers insight into the present, which is what the past does," he said.

Samori was silent, his steely eyes fixed on Talata. "You, unlike other scholars, don't have hunger for power," Samori said. "That's why I want you to be my envoy to Sere-Brimah, the man who enslaved my mother. He will listen to you. If I sent one of my sofas, he would probably decapitate him. You will go with presents. Tell Sere-Brimah that I want to be his ally, that I seek to work together with him."

Talata couldn't believe his ears. "But you once revolted against this man. He is still fighting you. Will he not see this as a trap?"

"What he thinks of it is of little importance. The world has to see that I've reached out a hand of friendship to him. Then we will see who the real agitator in Koniyan is. We will know the real enemy of the people."

"How soon can I leave? I want to return to Musadu immediately after my mission. My wife and son have not yet been found."

"I know, Haidarah. My sofas are still searching for them. If they are in Koniyan, then they will be found; but first, we have to deal with a few things before your departure. I could arrange for the sacrifice today."

"I would like Osman and Zaiwulo to go with me."

"The boys will remain. I want them to learn a bit about court life," Samori said.

Talata could not refuse him, though he feared that Samori would not make such a request without a reason. What did he want with the two boys in the long run?

Soon after Talata left, Samori joined his advisers in the larger courtyard. Each took his place around the Faama, and all refrained from inquiring about what had transpired between Samori and the scholar.

Zaiwulo chose an inconspicuous corner behind one of the sofa generals and sat with his back to the mud wall of the enclosure. This display of power and wealth, the size of the city, and the large presence of the sofas intimidated him.

Osman, on the other hand, sat in a prominent place, close to Kemoko-Bilali.

Together they went into detailed discussions of the affairs of the growing Samorian kingdom, especially the challenges that still faced them, with a slew of adversaries yet to defeat. Samori was silent all the while, slightly nodding his head or shaking it.

At one point, Samori coughed, signaling his readiness to speak.

"It's time to discuss the English in Freetown and the French on the other side of the Niger," he said. "What should we do regarding these two powers, Morifin-Djan?"

Morifin-Djan, small and with a smooth face, had spurred Samori on to become a leader. They had begun as a small band of young men in Maniambaladougou who sold their services to people. They cleared bushes for farmers, fetched firewood, tracked down horses or runaway brides, and even organized wrestling matches with other villages in Koniyan. They became so notorious that their parents intervened and separated them and Samori was sent to his uncles in Sanankoro. Years later, after Samori had served under Sere-Brimah to buy his mother's freedom, the Djeli had reunited the group and had ignited the fire of adventure in his best friend.

Morifin-Djan cleared his throat. "We should send a letter to their Faama-mosssou. What is her name again? Such a difficult name!" the Djeli asked the gathering. "Yes, Queen Victoria! We should send her a letter requesting a treaty."

"We could say that we regard her as our mother. Let's shower her with praises. The English are and will remain our best allies," Samori said, pleased.

"If we succeed at signing such a treaty with that woman, it will enable us to conquer Koniyan and all the territories around it."

Osman coughed to attract attention.

"Haidarah, you wanted to say something?" the griot asked.

"We've never paused to consider why the English are here, Faama, Osman said. "Why did they leave their land to settle so close to us?"

"But that's evident, Haidarah," Samori's brother Kemeh-Brimah said. "They want to trade with us. They've always traded with us."

"But what if at a certain moment they wanted more than trading? What if they decide to conquer our lands?" said Osman.

A deep silence fell on the gathering.

"How did you arrive at such a conclusion?" Samori asked.

"In one of my father's books, I read that it was outsiders who often brought about great changes and upheavals."

"The child speaks the truth, Faama," Morifin-Djan said. "This is the history of the Mandé people. Everywhere we went, we conquered. Why should the Toubabous behave differently? We should be on our guard."

Zaiwulo had to applaud Osman's courage and insight. He had managed to persuade Samori and his entire court to listen to him. Zaiwulo wanted to emulate him, and he knew how to go about it. He would begin by sticking to his writing slate and knowing every word written on its surface and every manuscript he could lay his hands on.

After the meeting, Zaiwulo borrowed a slate from a student in one of the houses in the palace. He sat in front of his lodgings and began to write what he had learned on its dry surface. Zaiwulo repeated the words and sentences he had written. Unafraid that he was attracting attention, he intoned every word, his voice rising and falling.

He went on till nightfall.

After dinner with his teacher and Osman, Zaiwulo took up his lesson again. At one point, he sounded as if he was imploring the words to come to him. He was hungry for knowledge. His mind was alive with the possibilities of what he could become.

Osman met him lying in bed and whispering his lessons. The lodging had two beds, the space was as large as Talata's study. An oil lamp burned in a corner of the room.

"I will be leaving as one of Samori's envoys to the English in Freetown," Osman said. "I will learn their language and excel in their world. Upon my return, I'll send you packing."

Zaiwulo ignored him, but he vowed to catch up with Osman. He was awake for most of the night. At dawn, he was the first one up. He left the house and went to sit in front of his teacher's house where he continued chanting his lesson.

•×•

Talata woke up to a voice with a gracious lilt in it. A voice that could stir hearts. In the life of every student, there came a moment when he realized that his fate was bound to the goal he'd set out to achieve. It often took years for most students to attain that keen level of awareness or to take that great leap, which was why Talata was surprised to catch a clear trace of it in Zaiwulo's voice so early on.

Talata came out to talk to him. "You are a gifted student, Zaiwulo," he said. "When I return from visiting Sere-Brimah, I will teach you myself."

The two were interrupted by Samori.

"Child of the forest, you are already a scholar," Samori said.

With his long French boots, a sword, and a rifle in his hands, the Faama was dressed for war. The weapons, black and glinting like his skin, suited him like armor.

"He's still a beginner, Faama," Talata said.

"But did you hear the hunger in his voice?" Samori said.

Uncomfortable with the attention, Zaiwulo kept his gaze down.

"My sofas and I are leaving today to teach Saransware-Mori a hard lesson," Samori said. The man has become a thorn in my side, Haidarah."

Talata knew the man. Like all powerful rulers in that part of the world, Saransware-Mori dreamed of becoming the next Sundiata Keita or Mansa Kankou Musa.

"You will wait until after our return, then you may leave to meet Sere-Brimah. But first, I want to discuss a matter with you."

"I'm all ears, Faama."

"Your son Osman wants to be one of my envoys to the English."

The world is crumbling around me, Talata thought. Sona and Karamo are gone. Now Osman wants to leave too. "Was it your request, Faama?" he said.

"It was his idea," Samori said.

"Zaiwulo, fetch Osman for me," Samori said.

When Osman appeared, he knelt before his father.

"Our Faama tells me that you want to be his eyes to the English?" Talata asked.

Osman did not speak.

"You see, Faama," Talata began. "I want him to assist Demba. You have capable elders and sofas who are better suited to this task than Osman."

"Wait until after my return to send the boys home," Samori said. "Today, Zaiwulo will go with me to Sirambadougou to confront Saransware-Mori."

Talata opened his mouth to speak but met Samori's eyes challenging him to defy him and incur the consequences.

The scholar kept silent.

25

The sofas gathered before the Samorian palace were in an array of clothing, from robes to bulbous trousers, to short tunics studded with amulets and cowries believed to deflect bullets and poisonous arrows. They were also in garments that smelled of medicinal herbs. Their headgear consisted of turbans, fezzes, straw hats pointed like beehives, velvet skullcaps, and caps of monkey fur. It was a jumble of loud and terrific colors. The tufts of hair on their otherwise-bald heads made them look like fearsome warriors. Most went without shoes to enhance movement and agility.

Samori faced them, mounted on Kawsu, his horse. The animal seemed calm, almost stoic in the face of the mounting tension. “Sofas,” Samori began. “We leave today to show Saransware-Mori who the true lord of Koniyan is,” he said.

“Admired one, we follow you. Whatever you do, Faama, we do, till death!” the sofas’ voices thundered across Sanankoro.

Zaiwulo was not afforded his own ride. Instead, he sat behind Kemoko-Bilali who turned to him and said, “Hold onto me, child. Whatever you do, don’t let go. Never let go, do you hear me?” Ensconced amid that seething army, Zaiwulo felt a certain sense of invisibility.

As the Samorian army marched out of the city, the Djeli Morifin-Djan Diabate broke into a song about the valiant sofas:

Not since Sundiata and Mansa Musa
Have the people of the word–Nko–the pure language,
Known such a fierce army.
Your enemy will flee before you!

The sofas consisted mostly of footmen. Horses were scarce, so many sofas rode in pairs for expediency. The cavalry was at the head of the army, followed by the footmen who could quickly cover long distances without tiring. The sofas had opted for a narrow path cluttered with high grass to surprise the enemy who might have heard of their deployment and taken measures to confront them.

They reached a valley located between two hills where the shadows were deep. The grass of the plains was bright green here, lush like a prosperous rice field.

They had been marching for hours.

"We will take a break here," Samori told his men.

His words were echoed by Kemoko-Bilali, Porokerrie, and the other sofa commanders. Porokerrie went around on his horse fueling the sofas' courage. "They say that the walls of Sirambadougou are impenetrable, but you will approach those walls from all sides and search for a crack in them. There's bound to be a crack. Sofas of Koniyan, you will find it and you will break through and capture Saransware-Mori!"

Besides the Djeli Morifin-Djan, it was said that Porokerrie was the one who understood the workings of Samori's mind best. He was heavily built but agile on his feet, and like most who coalesced around Samori, he had formerly been without purpose, restless, and in search of a dream. The Samorian ambition to succeed Sundiata and Mansa Musa had attracted him, for it encapsulated his own dream.

The sofas were singing a song Morifin-Djan had composed about how Saransware-Mori, on hearing about the sofas, had escaped to the hills with his tail between his legs. Listening to them display such exuberance, it seemed to Zaiwulo that war was like the harmless game he and his friends played under the full moon in Haindi, where swords were sticks they whirled around, and rifles were the oil lamps and torches they bore.

The pleasant shade lulled the sofas into a relaxed mood. War was still far away, hours away, they believed, which was why most of them did not hear the first shot. The sofa beside Zaiwulo had been inquiring about life in the forest from him when he keeled over, his body writhing in agony. Zaiwulo saw that half of the man's face had been blown away.

Saransware-Mori's army was upon them!

Volleys of rifle shots, spears, and arrows rained on them, but the sofas managed to regroup and move as a single block out of the valley and onto the hill. "Don't break up. Don't break up!" Samori shouted. "Don't break up, sofas!"

He aimed his rifle at a man on the other side of the valley. The man was wearing a short, yellow gown and a huge straw hat crowned with plumes. He looked as dynamic and as sinewy as his name—Saransware-Mori.

Samori must have missed the shot, for Saransware-Mori was still on his horse. Instead, it was Samori who went down. His horse Kawsu had been hit, and it fell to its knees. Samori buried his face in the muzzle of the dying animal, unwilling to let go or believe that it had met its end in such a manner. "Stand up, Kawsu. I say, stand up," he yelled. "What is the matter with you? Stand up."

Porokerrie braved it down the valley and dragged the Faama away. Zaiwulo watched the battle unfold from behind a thicket. From his position, he saw the sofas retreating in haste. The boy contemplated death: What did the impact of a substance released from a stick from afar feel like? What made it so lethal that when it hit a sofa as strong as an Arabian horse, he simply buckled and fell? What made it wreak such havoc?

The boy saw a riderless gray horse racing toward him. In the chaos of gunshot and smoke, he heard his mother's voice coming to him in a whisper. "Namesake of my father, stand up and ride that horse, she said. "Don't be afraid."

As if stung, Zaiwulo bolted out of his hiding place and confronted the fleeing horse. He aimed for the reins, and when he caught them, the horse dragged him in the dust and grass and then halted. The boy mounted it without hesitation. "Take me out of here," he told the horse.

Zaiwulo raced out of the valley, intending to follow the retreating army, but just then, from the corner of his eye, he saw a wounded Kemoko-Bilali lying on the field. He had been hit on his side, below the rib, and in his left leg. "Child of the forest, Saransware-Mori and his men will pay for this," the sofa general said, gritting his teeth to fight the pain.

Zaiwulo pulled hard at him, and the sofa general managed to stand up.

"Help me to the horse," the sofa said. Zaiwulo held onto the horse to steady it, and Kemoko-Bilali managed to hoist himself onto the animal.

They bolted out of the battlefield.

The sofas reached the main gate of Sanankoro at dawn. The wounded had slowed their progress. They met a city in chaos and rife with tales and rumors of their defeat. People debated whether to flee the city before the imminent onslaught that was to follow.

Samori, distraught by the death of Kawsu who was as invaluable to him as a family member, moved from one sofa to another, holding them by the shoulders and shaking them as though out of a stupor. It was the only way he saw to master his grief. "It's not yet over, people of Sanankoro. Return to your homes. Sanankoro has not yet fallen," he said. "We need fresh horses and supplies. We leave for Sirambadougou today."

The sofas were stunned. Never had their losses been as immense as in that brief encounter with the enemy. Half of them had been wiped out, and they were exhausted and needed rest. But Samori wanted to confront Saransware-Mori on his own terms.

Samori moved about attending to his men, often pausing to inquire about a fallen sofa or to see a wounded one, as if he alone were to blame for the defeat.

"Porokerrie," he called to his general. "Do you know why we lost the battle yesterday? No? It was because of this!" Samori picked a rifle and passed it to his friend. "We don't have enough of these."

"But what can we do, Faama? We are dependent on the English and the French for our supply of weapons. We have no choice."

"Yes, we do." Samori's steely eyes shone with excitement. "We will make our own weapons, Porokerrie! We will make our own weapons."

"But how, Faama?"

"We will copy the English and French rifles. The future of our world will be determined by those with the most weapons, and we will be the ones."

"But our smiths don't have the experience, Faama!"

"We have competent smiths. Don't the Djelis sing that smithery was invented by our people? We will build a stockpile of weapons to rival those of any other people on earth. Then we will see who will dare confront us."

26

"So you are good with horses," Samori told Zaiwulo. The two were standing around the main gate through which the sofas were transporting fresh supplies of food and weapons. Though the sun was still invisible, it had begun to shed off the mantle of night with colors draped against a drowsy horizon. "The sofas told me you guided your horse through smoke, rifle shots, and spears to rescue Kemoko-Bilali. Where did you learn horse riding?"

Zaiwulo dug his toes in the dust. His unease was heightened by Samori's intense eyes. I am not a fighter, he told himself and thought of his mother. Months before his departure, she had begun to teach him to recognize herbs. "The herbs talk to me, namesake of my father," she would tell him. Whenever a sick person was brought to her, his mother would go into a trance and disappear into the forest for a few hours, sometimes for a whole night. She would return with a basketful of herbs which she would pound in a mortar and feed the juice to the afflicted, all the while silent, her owl eyes directed inward.

"I was right about you, child," Samori said out loud. Sarankeyi was also right, he thought to himself. You are special. "You will remain in Sanankoro," he said. "We will meet again after the battle. This time, we will return victorious."

•×•

The Samorian army left that day to face Saransware-Mori and his men.

A week later, news of Samori's triumph during this second encounter did not come from Sirambadougou, the capitulated city, but from Bissandougou, his new capital.

Samori had decided to trade Sanankoro for a small village lying en route to Kankan to distance himself from his uncles and embark on a new beginning.

The story that reached Sanankoro—the one the Djeli Morifin-Djan Diabate composed and polished to perfection—told of how the Samorian forces descended on Sirambadougou at dawn. They met a city in a festive mood, unprepared for war, celebrating victory. The sofas had broken through its walls and sacked it with little resistance.

Samori, according to the Djeli, met Saransware-Mori lying in a hammock, in an empty courtyard, surrounded by corpses as though nothing was going wrong. The ruler of Sirambadougou had a steamy breakfast of millet porridge set before him, which he'd had no time to relish because the sofas broke through the walls of his palace, cutting down his men.

"Care to join me for breakfast, Samori?" he said.

"By all means," Samori replied.

Samori washed his hands in a calabash of rainwater and dipped his hand in the rich porridge that glistened with honey. It tasted good.

"You've lived a wonderful life," Samori said.

"Mine was a life littered with precious instances, such as the time you briefly served under me. Do you remember?"

"You taught me well."

"I should have remembered one of the lessons that I taught you: never rejoice until the enemy is dead."

"Yes, that was your mistake," Samori said.

"My wives are an example of what a king should expect from his women. They are resourceful and industrious. Appreciate their values. Don't sell them to the white people because they are priceless."

After a long silence, Samori said, "I didn't set out to fight you."

Saransware-Mori laughed. "That sounds like a lion saying it did not intend to hunt down sheep. I don't believe you, Samori."

Samori washed his hands again to indicate that he was done with the meal. He stood up to leave, knowing fully well that everything the old man ever held dear now belonged to him to do with it as he pleased. The conquest of men made that possible. He felt all-powerful.

"You can part with half your possessions," he said.

"No, Samori, take everything. What's there for a man to live for if he has been stripped of his dignity? I beg you not to spare my life, for I don't want to set eyes on a day when I am deprived of my former life. The suffering will be unbearable."

The sofas waited for a word to carry out Saransware-Mori's wishes, and Samori gave the word with some reluctance. But some people would claim that Saransware-Mori's life was spared, and he lived to become an ally of Samori.

•×•

Zaiwulo was thinking about this confrontation between the two rulers on his way to meet Samori in Bissandougou.

He had left Sanankoro with Osman and Talata and more than half of the Samorian courtiers.

They met Samori in his new palace which was still unfinished. The walls and enclosures were being erected, and homes were being built as if the Faama was in haste to distance himself from Sanankoro. The entire village was under construction. Samori wanted to turn what was once a tiny place of no consequence into his new capital.

Talata, Osman, and Zaiwulo negotiated their way between dirt mixture, wood, and heaps of cow dung and grass. They passed between long chains of men and women working to construct homes for the thousands who would converge on the village. The three entered a palace that was an affront to the one in Sanankoro. It was small and smelled of fresh reeds.

Samori was surrounded by some of his courtiers and the elders of Bissandougou. He was in a festive mood. "What do you think of my new capital, Haidarah?"

"I don't know what to say, Faama."

"Its location is perfect," Samori said. "It lies on the way to Kankan, that city of my dreams. But most importantly, Bissandougou does not belong to my uncles. Let them have their Sanankoro. Without me, the city will bleed dry and perish."

"Indeed, it lies on the route to Kankan," Talata said.

"That's where you had your education, right?"

"Yes, Faama. Kankan, the largest city in our part of the world, the city of knowledge and power. Yes, Kankan formed me."

"From today onwards, you will be my permanent envoy, Haidarah. One day, I will send you to Kankan to see if I can claim it as my own without bloodshed. But first, you will leave to see Sere-Brimah and secure his trust."

"I prefer to leave today."

Samori turned to his court. "Leave us. That goes for you too, Osman."

Zaiwulo stood up, but Samori said, "You can stay, child."

Osman hesitated for a moment, taken aback by Zaiwulo's sudden rise in esteem and the favors accorded him. Before leaving, he cast Zaiwulo an acrimonious look.

"Haidarah, you must be wondering why I have taken to Zaiwulo," Samori said. "It's because I see myself in him. The child appears shy, reluctant, but he is brave when required. He sees the world as a place of infinite possibilities, exactly as I see it. Moreover, he's of my mother's people. I'm asking your permission to allow him to stay with me."

"Faama, I want the boys to return to Musadu to assist Demba. I will do whatever you ask, but please let them go."

Samori's face, which had been all smiles, hardened into a frown. For a while, he was silent. When he spoke, he did not mince his words. "In that case, you will do everything you can to persuade Sere-Brimah to work with me, Haidarah. Don't return empty-handed."

They were interrupted by the sofa general, Kemoko-Bilali. He was drenched in sweat; his hands and legs were covered with dirt. Since their arrival, he had been supervising the construction work and the smiths tasked with manufacturing guns.

Once he had decided to turn Bissandougou into his new capital, Samori had assembled the best smiths in Koniyan and ordered them to reproduce the English and French weapons. They were to study the weapons and test prototypes made with old rifles, polished wood, and metals that had once been utilized to make hoes, hammers, pots, spoons, cutlasses, spears, arrows and other items.

"Our smiths have managed to reproduce the English and French rifles, Faama. Production has begun," Kemoko-Bilali said.

"Let's go and see. Come with me, Zaiwulo."

•×•

The smithy was located in the heart of Bissandougou. The workplace consisted of five large buildings that opened out onto two sides to allow smoke from the bellows. More than a hundred men were at work, trying to master the techniques of the English and French rifles.

The head smith was a stocky man in a tattered tunic with a missing front tooth. He stood to attention and coughed a greeting.

"Show me how far you are, Fakoli," Samori said.

Fakoli loaded a rifle with powder by ramming it through the muzzle. He added lead shots to it and handed it over to Samori. It was a replica of the Dane rifle.

The Faama aimed the rifle at a nearby tree. The shots only managed to graze it.

"Faama," Fakoli tried to explain.

"We will soon have a perfect rifle, Fakoli," said Samori. "Kemoko, make sure that Fakoli and his men are amply rewarded. Share parts of the spoils of Sirambadougou among them. Give women to those who are not married."

The smiths flung themselves on the ground before him.

"Thank you, Faama. You are goodness itself," Fakoli said.

Once they were back at the palace, Samori said, "You are still a child, Zaiwulo, but one day you will be in a better position to decide whether to stay with us or with your teacher. You belong here. Here is home. Here you will become what you always wanted to be."

"But Faama…" the boy fell silent.

Now that he had been thrown into this new world, Zaiwulo yearned for the world he had left behind. The life of a scholar, or the life boys his age would lead in the forest, farming, fishing, and being guided through the passage to adulthood. What would it mean if he became part of the Samorian world? Would he ever again be part of his forest world, again?

"Tell me what bothers you, child," Samori paused to glance at him.

"I want to see my mother and sisters."

"You will see them one day. They are also my people."

The words lodged deep in Zaiwulo's heart. Samori had once again referred to the forest people as his people. Although Zaiwulo was apprehensive of that aspect of Samori which embraced violence, he found, when he parted with the ruler and his wife Sarankenyi the next day, that he would miss the sense of belonging and home which the two had instilled in him.

Zaiwulo left with his teacher and Osman. Samori arranged for ten sofas to accompany them. Once they were beyond the bounds of Bissandougou, Talata turned to him and Osman.

"You two will return to Musadu," he said. "Ask Demba to continue teaching you, Zaiwulo. Osman, please assist Demba. Try to be good to one another, for you need each other. I will return as soon as I've met Sere-Brimah."

Part Two

SEPARATIONS

1880

1

The leaves of the flame tree were as fiery red as they ought to be, and the slender branches stirred at the slightest rise in the wind. Zaiwulo touched one of its branches as he passed through the courtyard where he had planted it.

"Sister Massah built this fence around it to protect it from domestic animals," a student told him. He was one of several young students who had eagerly gathered around Zaiwulo to hear his story.

"Where is she? I want to thank her," Zaiwulo said, and the student answered that she was away at the market, in the twin cities of Beyla and Jacodu.

"She goes there every week to sell her wares," the student said.

Sister Massah was becoming a trader in her own right, independent of everyone, Zaiwulo thought as he tended to the fence. He forced the poles that held it deeper into the earth and cleared the fallen leaves. Some of the students helped him.

"Is it true that kings take to their heels on hearing Samori's name"' one of the boys asked after Zaiwulo told them about Samori.

"They say he fathered more than a thousand children. Is that true?" said another.

Before he could answer, another student said, "We heard that the road to his palace is lined with enemy skulls and that he drinks their blood to make him invincible."

Zaiwulo tried to portray an accurate account of Samori, but he was met with doubts.

•×•

Zaiwulo took over the house he had once shared with his father. He was preparing for the night when he heard a familiar voice. "It's me, spoiled boy. Tell me how many girls wept when you left Sanankoro, and where is your teacher?"

It was Massah.

She had taken a bath and rubbed her body with scented oil. Her hair was plaited into four broad sections, each laced with cowries. Before she left her room, she wondered what it was about the boy from the forest that so excited her and made her go through all that trouble. I have Demba who cares about me, she thought. Why this foolishness, Massah? Not knowing the answer, she had shrugged and wrapped herself in a single cloth.

Zaiwulo inhaled deeply when he caught the mix of herbal soap and perfume that was Massah's scent. Although he knew that she was meant for Demba and hoped that the two would have a future together, he was emboldened by the playfulness in her voice. He decided to play along as he stepped outside to meet her. "There's only one woman for me, Massah, and that woman is you. Stop worrying now. I'm back."

Massah burst into laughter. "You were an infant just yesterday, and now, all you do is think about girls. A great scholar you will turn out to be."

"I will throw myself at your feet if necessary."

"Stop it, Zaiwulo. Why is Haidarah not here?"

"Samori sent him as an envoy to Sere-Brimah."

"What if that terrible man takes him prisoner? What will happen to this household? What will happen to us, Zaiwulo?"

"Sere-Brimah will not harm him, Massah."

"I hope not," she said.

"Thank you for taking care of my tree," he said.

She threw him a questioning look. "Who said I took care of your tree? You must be dreaming." Massah left him standing, confused by her words. As she returned to her part of the compound, he was so consumed by the guilt of having developed feelings for a person not meant for him that he went to see Demba.

As he neared the house, he could hear Osman saying to the blind man, "Rest, Uncle Demba. I'm here to assist you now. That Bush Boy managed to turn the whole Sanankoro against him."

"What are you saying, Haidarah?" Demba asked.

"He's not one of us, Uncle Demba."

"As long as he's here to learn, he belongs to us."

It alarmed Zaiwulo to hear Osman concocting stories to smear him. One day, I will fight back, he told himself. He called out, "I came to see you, Uncle Demba, and to thank you for taking care of the house."

"Is that you, child of the forest?" Demba said. "Come in. Come in." But then he changed his mind. "No, let's go for a walk."

Osman came out to join them.

"You stay here, Osman. We've talked long enough. I want to hear how Zaiwulo experienced Sanankoro," Demba said.

Zaiwulo held Demba's walking stick and led him toward the main gate. Students were still crowded around the hearths, throwing conjugations at each other like gifts. Zaiwulo realized that he could follow their exchange, even the most difficult ones. He longed for his writing slate.

"Haidarah shouldn't have allied himself with the likes of Samori," Demba said. "I'm incapable of running a house as large as this one for such a long time. I'm bound to fail. And Massah. I don't know..."

"But you've done well, Uncle Demba."

A shy look crept onto the blind man's face. He was silent for some seconds. "I don't know what will become of us. You see, child, our king thinks that Samori is holding Haidarah prisoner. He regards Samori as a warmonger, as a man who lusts for blood. That's the main reason why he's dispatched an envoy to Sere-Brimah to seek his friendship."

"But it was Sere-Brimah who sacked Musadu some years ago," Zaiwulo said, repeating what he'd been told about the man.

"When confronted with a bigger threat, you are left with no other choice but to ally yourself with former enemies. Our king has no choice."

Zaiwulo wanted to tell him that Samori was not the man he was portrayed to be in Musadu. He wanted to say that Samori had sent Talata to seek an alliance with a man who had enslaved his mother. That was a stark contrast to the king of Musadu whose envoys were out to cultivate allies in preparation for war, but Zaiwulo doubted that Demba would believe him. Moreover, Talata's action might be interpreted by the king as an act of betrayal.

"Musadu is in the grip of Samori," Demba said. "Our fear of him has become so pervasive that we are willing to embrace old enemies."

The two left the compound and strolled toward the city center. It was lit by torches and kindling burning from hearths. It bustled with life and festivities of every kind. The harvest had ushered in a period of merriment, including wedding and circumcision ceremonies.

"Haidarah wants me to read the manuscripts," Zaiwulo said.

"He meant the manuscripts in his home, not the ones in his study. The study remains locked until his return," Demba said. "I will teach you as much as I can, child, but you must realize that it takes students years to master a single book. Most come here as children, grow up, and get married without realizing their dreams of becoming scholars."

"I will do anything to become a scholar, Uncle Demba."

"That's good. Tomorrow, we begin at dawn."

The two turned around and headed home in the wake of a crowd leading a bride to the house of her bridegroom. Zaiwulo brushed his teeth with a chewing stick and retired to bed. He soon fell asleep.

•×•

The next morning, Demba took Zaiwulo to Talata's chambers located in the largest house in the compound. The manuscripts were arranged on planks. Most of them were leather-bound and stacked against the walls like sacks of rice or millet in a pantry. The books must be in the thousands, Zaiwulo thought. The air in the room reeked of sweat, musk, and dust.

"Imagine, child, that each manuscript was carefully put together by the best calligraphers in our part of the world," Demba said. "Some were written right here in Koniyan, while others were imported from places like Kankan, the Toucouleur kingdom, Kong, and places as far as Timbuktu, Djenné, and Kano. Imagine that each was bought with gold pieces. Then imagine being the owner of such volumes, such wealth. What a fortune!"

Zaiwulo browsed through the manuscripts until Demba, as if he knew the location of each manuscript, said, "Choose the one on the first plank on your right, close to the door. Bring it to me."

Zaiwulo pulled out the manuscript with reverence. The two took seats on the mat outside of the house.

"I see that it was written by Haidarah himself," Zaiwulo said.

"Yes, he wrote it while still a student in Kankan. Shall we begin?"

Zaiwulo read the first sentence in a singsong voice, and the blind man nodded and repeated the line. Then Demba quoted another line from memory to complement the first, and then the second and the third lines. He went on like this for a while, reciting line after line, culled from different sources, different books, all related to the first sentence.

"Nothing stands isolated," said Demba. "I will teach you to see the connection between things, between one branch of knowledge and the other."

The manuscript was Talata's vision on religion. Religion had to adapt to time and circumstances, he had written, its singular goal being to bind instead of divide. If it failed to do so, then we had no choice but to distance ourselves from it or replace it with something much more suitable.

The words sank deep into Zaiwulo.

Knowledge, Talata wrote a few pages later, was not confined to a group of people, to a place or a country, but belonged in principle to all humanity. No one had a monopoly on knowledge.

Zaiwulo was so immersed in the new knowledge that he failed to notice Naminata until her shadow fell on him.

"You returned and didn't tell me," she said.

She wore a scarlet tunic, a long wrapper, and sandals. Zaiwulo stared at her neck, at how the simple gold necklace emphasized its length.

She was glowing.

"Where is your teacher?" Naminata sat across from him, curling her feet under her so that her knees faced him. Her smiling lips were dyed black, creating a sharp contrast with her white teeth.

"He will return the moment he concludes his mission," Demba said.

"We need him here, Uncle Demba?" Naminata said.

Demba nodded.

"Yet you run the house better than Haidarah ever did. You underestimate yourself, Uncle Demba. One day, I will assist you."

"You, assist me? *You*, Naminata? Osman is here to do that."

"You will see," she said.

She turned to Zaiwulo. "Tell me everything that you experienced during your travels. Don't leave a word out. You must have left many girls in despair, like you did here."

"Naminata, you are making him shy," Demba said. "Go now and come back another time. He has lessons to attend."

"Just a few more moments, Uncle Demba, and then I will go home to bear my burden. That old man Foningama has become a nuisance. I can no longer bear it. I'm tired."

"What?" Demba was shocked. "A woman is never to say such things."

"I don't care what the world thinks of me."

"Then the world will punish you, Naminata."

"Before the world does, I will take action."

Demba shook his head.

Zaiwulo realized that Naminata would not leave until she had heard his story, so he stood. "I will be back soon, Uncle Demba."

On their way toward the entrance of the compound, Zaiwulo felt important beside Naminata. He was aware of the eyes fixed on her, and the necklace and gold earrings faded in the light of her beauty. He told her what he'd not told anyone, not even Massah. He told her about his first war, about Samori's power and ambitions, Talata's mission, and Osman's plans to take over from Demba.

"Be very cautious of Osman," Naminata said.

"I will keep an eye on him," Zaiwulo said.

"My old husband is afraid of Samori. If he's not lamenting the loss of his daughter Sona, then he's warning people about the danger Samori poses."

"I don't think Samori wants to conquer Musadu."

"I hope you are right. I wish Talata was here. His presence makes me grateful to be alive. But now that you are here..." She stopped.

When Zaiwulo was about to goad her on, she did something that astounded him. She hugged him with a tenderness that threw him into confusion.

He quickly turned around and returned to Demba.

•×•

"Naminata was once a slave, you see," Demba said.

"A slave? How, Uncle Demba?"

"The girl is smarter than many think. She managed to alter her destiny in such a way that her former master Foningama has become dependent on her. Her only fault is that she wants more than is possible. A girl in her position is never to desire the impossible."

The image of Naminata as a slave did not align with the free-spirited girl Zaiwulo had come to know, for she was not one to succumb to anyone's will. Didn't slavery include the breaking down of human will? he wondered.

Demba reached for his walking stick.

"I have to leave you, son of the forest. It was Haidarah's habit to distribute a portion of the harvest to the poor. That task falls to me now. You could come with me, and along the way, describe my future wife to me."

The two went in the direction of the women's quarters.

Massah had installed her wares in front of the house once occupied by Sona. Her girls were busy sorting them out.

"She's taller than I am, Uncle Demba," Zaiwulo said. "Her skin is so dark that when the sun shines on it, it glows. Her hands are callous from hard work, but she's the most beautiful woman in Musadu."

Demba laughed. "The most beautiful woman meant for a blind man. Wonders do exist in this world, child. I'm proof."

"Her eyes light up with joy every time she sees you," Zaiwulo said. Despite himself, he hoped that Massah would one day look at him that way. "She loves to listen to you recite poems. You are meant for each other, Uncle Demba," he said, and his heart sank.

"You talk about her as if you too love her, child."

Zaiwulo did not respond.

2

Talata was gone for months. His absence unleashed grotesque speculations about his fate. One version had it that Samori had kidnapped and threatened him with death to be his envoy to Sere-Brimah. Another had it that Sere-Brimah had held Talata prisoner and starved him to death. There were stories about him being held in a hole somewhere by a cruel ruler intent on punishing Samori. But Zaiwulo doubted the rumors. He knew his teacher was alive and would return. He took to lingering around the western gate, hoping to welcome him.

One moonlit night, as he was conversing with the sentries, Zaiwulo saw his teacher at the fortified gate. "Is that you, Zaiwulo?" Talata called out.

The sentries reacted as if they'd seen a ghost.

"It's you, Haidarah!" one of them said.

The scholar looked emaciated, a shadow of his former self. Zaiwulo ignored the rules that forbade excessive expression of emotion between student and teacher and threw his arms around Talata.

"How did you get here, Haidarah?" he asked.

"That is of little importance," Talata said. "I'm home now, and this time, I came to stay. I did what was in my power."

"We are glad that you've returned, Haidarah," the sentries said.

Talata thanked them.

"Any news regarding Sona and Karamo?" he asked.

Zaiwulo's silence was the answer.

"How have you been, son of the forest?" Talata asked.

"I followed your words to the letter. I can write stories and compose poems now. Demba taught me many things from the manuscripts. I've memorized and can recite dozens of your poems!"

"You are doing very well," Talata said. "Demba has been as assiduous as ever."

As Zaiwulo escorted his teacher through the main street to the Haidarah compound, he recited a line from one of Talata's poems, which Demba had taught him. Zaiwulo repeated the line over and over again. From one of the homes, a voice rose with the second line of the same poem. It was soon followed by another voice with the third line until a chorus of voices filled the night with the poem. Men and women poured out in droves to welcome Talata while Zaiwulo's voice continued to ring through the night.

He stayed with his teacher that evening and helped him settle down. He laid out Talata's clothes and asked the women to prepare his bath.

"Go to bed. You must be tired, Zaiwulo," Talata said.

Zaiwulo did as he was told, but he was up at dawn. Subsequently, he lingered around the study delivering messages from Talata to Demba. He swept the study, prepared the slates and paper, and even sharpened and made his teacher's reed pens with a knife. He made the tips smaller for annotations, larger for chapters and book titles, or regular, like the reed pens which he and other students used to write on wooden slates.

Osman who should have been with his father, doing the things that Zaiwulo did, chose to spend his days with his uncles in Beyla and Jacodu, sometimes returning late at night. Talata feigned as if his son's behavior did not affect him at all. He spent most of his days writing, an occupation that he hoped would reward him with some peace of mind.

One morning, while Talata was busy writing, he heard Zaiwulo outside.

"Come in, Zaiwulo. What is it?"

"The king wants to see you, Haidarah."

A messenger was waiting for Talata outside, and, according to him, the king had asked him not to return without the scholar. Talata, however, didn't want to be disturbed as he was deep in composition. Writing had become a necessity to him. During his travels where he spent most of his time negotiating treaties with rulers on Samori's behalf, he had longed for Musadu. Now that he was at home, he longed to feel his wife beside him, but because he could not translate that longing into action of any kind, he turned to his work, hoping for satisfaction, for some kind of solace.

That morning he had chosen to focus on the origin of his ancestor, the first Talata, and his youth in that desert city of Timbuktu.

He is unremarkable, this ancestor of mine, Talata wrote, *not endowed with great looks, but he loves life, which he conceals behind his love of books.*

He spends parts of his days in a small building he has been forbidden to enter. The building houses a special collection of manuscripts, kept by the Haidarahs of Timbuktu for ages. The family fears that the knowledge contained within the manuscripts might do him more harm than good, for he's not old enough, not prepared for the knowledge of the visible and invisible worlds. Yet every day, he disappears into the building. It's always dark inside, except for the light from chinks in the Moorish door. He devours one manuscript after another and leaves every time with a faint smile on his face, for he feels unique, in possession of forbidden knowledge.

Then one day, he finds what he's looking for. He finds the Haidarah Manuscript, the source of the legends. He flips open the first page with trembling hands, and his face lights up. He knows now that everything that's been said about the manuscript is true. It could make him great.

He runs out of the building with the manuscript secured under his garment. One of his uncles who is jealous of his successes catches him leaving the building and alerts the family. The family reacts with consternation. How dare a child nose into works that are beyond him? The Haidarahs of Timbuktu, which constituted three large families, distance themselves from him. His mother is his only ally. His punishment is banishment from the family, so he takes up residence at his teacher's home. No one in the family realizes he has the Haidarah Manuscript.

He is closely shaved, this ancestor, and a bit shy—especially in the company of women. Out to impress them, he often ends up speaking a language they barely understand. He craves admiration and pretends not to be aware of another storm heading his way, for he bears a secret which, if revealed, will alter his destiny forever.

Here, Talata paused, and a smile lit his face as he reached for his reed pen, dipping it in an ink composed of leaves and tree barks cooked until they turned pulpy. Talata continued:

One day, on his way to see his teacher, my ancestor encounters Aminah, his teacher's wife, in a narrow passage between two clay walls. The desert sun is searing, but he's accustomed to the heat that saps life out of the city during the day. At night, he turns the rooftop into a sleeping place and waits until silence has descended on the city to contemplate the star-studded skies. Or, he composes poems that are light at first but later contemplative, poems meant to stir hearts. Between the narrow passage, the sun pours light on Aminah's skin like gold through the hands of a trader. She's small, delicate, as if she would be swept away by the rising storm of dust that sometimes envelops the city. He walks past her with a thudding heart, and she flashes him a look that would stay with him forever. The two do not speak that day, but through her eyes, he reads what a thousand words could not express. Henceforth, the two meet between the alleys, sharing secrets, food, laughter, and smiles. And he begins to work on an epic poem about Aminah, placing the love story far in the past to disguise it.

The poem is read by scholars and students of various institutions of learning in Timbuktu, in Djenné, and beyond. It is considered unique. Out of curiosity, his teacher decides to read the poem. Between lines that were polished like the surface of a writing slate, the teacher catches a whiff of the now full-blown romance between his wife and his student. The resulting scandal compels Talata to flee the city of his birth.

My ancestor settles in Djenné, where his uncles reside. The clay architecture which is the hallmark of homes and buildings in Timbuktu is refined here. A sewage system runs along the narrow passages of the city. The fall of light on the smooth walls of its homes is like the scintillating play of light on water. On his way home from the market, in the vicinity of the great mosque, a man stops him—some people have arrived from the south to see my ancestor. His reputation as a scholar has reached them, and they have come to solicit his help. Their request, he thinks, might afford him room for growth, and he could be greater than he already is. He leaves, taking along dozens of manuscripts, including the Haidarah Manuscript, and he journeys south through the desert and the savannah to Musadu.

It doesn't take him long after his arrival to find someone to quench the desire denied him. She's a Kpelle woman, a descendant of Zoemuza, the founder of Musadu. This woman proves that a fresh start is possible, that an Aminah could be found at the fringes of the forest, far away from Timbuktu. She bears him three sons, and I belong to the line of the youngest…

Talata wanted to go on further, but the messenger still waiting outside the study was growing more impatient.

"Haidarah, you will end up angering the king," the messenger said.

Zaiwulo went with his teacher to see the king. The palace was the largest compound in Musadu. It had two interior walls and a labyrinth of enclosures, each screening off the other, as though the king intended to conceal his true whereabouts. The walls of the enclosures were of mud, unlike those in the Haidarah compound which were built from thatch. It was obvious to Zaiwulo that the king's fear of being murdered by his enemies often kept him awake.

The king of Musadu was standing in the shade of a tree, his eyes flashing with anger as if he had no desire to honor Talata by formally receiving him. He was surrounded by his courtiers and the elders of the city, including Talata's best friend, Soko Kenneh.

"Your Majesty, your hard work has enabled Musadu to remain a prosperous city," Talata said by way of greeting.

"I doubt it after what you've done," the king said, and sucked his teeth. "Why are you behaving as if you are the ruler of Musadu?"

Talata didn't know what to say.

"You returned and made no effort to see your king."

"Forgive me, Your Majesty."

"What is it with you and Samori? All the stories. Tell me."

"Mere rumors, Your Majesty," Talata said.

"Is it true that you now work for Samori? What kind of man is he who uses our people against us to achieve his goals?"

Talata paused briefly before answering. "I'm not one of Samori's followers. But I think that he's the one who will determine the future of our world, Your Majesty. It would be in our interest to seek an alliance of some sorts with him."

"So you support our enemy?"

"It's not about support, Your Majesty."

"But your words seem to suggest otherwise. Tell me, Soko Kenneh, did Samori ask your friend to convince me that he's the true ruler of the Mandé speaking people? That he's the heir to Sundiata the Great and Mansa Musa?"

Soko fell to the floor before the king. "Haidarah suffers, Your Majesty. His wife disappeared while carrying a child. He lost his youngest son shortly after that. Samori forced our scholar to leave Musadu and be his emissary."

The king sat on the mat. The elders took their places around him. He was silent for a while. "Haidarah," he said, finally, "we will resist Samori even if that means working together with Sere-Brimah, or with Gbanguno Saaye. We've dispatched envoys to Sere-Brimah and Saaye. We need their support against Samori."

Although he feared that the king was misguided, Talata said nothing. Zaiwulo, who sat behind him, worried about the security of Musadu. What if the king discovered that Talata had been sent as an envoy to Sere-Brimah and not forced at all?

Zaiwulo feared the worst.

"But we called you here for another reason also, Haidarah," his friend Soko Kenneh said, glad to change the subject. He was smiling now as he spoke. "You need capable hands to run your house."

"What Soko means is that you need a wife," the king said.

A ripple of restrained laughter swept across the courtyard. The men folded their garments and fingered their caps.

"A woman to turn you away from those books. What kind of Haidarah are you? Isn't it true that you are the one most enamored with women? Or am I mistaken, good people of Musadu?" the king said.

The gathering burst into hearty laughter.

"We are referring to my daughter, Massah," Soko said. "She ran your house with Sona's skills. Since your return, she's worked harder than ever."

Zaiwulo felt uneasy. He could hardly breathe.

"But you promised your daughter to one of my sons," Talata said.

"Circumstances have changed."

The elders nodded.

"Shouldn't we ask the girl for her opinion?" Talata said.

"Ask a girl for her opinion? What has gotten into you, Haidarah?" the king said. "We thought books made a man wiser!"

Soko turned to him and with finality, said, "Talata, from now till Judgment Day, I'm giving my daughter's hand first to God and then to you."

"You can leave now, Haidarah," the king said.

Like everyone present, Talata knew that if a bride belonged to God, one must accept her as wife without argument. He was not ready for a new beginning. His thoughts were always on Sona. The idea that another woman would take her place was unimaginable. He'd always considered Massah as a daughter, a girl intended for Osman or Karamo.

"You leave me with no choice," Talata said.

The men did not respond. On the way back to the Haidarah compound with his teacher, Zaiwulo thought of Massah and how she would react if told that Talata—not Demba—would become her husband.

What would that mean for the blind man?

3

"Zaiwulo, ask Demba to see me," Talata said when they arrived home.

Zaiwulo met the blind man heading toward his own chambers. "Haidarah wants to see you, Uncle Demba," he said.

The blind man, who must have caught a whiff of the sorrow in his voice asked, "What is it, child of the forest? Tell me."

Zaiwulo could not bring himself to share what he was certain would break the blind man. Demba approached the bolon with trepidation. He grabbed one of the four poles that held the roof, felt for the mat, and crawled toward his teacher until he was close enough to touch him. Demba fell to his knees.

Zaiwulo, who stood behind him, looked away.

"Don't kneel before your equal, Demba," Talata said.

"Me? Your equal, Haidarah?"

"Yes, I mean it."

The blind man shook his head. "I remember the first time we sat here long ago, Haidarah. You were not much older than I was, but you were already a great scholar. You picked me out of thousands and shared your knowledge with me. Within these walls, I became a better human being. No, Haidarah, I'm not your equal."

"You are being too humble, Demba. This house will remain standing when I am long gone because of you."

"You asked to see me, Haidarah?"

"Yes, the king and the elders of Musadu have decided to offer me Massah as a bride. What do you think?"

Demba was silent. When he attempted to speak, his voice broke, for he realized that despite his fears, he should have made his intentions regarding Massah public to avoid situations like this. Now, it was too late.

"She will make a wonderful wife, Haidarah."

"But I can't imagine myself being married to her."

"She's good, the best girl in Musadu."

Zaiwulo could feel Demba's pain.

"She is a bride of God, they said. So I have no choice. Sometimes I wish I had not returned. Sometimes, I wish I were not a scholar."

"You are being tested, Haidarah. We all are in our own way."

Demba stood up and excused himself.

"What should I do, Zaiwulo?" Talata said.

The two were interrupted by Foningama, Talata's father-in-law, who had refused to see his son-in-law or to receive him since his return.

"It's you, Foningama! How are you?" Talata said.

The old man sucked his teeth. "You drove my daughter out of Musadu to deny me from seeing her for the last time before my death."

"You are not dying yet, Foningama."

"You did not search hard enough for her."

"You are not being fair."

"You did not search the forest and other places she might have gone to. You gave up the search too soon. Now, in less than a year after her disappearance, you are about to take on as wife a girl whom my daughter raised to be wedded to one of my grandsons. Why, Haidarah?"

"This is not true. It's almost five years since Ma-Sona left. I–"

"You fooled us all into thinking that Samori forced you out of Musadu. But I know the truth. Samori is not to be trusted. In the end, he will not only destroy you, but will also destroy your precious Musadu."

"I don't want to have anything to do with Samori,' said Talata. "And about Massah, she was given to God first, so I cannot refuse her."

"You are a man of books. You can easily come up with a verdict to support your decision not to marry her. But you don't want to, do you? No. Deep down, you lust for her."

Talata attempted to mollify his father-in-law, but when he reached out to touch his shoulders, to calm him, the old man stepped back, shunning the gesture.

"Zaiwulo, fetch some water and kola nuts for my father-in-law," Talata said, and to Foningama, he said, "Please eat with us now that you are here."

"Don't bother, Zaiwulo. Your teacher takes pleasure in tormenting me. First, he marries my daughter without my consent, then drives her away only to replace her with a much younger woman."

"At least accept a kola nut," Talata said.

"Every day, I'm haunted by my daughter's voice blaming me for forsaking her. My time is near, and I will pass on without seeing her."

Foningama turned and left the compound.

4

Zaiwulo left to see Massah so he could persuade her to resist the decision taken without her consent. He was surprised to learn that she had moved to her parents' house that very day. When he inquired, he was told that a girl about to get married stayed in her parents' home until the night she was led to her husband's house. It occurred to him that he would no longer share jokes with Massah once she became his teacher's wife, and he decided to prevent it by persuading Massah to marry the blind man or not marry at all. On his way to see her, he met Naminata near the city center. She rushed at him, ready to pounce on him.

"Why are you avoiding me?" she asked.

It was true. He *was* avoiding her, for she always managed to get on his nerves. "You and I will never belong to Musadu," she once told him. "So stop trying to be like them. Remain true to your ways. Worship your gods in secret, and in public, pretend you are one of them. During another encounter she had said, "You let Osman lord it over you all the time."

"I hardly ever see Osman," Zaiwulo had replied.

"I've been watching you since your return," she said now. "Look at you, with those broad shoulders! It's about time you let go of childhood, Zaiwulo. You are ready to take on responsibility."

Zaiwulo did not respond.

"Where are you going?" she said.

"To see Massah."

"To see Massah," she snorted. "I'm the woman Haidarah should marry, not her. I'm the one who will bear him children who will not abandon him or fight him. I'm the right woman for him, and he knows that."

"What about Foningama?"

"I thought you understood me. Don't you believe me when I say that I am Foningama's wife in name only? The old man is always complaining about the loss of his daughter, expecting me to share in his grief. His time is near, and when he is gone, I will choose your teacher as my husband!"

"Musadu will never allow it. No one will allow it."

"You will see, Zaiwulo," she said and went her way.

She sounded as if she had figured it all out, but Zaiwulo wondered what power she possessed to force a whole city to succumb to her will.

Zaiwulo met Massah huddled with a group of young women around a hearth. Dusk was falling. The women were in a buoyant mood.

"I've not been away for less than a day, and you have come running after me," she said. "What if I were to leave Musadu?"

"I will follow you anywhere," he said, laughing.

"Hear him. Next thing you know, he will be asking for my hand in marriage. What should I do then, marry a kid? Come on now!"

Massah's father was sitting under a tree, conversing with some elders. Massah led Zaiwulo out of the main courtyard and along pens full of cattle and stables studded with horses. The homes rang with laughter which rose and fell like songs. Children chased after each other across the compound, and some clapped hands to various games.

"I don't want my father to see us, Zaiwulo. I fear that man so much that I'm often tongue-tied in his presence. They say I'm his favorite, but I can't remember him ever being kind to me."

"Massah, I came to talk to you about the marriage."

She stopped and glanced at him.

"You can't marry Haidarah," Zaiwulo said.

"But I will not marry Haidarah," she said in a matter-of-fact voice. "I will flee with Demba. We will leave Musadu."

Zaiwulo felt betrayed. He'd been worrying his head about her while she had plans that did not involve him.

Massah grabbed his hands. "You could come with us! My Demba is as good as Haidarah. Many people, including some great scholars, have been saying that he's better than his teacher but that he's too humble to show it."

"You should have told me this earlier," he said.

"I am telling you now."

"I can't leave Haidarah. He needs me."

"My friends are waiting for me," she said.

Zaiwulo walked away, disappointed. When he returned home, he fetched his writing slate and sat close to the oil lamp. He wanted to write down what had transpired that day. He wanted to describe the light of the fading sun on Naminata's face. If he could capture Massah's essence and her inner struggles, if he could put into words what he felt about her and return to it whenever he wished, would that not amount to a miracle? If he could write about his first days in Musadu, about his doubts and the precious moment in between, could he not relive those moments over and over again? Was that not what the Djelis did—those guardians of the word, men like Morifin-Djan Diabate and

Sundiata Keita's Balafaseke before him, storytellers who evoked moments to be relived by others?

But the words would not obey him. They eyed him with annoyance as if he'd done them an injustice by stirring them from their sleep. "Forgive me," he entreated. "I will return to you when you are eager to take me on journeys unimaginable."

Zaiwulo left to see Demba while wishing for more details about their escape plan.

"It's me, Uncle Demba," he said.

"It's our scholar who pretends he's not one."

The blind man was munching fried termites, a handful of which he shared with Zaiwulo. "Delicious, aren't they?"

"Massah tells me that you are planning to escape together," said Zaiwulo.

"We did not discuss such a thing. Maybe that's what she hopes," Demba replied. "But look at it this way, child of the forest. The woman I care about most will soon be uniting with the man who means the most to me in this world."

"But she's the woman of your life."

"That's true, but she's meant for Haidarah."

Massah had not told him the truth. Zaiwulo decided to convince Massah to see Demba before the wedding. She alone could persuade him to make public their secret or flee Musadu with him.

5

Massah was kept in a house surrounded by a group of women who, that night, would serve as escorts to her marital home. Regardless, Zaiwulo made up an excuse to see her. "I have a message from Haidarah for Massah," he said, and the women allowed him in.

He met Massah standing, wringing her hands in nervousness. She was dressed in a scarlet garment made from expensive fabric that her father had purchased from the English in Freetown. The burning lamp illuminated her oiled skin. The jewelry which decorated her arms, neck, and ears—gold bracelets, necklaces, and heavy earrings tied to red strings and woven into her hair—belonged to the family.

"You have to bring Demba here," she said. "I'm sure that I can convince him to talk to his teacher or persuade him to elope with me."

"What if you fail, Massah?"

She moved closer to him, and afraid of being heard, she whispered, "I've put other measures in place."

Zaiwulo touched her shoulder in excitement.

"What other measures?"

"We don't have much time. Go and fetch him."

•×•

Zaiwulo slipped away to see Demba and met him standing in front of his house, leaning against a tree. The blind man was reciting a poem to himself.

"You must see Massah right now, Uncle Demba," Zaiwulo said, as if it was an order.

"If you insist," Demba said.

Zaiwulo led him to Massah's door and waited outside.

The moment Demba took in Massah's scent, his legs began to quiver.

Massah turned to the women. "Mothers, sisters, please leave me alone with Demba. It's important," she said.

"Has Haidarah changed his mind?" one of them asked.

"Demba is here to carry a message from me to Haidarah," she said.

"Girls nowadays! Impatient and blunt!" The women murmured amongst themselves.

When they were alone, Massah reached out for Demba's hands and squeezed them hard to reassure him and allay his fears. She stared at him, as if doing so would make him see her and make things right. The blind man touched her face, tracing the contours of her forehead, her brows and eyes, the shape of her nose, the form of her lips, her chin, and her neck. A calmness descended on Massah, a feeling so deep that she thought with certainty that everything she asked of him would be granted.

"For God's sake, Demba, I beg you. Go to your teacher, face him, and tell him about us," she said. "If you don't, you will regret this forever."

Demba broke away from her and rubbed his sweaty face.

"You don't understand, Massah!" he said.

"You are his right-hand man, his friend. If you tell him about us, he will understand. He would never want to hurt you."

"But I owe everything I am and will ever be to Haidarah. Don't make me go against his wishes."

"Let's leave Musadu then. We could go to the forest. There, you could become greater than Haidarah. Yes, much greater."

"You are talking nonsense."

"If that's your answer, then I never want to see you again, Demba Kamara. You are a coward. If you abandon me now, I will do what I first intended to do. I'm warning you. Do you hear me?'

Though her grave tone surprised him, Demba saw no other way out of their conundrum. He stepped out of the house and joined Zaiwulo who was still waiting for him among Massah's women.

"What happened, Demba?" the women asked.

Demba ignored them.

He and Zaiwulo left and took the road which veered off towards the Haidarah compound. "Go home, son of the forest," Demba told Zaiwulo. "I want to be alone."

But Zaiwulo did not want to leave.

"If you follow me, Zaiwulo, I will make sure you have no future here ," he said.

Demba took the main street towards the eastern gate and walked on for a while. He sat under the thatched roof of an abandoned home. Misfortune could not be avoided, he thought now, not even by someone as prudent as he'd always been. He should have seen it coming when it became clear that Sona would not return. Massah was bound to replace her. Could he ever again face Talata knowing that he was married to the only woman he had ever loved? He reached the eastern gate, walked past the sentinels, and out of the walls. He waved off their concerns. He told the men he wanted to go to the river.

By the time he reached the Jon River, it was raining. Demba groped for shelter but found none.

Demba moved downstream until his joints ached. The sharp grass barred his way, cut into his skin, but he moved on. He broke into a Sufi chant his teacher had taught him. Of all the knowledge that Talata had imparted to him, the most precious and the most invaluable was the science of how the world functioned visibly and invisibly, and the ability to synthesize that knowledge into a handful of all-encompassing thoughts.

Talata had taught him to look beyond the obvious.

"I am like a bird bound for the sky. Where would I perch when my wings fail me? On trees not planted by me? On nests belonging to others? On fields not cultivated by me?" he sang.

Soon, like a Sufi prepared to fully give himself over to his master, Demba began to feel a sense of lightness. His body was being purified, the pain of being denied Massah was ebbing away, his whole being shedding off the miseries of existence.

Demba opened himself up to the realities of the other world, to become one with nature, to dissolve into nothingness, into the *Fana,* thereby attaining the *Baqa*, the divine.

6

Moments before Massah was led out of the house, Zaiwulo managed to see her again. "Demba is a coward," she said. "He refuses to talk to his teacher or do what is right."

Zaiwulo disagreed.

"So you support his decision?" said Massah.

"He has no choice," he said.

Massah spat at him and turned her back. "You are all afraid of Talata, but you will see. I will show that man who I truly am."

It worried Zaiwulo to hear her say this, but he was unable to alter the course of things. Massah was led out of her parents' home and toward a new life. She despised her father for sealing her fate in such a way. She despised Zaiwulo for failing her, and Talata for agreeing to such a terrible arrangement, and Demba for forgoing his well-being to please his teacher. Massah wondered where he would be at that moment—probably somewhere pitying himself.

The women sang as they escorted Massah to her new home. In their songs, they hinted at a life she did not wish to live, at secrets she did not want to share with Talata but only with Demba.

"*Let's take this fortune and carry her to our home*," the women sang. "*May she brighten the darkness of our days.*"

How she wished that she had the power to silence the singers or to turn into a bird and fly to an unknown world. The songs ceased only when they arrived in Haidarah's compound and were standing before the door to his chambers. What followed was a solemn silence. The women were serious now, as if the songs and ululations were trivial compared to what was to follow. Massah was left alone to confront her fate.

She fought against the chaos in her head, touched the knife she had wrapped in a piece of cloth around her waist. It was her ultimate recourse, one she was ready to turn to when left with no other choice. Massah stepped into the house. It was dimly lit, but across from her, at the other end of the space, was a face shrouded in darkness, the face at the cause of all her troubles. Massah stood with her back leaning firmly against the door, waiting for him to humiliate himself with a remark or a wrong gesture. Men were capable of such things, that much she knew.

But Talata did not move.

The silence dragged on for so long that Massah thought perhaps Talata had seen through her.

"What are you afraid of?" he asked.

His light tone surprised her. She decided to test him. If his intentions regarding her were good, then he would not touch her that night or any other night. If he lusted after her and wanted to possess her, she would simply kill him.

While the knife whispered profanities in her ears, Massah serenely stepped forward and sat on the mat facing him.

"I hope no one is listening in on us," Talata said.

When he stood up and moved past her to the door, he left a trail of male scent that threatened to dissolve her strength.

"The women are still here, so we need to be discreet about what we say or do here, don't you think?" he said.

He's waiting for the moment to fall upon me, she thought, like the men who fall on women at the river, disappearing with them into the bushes.

"People say it was my fault," Talata said.

She didn't know what he was talking about.

"They say that I chased Ma-Sona out of my house, that I hated her. They say that I forced her to leave me and Musadu. Do you also think so?"

Why was he asking her that question? Why was he not pouncing on her and pinning her to the hard mat, to the bed? She had to make sure not to be affected by the sadness in his voice. It could be a trap.

"I don't think so, Haidarah."

"Tell me about her then."

Perhaps she was wrong about him. Nevertheless, she kept her guard up. The knife could come in handy, if not that night, perhaps the next.

"I think about Ma-Sona day and night, Haidarah."

"What do you remember of her?"

"Her kindness, her goodness."

"Then let's talk about her."

Together, they discussed Sona and shared their experiences with her: Talata touched on Sona's role as wife, while Massah spoke on her role as a mentor, as one who had been preparing her for the future.

As the hours dragged on, Massah's fear began to dissipate, but the knife kept reminding her that the man who appeared innocent and was still in love with his wife could make the wrong move.

7

Zaiwulo couldn't shake off thoughts of Massah in the same room with his teacher. Because he did not hear screams of protest from Talata's chambers, he concluded that Massah had acquiesced to his desires. Zaiwulo lay awake for most of the night.

Sleep came around dawn, and it brought with it a woman in his dream. She breathed cold air that hurt him like a burning flame. Her presence was expansive, filling up the room, becoming part of him. Soon, he realized that the woman was his mother. Every time he attempted to reach her, ignoring the pain of her presence, she floated away from him. His efforts exhausted him. Between sleep and wakefulness, his mother seemed aloof, distant, unwilling to be close to him.

He woke up in tears, longing for her touch, for her presence. He had the feeling that he was not alone. And he was right. Beside his bed sat Naminata.

Zaiwulo buried his face in her lap like a child, and Naminata held him tight and steadily rocked him. "I came to tell you that Foningama has passed on."

Zaiwulo broke away from her embrace.

"Yes, the old man has died," she said.

Naminata told him how Foningama entered the house that night, trembling with fever. "Prepare a hot bath for me," he had told her. "My time has come."

Naminata had washed him thoroughly; she'd scrubbed his back, his arms, his shoulders and legs with soap before pouring water on his head. The old man moaned every time she touched him as his whole body was wracked with pain. She washed his member, which was shriveled as though it had known no strength. He was still, almost rigid, as though she were performing a shameful but necessary ritual. She moved her hands to his back, feeling the bones of his spine, and he leaned toward her, succumbing to the power she wielded over him. Foningama heaved a sigh that was both an expression of weariness and profound gratitude.

"Then I covered him in a thick blanket and led him to bed," she told Zaiwulo. "Seated beside him, I sang a song about a man who kept defying death by shedding his skin. I was not thinking about his condition, his imminent death, but about the wedding songs borne by the winds. Somehow, I felt that it was meant for me. Yes, for Naminata, for me."

She had leaned toward Foningama to feel the old man's breath, which was soft like feathers. She waited until he had drawn his last breath before she left the house. After crossing the city in the pale light of dawn, Naminata stood in front of Talata's door.

"Haidarah, your father-in-law has passed on."

"Is that you, Naminata?"

"Let us inform other people," Talata had suggested.

"While Talata went in search of Demba, I came to see you, Zaiwulo," she said. "Because you are the only one who truly knows me."

Zaiwulo left with Naminata to join the crowd rushing to Foningama's compound. The whole city was awake.

After the body had been washed and shrouded in a white cloth, it was placed on a wooden plank and taken to the mosque.

Talata, who was to lead the prayer, turned to the people. "Where is Demba?"

No one knew his whereabouts.

"Osman can take his place."

But Osman, too, was absent.

"Zaiwulo, you will second me then."

Zaiwulo agreed. As he prayed, Zaiwulo hoped that Massah would tell him the truth regarding what had transpired between her and his teacher. If she didn't, he would force the truth out of her. He had to know. But his thoughts invariably returned to Naminata. What would become of her now that her husband was deceased?

He was thinking about Naminata as he joined the crowd carrying Foningama's remains across the Jon River to the graveyard.

8

The funeral concluded and the crowd headed back to the city, sharing anecdotes about the life of the deceased. “Wasn’t Foningama a great human?” someone said. Many agreed. Another added that Foningama had set him up for life by giving him a *manangu*—capital—to start his trade in kola nuts.

“I owed Foningama some considerable sum,” another man said. “One day when I came to repay the money, he had looked at me as if I had insulted him and told me never to mention the debt to him again.

There was a lull in the praises.

“Have Beyla and Jacodu been informed?” a man asked.

“We’ve dispatched messengers to all major cities and towns in Koniyan,” Talata said. “They will attend the fortieth day.”

Zaiwulo recalled a night when he came out to pass water and saw a white form spread on top of the trees behind the house. The white form engulfed him, stifled his voice, and impeded his ability to move. On recovering his voice, he screamed. His mother had come to him. “It was death that you saw,” she said. She stayed with him until he fell asleep.

His train of thoughts was interrupted by voices from behind him. When he turned around, his heart skipped a beat at the sight of the person walking toward him. It was Talata's youngest son. Was life so capricious? Could you lose a person only to gain another at the same time?

"'Karamo, Karamo!" Zaiwulo called.

His reaction must have attracted the crowd of mourners, for people rushed to the source of excitement. Talata was amongst them.

"You've returned!" Talata said, embracing his son.

"Yes, Father. Forgive me."

"You are here now. That's what matters."

Karamo was not alone. With him was the Liberian, Benjamin Anderson.

"Thank you for bringing back my son," Talata said.

Karamo interpreted this.

"Your son is special," Anderson said.

Musadu welcomed Anderson at the main square in the city center where the market was held. Anderson was dressed in a gray-white gown befitting a ruler and given a seat beside the king. Mounted warriors carrying spears, bows, arrows, and rifles, raced about the square, firing their rifles into the air. The men exhibited various war maneuver. They contorted their faces and exaggerated their war cries, all in a bid to impress Anderson.

At a sign from the king, the horsemen cleared the square.

"Karamo," the king said. "Tell our Toubabous that once again he honors us with his visit but failed to carry out his promise."

The king leaned forward, his eyes fixed on Anderson. "Remind him that during his last visit here we wrote a letter to his king asking for help, for he has access to the white man's weapons. Now we need his help more than ever. We are threatened by the greatest enemy Koniyan and this part of the world has ever known: Samori Touré."

"Tell me about Samori," Benjamin Anderson said. "During my last visit, your greatest enemy was Sere-Brimah, who you told me plundered Musadu. In your letter to the president of Liberia, you asked for help to get rid of Sere-Brimah or protect yourself against his raids. What has happened since then?"

The king told him about Samori's sudden rise to power and his unbridled ambitions. "He has no consideration for our way of life. Samori wants to change everything."

The king turned to Talata. "Samori took our scholar hostage, didn't he, Haidarah?" he said, daring Talata to oppose him.

Talata mumbled something.

"There are other men who want to destabilize Koniyan: Gbanguno Saaye and our old enemy Sere-Brimah, but Samori is the most dangerous of them all. That's why we've decided to ally ourselves with Sere-Brimah and Saaye, or with anyone for that matter."

"I gave your letter to the president of my country, but he has a problem of his own. Recently, someone tried to kill him and usurp his power. My country Liberia is afraid that if we supply you with weapons, the French and the English might attack us."

"That means we are all on our own," the king said.

"I'm afraid that's the case. So be sensible and ally with Samori. That way when the white people come you will be able to fight them together."

"But we've had no cause to worry about the white people. As for Samori, we will never work with him. Do you know what he's done? He has allied himself with the

Kabbas, the rulers of Kankan. Those people loathe our way of life. Samori is capable of anything. From reliable sources, we've learned that he has set his eyes on our Musadu. He wants to incorporate it into his new empire. Never! We say, never!"

"What do you intend to do?" Anderson asked.

"We could be part of Liberia. You speak the language of the white people. You could ask them to leave us alone. When we are part of Liberia, Samori will never dare threaten us."

Anderson considered this for a while. "I will pass on your sentiments to my president. If it's in his power to help you, he will do so," he said.

And with that, the gathering was over.

•×•

Talata drew closer to the Liberian and invited him home.

On their way home, Zaiwulo threw questions at Karamo. "I came to stay," Karamo said. "So you have plenty of time to ask me anything."

"Fetch water for our guest, Karamo," Talata said after they had taken seats on the mats under the bolon in the main courtyard.

"Have you seen Osman or Demba today?" he asked Zaiwulo.

Zaiwulo shook his head.

"Where are they? Why are they avoiding me? Ask one of the students to search for them. Ask the women to prepare food for our guest."

When Zaiwulo returned from his errand, he joined Talata and Karamo. Karamo was sitting beside Anderson as if he was a guest in his own home.

The women brought water and some boiled cassava and fish prepared with okra for the Liberian. He took a knife and fork out of his bag and ate with the joy of one who'd been hungry for a while. Talata waited until he was done.

"What's your country like?" Talata asked him.

"My country was founded by Black people from across the seas, from a land called America. My people fled oppression and longed for freedom."

"Is it so beautiful that a son would trade his family for it?"

"Liberia is beautiful. But we are threatened by powers like the French, the English, the Germans, the Dutch, and others. We stand for the freedom denied us in America. We are against slavery and disapprove of keeping slaves like you do here."

"I want you to help me reclaim my son. I don't know whether he came to stay. If anything were to happen to me, I want him to run the house together with Osman, Demba, and Zaiwulo. The king doesn't trust me because he thinks I've chosen Samori's side. My stay in Musadu is therefore tentative. The king fails to see that Samori is the only one capable of uniting our people and preparing us for the future."

"I understand what you are saying. In my country, as small it is, the leaders keep fighting each other for power. Concerning your son, I have no influence over him. It's up to him to decide what to do."

"But he's still a child, can't you see that? How will he fare in a place with a different way of life? Can't you see the difficulties he will face?"

Even as he said this, Talata realized that he was demanding the impossible from Anderson. He should be sharing his concerns directly with Karamo. He decided to change the subject. "What brings you here again?"

"I've heard about the city of gold."

"You mean Buré," Talata asked. "I've been there."

"Tell me, are the stories true?"

"The stories are true. It's a prosperous place. More gold is extracted there than anywhere else in this part of the world."

"I want to continue my journey to Buré," Anderson said.

"That will be very difficult," Talata replied. "You need dozens of warriors."

"Dozens of warriors? But I came in peace."

"You will soon find out how much *that* is worth here. The people of Buré have reasons to be suspicious of newcomers."

"Thank you so much for the hearty welcome." Anderson took a Bible out of his leather bag. "My gift to you."

Talata browsed through the pages of the Bible in Arabic and read some verses aloud. "I have this in handwritten form, not a bound one. Some of the Biblical stories gave me insight into the verses of the Quran. Thank you for this."

"Who is this boy?" Anderson asked, referring to Zaiwulo.

"I knew his parents when I was in Haindi, in the forest. His mother prepared my food and bath. He reminds me very much of her."

It was the first time Talata had mentioned Zaiwulo's parents in his presence. Zaiwulo wanted to know more, but he decided to wait until Anderson was before asking his teacher further questions.

The Liberian stood up to leave, and Karamo joined him.

"What are you doing, namesake of my brother? Talata said to Karamo." Show some respect to your father! You've just returned. Stay."

Karamo sat down.

"Where is Osman? Where is Demba when I need him?"

"Perhaps Osman is in Beyla, Haidarah," Zaiwulo said. "I was told by some students that he spends his time there nowadays. I will fetch Uncle Demba."

"Send someone to Beyla to ask Osman to return immediately," Talata said. "Why is he in Beyla? His grandfather is dead, and he's not here."

Zaiwulo arranged a horse for one of the students to go fetch Osman from Beyla. As he went around the compound in search of the blind man, he thought that it would not be difficult to locate him. However, no one had seen Demba since the night before.

Zaiwulo returned worried. "I couldn't find Uncle Demba, Haidarah."

"He must be found," Talata said.

Finally, alone with his teacher after Karamo had gone, Zaiwulo plucked up the courage to ask him the one question that plagued him.

"Haidarah, why did my father bring me here?"

"What do you mean?"

Zaiwulo noticed his teacher's unease.

"Ma-Sona told me that you and my father made a promise to each other before my birth. I want to know what that promise entailed."

"That was long ago," Talata said, sounding dismissive. "It was to teach you what I know, yes, to make you a scholar. What else could it have been?"

This answer did not satisfy Zaiwulo. He was convinced that his teacher had left out the most important aspects of a past that involved him. Zaiwulo vowed to confront him with the subject again.

9

Osman was not in Beyla, but some people claimed to have seen him in Musadu. Why was his son avoiding him, Talata wondered. Was it because of the marriage? What worried him most was that Demba—the man who had given structure to his dreams—was nowhere to be found. From what he had learned, Demba had been seen walking through the main street of the city a few nights ago. The sentinels had seen him leave, heading in the direction of Beyla and Jacodu, but he had not reached the twin cities. What was he doing alone at night beyond the city walls? The world is crumbling around me, Talata thought, and he decided to act quickly before it was too late. "Zaiwulo, fetch Osman and Karamo for me. I need to speak to the three of you," Talata said.

Zaiwulo left the study in search of the two brothers and found them quarreling in the vicinity of the western gate.

"Don't deny it, Karamo," Osman was saying. "You decided to return and rub it in our faces. You have no idea how much you hurt Father. Your actions forced Mother to go in search of you. If she hadn't left, Father would not have married Massah. It's all your fault."

"All I wanted was to see how others lived, elder brother. I wanted to see the world," Karamo replied. "About Massah—"

"Shut up. I know what I saw. You and Massah! How could you do such a thing behind my back? How could you, Karamo?"

"What are you talking about, elder brother?"

"I will make you pay one day," Osman said.

As he turned his head, he saw Zaiwulo approaching. "When will you ever learn that you don't belong to us and never will? Go away!"

"Your father is asking for you," Zaiwulo said.

Osman sucked his teeth, stood up, and wiped the dust off his tunic before leaving to see his father. Karamo and Zaiwulo followed behind.

Talata was writing on a small wooden slate when they arrived. "Zaiwulo, please wash the slate and bring me the holy water."

When Zaiwulo returned, Karamo was telling Talata about the Liberian, Benjamin Anderson.

"My teacher is a man of consequence in Liberia, Father," Karamo said. "He's an adviser to its ruler. He's a writer like you, and like you, he's interested in numbers. He taught me his language and the knowledge of numbers. The numbers yielded to me, Father."

"There are no limits to knowledge. The more you acquire, the more the world opens to you. The world is opening up to you, namesake of my brother."

"I read all of Anderson's books, including many belonging to his friends. He was proud of me. I don't know what he was trying to prove, but he often told people that I was extraordinary. Perhaps he wanted to prove his hope that Liberians could work together with other people was not in vain. But some of his people, the ignorant ones, still regarded me as backward, as not belonging. Because of their contempt for me, I often longed to return to Musadu. I came to stay, Father."

"Don't say this to please me," Talata said.

Karamo was silent.

"Your mother left in search of you. Every day I worry about her and the child she was carrying. What happened to them?"

"I don't know, Father."

"Here is the nasi, Haidarah," Zaiwulo said, handing Talata the holy water.

Talata glanced at him with a smile.

"For washing the slate, you get to drink the nasi first," Talata said. "It contains words from the Haidarah Manuscript. It's my gift to you."

Talata's words sounded like a farewell message to Zaiwulo. He wondered whether he deserved such a gesture from the scholar, for he did not belong to the family. Zaiwulo drank some of the honeyed potion first, followed by Osman, and then Karamo.

The moment the boys left, Talata stood up to return to his chambers to see how Massah was faring. He heard someone calling him. It was Naminata. She was dressed as if she was about to attend a feast. Her hair was made-up and her ears adorned with silver rings.

"What are you doing here, Naminata?" Talata said.

"I came to tell you that once the ninety days of mourning my husband are over, I will announce the name of the man of my choice to the world."

"It's too early to be thinking about that."

"I can be a better wife to this man. I heard that his first wife left him and that he married the wrong woman."

"Please go home, Naminata."

"Ninety days, Haidarah."

Naminata left only when Talata entered his chambers. He expected to find Massah, but she was absent. He heaved a sigh of relief. The night had slipped by without him performing the obligation Musadu had imposed on him. He could simply not be the girl's husband. But Musadu was tightening its hold on him, gradually strangling him. He had to do something.

10

Massah was lying on a mat under the thatched awning of her house, her head resting on the lap of a woman who was plaiting her hair and singing softly to her. Other women attended to her like royalty. Her feet and hands were decorated with henna. Her scent was a fresh and beguiling mixture of soap, oil, and musk.

Zaiwulo, who had come to force the truth out of her if necessary, was struck by the sudden transformation she had undergone. He could not believe his eyes. Massah glowed in her newfound status as the mistress of one of the largest houses in Musadu. She seemed to have forgotten her Demba.

Osman and Karamo had followed Zaiwulo, and they stared in stunned silence at her. She seemed a stranger to them. On noticing them, Massah sat up.

"Haidarah, you've returned!" she said.

Karamo was at a loss for words.

"How was that land?"

Karamo was silent. Massah understood his shyness, and she shifted her attention to Osman. She loathed his arrogance, his obvious attempts to undermine his father, but most of all, his hatred of Zaiwulo. "Why are you staring at me like that, Osman?" she said and sucked her teeth. "Have you forgotten I am now your mother?"

It felt as if she had slapped him in the face. Osman threw himself at her and began to shake her, to slap her.

Zaiwulo jumped on Osman and wrested him away from Massah.

"What are you doing, Osman?"

"Don't touch me, Bush Boy," Osman said, his voice lacking the usual sharpness, as though shocked by the strength he had discovered in Zaiwulo. It unsettled him.

Talata was drawn to the commotion. "What is going on here?" he asked.

"Father, this girl insulted me!"

"What do you have to say to that, Massah?"

Massah collected herself and explained.

"You owe her an apology, Osman," Talata said.

"Me, apologize to this girl? Never."

"Osman, don't let yourself be carried away by anger."

Because he regarded his father's suggestion as humiliating—for there was no way he would bow to Massah— Osman turned around and walked away without any concern for the consequences of his behavior. Zaiwulo moved to bar his way, to fight him.

"Let him be," Talata said. "He will come to his senses."

Talata was mistaken. This latest episode was the final straw for Osman. His father had not only denied him being the Samorian envoy to the English, but in Musadu he was met with nothing but setbacks. From now on Osman would define his own destiny and grab whatever opportunities came his way with alacrity.

Osman rushed into his father's study, tore down the curtains, and stepped into the forbidden space. It was not hard to find the Haidarah Manuscript. It was heavy, as he had expected, but his anger fueled his strength and enabled him to leave the study with it. In the stalls, he saddled a horse, tied the manuscript to it, and galloped out of the city.

When Talata was told about his son's flight, he feigned disinterest.

•×•

"Your brother has gone mad," Massah told Karamo later that day.

"He has," Karamo agreed with her.

She turned to Zaiwulo. "Have you seen Demba?" she whispered.

Zaiwulo shook his head.

"Find him. I want to talk to him."

After days of searching, Zaiwulo finally found Demba at the Jon River. He was lying on the bank of the river, his hands folded around his chest as though he was fast asleep. Death had been merciful, Zaiwulo thought, for Demba seemed not to have suffered.

His first reaction was to rush to the city to tell Talata, but as he entered the compound and approached the study where his teacher had confined himself, Zaiwulo's feet weakened. If I tell my teacher or Massah about Demba's death, the grief might kill them both, he thought.

Zaiwulo decided to bury the blind man secretly. He returned to the river with a hoe and worked until night. It surprised him that the body had been spared by the animals of the night and the heavy rain. He thought that because Demba was special, the Earth and the animals had been kind to him. Zaiwulo conducted the burial with reverence, following the ritual he had seen Talata perform. His voice was trembling with prayers, but guilt began to mount in him with every line of the prayer, lodging like stones in his conscience. A voice kept telling him to tear himself away from that spot and run to the city, shouting the news of Demba's demise.

After he had poured the earth into the narrow grave, he wondered once again whether he had done the right thing. Was the uncertainty that would plague Massah and Talata regarding Demba's fate not worse than the truth? Could he deal with such a loss? Could he ever face his teacher or Massah with such a secret?

That night, Zaiwulo avoided Massah and Talata. He was still awake when, as the light of dawn poured into his room, he heard the blind man calling him.

"Child of the forest!"

It was Demba's distinct voice. Zaiwulo dashed out of the house. As he rushed to join the students around the hearths, he thought he saw the blind man walking before him, his feet barely touching the ground. This must be a dream, he thought. But in fact, Demba turned to him with a smile he had never seen on his face when he was alive. "Don't be afraid," the dead man said. "I am at peace here, so don't burden yourself with the weight of my loss."

Zaiwulo reached out to touch the blind man but felt the mat under him and realized that he had been dreaming.

Just then, one of the students called to him. "Haidarah wants to see you," the boy said.

Zaiwulo entered the study and met his teacher wasting away. His burden seemed much heavier than his own.

"Are you well? You seem lost," Talata said.

Indeed, Zaiwulo was looking around him, as though expecting to see the blind man seated behind his teacher, with that strange smile on his face.

"I did not sleep well, Haidarah," said Zaiwulo.

"You are not the only one," the scholar said. Talata closed his eyes and yawned softly. He shifted from his seated position, and, as if he longed for sleep, stretched out his feet, away from Zaiwulo. "Since his return, Karamo has hardly left Anderson's side. Please fetch him for me," he said and sat upright again, as if he had caught himself breaking a protocol.

On his way, Zaiwulo paused to see whether the blind man would appear again. He was glad that Demba had justified his action, but he was still wary of facing Massah for fear that she might read the secret on his face.

Zaiwulo found the Liberian seated outside of his lodgings, bending over his notes and plying Karamo with questions about Koniyan, its people and their customs. Every morning, Anderson went around the city asking the authorities as well as the common people about Musadu and its history. He relied on Karamo to interpret for him.

"Zaiwulo," Anderson said without looking up from his notes. "They tell me that you've met Samori. What type of man is he?"

Zaiwulo understood the question. There were rumors that Samori had conquered most of Koniyan, except for a few places like Beyla, Jacodu, and areas belonging to Saaye. The conquered people had sworn allegiance to him, but it was evident that sooner or later, he would turn his conquering gaze toward Musadu and its neighborhood.

"He's the most powerful person I've ever met," Zaiwulo said. "But he means well for his people. You should consider working with him."

"Why do you think so?"

"Because he protects his people against the enemy," Zaiwulo said.

"Even against the whites?"

"I think so. He works with the English now, and he intends to do the same with all people," Zaiwulo said. "He has ambassadors in Freetown."

"I've never thought of Samori in that light."

"If there's anyone who can help you reach Buré, the city of gold, then it's Samori. You should ask for his help," Zaiwulo said.

"According to the people here, the journey to Buré is fraught with dangers, and it takes months to reach it. They say you need an army for protection, but I don't believe it. According to my calculations, Buré is a few days away."

Zaiwulo did not respond.

"You think Samori can help me reach the city?"

"If your country is willing to work with him."

"You have the talent to persuade people, Zaiwulo. You will make a good adviser. You admire Samori, but that can be dangerous. Admiration clouds judgment. Are you hoping to join him one day?" Anderson asked.

"No, I want to be a scholar."

Anderson laughed. "In the next few days, I will prepare to return to Liberia. I will tell the president about your advice to work with Samori. Next time I return, I will head straight for the goldfields of Buré."

"Karamo, your father wants to see you," Zaiwulo, said as he remembered Talata's errand..

"Excuse me, Mr. Anderson," Karamo said.

Zaiwulo and Talata headed back together to Talata's study.

"Today, I received a request from Samori to accompany his daughter Jawulen-N'nagbe to Kankan," Talata said. "He wants to give his daughter as a bride to my brother Karamo-Sidikie. It's a gesture of alliance with the people of Kankan."

Talata turned to Karamo. "Namesake of my brother, you've seen the world. Your experience is invaluable to the people of Musadu. Something terrible must have happened to Demba or he would have been back by now. I want you two to take care of the house in my absence."

Karamo did not respond, so Zaiwulo did. "I'm honored by your request, Haidarah. But what about Osman? He's so capable."

"Osman has turned his back on me. People keep disappearing out of my life. Karamo, I want you to stay and help Zaiwulo run the house."

The request, perhaps the greatest honor that could ever be conferred on Zaiwulo in Musadu, came as a surprise to him. He did not want to fail his teacher. "Haidarah, give me time to consider your request," he said.

"I know it's a huge responsibility," Talata said.

Zaiwulo decided to take a ride on his horse to think over the huge responsibility entrusted upon him. He had not ridden Haindi for a while, but the horse welcomed him as if he were a lost friend. "Forgive me for neglecting you, Haindi," he said.

On leading the horse out of the stall, he brushed its flanks with his hands and the animal huffed in appreciation.

Zaiwulo rode past the twin cities of Beyla and Jacodu, beyond towns and villages with names that sounded like songs: Baladu, Mavinkonedu, Kolelah, Saydu, and Konokoro. As he rode on, he recalled his mother's face: Black like a cooking pot, her solemn and owlish gaze as she stood pounding herbs collected from the forest, herbs the ancestors had picked out for her. He thought of his sisters who, after their father had denied him food for one reason or the other, often went out of their way to share their food with him.

Images of Haindi crowded his memory. The women bathing in the nearby river. The silence that descended on a gathering of elders The songs of boys and girls his age. Zaiwulo fed hungrily on those images and projected them against the image of a young man on a horse, on the cusp of taking up a great, enviable position.

I will not fail you, Haidarah, no matter what happens, he vowed to himself.

The horse must have felt his determined mood, for it neighed loudly and raced across the plains as if in competition with time.

11

On his way back to Musadu, Zaiwulo stopped at a tiny village that looked quiet and innocuous. The first house was occupied by an old woman with a face so wrinkled with age she seemed like the work of a sculptor. "Please help me with a meal, grandmother," he said. The old lady nodded and pointed at an elevation under a house close to her own. Zaiwulo tethered Haindi to a tree and waited under the house. It was then he saw the girl.

She was slender, bright, with amber-colored eyes, and pert breasts like dollops of pounded cassava stuck to the flat surface of a pan. From waist to knees, she was covered in a single piece of cloth. Her elegant arms held an earthen bowl of food on her head, the effort tightening the skin around her ribs, making her look so fragile, so intensely vulnerable that his heart ached to touch her, to protect her.

"Here's your midday meal," she said in a quavering voice, clearly afraid of him.

"Where are your parents?" he asked.

"They died in a raid last year," she said.

The answer took him aback. He wanted and wished her to have parents who doted on her, who spoiled her, and who watched her grow to become independent of them.

The girl sat under the tree to which he had tethered Haindi and watched him eat the boiled cassava she had prepared. "Men like you came to our village last year," she said, as if he had asked her. "They raided it, burned our homes, killed many people—including my parents—and took others away to be sold into slavery."

"What do you mean by men like me?"

"Horsemen dressed like you."

"I am a Samorian sofa," he said to impress her. "We don't raid villages or kill people. We negotiate first."

She made no response.

Why am I lying to her, he thought. Do I truly want to become part of Samori's world? Zaiwulo shook his head. I shouldn't have lied to her, he told himself. Because he wanted to reassure her that he meant well, he left in search of firewood. On his way, he came to a river aplenty with fish, and he decided to fish for her. At sunset, he returned with enough firewood and fish to last the old lady and her granddaughter for days.

The old lady spoke to him for the first time. "Where are you from, young man?"

"I come from a land where we thrive on fish, meat, greens, and rice every day. My father was a hunter, among many other things, and my mother was a herbalist. She could cure a broken bone and heal those struck with madness."

"You must have been wealthy, child."

"Meat and fish easily came to hand, grandmother."

"You must be tired. Stay the night with us," the old woman suggested.

Zaiwulo retired to bed hoping to see the girl with a bowl of boiled groundnuts and fried grasshoppers for him, or with stories other than her loss. Instead, it was his mother who appeared to him. "They are coming for you, namesake of my father. Run for your life. Run before it's too late."

Zaiwulo woke up to the presence of men around him. They grabbed him, threw a cloth over his head, tied him up, and led him out of the house and into the unknown.

The journey lasted for hours. No one spoke. Not even when the men built a fire close by and tied him to a tree.

"You are a Samorian sofa," one of them broke the silence and spat in his face.

"I am not," Zaiwulo shouted.

The men ignored him.

"They say Samori's sofas are invincible. Let's see how you survive this. We should have cut off your head the moment we captured you, like your master Samori did to the people of our village. But first, we will make you suffer. Yes, you will suffer."

"I am from Musadu, a student of Talata Haidarah!"

The men laughed.

"Lies. A sofa's trick."

The men gathered around the tree.

Zaiwulo closed his eyes. "Mother, if you can hear me, don't abandon me."

The men began to shake the tree.

"You are not abandoned, namesake of my father," a voice came to him so faintly that Zaiwulo doubted whether it could be his mother's.

Soon it was raining down red killer ants. They converged on Zaiwulo. He thought that by gritting his teeth and by thinking about his mother and sisters, about Massah and Naminata, he could withstand the assault. However, when the ants began to bite him, he forgot his prayers. He was gripped by an unusual fear. Out of the paralyzing dread of his imminent death, Zaiwulo screamed and fell into a faint.

When he came to, Zaiwulo could not open his swollen eyes. His body was in the throes of an unbearable pain.

He felt that he was being dragged, lifted, and placed somewhere. Myriads of needles seemed to pierce his body. He fell unconscious again.

When Zaiwulo woke later, his head was filled with sharp flames. He felt hands moving across his body, coarse at first but gradually, it felt pleasant. His mother's hands, he thought. He managed to shift his eyelids a bit to see the old lady rubbing him with medicinal oil like his mother did whenever he came down with fever. He moved his head and saw the girl. They did not talk to him, and every time he attempted to speak, the old lady would place her hand on his mouth. Fatigue soon seeped in, and he fell asleep.

Zaiwulo woke up again, this time in a house filled with a brilliant light that streamed through the open door and the chinks in the roof. Outside he could hear his horse neighing, missing his presence. He ached to touch it, to let it know that he was alive. He was not in a village, Zaiwulo thought. He could hear no other sound except for that of birds. It must be a farm.

"Give him something to drink," said the grandmother.

The girl approached him with a calabash of water, from which she took a handful and let it course into his mouth. She went on like this until he had his fill.

After the grandmother and the girl were gone, Zaiwulo longed for their presence, but they seemed to have agreed to let him rest. Sometimes, he would hear the old lady whispering earnestly to her granddaughter. He thought perhaps they were afraid that the men would return. Sometimes, the women came only when it was almost dark, and when he had begun to feel giddy lying dormant all day. The girl fed him lukewarm soup in small rations. Hunger was a welcomed surprise, an indication that he was recovering. Before the grandmother and the girl left, he caught a faint trace of a smile on the girl's face.

A few weeks later, Zaiwulo could sit up, turn around on his mat, and move his legs.

The day he took his first step, the two women celebrated with a sumptuous dish of toe and meat. When he began to talk, his first words were about his horse.

"Thank you for caring for my horse," he said.

But the girl and the old woman kept their distance.

One morning—months into his recovery—the old woman and her granddaughter gave him a bundle with food and some clothes. They parted with him without much fanfare, shunning every attempt at sentiment.

Leading his horse by the reins, Zaiwulo walked with the two women to the river where he had once fished for them.

They did not hug him.

Haindi looked fresh and anxious to take him home. His tormentors must have been more interested in him than in the horse, he thought.

12

Zaiwulo had no sense of direction.

So he decided to ride on, arriving at a farm as the shadows of dusk fell over the earth. There was no one about. Zaiwulo felt alone, insignificant beneath the star-studded sky. He let Haindi graze and went in search of food. In the largest hut, he found a supply of rice, a portion of which he pounded in a mortar with a pestle until it was clean.

The farm's borders were hedged in with fences of branches and grass as well as traps made of simple sticks where hooks had been attached, snapping at any encounter with prey. From one of the traps dangled an opossum. The animal was still alive. It snapped at Zaiwulo's fingers as he tried to release it. He clubbed it to death. The meat served as a base for the sauce of greens he had plucked from the gardens around the main farmhouse.

Seated outside with the fading sun in his face, Zaiwulo ate from a large earthen bowl and thought about his near-death experience at the hands of his captors. He itched to put down his experience and encounter with the girl on a slate or a paper. Zaiwulo imagined her life with another man. He imagined her laughter, her smile, her unconditional love for that man, and wondered whether life was not but a passage cluttered with missed opportunities. He decided to dispel these uneasy thoughts by envisaging a future in which he was surrounded by his own students, by his mother and sisters, and by a wife with the looks and generosity of the girl now lost to him forever.

When he fell asleep on the floor of the main hut, with threshed stems of rice as bedding and nothing to cover him, Zaiwulo saw a sturdy, bow-legged man leading a giant warhorse toward him.

Drawing level with Zaiwulo, the man stopped. He dismounted and limped to him. His face looked familiar to Zaiwulo, as if he'd seen him somewhere before, but he could not place it.

"Tell me what you are called, son," the man ordered.

Zaiwulo told him.

The man shook his head. "No, there's another name. What did they call you in the forest? I mean your real name?"

Zaiwulo thought for a while.

"My mother called me Son of the Buffalo," he replied.

The man smiled. "Yes, that's the name," he said. "In a previous life, very far away from here, across the seas, I was called The Man with the Two Horns. When I was born again, in this part of the world, I went by the name Son of the Buffalo. That was because my mother was the ugliest of all my father's wives. Later, I became known as Sundiata the Great. Or Mari Jata, The Lion King." The man stared solemnly at Zaiwulo. "Beware of the upheavals that are to come. When they do come, our world will never be the same again."

The bow-legged man mounted his warhorse and rode down the road until he was swallowed up by dust.

The dream haunted Zaiwulo. Who was this Sundiata, this Son of the Buffalo, this Man with the Two Horns? And what was he talking about? What upheavals?

When the sun drew a pale line across the horizon, Zaiwulo continued his journey. He rode all day, only now and then stopping to let Haindi rest and feed.

Days later, he arrived at a place with some hamlets and farms.

"Where is this place?" he stopped to inquire.

"Kankan," a man answered him.

The city stretched like a plain before him. He was allowed through its fortified gates, and he saw whitewashed homes, some of which were plastered gray-green with cow dung. The streets were wide and crowded.

Kankan was a city of trade.

The city connected the coasts of Sierra Leone and Liberia and the forests in the south with the savannah and the desert in the far north. The gold of Buré—a legendary place known in places as far as the forests and Liberia, including Sierra Leone and the French Senegal—was traded here deep in the night, beyond the gaze of ordinary people. Here English, French, German, Portuguese, Dutch, and Danish rifles exchanged hands like currency.

Zaiwulo knew that Talata's brother lived in this bustling city. He inquired here and there before he was led to the Haidarah compound, near a huge marketplace.

Karamo-Sidikie was one of the notables of the city. Zaiwulo noted the resemblance between the two brothers: Talata exuded an aura of privilege and wealth, which belied his calling as a scholar, while his elder brother appeared gaunt and ascetic.

With a rich, timbered voice, Talata's brother said, "You are most welcome. Your teacher is here. He will be very glad to see you."

He led Zaiwulo to the main courtyard of a compound where Zaiwulo met his teacher, surrounded by older students.

"I thought you too had abandoned me," Talata said. After listening to Zaiwulo's story, he said, "I will arrange for you to return to Musadu as soon as possible. You are needed there, not here."

Talata then recounted how Karamo had chosen to return with Anderson to Liberia. His son did not even bid him farewell.

"I was told that he left at dawn and waited for Anderson in Beyla," Talata said. "What is more, Samori sent me a message saying that Osman came to him with a letter in which he claimed that I had permitted him to join his emissaries to the English in Freetown. I never wrote that letter. He attempted to steal the Haidarah Manuscript. Fortunately, he took the wrong book. Zaiwulo, you are the only one left now. You are too young to be saddled with the responsibility of running such a large household, but I need you in Musadu. I entrusted a few capable people with this responsibility, but it is temporary. You must return as soon as possible."

"Have you considered moving the manuscript to Kankan?' his brother Karamo-Sidikie asked. "It's safer here than in Musadu."

But Talata shook his head.

"The family entrusted it to me. You all entrusted it to me. I will take care of it. It will never get lost, elder brother."

"Yes, we are the manuscript, Talata. If it gets lost, it would be the end of us. It must never get lost."

That night, Zaiwulo's teacher led him to a house in the compound, not far from the main entrance. "I slept here when I was a student in Kankan," Talata said. It's small but clean. It will be your lodgings."

On one of the slates that were piled up against the wall, Zaiwulo recognized his teacher's handwriting. The damp smell suggested that the house had not been in use for a while. Instead of a bed, there was a worn-out mat. Zaiwulo could not reconcile that simple accommodation with the elegant and now world-renowned Talata. Perhaps, a human being was not defined by a house or a privileged life, but by the caprices of time.

How would time define him?

As a great scholar? Or as a man who would one day trade the lush of the savannah for the shades of the trees of the forest?

13

"Do not tell anyone else about your dream, not even your teacher," Karamo-Sidikie said to Zaiwulo. "Sundiata was the greatest ruler the lands of the black-skinned people have ever seen. From the expanse of the desert to the depths of the forests, his name resounded like a hymn to man's greatness. He named his capital city after the man he admired most, Alexander the Great. Alexander, The Man with the Two Horns, conquered East and West and defeated the feared and gruesome Gog and Magog, who were out to destroy the earth. Sundiata wanted to emulate him. His story has lived on for centuries. That he appeared to you in a dream is extraordinary."

The two were sitting in the shade of a mango tree whose branches labored under the weight of the succulent fruits. The heady and metallic smell of the fruits lingered around them.

Karamo-Sidikie was not much older than Talata, Zaiwulo noted, but his slender jaws and drooping eyes, which were overcast with well-earned wisdom, conveyed the perspicacity of the aged. His bony hands were resting on his lap. There was a faint suggestion of a smile on his face.

"While your teacher goes about his business," Karamo-Sidikie said, "I will take over teaching you while you are here. Shall we begin?"

This suggestion, coming from a scholar of such caliber, was an honor that humbled Zaiwulo. He mumbled his gratitude.

Karamo-Sidikie and Zaiwulo had not gone far with the day's lesson when Talata showed up. "My teacher Karamoko-Mori, the King of Kankan, has agreed after weeks of hesitation to grant me an audience," he said.

"You say this as if he still considers you as an opponent, Talata," his brother said. "But he's changed."

Karamo-Sidikie was referring to the differences between teacher and student that had driven them apart. "You are mistaken when you think that he fell out with you because you were a Qadiriyya Sufi and he a Tijaniyyah Sufi," his brother continued. "You know as well as I do that the founders of the two orders preached only love. The problem lies in the interpretation of their teachings. Some Tijaniyyah adherents consider us Qadiriyya Sufis as tolerant of animists and other practices. They claim that Islam should be practiced in its purest form. But what pure form? Was there ever a pure Islam, even during its inception? If love is the essence of everything, as the Tijaniyyah and the Qadiriyya hold, how can it not be all-inclusive? This is the question I confront people with to explain my presence in Kankan as one of the few Qadiriyya Sufis among the majority Tijaniyyah Sufis. Why should it not be all-inclusive? Are we talking about Islam, Talata, or are we talking about something else? Power perhaps or simple vanity?"

"Well said, elder brother, but I was forced out of Kankan," Talata said. "Why should we declare war against the animists, whom we consider as infidels? We are animists, elder brother. We descend from them. Our ancestor married an animist. We've become who we are thanks to people we now call kaffers—nonbelievers. Who are we to judge them?"

"Your case was different," his brother said. "Knowledge came to you at an early age. You wrote great commentaries and treaties before you were twenty. You mastered the works of the great philosophers. You should have been careful with your gifts, with your fame, but you flaunted them, perhaps because you were too young to understand and fully appreciate your gifts. You know how long it takes people to acquire a fraction of what you have. They serve their teachers all their life, expecting nothing in return but a fraction of their blessing, their Baraka. You were spared all this, so be very grateful."

Talata nodded pensively, but he had trouble letting go of the past in which he was often at odds with his teachers and their extreme views.

•×•

The ruler of Kankan, Karamoko-Mori, resided in a palace larger than Samori's in Sanankoro or Bissandougou. The walls were smoother and the trees threw large shadows on the courtyards which were covered with mats. Zaiwulo followed Talata and his brother across a courtyard to where, at the far end of a grand carpet, sat the king.

Men gorgeously attired in bright, colorful gowns surrounded the ruler of Kankan. The king himself wore an embroidered scarlet gown, and a shawl of pure white cotton covered his head and shoulders. Zaiwulo could see that he was old, lean, and languid, exactly like his tremulous voice which greeted them as if he was in the grip of a degenerative illness.

"Haidarah, Haidarah," he whispered.

"Your majesty, my teacher," Talata said, and he knelt and reached out for his teacher's hands. The king grabbed his hands, and a long greeting session followed, during which Talata heard himself mentioning almost every member of his large household.

There was a brief pause, and then the ritual began again, until one of the courtiers said, "Before you were here, Haidarah, I told the others about your family's relationship with women! It is one to be envied. Your ancestor, our Prophet, must have left you a formula which makes women irresistible to you, or was it the other way round? Tell me, Haidarah."

Smiling, the men touched their caps.

"I am sure that your house is full of them," another man said. When Talata refuted this, the man said, "Karamo-Sidikie, you know your brother better than any of us here. Tell us, is it not true that his house is brimming with those wonderful beings?"

"You know us," Karamo-Sidikie said.

"We are glad to see you, Haidarah," the king said. "It seems like only yesterday that you came to us as a student. Your father and I were best friends, that's why he entrusted you to us before his death. And look at what you've become, a great and famous scholar. The only thing we regret is your attitude toward the animists. I still believe that we should fight them by all means, that we should kill them if they refuse to accept the true faith. Death or the true faith, Haidarah. There's no other way around it."

So nothing has changed, Talata thought, his gaze fixed on the carpet. A long silence ensued, and he felt every eye on him.

"Do you still think that those unbelievers should be left alone while they go on undermining our society with their vile practices? I say, let's get rid of them. We are going to declare holy war on them, again."

As he listened, it occurred to Zaiwulo that the king was referring to his people, to people like his parents, who worshiped different gods. He was referring to those who were one with nature, to people he would not hesitate to slaughter in the name of religion.

"Your majesty, we have to be an example to the animists," Talata said. "Our good behavior should be our best weapon. Our faith thrived here because we managed to mix it with that of the animists. We are them."

"Are you claiming that we are animists? How dare you say that?"

"You and I don't even know where heaven and hell are. What we know for sure is that the animists are like us. Our essence and longings are the same."

The king burst into a fit of coughing which lasted for a while.

"Haidarah, what am I hearing? Your brother has become one of them, an apostate," the king told Karamo-Sidikie. "It's written that those who tolerate the behavior of the unbelievers should be considered one of them. Your brother should be castigated, don't you think so?"

"Your majesty, my brother is still young and inexperienced," Karamo-Sidikie said. He approached the king and held his hands. "Thanks to you, he's acquired some knowledge which is of no consequence compared to your vast knowledge and wisdom. Please forgive your student."

Talata decided not to pursue the subject further. He did not want to risk putting his mission for Samori in jeopardy. He had not come to evoke the past but to talk about the future. "I owe what I am to you, my teachers," he said. "Wasn't it written somewhere that obeying your teacher was like obeying God? Where would I be without you?"

"Beautifully said, Haidarah," the king said. "Please sit."

The conversation meandered on, moving between playfulness and seriousness. The king appeared to have forgiven Talata. Then it took on a political turn as Talata answered questions about Musadu, about Saaye, Sere-Brimah, and Samori.

At the mention of Samori's name, the court fell silent. Everyone expected Talata to say something about Samori, but, unsure of what the king and his court thought of the man, Talata held his peace.

The king spoke. "We've heard that Samori is now the sole ruler of Koniyan and beyond. His horrible deeds are unspeakable." He coughed hard again. Tears sprang to his eyes.

"Your majesty, Haidarah should not be spared the details. He should know everything," said one of the courtiers.

"Samori doesn't negotiate with people anymore. He decapitates his enemies," another said. "We've heard that he sleeps on a bed of bones and drinks from a skull. They say he's not even human. He's the devil himself."

"He's like a swarm of hungry locusts. He usurps lands. Samori wants to conquer the world. He wants to be greater than Sundiata Keita or Mansa Musa, greater than The Man with the Two Horns. Dear Haidarah, what do you think of this Samori?"

"Have you met this man?" the king said.

"Yes, I have. Some of the things that are said about him are exaggerated."

"What do you mean?"

"He wants peace. In fact, he's the one who sent me to you, as your servant."

"How can a Haidarah be our servant? It's through your ancestors that we gained knowledge, that we saw the light," said the king.

"Splendidly spoken," someone said.

"It's the truth," another said.

Talata knew that those words were nothing more than traditional formalities. He accepted them affably before sharing his message. "Samori is convinced that his future lies in working together with you, my teachers. That's why he decided to give his daughter's hand in marriage to you, the Kabbas of Kankan. But the man who will bear the responsibility of taking care of her is your servant, my brother Karamo-Sidikie."

The king was silent.

"We thank you and Samori who sent you. A wife forges a union between two people. She brings joy to a house and ensures its continuity. Through this marriage, the Kabbas, the Haidarahs of Koniyan and Kankan, and the Tourés of Samori will become one. It says a lot about this man. With a single marriage, he plans to ally your brother and all of us to him. What an extraordinary thing," said the king. "This morning, we received a letter from Prince Agibou of the Toucouleur Kingdom, Omar Tall's son, the great man who declared holy war to rid this area of unbelievers.

His son Agibou complained about Samori's incursion into his territory. The prince thinks that Samori is our ally. He wrote that Samori dared to enter his court by pretending that he was a trader. Before the prince could discover his true identity, Samori held him at sword-point and compelled him to cede some of his territories to him. Who is this man who crosses borders and unites three houses with a single marriage?"

"I think Samori is the man of our time," Talata said.

"But can we trust him?" said the king. "What does he want? Now I know why he sent his wife Sarankenyi and her son to us with the request to teach the child. It will be difficult to refuse him in the future once we've accepted his daughter. What do you know of his wife Sarankenyi, Haidarah? She says she came here to be with her son."

"Sarankenyi represents her husband, your majesty," Talata said. "I wouldn't be surprised if it turns out that the marriage was her idea."

"So we are dealing with a special woman."

"She's capable in every way."

The king was silent. "We are going to keep an eye on her," he said. "Tell Samori that we set a great store by our independence. We don't want anyone lording it over us."

"I will convey your message."

The king then shifted his avuncular eyes toward Zaiwulo and asked: "Who is this young man? "Is he one of your sons, Haidarah?" He beckoned to Zaiwulo. "Come closer."

Zaiwulo crawled onto the carpet and bowed. "I am Haidarah's student, Your Majesty."

"Why is he the only one here, Haidarah?"

Talata told the king about his sons.

"So your trials have already begun. Don't waver, Haidarah."

With those words, the ruler of Kankan gathered himself up with the aid of a walking stick. As he tried to move, he went into a coughing fit. His courtiers rushed to his aid to prevent him from falling.

Zaiwulo slipped away. He was surprised to hear that Sarankenyi was in the city, but he was more interested in her son.

14

Sarankenyi stepped out of a house with walls painted white and black against a light green background. Veiled in a blue silk garment edged with golden filigree, she wore the refined bearing of royalty and exuded serene dignity. When she saw Zaiwulo, her face lit up with a smile, exposing her fine teeth cast against a backdrop of darkened gums and lips. It made her smile even more disarming and enchanting to Zaiwulo.

"What are you doing here?" she said.

A boy darted out of the house and threw himself at her. Sarankenyi cuddled him. "My son and your brother, Sarankenyi-Mori," she said and urged the child on. "Go on, greet your elder brother, Zaiwulo. Shake his hand."

The boy's hand felt soft and plump. Folds of fat had created curves in his neck and dimples in his knees.

"I want him to be a scholar like you, Zaiwulo. That's why I brought him to Kankan, the center of knowledge." Turning to one of her maids, Sarankenyi asked her to spread a mat out in the courtyard in the shade of a tree for them to sit on. "You have to eat something," she insisted and directed her maids to prepare something for Zaiwulo.

Sarankenyi seemed in her element in a place that must feel strange to her, Zaiwulo thought as they settled under the tree. He looked around him. The houses, all four of them, were filled with people related to Sarankenyi.

"We've not seen each other for so long, my son," she said.

"Mother," Zaiwulo began, "I've not neglected you. Were it not for the long distance, I would have come often to see you."

Zaiwulo was glad that she called him "son," for his mother once told him to regard any woman who treated him well as his mother.

"My husband talks about you often. He praises your courage and hunger for knowledge. The last time we saw each other, he promised to convince Haidarah to give you up to him. He's come to regard you as a son."

Zaiwulo did not doubt Samori's interest in him, but he had never thought Samori would want to include him in his family.

"I know why you are here," Sarankenyi said. "My husband seeks an alliance with the Kabbas and the Haidarahs of this city. I suggested that he could achieve that by marrying off one of his daughters to them. The one thing I've learned since arriving in this city is that it would be very difficult for my husband to include it in his empire. The people here regard him as a mere hawker. They fail to see that times have changed, that a slave is no longer bound to remain a slave, a hawker a hawker, a smith a smith. Such ways of life defined our people for so long, but my husband came to change all of that. However, they will never grant him what he wants, because he's not one of them, not of nobility."

"Where is the Faama now?"

"He's at work conquering the lands of the Toucouleurs, a people he admires even as he envies them their vast kingdom."

"The rulers of Kankan are indeed reluctant to be his allies," Zaiwulo said. "We met them today."

Sarankenyi stared intently at him. "Isn't it time that you had a wife?" she said. "I could pick out the best for you, a beautiful and industrious girl who will make us all proud."

Zaiwulo did not know what to say.

"Someone should lean on those broad shoulders of yours every once in a while. Kabako—what a wonder! You are as tall as my husband, and then, those eyes. In them lie everything."

Two maids arrived with the food, arranging it before Zaiwulo like a game of cowries: toe, eddoes, fruits, rice, fonio, and sauces of different kinds—a display of sumptuous wealth.

Little Sarankenyi-Mori strolled up to his mother and sat on the mat, snuggling close to her. He whispered something in her ear.

"You must be hungry," she said. "Join your brother."

But the child refused to leave her side.

"After lunch, you can spend some time with your elder brother—Zaiwulo, will you please take him later to the city?"

Zaiwulo nodded. When the child did not budge, Sarankenyi held him up and slapped him hard across the face. The child tottered and fell on the ground, but Sarankenyi was not yet done with him. "Not a single drop of tears," she yelled. "You think I brought you here to play! You think that because I am your mother I can tolerate such weakness. Stand up. Move when I tell you."

Sarankenyi-Mori sought refuge behind Zaiwulo. When his mother attempted to reach him, Zaiwulo prevented her from reaching the boy.

"I should teach him to be a man," she said.

"It's enough, Mother."

"What's the use of a lazy child?"

"You will do what Mother says, right?" Zaiwulo said to the boy after Sarankenyi had calmed down. "Come, I will take you into the city."

On their way to the main market, clouds of sandy dust that smelled of pepper rose and moved in their direction. Zaiwulo pulled the child aside to escape it, but even with all the care he took, the hem of the boy's tunic was stained orange-brown with dust.

Kankan was a city of dust.

At the market, the two saw a group of women sweeping the particles and piling it up in mounds. Zaiwulo told the child about the goods. He talked about the rice and millet, how they were cultivated in paddies in the savannah and in large areas that were cleared and burned in the forest. He told him about the dyeing process for cloths and about the prices of gold, silver, copper utensils, and earthenware. The child gasped in wonder at everything.

In that chaos of the marketplace, Zaiwulo heard a language that sounded familiar. He ran with Sarankenyi-Mori toward the voices, but he realized that his ears had deceived him. The language was a distant variation from that of his own people. He felt disappointed.

"Look, elder brother, look at that man," Sarankenyi-Mori said, pointing to a man playing the flute. The man alternated his music with acrobatic moves and somersaults. The attraction cheered Zaiwulo up.

At sunset, he brought the child home.

"What did you do all afternoon?" Sarankenyi asked.

With great enthusiasm, the child told her about the visit to the market, the encounter with the flute player who somersaulted from the rooftop of houses, and how Zaiwulo had taken him to other places.

"Until your elder brother leaves Kankan, you will spend all your afternoons with him, you hear me?" his mother said.

"I will take over teaching him," Zaiwulo said, thinking about the period many years back in Musadu when he discovered the alphabet for the first time and how he had felt. "Don't be too hard on him, Mother."

"The world is out to crush him. Yes, Sarankenyi's child has no right to live, my enemies say. That's why I must be hard on him."

•×•

On arriving at the home of the Haidarahs of Kankan, Zaiwulo met the two Haidarah brothers sitting on a mat in the main courtyard.

"I was at Ma-Saran's," he said.

"Stick to what we tell you to do here," Talata said. "That woman thinks only about herself. I've seen her behave as if she is a Faama-moussou, dictating each of her husband's actions." Turning to Karamo-Sidikie, Talata said, "Have you met her, elder brother?"

Karamo-Sidikie laughed. "Who hasn't met Sarankenyi? What a brave woman, Talata. She reminds me of your wife, Sona. I hope that she has returned by now."

"If so, we would have been notified of her return," Talata said.

"We will pray for her safe return."

Sona's image rose before Talata, her presence, her abilities, and the intimate moments he shared with her. The scholar changed the subject for fear of quaking under the pressure of his longing for Sona. "The Kabbas's attitude toward me has not changed, elder brother, and perhaps, it will be the same with Samori," he said. "If Samori conquers Kankan, will the Kabbas succumb to his will? Would they not persuade him to accept their extreme view of religion? If that happens, then there will be no place left for you and me here. I must warn Samori."

"You worry too much, Talata."

"What if they deny him access to Kankan?"

"I know for sure that the Kabbas will find a way to work with Samori."

"If it comes to a head, I don't want to play any role in it, elder brother. I will return home to Musadu, to my manuscripts."

It worried Zaiwulo to see his teacher racked by misfortune, but he could do nothing to alter the situation. That night, alone in bed, Zaiwulo thought of Sarankenyi's words. She'd hinted at marriage, but the women he desired were beyond his reach. How would he find the right woman and who would she be?

In Haindi, the forest, his passage to adulthood would have been celebrated. He would have been initiated into the secrets of the Poro Society, which would have prepared him for manhood and the future. But here in the savannah, there was no one to teach him. What he had learned from Talata, the stories, and the manuscripts were of no use regarding his approach and understanding of women.

Perhaps, he would have time to consider his well-being after taking over the affairs of the Haidarah household in Musadu.

15

The sentries at the main gate in Musadu gathered around Zaiwulo's horse and pulled him off it. Haindi reared up in resistance against the man who tried to lead it by the reins. The horse was as exhausted and as edgy as Zaiwulo. The man soon let go of the reins and, dusting down his tunic said, "Talk some sense into that horse, or I will kill it."

Zaiwulo walked up to Haindi and rubbed its flanks until the animal calmed down. "Once we are home, Haindi, I will feed you salt and grass, and you will rest for as long as you like," he said. The men's hostility upset him, so he turned to them. "Why are you behaving like this? What happened? Tell me. You all know me."

"We are bringing you to the king," one of them said.

The men surrounded him and led him through the city like a prisoner, while Haindi followed him. His heart skipped a beat on passing the Haidarah compound, which was shrouded in funereal silence. The usual crowded marketplace was deserted.

The horse neighed when Zaiwulo disappeared beyond the thick walls that enclosed the king's palace. Zaiwulo was locked up in an enclosure with no roof or tree and exposed beneath a clear sky and fierce sun. He could hear Haindi's sniffs and grunts. The horse's hunger and distress were palpable. Out of frustration, Zaiwulo hit the wall with his bare hands, so hard he hurt himself. As he waited and tried in vain to avoid the harsh sun, he heard movements beyond the wall.

"Wonders never cease!" someone said. "You say he's here? I can't wait to see him."

The heat exhausted him, but he remained standing, determined not to break.

Hours later, his head throbbing with exhaustion, he was picked up by a group of men. They grabbed him and led him to the king.

"Here he is, Your Majesty," one of the men said, and to Zaiwulo, he muttered, "Behave accordingly or it will be your last day on earth, do you hear?"

The elders of Musadu flanked a mat. The king sat at the end wearing black-and-white tunic and bulbous trousers. A rifle and a sword rested on his lap, and from his neck dangled an amulet as huge as a sofa's palm.

"Where's your teacher?" the king asked.

Zaiwulo realized that he would have to weigh every word. "I don't know, Your Majesty. I was captured and held prisoner by people who mistook me for a Samorian sofa. I managed to escape."

"He's not telling us the truth, Your Majesty," one of the elders said. "I am certain that he's been told to say exactly this."

Zaiwulo shook his head, and he went on to tell them a detailed story of his capture and how the two women had helped him.

"Your teacher," the king said, his voice laced with restrained anger. "Your teacher has decided against our wishes and allied himself with Samori. He abandoned Musadu and neglected his family to escort the daughter of that scoundrel to marry his brother in Kankan. All along, your teacher was Samori's secret envoy to Sere-Brimah whom he tried to bribe with gold and false promises. Your teacher is a traitor. We know that now and more. The traitor has declared war on us, like his master Samori."

Zaiwulo raised his eyes and looked at the king, which was forbidden. One of the sofas shouted at him. "Never look the king in the eye! Do it again, and I will pluck your eyes out and stuff them in your mouth," he said.

"We will defend Musadu with our allies," the king said.

The king stood and fired his rifle in the air.

"You will write a letter to your teacher," he said. "Tell him to return immediately to Musadu. His wife Sona is back and wants to see him."

Sona could not be in Musadu, Zaiwulo thought. The king must be using her name as bait to lure Talata back to be punished. It was a trap. He would find a way to warn his teacher.

The men fetched him a sheet of paper, pen, and ink, and Zaiwulo composed the letter in a different style, hoping that his teacher might notice the change:

To my esteemed teacher, guardian of our world.

Peace comes from me, your humble student, to you, the beacon of what is good in humanity.

I'm now in Musadu, and I bear glad tidings. Ma-Sona is back. I am looking at her now as I write, and she's eager to see you. Musadu and its surrounding towns and villages anticipate your return. And I, your devoted student, plead with you to come home. I am the one who dictated and composed this letter and not someone else.

Yours in service,
Zaiwulo of the forest

Zaiwulo hoped his teacher would notice the peculiar style and exaggeration in the tone of the letter. The moment the ink dried, the letter was folded in a piece of cloth and entrusted to ten riders to make sure it reached Kankan and Talata.

"You will be held within the palace walls until they return with an answer," the king said, by way of a verdict.

Once again, the men shoved Zaiwulo into the implacable sun.

16

Massah learned about Zaiwulo's imprisonment. One of the girls in the house told her while she was sorting out her goods with the traders who were to hawk them in the forest.

"Zaiwulo held by the king?" she asked.

While most people rested, Massah had defied the afternoon heat to oversee the loading of goods into sacks bound for the forest and the coast of Liberia. Her wares consisted of clothes, jewelry, and salt—an invaluable commodity that the forest people equated to gold. Massah would trade her goods for kola nuts, fibers, beans, and a host of other items. The black tunic and white wrapper she wore were soaked in sweat. A veil of weariness clouded her face. Her lips quivered when she turned to the leader of the traders. "You cannot leave today. Something has happened." Tears pricked her eyes.

"If we don't leave today, Massah, we will lose time and money," the head hawker said. "The sooner we leave, the better."

Though she agreed with him, Massah wanted to see if she could be of assistance to Zaiwulo. Her father, Soko Kenneh, had given her the silent treatment since Talata's departure. He had accused her of driving him away. Massah had told her father everything, including her involvement with Demba, hoping that he would appreciate her honesty.

But the man had grabbed her by her hair and thrown her out of his compound. "Return to your husband's place at once," he said.

"Father!" she protested, but he slapped her.

"Don't ever show your face here again," he said. Massah had vowed to never return to her father's house or to solicit his help.

Now, she told the head hawker about Zaiwulo.

"You treat us with respect, and that's why I've begun to regard you as my daughter," he said. "Listen to me: don't get involved. It's beyond you."

"But I know that he's innocent."

The man shook his head. "You are a young woman with a great life ahead of you. The king and the elders will not appreciate your efforts."

"But I must do something," Massah said as the tears came.

The head hawker embraced her.

"There are certain things in life that are best left alone," he said.

But Massah knew that failing to help Zaiwulo would forever weigh on her conscience. If something happened to him, the guilt would be unbearable. She decided to go see her father.

On her way out of the compound to see him, she thought of dropping by to see her old mistress Sona who had indeed returned home.

Sona was wearing a worn-out garment and was sitting on a mat outside her house. Her hair was disheveled and she had a vacant look on her face. She was spinning cotton, a task she had begun doing to distract herself from her troubles. All day, she would spin the loom with one hand and with the other, pinch the cotton into thread. Sona had refused to share her story with anyone or to explain the absence of the child she had been carrying the day she left Musadu.

"Sister Sona," Massah said. At first, Sona did not respond, as if she'd not heard her. "Sister Sona," Massah repeated. This time, Sona looked up. "The king holds Zaiwulo prisoner in his palace. We should do something. You could talk to the king."

"The boy has become a man," Sona said and toyed with her loom. "He can take care of himself."

"But they might kill him!"

"We live in a mad time, Massah."

As if the interruption irritated her, Sona turned back to her work, leaving Massah with no choice but to go and see her father. She was told that he was with his herdsmen at one of his farms beyond the hills. She decided to brave the long distance to see him.

At the western gate, the sentries stopped her.

"I must see my father," she said.

"Return home, daughter of Soko," the sentries ordered. "There are people out there searching for young women like you to sell into slavery."

But she begged the men for so long that they allowed her to go on.

Outside the gate, kites were making their rounds, alighting on treetops from where they intently eyed her. The smell of grass was sharp and heady. Flies buzzed around her. Massah thought of Demba and tried hard to stifle her concern. She was still in the dark regarding what had happened to him. It made it difficult for her to contemplate any decision about the future. She had often pondered leaving Musadu, but where would she go without the protection of a man? Throwing herself into trade had been her only means of escaping her troubles. But at night, alone in bed, worries about Demba's fate still kept her awake. Sometimes she would leave her bed and go to stand outside his house for hours. There, she would wrestle with her demons until sleep came and she would return to bed.

The incessant buzzing of the flies irritated her, so Massah loosened her wrappers to attract some fresh air, for she was all sweat now. She quickened her steps, her lips sealed in defiance of the fierce sun.

After a while, she reached the herdsmen. She heard her father's decisive voice instructing his men. As she climbed the hill to reach him, she realized how absurd her efforts were to seek his help. Surely, he would chase her away.

When he saw her, her father left his herdsmen and went to her.

"What are you doing here, Ma-Massah?" he asked. "You know it's not safe outside the walls. What happened? Tell me."

Massah told him about Zaiwulo and her fear that he might be killed for being one of Samori's henchmen. Her father listened intently to all she had to say. Instead of an angry reaction, she saw concern in his eyes. He took her by the arm and led her to his horse, which had been grazing nearby. They returned to Musadu and headed straight for the king's palace.

Massah waited beneath the shade of a baobab tree. She thought of the terrors of her wedding night, the moments with Demba, and how Zaiwulo had always been kind to her.

Massah did not see her father and Zaiwulo emerge from the gate, but she felt Zaiwulo's presence and turned. He was taller and bigger than she remembered, with stubs of beard spread on what was once a smooth chin. He held the reins of his horse Haindi like a warrior. His scent and his gaze, which she felt burning every aspect of her body, sent a tremor of weakness through her body. But she withstood it because she was aware of her father standing behind Zaiwulo. "I did everything to free Zaiwulo," he said. "The king holds me responsible for him. If he escapes, I will be held prisoner in his stead, so make sure he doesn't leave the city, Ma-Massah."

Zaiwulo walked between the horse and Massah in the direction of the Haidarah compound. Careful not to express what he truly felt for her at that moment, Zaiwulo, instead, told her about the village where he'd been captured, and of the old lady and her granddaughter.

"If you hadn't been captured, that old lady might have offered you her granddaughter's hand in marriage," she said, laughing.

"I would have refused."

She glanced at him and shook her head. "You… refuse a woman?"

"I thought I would never see you again, Massah. Did you think of me?" he asked.

She blushed and walked on in silence.

17

The moment he entered the compound, the women of the Haidarah household rushed to Zaiwulo and hugged him. Some were in tears. "We were so worried about you, brother," they said. "Where is Haidarah?"

"He's in Kankan," he said.

The flame tree he planted years ago was now taller than he was, and its branches now threw long shadows across the compound.

"We took good care of the tree, for we believed that with it here you would always return to us," Massah said.

"You managed to hold the house together, Massah."

"That's not true. Look around you, the house is almost empty. Most of the students have left, and some took precious manuscripts with them."

"What about Talata's study?"

"They left it as it was, perhaps out of fear that something terrible might befall them. The king asked some men to block the door with wooden poles to deter intruders."

Zaiwulo breathed a sigh of relief. The loss of the Haidarah Manuscript would have been unbearable to all, especially his teacher.

"Bring Haindi to the stalls," he told one of the boys.

Massah noticed how easily his orders were carried out and that he now exuded a natural authority. Zaiwulo had become a man.

"Has Ma-Sona returned? I was told that she has but I did not believe it."

"Yes, she's back, and we are all grateful."

Zaiwulo went to see Sona and found her leaning over her loom.

"Ma-Sona," he said.

She looked up. Her once-mischievous eyes looked vague, empty. Unable to bear the grief in her eyes, Zaiwulo turned his gaze to a group of young women pounding cassava.

"I heard the king held you prisoner," Sona said. "But I said that you would escape if you were a man. Now you are a man, Zaiwulo."

"What happened to you, Ma-Sona?"

She stared so long at Zaiwulo that he thought she would end up screaming at him or attacking him. However, all she did was to go on spinning. Zaiwulo didn't dare ask her about the child that he'd helped bring into the world. Her answer might break them both. What would Talata do when he returned to find a wife who was not even half of her former self? Would Sona ever recover from what had reduced her to such a sorry state? What had happened to her child?

Zaiwulo left Sona and went to his old chambers. Massah had dusted it and laid out fresh clothes on the bed. She had filled a jar with water and left a bowl of boiled groundnuts for him. Beneath the earthy scent of the groundnuts and the dusty scent of the room, lingered her soapy scent. She had also prepared his bath, which he took in an outhouse with the sky as cover. The bath invigorated him.

Later Zaiwulo shaved and oiled his body with shea butter and left the house in a long white garment—he was a tall, handsome man with a slight stoop in his back. Unaware of it, he would touch his red cap like his teacher. Even his steps were deliberate and unhurried, in the manner of Talata.

He heard the women talking about him in terms that appealed to him. "Look, he's become a man!" one of them said, and he smiled.

In his teacher's home, Zaiwulo took stock of the damage. What was left of the manuscripts had been piled toward the entrance. He went to work arranging them according to the subject matter, and while at it, he browsed through some of the titles. Most were authored by his teacher, with subjects ranging from law to esotericism, but there were also stories of his formative years in Kankan. Some were mere jottings, others serious meditations on life. The Haidarah Manuscript was in the study, but who was he to touch that sacred book, let alone try to open it?

As dusk neared, he returned to his room. A girl brought steaming toe with a sauce of meat, fish, and chicken.

"Sister Massah sent it, elder brother," she said.

As he ate, his dinner was interrupted by Naminata.

"So you are back, Zaiwulo."

"Naminata, how are you?"

"I brought you some food; now you can stop eating that woman's food," Naminata said. "Massah is destroying this house."

"Massah has kept this house running in Haidarah's absence."

Naminata set the food down on the mat and sat across from Zaiwulo. "I've decided to move to this house to protect it from falling," she said.

"But I will not accept your presence here. No one will."

"You cannot stop me, Zaiwulo."

He stared at her. "I think you should leave."

"Not before you've eaten my food."

Leaving the half-eaten toe and sauce Massah had prepared, Zaiwulo tasted the bangoo dish which Naminata had placed before him. Boiled cassava cut into pieces and served with a sauce of peppered fish and souma. The soft spices made of herbs gave sauces their unique flavor. It was so delicious that he found himself reaching for more until the bowl was empty. When he was finished, he washed his hands.

"Thank you for the food, Naminata, but I have work to do right now," he said and waited until she left.

The food made him sleepy, and he yawned. However, instead of resting, he returned to his teacher's chambers to attend to the manuscripts. He had decided to arrange them chronologically, beginning with his teacher's first years in Kankan and his attempt at poetry. The earlier poems were clearly influenced by the work of the great poets, but as he read on and recited some of the lines aloud, Zaiwulo began to see his teacher gradually emerge as a confident, erudite, young poet out to enthrall. So this is how it's done, Zaiwulo thought. This is how to become a poet.

When his eyes began to hurt from reading, he felt like stretching out on the bed and sleeping till dawn. Instead, he went to see Haindi and took a small block of salt with him. The horse licked the salt off his hands, its rough tongue brushing against his palms and giving him a tingling sensation.

"You and I must be strong and hold this house together, Haindi," he said. "It will be difficult, but we will do our utmost best."

On his way to his house, Zaiwulo heard the town crier yelling as he walked through the city delivering his message to the different quarters. “Musadu needs all its men to fortify its walls against Samori. I call on everyone to appear at the king’s palace tomorrow morning,” the man cried.

Zaiwulo decided to show up at the palace in the morning as a token of goodwill. Staying home could be interpreted as having chosen the Samorian camp.

He could not risk the wrath of Musadu.

18

Massah came to Zaiwulo in his dream. She was more beautiful than he'd ever seen her before. The jewels she had inherited from her mother adorned her wrists, her ears, and her neck and in the semi-darkness she glowed like cowries strewn along a path. He held his breath as she walked to the mat and stretched herself out on her back, her slender right arm resting on her navel, anticipating him. Meanwhile, he had stripped himself of his tunic, his trousers. He was never more aware of his manhood than at that moment. Zaiwulo lifted her loins with one hand, and with the other slowly guided his member. She seemed pliant, supple, ready for him. She reacted to his every move, and when they came together, their breath rising and falling, she moaned his name. She was the bow and he was the arrow. The bow was stretched to its maximum, and the arrow, hard, beyond respite, beyond hope, exploded in the narrow chalice of her world. And with a cry, he awoke.

For a while, Zaiwulo was disoriented. It felt like he was in a dream but, at the same time, not in a dream. His mat was damp, and he was unsure if it was a witness to the dream or reality. He could not tell. He smelled that blend of herbal soap, musk, and shea butter that was Massah's unique smell. This state of confusion persisted until he noticed her presence outside. He heard her breathing as if she was fighting the urge to enter the house. Or perhaps, she had been with him the whole time and had now left. Suddenly, her footsteps withered away, vanished from his existence. Zaiwulo heaved a sigh, for he did not want to act out the dream, or whatever he thought he had experienced. The consequences might be far-reaching.

After that, Massah avoided Zaiwulo.

A few days later, he returned home from working on the walls with the intention of seeing her, but, at the sight of him, Massah bolted. He had wanted to ask what had led her to his door at that hour.

The women greeted him. "Has the day been good to you, brother?" one of them asked. He answered that it had been and in turn he inquired about the women's day. They were all pleased with him.

The next day, Zaiwulo found Massah surrounded by a bevy of young apprentices. He attempted to start a conversation. "According to the king, the work on the walls will go on for weeks."

Massah did not respond. The girls giggled as though they were privy to the trouble he was having with their mistress. Embarrassed, he left.

Zaiwulo had begun to teach the young students every day after working on the walls. They had taken to gathering around the three hearths in the main courtyard and always recited at the top of their voices. When they saw Zaiwulo, their voices rose, each competing with the other to impress him. His eyes swept across the three hearths and rested on a child he suspected was having difficulties with his lesson.

The child reminded him of his first days in Musadu, so he walked up to him. "Have you eaten?"

The child shook his head. The older students had denied him food because he was a slow learner. His name was Vali. Zaiwulo turned to his students. "If Vali complains of hunger again," he said, "I will make sure that none of you eat."

Zaiwulo used Vali's hunger as a pretext to see Massah. On their way to her quarters, he asked the child, "Where are you from?"

But the child didn't know.

"Who were your parents?"

The child couldn't remember them. "There was a woman everyone said was my mother," he said, "but I didn't believe it because every time she looked at me, I thought she was about to slap me."

When Massah's girls saw Zaiwulo, they burst into laughter. They'd seen through him. Ignoring them, he went to Massah. "The child needs food, do you have some leftovers?"

Without answering, Massah shoved an earthen bowl with food before the child, denying Zaiwulo the opportunity to pursue a conversation of any kind with her.

He couldn't stand it any longer.

"Why are you behaving like this?" he said.

"Like what?" Massah said.

"Your silences?"

She flashed him a look full of anger. "It's you who's behaving like nothing happened."

"What do you mean?"

Massah ignored him.

Zaiwulo was about to leave when a girl brought a message that Ma-Sona wanted to see him. He left immediately for her house.

"Last night, I thought I heard my husband's voice," Ma-Sona said. "When I went outside to see him, I found it was you. You were reciting exactly like him. I need him here with me, Zaiwulo. I need to hear his voice. I need my children here, all of them. I want life to be as it was before; I want to be with my Talata."

"Ma-Sona," Zaiwulo said.

"I was in town today, Zaiwulo, and I was surprised by how fear of Samori had taken hold of everyone. I reminded them that Samori had to first defeat his greatest enemies in Koniyan, Sere-Brimah, and Gbanguno Saaye before turning his attention to Musadu. But no one would listen to me. If we fear Samori so much, how will we ever stand up to him?"

Zaiwulo noted a faint trace of the poise that once characterized Ma-Sona. She sat down on her bed and folded her hands on her lap.

"Do you think I will ever see my Talata again?"

"Yes, you will, Ma-Sona. He talked about you all the time."

She was silent for a while, and then she smiled. "We are always dragging you into our troubles, Zaiwulo. Tell me, how are you?"

"What do you mean, Ma-Sona?"

"What are your troubles?"

He wanted to tell her that at night, he often lay awake thinking about the welfare of the household—especially about Massah's welfare and her strange behavior. But perhaps she would want to know more about his concerns for her.

"I will do my best to keep the house running until my teacher returns. I will do my best to protect the Haidarah Manuscript."

"No one can bear such a huge responsibility alone, not even my husband. He depended on all of us in this house, in Musadu, and the whole of Koniyan. I wish I could help you, but I'm a broken woman."

"I will not waver, Ma-Sona."

"Sometimes you become a man before you are ready for the task. Now you are head of the Haidarah household. Be strong."

She held his hands for a while before letting him go.

Zaiwulo stepped into the moonless night. Despite the darkness, he managed to negotiate his way through the various houses and enclosures. Sometimes, he would pause to listen to the women's laughter, aware that in his presence they could afford to laugh. He went to the part of the compound where the younger students slept to check on Vali. Zaiwulo hoped that the students had either accepted him or had, at least, left him alone.

The unease in the city and fear of Samori made Zaiwulo vigilant. Thanks to Soko Kenneh's mediation, he had some kind of freedom. But he was aware that as fear mounted in the city, some people would begin to look for someone to blame for Samori's desire to conquer Musadu. With what he knew about them, he was sure that they would probably look in his direction.

•×•

In the meantime, Zaiwulo had his hands full with the rivalry between Massah and Naminata. Naminata had done what she'd promised to do. She had moved into the Haidarah household without his knowledge or approval.

Zaiwulo had only found out when Massah's voice woke him. "That crazy woman sleeps here nowadays. Did you know that? It's your fault. Get rid of her. Send her away!"

Naminata fired back. "You are the destroyer of families, not me."

"You don't belong here, Naminata."

Massah pushed Naminata who fought back and the two landed on the ground. Naminata sat on Massah, and began to hit her with all her might. Zaiwulo acted swiftly and tore Naminata off Massah, causing Naminata to go berserk. She clawed at his face, and her legs flew about. She hit him, screaming as if he was violating her. She called her ancestors to wreak havoc on him and his descendants. This fueled his rage.

Zaiwulo dragged Naminata out of the compound and onto the road, ignoring entreaties from the crowd that followed them to let her be. He kept pulling her until they reached the compound of her deceased husband Foningama. There, he let her go.

Naminata pulled herself together and turned to the crowd. She stood tall and imperial, beautiful, and fiercely defiant even at her most vulnerable moment. Those who saw her would later swear that they had caught a look on her face that could only be associated with evil spirits.

With a bound, Naminata was at the well at the center of the compound.

She plunged into it without hesitation.

Everyone stood still as if nailed to the ground.

"Naminata," Zaiwulo shouted before jumping in after her.

The crowd stirred. Someone threw a rope down to Zaiwulo. He tried to tie Naminata to the rope, but she fought him. Her nails sank into his flesh, and she bit him until he bled, but his will to save her was stronger than the pain she inflicted on him. In the end, he managed to tie her to the rope and she was pulled to safety.

Zaiwulo would not leave her side.

He stayed with Namintata in the house where she had been rubbed down with medicinal oil and put to bed. He sat beside her until she fell asleep. In the middle of the night, she awoke but fell asleep again. He left her in the morning to work on the walls.

Zaiwulo thought of Naminata as he churned mud and grass with his feet and plastered the city walls with his hands, and as he strengthened those walls with slender poles. He was haunted by the sad thought that he had driven her to commit such a desperate act. He alone was responsible, and he alone had to take care of her to rid himself of the gnawing guilt.

19

Naminata was shelling roasted groundnuts in a winnower resting on her lap. She had recovered enough to resume her old chores. Nothing about her composure, or choice of clothes betrayed the incident of the day before. Seated in front of the kitchen, she rolled her hand over the groundnuts, and moved the cleaned ones to one side of the winnower, applying the same pressure as when preparing tiny pellets of rice to be cooked as porridge for breakfast—the famous monnie. She seemed unaware of the hostile glances thrown her way, but now and then, when Naminata caught a glance, she would suck her teeth hard. When Zaiwulo joined her, after returning from work, he was surprised by her composure.

She shared a handful of roasted groundnuts with him.

"They are delicious, Naminata," he said.

"Yes, my food always is. That's why you keep returning. Just imagine if you were to have such food every day, Zaiwulo."

"How are you feeling now?"

She glanced up at him. "Much better, but I am worried about you."

"Worried about me?'

"You are here defying a whole city because of me, but don't you know that there are fights you are yet to fight, fights you must win?"

"What fights, Naminata?"

"Wait until Osman and Karamo return. They will throw you out of their home and send you back to the forest."

Zaiwulo had given little thought to Osman and Karamo, what with all the work that occupied him, but Naminata had a point. What if he was told to leave a house to which he had no claim? Would he return home?

"They will never allow you in their house, never Zaiwulo. Together they will turn against you, and everyone will take their side. Don't you see that?"

She shook her head as though he was a hopeless case.

Later that evening, Zaiwulo left and went to see Sona. "I want Naminata to come and live here, Ma-Sona," he said.

Sona, who had been lying in bed, sat up now.

"She's mad," she said. "No woman in her right mind would attack another woman the way she did and would certainly not throw herself in a well."

"She's not crazy. She's desperate."

"I thought you had your hands full with running the household. Clearly, you intend to make life more difficult for yourself. She can come and live with us."

"Thank you, Ma-Sona."

•×•

Early one morning, a few days later, after Naminata had moved to the Haidarah compound, Zaiwulo received a message.

A group of elders, including Soko Kenneh, wanted to see him.

The men received him around a burning hearth in Soko Kenneh's compound.

"Naminata's actions prove that she's lost her mind," Soko Kenneh said. "One of us has to take over caring for her."

"She belongs to the Haidarah household," Zaiwulo said.

"You have no say in that," said one of the elders. "We are discussing this with you out of respect for the man you represent."

"It's my responsibility to protect her. Because of my actions, she was driven to commit that terrible act. She has suffered enough."

"The girl was once a slave with few rights. After the death of Foningama, it befell us to decide her future. If you don't listen to us, we will inform the king," another elder said. "He's sure to act."

"Make sure the girl's ready when we come to pick her up. If not, I cannot protect you," Soko Kenneh said.

"I will not let her go, Uncle Soko. Never."

"What arrogance!" another elder said. "You lack manners, child. We summoned you out of respect for your teacher and all you do is spit in our faces. Remember you are not one of us."

"We will send people to fetch her tomorrow," Soko said.

The elders sent Zaiwulo away.

When he told Naminata, she flared up.

"After Foningama's death, each one of those men came to see me. They wanted to have me, but I refused them all. Hypocrites, all of them."

"I will protect you, Naminata. You belong here."

"I would rather kill myself than yield to them."

Though her grit inspired him, he feared that he might not have the courage to stand up to those elders.

Later, when he went to see Massah, he met her in a foul temper.

"You are as crazy as that woman who's attached herself to you like a leech. Saving her was not enough. You had to play the husband."

"All I wanted was to protect her; don't you see that?"

"I thought you were an exception. I thought you understood me, but you are just like the others. I don't know why I trusted you."

Her hostility bothered him.

"I will never forgive you for what you did to me," she said.

"But what did I do?"

"You know what you did. Don't pretend you don't."

"Tell me, Massah."

Zaiwulo tried to calm Massah but his actions were in vain. She bolted out of the house and rushed in the direction of Sona's place. How would his teacher have reacted in the face of all this? Would he have gone on to confront the elders of Musadu or would he have succeeded at settling the dispute? Zaiwulo began to doubt everything that he had once believed. He could not sleep a wink that night, and because he was awake, he was one of the first to hear the war cries.

Samori's sofas were invading Musadu.

20

Zaiwulo's first thought was to save the Haidarah Manuscript, so he broke through the poles that had been built across the door to the study. Once inside, he lifted the curtain which separated the study with reverence. After raising the second curtain, he stepped into the world of manuscripts. He searched around in frenzy, and his gaze alighted on a manuscript wrapped in brown leather.

There was nothing special about it. It looked like any other book. Without unwrapping it—sure it was the one—Zaiwulo carried the manuscript in his arms and ran out to gather his people. The chaos that greeted him was so complete that he stood stock still, uncertain of his next move. Zaiwulo heard rifle shots, he saw smoke rising from burning homes outside the compound. Horses were neighing and war cries sounded beyond the walls. Women rushed about with their belongings, followed by their children.

Zaiwulo willed himself to be calm for their sake as much as his own. "Follow me," he told them.

Zaiwulo led the women and children to the main courtyard where he met other members of the household huddled together like a herd of cattle paralyzed by terror.

Naminata was not with them.

"Where's Naminata?" Zaiwulo asked.

"No one has seen her," Sona answered. "Let's leave now, Zaiwulo."

Zaiwulo searched the compound and found Naminata sitting before one of the houses, her hands folded and resting on her lap, unbothered.

"I am not leaving, Zaiwulo," she said.

"Those horsemen have no mercy for anyone."

"Haidarah will return one day and meet me here. We will build this house together once again. It will happen, Zaiwulo."

"I will take you to Haidarah. We are going to Kankan, where he is at this moment. You will be safe there."

"He's not in Kankan. I dreamed about him last night. He was on his way to Koniyan, to me. That's what I saw."

Zaiwulo realized it was futile to try to persuade her. The men with whom he had once rubbed shoulders were now closing in on them. He knew that they had an unbridled proclivity for violence and would not hesitate to cut anyone down. If he chose to save the Haidarah family, he would never be welcomed in Musadu again. But by staying, he would be exposing the household to danger.

Zaiwulo made his choice quickly, and on impulse, he entrusted Naminata with the Haidarah Manuscript.

He didn't need to explain.

"Of course I know about the Tareequ," she said. "People think I am a mad woman. No one will hurt a mad woman. So leave it with me, Zaiwulo."

Zaiwulo used the tumult and chaos reigning in Musadu as a cover to lead the family, which consisted of more than a hundred souls, to the edge of the valley where the household's refuse was dumped. Here, the city wall was shrouded in a cover of trees and bushes, making it appear higher than it was. With a ladder and the help of his students, Zaiwulo managed to move the women across the wall first, followed by the children and then the students.

He was the last to jump over the wall. Only then did he realize that he'd forgotten about his horse.

"Haindi," he cried.

"Human lives are more precious than those of horses, Zaiwulo," Sona snapped. "Forget about your horse."

He had no time to argue with her and no way to rescue the horse. Columns of smoke covered the city. From the spot where the ladder stood, he could see people jumping over the wall, some landing in such a way that they were unable to stand. He had to separate the family from those hordes of refugees.

Zaiwulo led the family through razor-sharp grass, swamps, and bushy paths toward Beyla and Jacodu. He had no intention of stopping there. Samori's invasion of Musadu meant that the twin cities and all the towns and villages along the route would not have been spared.

After hours on the road, he ordered his charges to rest under a hill where the grass was low, yellowish-green, and gave off a sharp, feverish scent. Massah had separated herself from the group. She was ill and kneeling on the side of the road, throwing up.

"I will see to her," Sona said.

"We will go in search of food for the women and children," Zaiwulo told his students. "We need food to survive on the road."

They found a stream where they quenched their thirst. The earth, when they dug into it, yielded some edible roots and wild yams that Sona and the women boiled and shared among the group.

"How is Massah doing?" Zaiwulo asked.

"That girl is hiding something from us," Sona said. "She keeps insisting it is the food, but I know what I saw."

"What did you see, Ma-Sona?"

"When last was your teacher in Musadu?"

"Months ago."

"Are you sure?"

Zaiwulo nodded.

She shook her head, puzzled. "Keep an eye on Massah."

"We will stay here till late afternoon," he said. "In about a week or two, we will have passed Samori's capital, Bissandougou. Then we will take the main road to Kankan. We will be safe then."

They spent the night on an old, abandoned farm. With the help of the students, Zaiwulo set up impromptu shacks by cutting down trees, branches, and by gathering grass. It was dark before the work was done. Zaiwulo guarded over the farm with the assistance of the older students. As the night stretched on, he wondered if Naminata had survived. Was the Haidarah Manuscript safe with her? What about the other books? Had he done the right thing?

The next morning, Zaiwulo led the family out of the farm and onto a grassy path. They walked on for days. They passed Samori's capital, Bissandougou, without entering it and were out of his sphere of influence. A sense of optimism reigned in the group. Kankan, where Talata resided, was within reach. Once there, Zaiwulo would no longer be responsible for such a large group of people. There, he could turn his full attention to scholarship.

Zaiwulo was sitting on a strip of grass when Sona approached him. She sat beside him. "What do you expect after meeting Haidarah?" she asked Zaiwulo. "Musadu has probably been destroyed, and Kankan has always been hostile to your teacher. Those scholars prey on each other but profess lasting brotherhood. The search for the right path can make enemies of friends. They will tolerate him for a while and then he will notice, through their backstabbing, that it is time for him to leave their city. What will he do then? Return to a home empty of his books and students? Will there be a place for us after the destruction of Musadu? I doubt it, Zaiwulo." Sona patted his shoulder. "Thank you for saving our lives."

Zaiwulo was humbled by her words. The old Sona—the one who had once been a mother to him—had returned.

As Zaiwulo and the Haidarah household approached Kankan, they could already see its walls and were shocked by the sight before them. Thousands of Samorian sofas were walking along the dusty roads leading to the city. Samori was campaigning on multiple fronts.

Kankan was under siege.

Part Three

EMPIRE BUILDING

1885

1

All morning, the sofas had been waiting for a sign from Samori to launch fresh attacks on the walls of Kankan. During a routine inspection of sofa positions, one of their commanders, Kemoko-Bilali, encountered Zaiwulo leading a group of disheveled people toward the city.

The sofa general rode up to Zaiwulo, wearing a smile that froze before the hard expression on Zaiwulo's face. The boy who was now a man was angry, and his once-amiable face was a riot of contempt. When Zaiwulo ignored his greeting and walked on, Kemoko-Bilali dismounted, worried.

"It's me, your friend, tell me what is wrong?" he said.

Zaiwulo stopped, and in a voice marked with rage, he recounted how the Samorian forces had attacked and destroyed Musadu.

"Come with me," Kemoko-Bilali said.

The sofa general had not changed. His colossal body seemed to burst out of his light-yellow tunic. He shared a common history with Samori which cemented their friendship. Both men were once slaves: Samori to Sere-Brimah, and Kemoko-Bilali to a king who, for sport, fired his rifle at wounded men he had captured in war. Kemoko-Bilali had been a recalcitrant child, getting into frequent fights with the children of his master. One day, when one of them insulted his mother, Kemoko-Bilali killed him. He fled with his mother, moving from one place to another, trying to conceal himself. An impossible feat for a man with his voracious appetite for action. Then he met Samori who understood his deepest fears. They were similar to his own.

The Samorian sofas could hardly suppress their impatience to conquer Kankan. The wide expanse around the city teemed with herds of cows, sheep, and goats. Women trafficked huge bowls and calabashes filled with food. The men, armed with rifles, swords, daggers, cutlasses, arrows, and spears, walked and rode along the roads. The sofas had been waiting for months for the walls of Kankan to cave in and reveal treasures beyond their dreams.

Dust mixed with their frustration rose and lingered in the air like a thick mist.

Kemoko-Bilali led Zaiwulo and the Haidarah household to Samori's *diassa*, one in a series of tiny forts Samori had built around Kankan. They served not only as strategic locations from where to launch his attacks on the city but were also resting places, homes to his large army, their helpers, and the women who accompanied them. The forts were surrounded by wooden walls. From a distance, they appeared to Zaiwulo like tiny villages scattered around the city walls.

Without waiting to be announced and breaking protocol, Kemoko-Bilali led Zaiwulo into Samori's diassa.

The emperor was holding court with his advisers, including his Djeli, Morifin-Djan Diabate, Samori's favorite son, Jawulen-Karamoko, his friend Porokerrie, his brothers, and many others. There were also new faces that had gained favor in the eyes of the Faama and were now his courtiers.

One of them was Osman.

Samori was dressed in a simple white tunic and a pair of black bulbous trousers. His broad forehead was bordered by a black fez. Zaiwulo noticed that the folds around his nose were more pronounced. The years and the conquests had taken their indelible toll on his face. His vigor and ability to bend and subdue the wills of others to his was, however, unaltered.

"Son of the forest." Samori stood up to hug Zaiwulo, which was unusual. No one had ever seen Samori embrace even a family member in public. "What brings you here?"

"He says our sofas attacked Musadu," Kemoko-Bilali answered.

Samori looked baffled. "Why would I attack Musadu?"

Zaiwulo answered, his voice steady, "For months, we'd been hearing rumors about your plan to attack Musadu. The king of Musadu held me prisoner because Haidarah had sided with you. Then the war came."

Samori sat down and his Djeli spoke, "Why would we invade the home of our allies? Haidarah has been nothing but a valuable asset to us, child. This must be the work of Sere-Brimah or Gbanguno Saaye. The two want to turn the whole of Koniyan against our Faama. Sere-Brimah has invaded Musadu twice before, this must have been his third attempt."

"Did you come alone?" Samori asked.

"No, I'm here with the Haidarah-household. Ma-Sona, Haidarah's wife, is also with me."

Osman jumped to his feet. "May I see my mother, Faama?"

Samori nodded and Osman rushed outside to his mother. They fell into each other's arms. Sona lost her balance, and Osman had to prevent her from falling. She kept looking at her son, touching his face, his shoulders, his hands, and then embracing him again, making sure he was real. Both were in tears.

"Mother, you are here. Everything will be fine now. Everything will be as it was before. Where have you been all this time?"

It was quiet in the diassa as everyone listened to Sona tell her son how she had lost her third child. "I gave birth to your brother, the one I was carrying when I left Musadu. We went from village to village, from town to town in the forest in search of Karamo. After a few years, I decided to head to the coast of Liberia with a group of traders so I could continue my search. On our way, we were attacked by slavers, and we were pursued by one of them. He caught up with us and killed your brother. After tying me up, he led me toward the coast to be sold into slavery. It happened that in the town where he had chosen for us to rest, Benjamin Anderson and your brother Karamo were present. They were on their way from Musadu to Monrovia. They rescued me and took me with them. I became mad at the world. And your brother Karamo…"

Sona fell silent, unable to continue. After a while, she said, "Karamo has changed. Not only has he abandoned our way of life, but he has chosen the language of the Toubabous and is forgetting his own. Furthermore, he has opted for the ways of the Nazarenes. I found him in their place of worship, but he insisted that he still carried Musadu in his heart. I didn't believe him. I went in search of one of my children only to lose both. I am glad you are alive, Zumana!"

Samori left the diassa. Zaiwulo and the entire court followed him.

Samori tried to commiserate with Sona. "What a loss, Ma-Sona. The loss of one child is unbearable, let alone two. What a loss."

He drew up to her to embrace her, but Sona stepped back. She pulled herself together, checked her sobs, and wiped her face with her hand. "You destroyed Musadu," she said. "I don't want your consolation."

"You are mistaken, Ma-Sona. Invading Musadu would amount to a declaration of war against your husband, who I regard as a friend. He's here in the city. I hope its rulers will capitulate soon so that you can unite with him, and I with my daughter and my wife Sarankenyi."

Sona weighed Samori's words. Could she believe him? She asked him to elaborate on the situation in Kankan.

"Kankan is divided. The majority support my efforts to rid the city of the Kabbas. That's why those in power will not hurt your husband or my wife. They will protect them. Their lives depend on it. That's why we will succeed in capturing Kankan. Those rulers will yield."

"But why is my husband not with you?"

"It's his choice. He disagrees with me in my dealings with the Kabbas. He would rather that I didn't besiege Kankan. But Kankan is the prize. If Kankan falls, all the kingdoms in this part of the world and far beyond will also fall."

As he said this, Samori recalled his conversation with Talata a week before. The rulers of Kankan had sent the scholar to see him. Across from Samori in his diassa sat Talata. The scholar looked exhausted.

"Faama, wait until your enemies Sere-Brimah and Saaye have fallen to conquer Kankan. Kankan will cave in when those men fall," he said.

"Haidarah, that's precisely what I want. If Kankan falls, all my enemies will fall. Then, I won't need to wage war anymore."

"The siege is taking its toll. People might turn against you."

"That's why we need to hasten the conquest. I will give Kankan an ultimatum, and then I will do anything to break through the walls. Kankan is the biggest prize of them all, Haidarah. The biggest."

"But even if you succeed in conquering Kankan, you still have the problem of getting the people to accept you as their Faama."

"What do you mean?"

"They are different and difficult, especially the rulers."

"I plan to treat everyone equally. Taking part in the governing of my empire will not depend on how special a family is but on the merit of each individual. You've seen examples of it, Haidarah. I'm an example, as is my Djeli, my generals, sofas, and many others are. We became what we are not because of our families or wealth but because of our deeds."

"But I'm afraid that not everyone will regard it that way. I'm afraid that you will be undermined by those who claim to be your allies."

Samori had tried to persuade Talata that he would use common sense in governing Kankan and his empire, but he had sensed that the scholar was not convinced.

Now, he turned to Sona. "You don't need to worry about your husband, Ma-Sona. I will ask him to be the new ruler of Kankan."

"My husband hated fights, even during our marriage. Would he agree to rule a people he once disagreed with?"

"I know what you mean, Ma-Sona, but times have changed. I promise that I will reunite you with your husband."

"Thank you so much, Faama."

"We will build you a home, Ma-Sona."

Zaiwulo was about to go join the sofas, but Samori stopped him.

"Come with me, Zaiwulo," he said.

The sofas arranged a horse for Zaiwulo. Together with Samori, he rode toward the city walls which were strewn with archers and snipers engaged in smatterings with the army of Kankan.

"I am at war with Kankan because its rulers have been arming my enemies," Samori said. "It's about time we wrested this city from them. If we succeed, Koniyan and all the lands around it will fall. In their place, an empire will rise that will compete in glory with Sundiata Keita and Mansa Musa. Then, the world will take note of us."

They stopped at strategic locations where Samori breathed enthusiasm into his men, and then they rode on. As Zaiwulo listened to Samori, a clear picture began to emerge before him of a man who was once a trader, then a slave, then a warrior, then king, and who was on the verge of becoming an emperor.

"I will introduce a single system into my empire," Samori said. "It will be the Islamic system, not because I am a great believer, but because its laws are uniform."

The two men dismounted, and Zaiwulo tethered the horses to a tree in an area with low grass.

"But what if the laws were broken?" Zaiwulo asked.

Samori was thinking about those parts of the empire that had not been converted to Islam, and about those Muslims who were believers in name only and who drank wine and mixed Islam with their traditional beliefs.

"You astound me, Zaiwulo, and there are few who do so. What to do with non-Muslims who break the law in the empire?" He reached out and held Zaiwulo's hands. "Well, child of the forest, we will be flexible and listen to them."

Zaiwulo was silent, thinking.

"Speak your mind," Samori urged.

"Flexibility will not depend on you alone, Faama, but on those who execute the laws. If they are wise and just, your empire will be one of the greatest in the world. Maybe even greater than Sundiata's."

Samori looked at Zaiwulo for such a long time that the young man thought he had incurred the Faama's wrath. "You've read and seen a lot," he said.

Zaiwulo did not respond.

"And you don't speak until you've carefully weighed your words."

Zaiwulo was still silent.

"I want you on my side, son. When Kankan falls, I will ask your teacher to let you go. I need you. I will get you the books and the students you need, if you choose to stay with me."

Zaiwulo could hardly contain his joy. He knew what it meant to be a scholar, which was his only dream. He was not cut out to become a warrior, for he felt he was a man who espoused the written word. Samori understood that.

"Come, let's get back to the diassa," the Faama said.

2

On his way to join the Haidarahs of Musadu, Zaiwulo crossed the main camp. The camp was a ragtag compilation of shacks and huts pressed against each other, with narrow alleyways cluttered with dirt and refuse. Particles of dust formed a hazy canopy over the camp. Children, swathed in this ochre powder, chased after large flying insects tied to strings, cheering when the insects reached the heights of trees. From a hut nearby came the voice of a woman fighting with a man. Her screams were soon followed by a terrible roar from the man, which drew people to the hut. The woman came out with the man's member in her hands. "It's because of this that he's always treated me like a slave," she said and threw it in the dust. Some men fell on the woman, and her family rose to her defense. The man was rushed to a herbalist somewhere in the camp.

The sofa general Porokerrie, who was in the vicinity, intervened and led the woman away. The men seemed intent on beating her to death. The image of the woman with the man's blood-soaked manhood in her hand haunted Zaiwulo.

Further down the road, people were hurrying about, anxious to wrap up the day's work before nightfall. Sofas were riding to take up positions around Kankan's walls. Some women were sitting along the roadside. Zaiwulo greeted them and they answered in amicable tones. "That's the favorite son of our Faama," one of them said.

The Haidarah family were gathered before the new shacks the Samorian sofas had put up for them. They were listening to Osman. He was telling them about his experience in Freetown, Sierra Leone.

"As I was saying, Mother," Osman went on, ignoring Zaiwulo who had joined them, "I went to Freetown to learn English and to get to know the English people. I mastered the language in less than a year."

Sona nodded in admiration. She seemed to have replaced her garment of grief with one of tentative joy. She hung onto her son's every word.

"I wanted to know why the Toubabous traded their lands for this part of the world, Mother. There must be other reasons besides trade. I told the Faama that as long as we continued to supply the English with gold and silver, they would not fail to deliver us weapons. We are allies now. Their Faama-Moussou, Queen Victoria, presented us with arms. It's just a matter of time before we conquer all territories in this part of the world. But I also warned him that the English, like the French and all the whites in these parts, might one day begin to perceive him as a threat. They might want more land, more wealth. A clash would then be inevitable."

"What will happen to us then, if the Toubabous were to decide to claim more land? Would we have a say in all of this?" Sona said.

"I don't know, Mother, but our world is rapidly changing. Whoever thought that a man from Koniyan would dream of besieging Kankan? We need to prepare ourselves for the changes to come. That's why I can't wait to see Father. I want to know his opinion on all of this."

Sona was proud of her son. Unlike his brother, he'd chosen to return, but she feared that he might get involved in matters beyond his power. "You have to be patient. Your father might be against all this," she said.

"Once he's heard me out, he will understand, Mother. He's a man of learning. We have to move with the times. I want him to see what I've seen."

They were interrupted by a group of women carrying huge pots and pans of food for them. "Our Faama greets you and expresses his excuses for the food taking so long, Ma-Sona. He asks for your forgiveness," said one of them.

"He asks for our forgiveness? But we've already forgiven him long before he asked for it. He received us here with open arms and built us a home. He's a true Foningama, a true Touré-keh."

As the family coalesced around the food, the novelty of Osman's adventures wore off before the family's hunger.

"Massah is not with us," Zaiwulo said.

"No," Sona said.

"I will fetch her."

Zaiwulo found her in one of the shacks. "Massah, Massah," he called.

She came out in a single wrapper, which covered her from chest to knees. She wore no ornaments, no bracelets, necklaces, or bangles. The real Massah, barefooted, her hair undone, yawning as if he had awoken her, was never as appealing to him as at that moment. But he thought of Demba, who had deserved her, who had loved her more than he ever would.

The fullness of her face, which he thought was beautiful, was in fact, the effect of tears. The thought that she would soon be back with Talata as his wife affected her. Massah planned to convince Zaiwulo to flee with her, far from that part of the world. She knew he loved her and had been smitten with her for years. It was out of that certainty that she now said, "Beware of Samori. One doesn't have to be smart to see that he favors you and wants you to join him. However, he's a man of war and you are not, Zaiwulo."

Zaiwulo was touched by her concern.

"Why don't you return to the forest?" she said. "You are a scholar now. You could start your own school there. The time is right!"

"I know nothing, Massah, nothing. I quiver before Haidarah's vast knowledge. It will take me years—"

"You don't have to be as educated as your teacher now. It will come with the years. I'm sure of that!"

"I don't know. I don't know."

"I could go with you. I'm sure that Demba is dead or has decided to have nothing to do with me. Look, you are not a child anymore."

Hearing Demba's name, Zaiwulo's face clouded over.

"Did I say something wrong?"

Zaiwulo remembered the blind man's words in the dream, reassuring him that he had done right by him, but marriage was another thing. Moreover, Massah remained his teacher's wife. Was eloping with her the only option? "I want to make sure that Haidarah is all right," he said.

"He will never let you leave. Can't you see that?"

"If I leave now without telling him, it would feel as if I've abandoned him, Massah. I have to see him first."

"Listen to yourself!" Massah said. "Why wait for others to decide for you? You led us out of Musadu and to the safety of this place without asking for anyone's approval. You took on a whole city for the sake of a mad woman. Now you refuse to take a decision regarding your future? I will stand by you. You will not be alone, my Zaiwulo. Osman has already taken over the running of the household and has ignored you. Demba always wanted to please others but not himself. Don't make the same mistake."

At that moment, Zaiwulo wished that he were not Talata's student, that he did not know Samori, so that he could be with the girl of his dreams. He pondered holding her hand and fleeing with her that instant. Instead, he attempted to conceal his hopelessness. "The food is here. I came to fetch you."

"You should not have bothered me."

Massah entered the hut, ignoring his entreaties. When Zaiwulo returned to join the diners, Osman glared at him. Zaiwulo could see flames of jealousy flashing across his cloudy face, but he ignored him.

"What happened to the manuscripts?" Osman asked.

"We had to flee. We had no time," Zaiwulo said.

"And the Haidarah Manuscript?"

"I entrusted it to Naminata."

Osman jumped up, trembling with rage. "Mother, why did you allow this Bush Boy to give the Tareequ to a stranger? Our entire existence revolves around that manuscript."

"Don't fight, Zumana," said Sona. "In the time of war, we take decisions that we later regret. Zaiwulo made the right decision. The Tareequ is safe."

"But you allowed him to take such a decision, Mother!"

"Your father asked him to run the household."

"Father didn't do that. He shouldn't have done that."

"Zumana, enough of this nonsense! Go on with your dinner."

Osman sucked his teeth and sat down. "You will pay for all of this, Bush Boy."

Despite their history, Zaiwulo, for the first time, saw Osman as spoiled, as a man who was used to having his way. Not with me, Zaiwulo thought. He vowed to stand up to Osman next time and to show him that he was his equal in every way and more.

3

The cold came with the night.

Out in the open with hundreds of sofas, Zaiwulo felt the first intimations of illness after being exposed to the full force of a chilly and dusty wind. He coughed, sneezed in response to the cold that burrowed under his skin and settled in his bones. To chase it off, he clicked his tongue, and his new horse—a pony borrowed from a sofa—broke into a gallop. They rode on until Zaiwulo began to sweat. He was part of seven units that Samori had selected to guard over the camps and to report unusual activities near the walls around Kankan. With him in his unit were Osman and Samori's favorite son, Jawulen-Karamoko, who was their commander.

Jawulen-Karamoko had a keen sense of the future regarding his father's empire. "Once Kankan falls," he told Zaiwulo, "we will conquer the city of gold, Buré, and all the lands in this part of the world."

Jawulen-Karamoko was handsome and taller than his father and was endearing to women. A story made the rounds that women fought each other to gain his favor.

The three dismounted.

They had come closer to the walls than any sofa had dared before. There were no signs of the defenders of Kankan, who were often seen scattered across the battlements with their rifles, bows, and arrows at the ready.

"They've let their guard down," Jawulen-Karamoko said. "Let's climb the walls to see what's happening."

"We don't know what lies beyond the walls," Zaiwulo said. "It might be a trap. I suggest we inform your father first."

Jawulen-Karamoko laughed. "Inform my father? That old man has lost his edge. Before we laid siege to Kankan, I suggested we conquer Buré first, but he believed that Kankan was much more important than Buré and its goldfields. He fails to see that if we don't take Buré now, it will be impossible to do so later. By then, even a siege might not break it. So why consult him?"

"I insist we do so first," Zaiwulo said.

"When we take Kankan, we will kill all the Kabbas. No one will ever sing their names in these plains again." He patted Zaiwulo on the shoulder. "I hear that the city is full of beautiful women. How many would you want?"

"There's only one woman in Zaiwulo's life," Osman said.

"Just one?" Jawulen-Karamoko said. "What is wrong with him?"

"And that woman is not even his wife," Osman continued, shaking his head.

"Shut up, Osman," Zaiwulo said.

But Osman was just warming up. "That woman is his teacher's wife," he went on. "Her name is Massah."

"Our father's? Haidarah's wife?" Jawulen-Karamoko stood aghast. He spat in the dust, swore and spat again, warding off the evil that was Zaiwulo.

"Don't believe a word of what Osman is saying." Zaiwulo walked up to Jawulen-Karamoko, who pulled away.

"If you come any closer, Zaiwulo, I will cut you down and no one will ever care, not even my father," Jawulen-Karamoko said. "Why would you do such an abominable thing? What type of person are you?"

"Those people from the forest are so vile," Osman said, barely able to contain a smirk.

"My father will hear of this," Jawulen-Karamoko said. He mounted his horse and rode away with the rest of the unit.

Zaiwulo was left alone with Osman.

"Do you know why you were brought to Musadu?"

Zaiwulo waved his hands in warning. "I don't want to know, Osman. Stop it."

"You must have wondered why your father left you without so much as saying a goodbye. Why would a father do that?"

"Shut up! I say shut up." Zaiwulo's voice broke. He hauled himself at Osman and the two fell in the dust.

"You say you are a fighter, show me!" Osman said. "You were brought to Musadu to be a slave, Bush Boy. You were sold to my father in exchange for money, in exchange for something less than money, for nothing. For nothing, Bush Boy!"

He sat on Zaiwulo, crushing his face into the dust. With all his might, Zaiwulo threw Osman off and aimed for his eyes, intent on gouging them out, but Osman would not allow him. He managed to entangle one of his legs between Osman's and flung him down. Blinded by rage, Zaiwulo blows were indiscriminate, unfocused, ineffectual.

"Is that all you've got?" Osman said.

Zaiwulo saw a piece of metal with sharp edges lying beside him. He picked up and brought to rest against Osman's throat.

"Go on, do it, you slave," Osman hissed.

The muscles of his neck yielded to the pressure of the weapon. Zaiwulo could see blood now, but he realized as he squeezed that killing Osman would not rid him of his terrible despair. He lifted the metal.

Meanwhile, Jawulen-Karamoko had returned.

"Stop, you two! Stop, right now," he said.

Zaiwulo released Osman and stood up.

"My father wants to see you, Zaiwulo."

Zaiwulo met Samori alone in his diassa. The emperor's eyes burned and his seething demeanor made Zaiwulo short of breath.

"Good evening, Faama," Zaiwulo managed to say, as he lowered himself on the mat across from Samori. His effort was ignored. Zaiwulo began to sweat.

Samori sucked his teeth and spat out that crushing insult—Packie— which sounded like a tree branch breaking in a silent forest. "What is this nonsense I hear?"

Zaiwulo told him about the secret Osman had revealed, the secret that bound his father to Talata, the forest to the savannah. As he recounted his story, he could feel Samori's growing weariness and impatience.

"And Soko Kenneh's daughter, Massah."

Zaiwulo swallowed hard. "She's my wife, Faama."

The words were out before he could suppress them, but he had no regrets, for if he told Samori the truth, that he was enamored with Massah, his teacher's wife, the emperor would banish him or worse. He would kill him. Zaiwulo now realized that Massah's request to flee together had partly to do with her fear of being Talata's wife and the rest with her love for him. But he had not believed her. He had been blind to her plights. What if Samori discovered the truth, which was bound to happen soon? What if Talata told him?

"What you are now, Zaiwulo, is what I was growing up," Samori said. "You could read my feelings on my face. I was so eager to please. Such honesty often endears one to people but could be used against you by your enemies. I became a slave to purchase my mother's freedom, and I fought wars to please her master. After escaping slavery, I fought wars to please my uncles, but while they relished my efforts and generosity, they went on undermining me. Sometimes, you have to wear your feelings behind a mask of indifference to prevent your enemies from hurting you. Osman is jealous because he thinks that you've taken his place in his father's heart. That's why he invented a story to hurt you. It's not true, so don't break your head over the past. It's what you do now and tomorrow that counts. Look at how far I've come! My town of birth is smaller than one of these camps, but here I am standing before the gates of the biggest city in our part of the world. And I will not rest until I've taken it. Forget the past, Zaiwulo, for it is a yoke that prevents you from becoming what you want to be. Use the past only to strengthen yourself, to learn lessons to be used in the future."

Samori's candid words touched Zaiwulo, and although there was more to Osman's claims than mere jealousy. Zaiwulo chose not to express it. "Thank you, Faama," he said.

"Fetch Osman and my son," Samori replied.

The moment the young men entered the diassa, Samori said, "Jawulen-Karamoko, never repeat what happened today. If you do, you will end up where you never wished to be. And you, Haidarah, I thought you were a sensible young man. No one has a place in my world who thinks he's better than the other. If you go on like this, I will send you back to your father. In fact, you will return this week to the English in Freetown."

Before leaving, Zaiwulo told Samori about the absence of the Kankan army around the walls.

"That's very strange," Samori said. "We will look into it tomorrow. Go to sleep and try to forget about what happened today."

As he left, doubts gnawed at Zaiwulo. If there was no truth to what Osman had said, then why were his father and Talata so evasive about the reason for his being in Musadu? Why the secrecy? Zaiwulo had had enough of the half-truths.

That night, he made a decision. He would join Samori. In a world where a slave could be equal to the man who was once his master, a world in which a slave could be a general like Kemoko-Bilali, and where a man with no claim to royalty could become an emperor like Samori, he would feel at home. In that world, no one would harass him with issues regarding his past or the caste to which he belonged.

In the Samorian world, he would be free.

4

The battlements were indeed deserted. Zaiwulo and Samori, who had left early in the morning to inspect the walls, rode along its length without meeting a single Kankan defender.

"What to make of this?" Samori said. "Let's return to the diassa to discuss our next step."

On their way back, Zaiwulo and Samori met the sofa general, Porokerrie.

"There's an emissary from the people of Kankan, your own daughter, Jawulen-N'nagbe, Faama. She's waiting to see you," Porokerrie said.

When Samori entered the diassa, which was already crowded with his advisers, Jawulen-N'nagbe stood up. "Father!"

The emperor nodded to her.

The Djeli Morifin-Djan spoke on Samori's behalf. "It's been a long time, daughter," he said. "The Haidarahs must be taking good care of you."

"They've been good to me, Uncle," she said.

Jawulen-N'nagbe had inherited her father's lean frame and smooth face, but her skin was bright, which was why she was called N'nagbe—The Bright One.

"Father, the people of Kankan sent me," she said. "The Kabbas have fled the city. The people are ready to receive you as their Faama."

Morifin-Djan Diabate spoke, "Kankan is there for the taking, Faama, so don't hasten to it like a conqueror. Enter it like its true Faama."

Later that day, Samori presented Zaiwulo with a set of clothes: a new and embroidered tunic and trousers, a garment and scarlet shawl to go with them, and new boots and slippers. "You will need these," he said.

Zaiwulo joined the Samorian entourage, and as they approached the main gate on horseback and foot, thousands greeted them.

"We will spare lives, Morifin-Djan," Samori said. "We will ask every household to part with a bullhorn of gold dust or with anything they can afford."

The Djeli nodded and conveyed the Faama's words. The moment Samori and his entourage reached the city center, Zaiwulo parted from it and led Talata's household to the Haidarah compound. He could not wait to see his teacher and to ask him questions regarding his origin. Until then, he would remain restless.

Kankan had changed. The siege had taken its toll. Once neat and well swept, the homes were now swathed in dust. The markets were gone and the streets were filled with refuse. The nauseating stench of death and illness lingered in the air. Zaiwulo covered his mouth and pinched his nose to prevent himself from throwing up.

Karamo-Sidikie looked emaciated. His cheeks were hollow, his fingers like bird claws. It seemed like he had suffered the most out of all the people in Kankan. Standing in the main courtyard, he seemed disoriented, and his eyes darted about until they settled on Zaiwulo.

"There you are, finally," he said, as if he'd been searching for him all day. "Now that the siege is over, we can go back to teaching you. Son of the forest, let's get to work."

"Haidarah, where is your brother?" Zaiwulo said.

Karamo-Sidikie did not answer but turned his attention to the Haidarahs of Musadu. He walked up to them. "My sister-in-law has returned at last," he said. "It's been a long time, Ma-Sona. I was beginning to wonder when you would return to perform your wifely duties. During the siege, I was caught between my father-in-law, Samori, and my teachers, the Kabbas. How can one please two rivals with such opposing ambitions? Look at me! Due to your neglect, I've grown so old in such a short time. Where have you been all this time?"

Sona laughed. "The people of Musadu would not let go of me, Haidarah. Your reputation as a generous husband precedes you."

"Now that you are here, I will begin to grow more flesh on these bones, and people will begin to envy me for my good health. I will eat no other food but yours."

"And I will cook for no other man but you, Haidarah. Your brother will have to find another woman."

Karamo-Sidikie fell silent.

"Well, where is he?" Sona asked.

"My brother fled with the Kabbas. He was against the siege of Kankan and is now on his way to Musadu."

Zaiwulo was upset by this news.

"I did not expect to hear this, Haidarah," Sona said. "We will not stay here any longer. I don't want to spend a day without your brother. I want to see him."

"I will ask the Faama to arrange sofas to escort you back to Musadu. But first, try to rest and eat of the meager food we managed to save."

While the family settled down, Zaiwulo left to see Samori, but on entering the palace that had once belonged to the Kabbas. He changed his mind and decided to meet Sarankenyi first. She had allocated one of the largest courtyards to herself, in the heart of the huge palace. There, she met the most successful women of the city whose husbands had declared allegiance to Samori and had protected her against the Kabbas.

"I've been waiting all day for you," she wore the most disarming smile as she left the circle of women. When she hugged him, Zaiwulo smelled a mixture of pleasant incenses that threw him into confusion.

"Where's Sarankenyi-Mori, my brother?" he asked.

"The day you left Kankan, your brother fell back into his old habits," she said.

She asked one of the maids to fetch her son. Sarankenyi-Mori came running and fell into Zaiwulo's arms.

"See, he truly missed you," Sarankenyi said.

"When are we going horse riding, elder brother?" the boy asked.

"Tomorrow, I will take you beyond the walls."

"Why not now?" Sarankenyi-Mori said.

Zaiwulo felt Sarankenyi's intent eyes on him.

"What's wrong, my son?" she said, searching his face.

He avoided her stares.

"Look at me, tell me," she insisted.

"Mother, I've decided to join the Faama. With him, I feel at home. Look at how he treats his sofas. I can be a scholar and a sofa at the same time," Zaiwulo said.

"Does this have to do with your teacher's flight?"

Zaiwulo shook his head.

"I think my future lies with the Faama."

But Sarankenyi did not believe this to be the real reason. She searched his eyes in an attempt to catch a glimpse of the worries he had learned to conceal since the confrontation with Osman.

"Let's go and inform him then."

5

"I want to see my husband," Sarankenyi told the men who were guarding the entrance to Samori's part of the palace.

The men hesitated. "Ma-Saran, things have changed," one of them said. "We have to announce you first."

Sarankenyi sucked her teeth. "When last did I need anyone's permission to see my husband? Move aside, I say."

"But your husband is now the Faama of all Faamas, the king of kings, not just your husband," the guard replied.

"Even if he becomes a god, he remains my husband. I will see to it that you are all removed from your positions." Sarankenyi brushed past the man. "They seem to have forgotten that I was the one who helped their Faama to victory," she told Zaiwulo. "I turned the people of Kankan against the Kabbas after all efforts, including the siege, had failed."

Sarankenyi walked ahead of Zaiwulo. As they turned a bend, they were greeted by more than two dozen pairs of male eyes. Samori and his courtiers were sitting together. The gathering included Osman and the most important members of the new Samorian court, including his brothers and sons. They were all silent. The men glared at Sarankenyi with such hostility that she froze. Zaiwulo could see her fighting her tears, and then she did something that astounded him: Sarankenyi collected herself and walked on towards the men.

The distance between her and the men seemed long, but she covered it, holding herself upright, without flinching, without quaking. She took her place on the right side of Samori who was stunned, like he had been slapped in the face, and then, his face relaxed into a smile.

"Ma-Saran, we were just discussing our next step."

"Go on, beloved," she said.

Kemeh-Brimah, who had been talking when Sarankenyi and Zaiwulo interrupted them, didn't know what to do with a woman in their midst, especially a woman that some of them, if not all, loathed.

Samori gestured to Kemeh-Brimah, as if nothing was amiss.

"Sere-Brimah, the man who enslaved our mother, is now at our mercy, elder brother," Kemeh-Brimah said. "His head is ripe for plucking. Give me the go-ahead, and I will bring you his head."

Samori was chewing on a small stick that functioned as a toothbrush as well as a stimulant. He laid the stick aside on the mat and leaned forward. "By all means, do it then. Bring me his head."

Morifin-Djan Diabate repeated his words, and they were taken up by the sofas in and around the palace. A round of rifle shots followed.

"But first, we need to consolidate our hold on Kankan," Samori said. "Everyone in the city and in all the towns and villages belonging to it, everyone in the lands that are not part of Kankan but that have capitulated with its fall must pledge allegiance to the new empire."

He turned with a questioning glance to his Djeli. "What should we call this new empire, Morifin-Djan Diabate, my best friend? What should we call it?"

"We will call it what the great Sundiata Keita, Mari Jata, The Lion King, King of Kings, once called his empire. We will call it Wasulu, a name that will sound and resound throughout the world until the end of time. The Empire of the Proud."

"So be it, my friend," Samori said. "So be it."

The sofas repeated the name of the new empire over and over and fired their rifles until the grounds shook, and when the noise died down, Samori asked, "Where are the Kabbas?"

"We've dispatched sofas to places as far as Dakar, Kong, Segou, Bamako, Dabakala, Sikasso and beyond to see whether they are hiding out there. We will find them, Faama," Porokerrie said.

"As long as they are not captured, our hold on Kankan will be tentative." Samori said. "What about our great scholar, Haidarah of Musadu? Is there any news about him?"

"We will find Haidarah, elder brother," Kemeh-Brimah said. "Don't worry about the Kabbas. With Sere-Brimah on his knees and Saaye still confined within the walls of Gbanguno Mountain, the empire our ancestors didn't dare dream of is being realized by us."

"What about our rifles, Kemoko?" Samori asked his sofa general.

"We've succeeded at copying the English rifles, Faama. But we need more weapons than we can produce. Moreover, we've received reports of a new weapon made by the French. They say it's more lethal than any the English have ever made."

"So the French pose a danger?"

"Our limited knowledge of the French means that we have to be on our guard regarding their presence in this part of the world, Faama," Kemoko-Bilali said.

"It's about time that we sought an alliance with the French. We should send them an emissary as we've done with the English."

Morifin-Djan Diabate turned in Zaiwulo's direction. Samori nodded.

"With the French and the English as allies, your empire will rival that of Alexander the Great, Faama," the Djeli said.

"But what if the English have other plans?" Osman said.

"Haidarah, you often ask the right questions," Samori said. "We can always satisfy the Toubabous with gold. They are only here to fill their pockets and for nothing else."

The Djeli exchanged a knowing look with Samori.

"But we have to take the right measures because the Toubabous remain unpredictable," Osman said. "We should turn our attention to other kingdoms. We should approach Agibou of the Toucouleur Kingdom, Tieba of Sikasso, the rulers of Kong, and the Ashanti people. The more allies we have, the more difficult it becomes for our enemies to defeat us."

"Haidarah is right," Morifin-Djan said. "I think it's time for us to make arrangements with the English regarding the borders."

"The English will have difficulties coming to such an agreement, Faama," Osman said. "It would mean recognizing your hold on territories deep in their sphere of influence. Perhaps we should have a permanent sofa presence at the frontiers. We should be ready."

"The English have always treated me well, even during my trading days. But you are right. Let us send some sofas to take up posts at the far reaches of those lands. If possible, let them reach out to the Mendes and Temnes, who are related to us, for an alliance."

"You are right, Faama," Osman said.

"You will leave tomorrow, Haidarah. Make sure you meet the English governor in Freetown and sign some form of agreement with him."

"Have we forgotten something?"

Sarankenyi spoke for the first time.

"The ceremony, beloved," she said. "The people of Kankan are waiting to see their new benefactor. We talked about this."

"Yes, the ceremony will be held in due course, Ma-Saran," he said, barely concealing his discomfort.

The men expected Somari to shout at Sarankenyi, but he was the only one who knew how invaluable she was to the new empire. It was due in no small part to Sarankenyi's efforts that the empire had thrived and Kankan had fallen.

"Tomorrow, we will ride out to meet with Sere-Brimah," Samori said.

Though she disagreed with him, Sarankenyi decided not to humiliate him before those men whose disapproving looks she'd withstood throughout. She waited until the men had departed to leave for her part of the palace.

"You are still here," Samori said, when he met Zaiwulo lingering at the entrance to the enclosure. The Faama sounded tired. "Saran is my other half, Zaiwulo, the one who made the conquest of Kankan possible. She deserves a permanent place in the court, but she's a lone woman in a world of men. I don't know how to make her see this."

"Maybe she wants you to acknowledge her role, Faama."

"I do acknowledge it, but I fear for her. I don't want those men around me, some of whom might be my enemies, to hurt her."

"She can take care of herself, Faama."

"Yes, she can. She's proven this."

"So let her have a say in the running of the empire."

"I will let her. She deserves it. You are wise beyond your years, son."

Zaiwulo was silent, humbled.

"Now that Kankan is ours, there's the question of who should rule it," said Samori. "I wanted to ask your teacher, but I think he will refuse me. He is angry with me. He is a man of peace in a time of war. His brother Karamo-Sidikie also refused, but at least he suggested one of his relatives who knows the law."

"Faama, I want to go with you to fight Sere-Brimah."

Samori frowned. "I hope it has nothing to do with your fight with Osman the other day. Even if what he said was true, you are a free man now. You are also well educated—a Karamo—which I cannot say of many others in my court. Let the past rest."

"I've decided to join you."

"Dwelling on the past is not a good reason to become a sofa."

"But most of your sofas were once slaves. Most of them belonged to the lowest caste. They became great with you."

"You want to be a sofa because someone said you were a slave and you believed it. It's when you stop believing that you are a slave and begin to regard yourself as a free man that you can join us. I was about to send you to the French, but I'm beginning to doubt my decision. You are not ready."

"But I belong here with you, with the sofas."

Samori turned his back on Zaiwulo, leaving him heartbroken. On his way out of the palace, Zaiwulo met Massah with Sarankenyi. The two women were laughing as if they'd known each other all their lives.

Sarankenyi turned to him. "You didn't tell me that you already had a wife. So that's why you were silent when I suggested finding you a wife? You made a wise choice, son. Massah is a capable girl. We've known each other but for a day and already she wants to work with me. Together, we will control the trade route from here to the coasts and the distant desert."

Zaiwulo could not believe that Massah had dared to concoct the same lies that he had told the Faama.

"She wants to stay here in the palace, closer to me, to learn more about the trade, and I will be very glad to help her."

Massah was standing with her back to him, perhaps to avoid any confrontation with him. He wondered how Massah would react if he told Sarankenyi that she was not his wife? Though he longed for her and cursed himself for those thoughts, he thought that it was impossible to be with her.

"Is something bothering you, my son?" Sarankenyi asked.

"No, Mother. I can't stop thinking about the war with Sere-Brimah." He hated himself for lying to her, but would she understand if he told her the truth? Would anyone understand?

Sarankenyi shook her head. "You are here with us, and you are loved by the greatest ruler our world has ever seen since Sundiata. Cheer up, my son. Don't think too much. It only hurts."

"Nothing is the matter, Mother."

Sarankenyi watched him leave. "My son has changed, Massah," she said. "Why do children nowadays grow old before their childhood is over? Your husband has changed. What does that mean for us?"

For most of that night, Zaiwulo was awake playing out various scenarios of his life. When he fell asleep, he saw the bow-legged man again. The great Sundiata limped towards him.

"I came to warn you, son," Sundiata said. "The time in which our world will change forever is very near. Be prepared to protect our world. You are as old as I was when I took on the giant Soumangourou, the greatest threat to my world. Be brave, Son of the Buffalo."

Zaiwulo woke up knowing what to do.

On hearing the signal from the sofas who were about to ride out of Kankan, he left the house to join them. Despite Samori's objections, he was determined to become a sofa.

It was his destiny.

6

Sere-Brimah's palace was located on a hilltop from where Zaiwulo, mounted on a new horse, turned toward the horizon resplendent with brilliant shades. Once upon a time, such a sight might have led him to attempt to compose a poem or reminded him of sunset along the river Jon in Musadu, but now he clamored only for action.

Zaiwulo dreamed and woke up with battle on his mind. For most of the campaign, which had begun a few weeks ago, he had avoided Samori, and although he interacted with many sofas, none had broached the subject of his conflict with the Faama. So, he had concluded that perhaps the Faama had not discussed it with them. However, as a precaution, he kept his distance and mingled with sofas of lower ranks.

The men were fond of him and his storytelling abilities. Now that he had abandoned his efforts at chronicling his life story in prose or verse, he discovered that he could tell stories with astonishing ease.

The night before, after a day of intense battle which left parts of the walls of Sere-Brimah's capital damaged but still standing, Zaiwulo had sat with the sofas out in the open around the hearths. The men were eager to hear his stories. He told them about Alexander the Great and his exploits to the farthest reaches of the earth, where he had met the legendary Gog and Magog. These were beings who were as tall as trees and with thunderous voices. Their breaths were a riot of flames that consumed everything in their path. Alexander had fought them in a battle that had dragged on for dozens of years.

"What a wonder," said one of the sofas.

Zaiwulo told them that Alexander the Great, who conquered East and West, inspired Sundiata Keita the Great who had emulated and even named his capital after him. He told them that he had read Alexander's story in a book Karamo-Sidikie of Kankan had lent him. "The book is full of many amazing stories. Some more amazing than those of Alexander's."

"Do such stories exist?" a sofa asked.

"Yes, they do," Zaiwulo said.

"Did the book mention anything about the women in those lands where the skies rain with a white substance as light as feathers?" Jawulen-Karamoko asked. He had left the hearth belonging to the generals and had taken a seat beside Zaiwulo. He was smiling.

"I've read about those lands, elder brother," Zaiwulo said.

"Tell me about their women. Is it true that their bodies are as white as cow milk? That they whisper when talking to their men? A man from across the Niger told me that the women there are docile, unlike ours."

"I didn't read anything about the women there."

"Yet it is true, little brother," Jawulen-Karamoko said, and he turned to the sofas. "Imagine having such women as wives."

"But our women are the most beautiful in the world," Zaiwulo said.

Jawulen-Karamoko smiled. "My little brother does not agree with me," he said and fell silent, as though Zaiwulo had embarrassed him. "What are you doing sitting here, little brother? You belong to our hearth."

"If I am ever going to be a good sofa, elder brother, I have to learn from the bottom up," Zaiwulo said.

Jawulen-Karamoko nodded and jumped to his feet. "You will make a great commander one day. When I am emperor, which is bound to happen, we will fight side by side, conquering places never heard of before, just like Alexander the Great.'

Jawulen-Karamoko left them. By the time the fire had died down, most of the sofas were already spread out on the grass, trying to catch some sleep. Zaiwulo, too, bundled himself on the grass. He wondered what he had to do to distinguish himself in the campaign the next morning.

The sofas were up before dawn. With the singular determination of those who were sure of victory, they assaulted the city walls. As they worked, parts of the walls cracked and broke. Zaiwulo found one such tiny gap, and he and his horse slid through. Slowly and carefully, his eyes searched everywhere for snipers. As he rode, he happened upon severed heads scattered along the walls. Trails of blood terminated at a pile of bodies lying on top of each other, forming a barrier, but the Samorian forces broke through it with ease.

Zaiwulo maneuvered his horse out of an area where the battle was heaviest, where limbs, arms, and heads flew about him, where heads crunched under the weight of horses and rifle butts, where bones cracked like groundnuts popping out of shells.

He wanted to reach Sere-Brimah's palace first.

When the rifle shots and war cries were behind him, Zaiwulo bumped into a man who had his rifle aimed at him. Before the man could fire it, Zaiwulo was upon him.

The two went at each other like darting arrows in the thick of a battle. Their horses crashed into each other, and the two fell with a great thud.

Zaiwulo grabbed the man's neck. Ignoring the chest wound that he had sustained in the fall, he held tightly onto the man's neck. Letting go would mean certain death, he thought. So he went on squeezing until the other's resistance petered out and then ceased. So this is war, Zaiwulo thought. War was the will of one pitted against the other, the resolve of one against the equally powerful resolve of the other to survive.

With little time to consider the fact that he had killed a man, Zaiwulo jumped on his horse and raced toward the palace on the hilltop.

He was surprised to find it deserted.

The eerie silence failed to affect his resolve. Zaiwulo of the forest dismounted and raced with his rifle and sword to the palace. Sweat poured down his body and his chest wound sent sharp needles of pain through him, but he ignored it. There was no pain, he told himself and believed it. There was no pain.

He searched everywhere for a sign of life and found it in one of the enclosures. Dozens of women and children were huddled together. As he walked toward them, they suddenly lurched forward and fell on the ground before him.

"Have mercy, don't kill us," they cried.

The women clung to him, but he wrested himself and moved on. By then he had covered most of the palace grounds, but there was no sign of Sere-Brimah. He was moving in circles, but then he realized that he had overlooked a tiny enclosure. He approached it.

A man sat leaning against the wall, one of his knees bent toward his chest, the other stretched out on the floor. It was Sere-Brimah.

Sere-Brimah's lips twisted into a grin when he saw Zaiwulo. He was sturdily built. His legs were as round as a calabash, his stomach taut. He looked unkempt in his worn-out tunic. His gray cap was balanced carelessly on his head and his teeth stained from kola nut consumption. This cannot be the feared Sere-Brimah, Zaiwulo thought.

"So, he sent you in his stead," Sere-Brimah said. He had a deep voice with a scratchy edge to it. "I guess he told you that I enslaved his mother, that I made her work day and night, forced her to lie with me, that I am the greatest agitator in this part of the world and that I slaughtered more people than he ever will. These might all be true. These might all be all lies. What does it matter now? When the Djelis sing our stories a century or two from now, mine will be that of a defeated man. Won't it, young man?"

Zaiwulo did not answer.

"Tell me who you are, young man."

"Who I am is of no consequence, Your Majesty," Zaiwulo said. "I came to deliver you to my Faama."

"You look so young, but you're already so courageous! There was a time in my life when I would have trained you to better conceal that softness in your eyes which you think you can hide so well but not from men like me. The softness is your fear of death. I would have made the fear disappear and replaced it with the ruthlessness that has made me who I am today. I would have made you like Samori—better than Samori even."

"You are trying to buy time, but it's over."

Sere-Brimah gathered the hem of his tunic between his legs.

"You know what to do then. The instruction must have been clear: bring Samori my head. My skin has become softer with age, my bones crack when I walk like the wood of a leaking canoe. One clean blow will do the job. Get on with it. Hurry up. Because for men like me whose name was enough to decide a battle, to compel a whole city, a whole people, to surrender unconditionally to him, death is better than shame."

"My Faama will be the one who will decide what happens to you," Zaiwulo said. "So please stand up and follow me, Your Majesty."

Sere-Brimah laughed. "I've lost the function of my legs, young man. You will have to fetch me a cane and help me stand up."

Zaiwulo thought that the king could not be serious or was lying to him. However, when he took a closer look at the old man, he realized that he was speaking the truth.

Zaiwulo approached him. As he bowed to hold the king under his arms, he felt the pain from his chest wound and paused to consider it. It was not deep. A bullet had grazed his skin. Zaiwulo pulled Sere-Brimah to his feet, and the rancid scent of sweat and old age invaded his nostrils. He led the old man through the palace and to the main gate.

There, Samori and his sofas awaited them. Zaiwulo let go of the old man.

Sere-Brimah pulled himself to his fullest height and, swallowing the pain of the effort, dropped his cane. "We meet again, Son of Lafiya."

"Today, I prefer to be called Son of Masoronah in memory of my mother. You remember her well, don't you?"

"Who can forget such a spirited woman? You take after her and not after that drunken father of yours. Did you know that I asked her to marry me, to leave that weak man, your father, to be with me?"

"I don't believe a word, Sere-Brimah."

"Once, long ago, you would have believed me," said Sere-Brimah. "I made you, Samori Touré. I molded you into the fighter you are now. It's only natural that you are stronger than I am. The young always outperform the old."

"Our story is well known. You should have let go of my mother when I offered you my services and became your slave."

"Didn't it occur to you that as long as your mother was with me, you would keep fighting my wars for me? Sometimes, a ruler must be ruthless. I heard that you let the Kabbas escape. It's a terrible mistake. Those men preach peace, but they are as bloodthirsty as you and I."

"Time for advice is over, Sere-Brimah. The Kabbas are my concern. What I do with them is my business."

"What do you intend to do with me?"

Samori turned to Zaiwulo. "You are the one who saved his life, going against my explicit instruction to have him decapitated. Tell us what you intend to do with him, Son of the Forest."

"I don't know, Faama," Zaiwulo said.

"You don't know? You joined my sofas without my permission, captured the man who enslaved my mother, and then refused to do what I asked of every sofa. Now you don't know?"

"But Faama, I wanted to please you."

Samori turned to his sofa general. "Kemoko-Bilali, listen to your young friend here. He says that he wanted to please me by refusing to carry out my order. What have you been teaching him? Doesn't he realize that such behavior is punishable by death? Now he refuses for the second time to carry out my order. Is he deaf or incapacitated?"

Kemoko-Bilali cleared his throat. "He's just a child, Faama."

"Give me your rifle, Kemoko-Bilali. We will see whether he's deaf or incapacitated. A child, you say? Come on, give me your rifle."

The sofa general hesitated. Samori snatched the rifle from him, walked up to Zaiwulo, and aimed the barrel at his head.

"Sofas, look at what your Faama is doing to his most courageous fighter," Sere-Brimah said. "You keep surprising me, Samori."

Sere-Brimah turned to Zaiwulo. "I want you to make a clean cut across my neck. Show me the courage I saw a while ago in the palace."

"You've heard him. Snatch it off!" Samori roared.

"But I cannot kill you, Your Majesty."

"Faama," the Djeli Morifin-Djan said.

Not once had Samori defied his best friend.

"Another step, Morifin-Djan Diabate, and I will strip you of all your ranks and send you back where you came from. Not another step!"

A murmur spread among the sofas.

"I can't do what you asked, Faama," Zaiwulo said. He fell to his knees and turned to Sere-Brimah. "I cannot cut your throat, Your Majesty!"

"In that case, please spare me a fate worse than death. Spare me the fate of my people seeing me every day in this condition," Sere-Brimah said. "Banish me to a place where no one has ever heard of me."

"Choose a place, and we will grant you a safe passage," Zaiwulo said.

Samori nodded and handed over the rifle to Kemoko-Bilali. "Zaiwulo, you are one of those to whom I'm most attached, but never disobey me again," he said. "If you do so, I will cut the rope that binds us."

"Who is this young man, Samori?" Sere-Brimah asked.

"He is of my mother's people. He carries her heart," Samori answered. He mounted his horse and turned it around, about to leave.

"What do we do with the city, Faama?" the sofa general Porokerrie asked.

"Burn it to ashes. A place where my mother was enslaved deserves to be forgotten. It never existed. We are heading back to Kankan."

7

Thousands of people gathered in the large square in the heart of Kankan where the markets were held to receive the new emperor. Zaiwulo and a few hundred sofas were assigned the task of maintaining order and preventing the crowd from running amok. Some of the inhabitants of the city were yet to accept the new ruler, so all rebellion had to be crushed.

Most people stood squinting in the fierce sun, and the air was heavy with the cloying scent of incense, shea butter, and sweat. Now and then, subdued murmurs would sweep across the crowd. People were speculating over Samori's appearance.

"I heard that he's as tall and as big as the giant Soumangourou, who faced Sundiata in an epic battle that led to the founding of the greatest empire on earth," someone said.

Another said that on entering Kankan, the emperor had intercepted its ruler, Karamoko-Mori, who had not fled in time. To display his generosity, Samori had pardoned and allowed him to go into exile. Rumors spread about how Samori had captured the sons of the Kabbas and enlisted them into his army, and how their wives were now his wives. Each day, after attending to the affairs of the empire, he would retire into the palace, where he would receive the Kabbas' women in turn, so that now, he had sowed his seed in half of them. The gold he had acquired from the people of Kankan and all the lands around it as compensation for not punishing them, filled up more than a hundred houses.

Samori had conquered Buré, the legendary city where the elders were fitted out with gold tunics and caps, and women walked with their hands held to their backs to ease the pain of bearing so much jewelry. The numerous shafts and creeks where the gold was mined by thousands of men and women day and night contained gold nuggets and gold dust that filled granaries the size of Kankan. Samori had become the emperor of gold and could purchase any weapon of choice from the English and the French to the German and Dutch rifles, pistols, and other arms.

Zaiwulo's attention shifted to the Djeli Morifin-Djan Diabate, whose voice rang out with the emperor's name:

Who dares challenge you now, Faama?
Who dares speak a note higher than yours?
When those left of your adversaries compete against each other
in their efforts to please you… The world awaits you, Faama
of all Faamas.
So do with it as you please.

The Djeli then announced Samori. The emperor sat on a splendid white horse with a bridle of gold, the edges of the clothes that covered its back lined with golden filigree. On the path cleared of people, the horse rode toward a platform decorated with large pillows.

Samori wore a white cap, his face half-concealed behind a white veil, his fingers studded with gold. His sword, fashioned by those very smiths who produced the first rifles of the new empire, danced in step with the horse. Behind him, also mounted, was his large entourage which consisted of sofa generals, friends, and family members. There were more than a thousand people, all handsomely attired, their horses polished so well that their manes and flanks glinted. It was a calculated performance. Samori wanted not only to display power and grandeur but also to dissuade the revolting populace of Kankan from entertaining any ideas of insurrection.

The panoply of colors that was the crowd fell to its knees on seeing Samori. The colors were like a majestic canopy sailing down the Niger, all full of bubbles and depressions, a large piece of cloth borne by invisible hands. Without qualms, without a moment of doubt, Samori was convinced that with such conquests, such wealth, and such means, he could take on the rulers of all the lands of the Black-skinned people. He was certain that he could take on the English and the French, the Germans and the Dutch, the Portuguese, or any other white force that posed a threat to his existence. He could bring down Tieba of Sikasso with his famous city walls, the Tata. He could extend his empire to the depths of the desert and beyond, he could unite the vast forests with the infinite desert and become greater than Sundiata Keita and Mansa Musa, greater than Alexander the Great, or any ruler who ever lived.

Somari alighted from his horse and strode up to the throne. Only then did the crowd stand up. Everyone waited for a sign from the new master, and Samori turned to his Djeli with a slight nod.

Morifin-Djan Diabate spoke:

"Thanks a thousand times to you the rulers of all the lands assembled here today. Our Faama invited you here to swear allegiance to the Wasulu Empire, to the Faamaya

Empire, the largest since Sundiata. The oath you are about to take will not only bind you to him, but it will also bind your lands to his empire. By vowing to support him, you are being bound by *Kafu*—a Mandé word that is stronger than the bond between a child and its mother."

The women brought degue in large calabashes, earthen bowls, pots pans, and jars. They set the food before Samori who had not shared a word with anyone since the onset of the ceremony. The rulers of the lands Samori now controlled stood up and filed out in a long queue before the throne.

"Not since Sundiata have our lands been graced with a ruler as powerful as you are," said one of them before reaching for a handful of the degue and swallowing it.

Another edged forward. "Come what may, Faama of Faamas, we will stand by you,"

Samori nodded solemnly to each ruler until they had all tasted the honey-sweetened gruel. He always allocated the governing of conquered territories to the people conquered. They were usually assisted by some of his sofa generals. Now he was set to bring about change in that order. He nodded to his Djeli. Morifin-Djan Diabate ascended the platform, and Samori whispered instructions in his ear.

The Djeli turned to the crowd.

"Our Faama has decreed that, henceforth, slavery is forbidden in the new empire. All slaves are free. If anyone is caught selling people to the whites, he will be decapitated. Moreover, the rulers present will return to their lands accompanied by a scholar and a sofa general who will make sure that the laws of the empire are implemented. The scholars will interpret the laws under the leadership of Haidarah of Musadu—if he is found— and with the help of his brother Karamo-Sidikie. Henceforth, uniform laws will govern the new empire. The rulers and the generals will make sure that the laws written by the scholars are implemented to the letter. Order is the single goal of these laws," the Djeli said. "Order and nothing else."

"So you mean to deny me, or should I say to deny us, the drinking of dolo, Samori Touré?" a voice asked.

The crowd stirred. Everyone was curious to know whose voice it was.

Zaiwulo recognized the voice. It was Lafiya's, Samori's father, who, by now, was walking with his stick to the center of the square.

"Is your latest conquest about forcing people to become what they are not? I don't recognize my son in the man sitting on that throne. Why the obsession with scholars? What can they give you that you don't already have? You are sending them to people they don't know and to ways of life that are strange to them. How will they interact with those people? How will they implement laws if they don't know the people who are to obey those laws? I thought you came to bring about change, the change that made you, the son of a weaver and from a family of traders—a simple Djula—an emperor today. I thought you would institute something new in Kankan after defeating the Kabbas. I thought you would denounce their ways, but you are about to become like them. Why?"

Zaiwulo wanted to assist the old man, for he saw how frail and unstable his steps were, but before he could reach him, Lafiya went into a coughing fit. The old man stumbled and fell over in the dust. People rushed toward him.

Zaiwulo gasped when the crowd surged forward. A stampede ensued.

Samori and some sofas rushed to Lafiya to take him away. Zaiwulo was with them. Other sofas calmed the crowd. While Karamo-Sidikie prayed for the old man, some herbalists attended to him.

Zaiwulo left to see Massah. He met her preparing monnie in a winnower. She was in a scarlet tunic and wrapper. Her hair was plaited in two large rows. Every part of her body was more pronounced. Her gleaming face was fuller, her legs rounder, her whole body and slender arms were bursting with life. Her eyes had taken on a softer aspect. The weariness was gone. Massah was surrounded by maids who were helping her with chores and other maids who purchased and sold her goods in the market. As he told her about Lafiya, he attributed the changes in Massah's body down to the transformation in her fortune, to the good life in Kankan.

"Will he make it?" she asked.

"Karamo-Sidikie and the herbalists are with him now," Zaiwulo said.

"Have you any news about your teacher Talata?" she asked.

Zaiwulo noted a hint of satisfaction in her voice. On his return from the war with Sere-Brimah, he had been told that Sona had left for Musadu but that Talata was not in Musadu, neither was Naminata. Was his teacher hiding somewhere in Koniyan, waiting for the right moment to return to Musadu, he had often wondered. Where was Naminata?

"I hope he's back in Musadu," Zaiwulo said.

"You look hungry," Massah said. "I will fetch you some food. This monnie is for your breakfast tomorrow. You and your obsession with food!"

When she returned, Zaiwulo couldn't take his eyes off Massah. He watched the movements of her hands as she dished out the food. Massah laughed.

"If people were to see you like this, they might think I've bewitched you or mixed your bath with the nasi Karamo-Sidikie prepared:

"I saw it, and I am sure you've bewitched him, Massah," Sarankenyi said laughing. She had caught them by surprise. "The way he looks at you!"

"We were talking about Grandpa Lafiya," Zaiwulo stammered.

"If I didn't know you well, I would have said that being here is a weakness on your part. See your wife as often as you can, as long as you don't neglect your dear mother. Come here!" she said, but Zaiwulo did not move. "I hope with all my heart that his brother Sarankenyi-Mori takes after him and becomes a man like him. Look at him, Massah!"

"My brother will be all right, Mother," he said.

"You think so?" she said. "Every time I see him, he looks so weak that I wonder whether he will even make it in life, let alone succeed his father."

"You worry too much, Mother."

"We have enemies who want our blood."

"He will be fine.'"

One of Samori's personal guards came to fetch Zaiwulo. "The Faama wants to see you."

It was the first time he was seeing the emperor since the campaign against Sere-Brimah. Zaiwulo worried about how he would be received. Was Samori still angry with him?

Samori sat in a gathering with his Djeli Morifin-Djan, his brother Kemeh-Brimah, his friend Kemoko-Bilali, and other generals and family members.

"We've located the kabbas," the Djeli told Zaiwulo. "They are in Kenyera."

Samori turned to Zaiwulo. "You and my brother Kemeh-Brimah will lead an army to Kenyera to ask its king to give up the Kabbas," he said. "I would have accompanied you, but my father is passing on, and I want to be by his side."

"We will bring back the Kabbas, elder brother," Kemeh-Brimah said. "Once the people of Kenyera see us at their gates, they will hand them over to us. You don't need to worry."

"Come closer," Samori told Zaiwulo.

Zaiwulo edged forward and sat on the mat across from him.

"In the campaign against the man who enslaved my mother, you not only proved to be courageous, but you also surprised me with your intelligence and wisdom. I was hard on you to test your resolve. But you did not disappoint me. Sometimes, you need to defy your leader and do what is right."

Samori dismissed his court.

"Come with me, Zaiwulo."

Samori took Zaiwulo to the stables studded with new horses. As he moved from one stable to another, a horse caught Zaiwulo's eyes. It was a black horse, an Arabian with a forehead streaked with white. It sniffed, snorted, and pointed its ears in defiance.

"I wanted the horse for myself, but it suits you," Samori said.

Samori left Zaiwulo alone with the horse. The horse glared at Zaiwulo as if he was an enemy that had to be crushed. He wondered whether he would ever manage to ride it.

A few days later, Zaiwulo went to take leave of Massah. She was laying out pieces of clothes and other goods that her traders would sell in lands as far as Kong, Sikasso, Bamako, and Bobo-Dioulasso. She stopped working when she saw him. She was becoming more beautiful with each passing day, and now, she looked like a young woman in her prime. The beads of sweat on her face mixed with her body oil and glowed, emphasizing her good health.

Zaiwulo longed to touch her, to embrace her, to be with her.

"I'm leaving today with Uncle Kemeh-Brimah in search of the Kabbas. We believe that they are in Kenyera, a city very far from here."

"So you are going to war again?"

"It will not come to war. The king of Kenyera will extradite the Kabbas. We will only threaten them with war, Massah."

"You chose to join the sofas. Now you are being accompanied by one of the most bellicose sofas, and you claim it will all end peacefully?" She threw her hands in the air in disbelief.

"Should we talk about something else?"

Massah sucked her teeth. "No, Zaiwulo. You are not going to avoid this stupid choice of yours by pretending it's nothing. It is everything. We should have been elsewhere by now. We should have been in the forest, at your birthplace."

"When this is over, I will take you to a place of great safety."

"This will never be over. Don't you see that? The more Samori conquers, the more he craves. His hunger is insatiable. It will never stop. If you follow him, Zaiwulo, you end up being like him."

Zaiwulo turned around, about to leave.

"Don't turn your back on me, Zaiwulo. Look at me."

He turned, and she grabbed his hands. "Promise me that wherever you go, you will never leave me."

"I will never abandon you, Massah. Never."

She let go of him. Before bending the corner, Zaiwulo had the urge to turn around, but if he did so, he was sure that her eyes would crush him, so he walked on.

8

Zaiwulo's new horse growled and stamped its hooves while flashing angry glances at him. Horse and rider were standing above a hill overlooking Kenyera. The horse had remained defiant, even after both had raced through the plains of Kankan in preparation for the march to Kenyera.

That day, a rush of unalloyed joy had welled up in Zaiwulo. He had become one with the horse. His heartbeat was in tune with the steady rhythm of its gallops, but for no apparent reason, the horse had suddenly thrown him off, betraying his trust. Zaiwulo had survived the incident with minor injuries. Every time he brushed it down, hoping to win its affection, the horse's body would swell with fury under his touch. Even now, after weeks on the road, it refused to eat from his hands but preferred to graze out in the open.

"You are not easy to deal with, Sundiata," he said, as he prepared to inspect the hills around Kenyera where he and Kemeh-Brimah had stationed their army. "But I will not give up on you."

Zaiwulo thought of Massah. He was suddenly overcome by the fear that their secret might have been revealed, that Talata was with Samori, that sooner or later he would receive a message that he had been banished from the empire and that he would never see Massah again.

Zaiwulo had set out with ten of his men that morning.

Kenyera was a collection of villages and towns that were enclosed by walls. For any conquest to be possible, he thought as he gazed down the hill, those walls had to be scaled and the interlocking villages and towns had to be attacked by stationing sofas at all exits, with the bulk of them concentrated on the main gate.

Earlier that day, Kemeh-Brimah had once again dispatched his envoys to Kenyera to let the king know of their presence and their demands. "If the king refuses again, and if all efforts fail, we will storm the city and capture the Kabbas," he had told Zaiwulo.

The envoys were not back by the time Zaiwulo completed his inspection and returned to the camp, but there was news from Kankan.

Shortly after their departure, Samori's father had passed on.

"The old man lived a long life, son," Kemeh-Brimah told Zaiwulo. "He lived to see us as rulers. Now we look to the future."

The sofas had also brought a letter for Zaiwulo from Talata. This meant that Samori knew the content of the letter, he thought. Samori had indeed read the letter, according to the messengers, and he regretted Talata's choice. He still hoped that the scholar might return from the forest where to play a role in the governing of the empire.

Zaiwulo's hands trembled as he unfolded the starched cloth on which the words had been written.

I couldn't find papers, his teacher wrote, *so I had to make do with this piece of cloth.*

How is life in Musadu? What happened to my books? Were they spared? Are Demba and my son Osman with you? Is Osman still making life difficult for you? Yes, it's true that I escaped from Samori. I tried to mediate between him and my teachers, but both parties were stubborn. Many times, I advised Samori to find a way to conquer Kankan without resorting to violence, but he refused. Failing to bring about peace, I was left with no other choice but to flee Kankan. While in Beyla and Jakodu, I heard that the king of Musadu was waiting to kill me and that Samori had sent his sofas to cut off my head. I couldn't wait to find out whether this was true or not.

Just before my departure, I was joined by Naminata. She came bearing the Haidarah Manuscript on her head. Great was my joy that she had managed to save our precious heritage. Together, we sought shelter in the forest. They say love manifests itself in many ways, that it's a magic that touches and transforms lives. The great poets had written about it. I've written about it. What I didn't know was that it would affect me in that way. What a struggle Naminata must have undergone to save the manuscript. I didn't dare ask her for details and to this day, I am not inclined to do so. The most important thing is that the manuscript is safe with me here, in Bopolu.

The king of Bopolu holds me prisoner but insists he is being honored by my presence. He claims without proof that we are related through my wife Sona, a Kamara like himself. And he believes that I am capable of making him more powerful than his father Sao Boso Kamara. King Sao Boso was the one who helped the Blacks from America, like our Benjamin Anderson, to settle in these lands and found Liberia.

The Bopolu king believes that I possess a secret formula that can transform him into what he is not and will never be! If I possessed such powers, then why didn't I use them to prevent my house from falling apart? I told the king that I was incapable of performing such miracles, but all in vain. I am stuck here. You, Demba, and Osman, should keep the house running. When peace reigns in Koniyan again, I will return.

Zaiwulo reread the letter. Naminata was alive! He thought of her wars with the Haidarah and the Foningama households, her wars with Musadu. She had managed to wrest herself away from a terrible fate. What a woman! One day he would go in search of her, and he would hold her hands and ask her forgiveness.

Talata needed him, but he had made his choice. In the Samorian world, he was not judged by his background but by his deeds.

In the distance, Zaiwulo heard the sound of horses.

"The king of Kenyera has refused again to give up the Kabbas," the envoys said. "He challenged us to come and get them."

Kemeh-Brimah laughed. "This is a declaration of war."

The next evening, as the sofas prepared for war, Kemeh-Brimah sought out Zaiwulo. "Join me around the fire, son," he said.

Despite the weeks together, Zaiwulo was yet to feel at ease in his presence, for Kemeh-Brimah was already a legend. Many Djelis claimed that he was more formidable than his brother Samori. Stories made the rounds of his heroic exploits. The Djelis sang that after all attempts at capturing a town in Koniyan had failed, Kemeh-Brimah had singularly broken through the gate and had captured its king, thereby ending the siege and the war.

"Even after a thousand wars, Zaiwulo, you will never get used to the reality of being on a battlefield." Kemeh-Brimah said.

"But I see no fear in you, Uncle Kemeh-Brimah," Zaiwulo said. "In fact, I see no fear in any of the sofas, but I am always full of fear."

"We all suffer from one form of fear or another. The fear that with each war we might never see our loved ones again makes us stronger instead of weakening us. I confess that I hate war with all my heart."

"But why do we wage war then?"

"Let me tell you a story, son. Perhaps it might help explain all of this." Kemeh-Brimah leaned forward. "During our childhood, my brothers and other family members often fought over food. It was never enough. Hunger was an enemy intent on crushing us. Sometimes we thrived on toe without sauce for days. Our single dream was to rise above our station. In the end, we succeeded. Not only did we banish poverty out of our lives, but we went on to prove that attaining high status in society was not confined to one set of people and denied others, as has been the case for ages. We proved that a hawker could be whatever he wanted to be, a warrior, a king, or even an emperor. True peace is achieved only when one is open to the possibility of war."

Kemeh-Brimah fell silent. "How do we attack Kenyera?" he asked Zaiwulo.

"By stationing sofas at all the exits of the towns and villages, and with our main force concentrating on the main gate, Uncle Kemeh-Brimah."

"That's what we will do," Kemeh-Brimah said. "Come, let's make some preparations, as I'm sure the people of Kenyera are doing the same."

The sofas rode out to the city walls at dawn.

As they approached, Zaiwulo thought that he could hear women beyond the walls, perhaps preparing for breakfast. He scratched the spurs tied around his bare feet against Sundiata's flanks. After a slight hesitation, the horse broke into a trot toward the walls.

The main gate stood open. There was no one about.

"Come, let's enter and see," Kemeh-Brimah suggested.

They rode into the city without encountering a soul.

"It's a trap," Zaiwulo said.

"They've taken to their heels," Kemeh-Brimah said.

The sofas rode on deeper into the city but found no one.

"Yes, it's a trap, but it's too late now," Kemeh-Brimah said.

Something landed in the sofas' midst with a terrifying explosion that left a huge gap in the ground. Zaiwulo was lifted off his horse by a force that hauled him so hard against the ground that he could not move, as though he'd lost the function of his whole body. The acrid smell of cannon fire was suffocating. Zaiwulo realized that if he failed to move, he would die under the weight of the debris. A serene calmness descended on him, deafening the noise around him, luring him towards slumber. So this is death, he thought. This utter silence, this deep sleep.

"Wake up, namesake of my father," he heard a distant voice calling out to him.

It was his mother's. Opening his eyes, he saw his horse Sundiata clearing away the debris with its hooves and wiping his face with its tongue. "Sundiata," he cried.

Although his body ached, Zaiwulo clambered on the horse and, emboldened by his sudden brush with death, raced in the direction of the source of the carnage. Like one possessed, he broke through the wall of dense smoke. In the clearing before him, on a hillock, he saw a group of white men with rifles pointed in his direction. Around them, collected in a single block like a wall, were Black soldiers. The men had weapons which he would later learn were cannons. These weapons had caused havoc amongst his men.

As if he had read Zaiwulo's mind, Sundiata turned left and raced out of the battlefield and into a fog of smoke. They rode out of Kenyera and into the plains.

Every time he paused to catch his breath, Zaiwulo could still hear the sounds of the strange weapons and the howling of his sofas. He rode on without stopping. Dusk fell on that grass country and he was still riding. At one point, deep at night, he found he had been riding in circles. He decided to stop and rest for the night. In the morning he followed the same trail back to Kenyera in search of his men.

He had to know their fate.

The savannah grass in that place was thin like scrawny corn. It was a disheveled country with dwarf trees. The anthills were a shadow of themselves. The earth was hard as if a famine had struck, and it hurt Sundiata. So Zaiwulo rode slowly until he happened upon the dead and the wounded lying around unattended. Flies buzzed around them. Death had the sour smell of old blood and neglect. The odor held everything in its thrall.

"They were white men," Zaiwulo said. "I saw them. They were white," he kept saying, as if it was enough to explain his deepest fears.

He dismounted and rushed to Kemeh-Brimah. The sofa general had been shot and had broken one of his legs, which was tied to a long stick. Kemeh-Brimah sat up against a tree, gritting his teeth to fight the pain.

"Who were those white people, Uncle?" Zaiwulo asked.

"White people? What are you talking about?"

"They were white and Black men. I saw them."

Kemeh-Brimah considered this. “I don’t know, son,” he said. “The king of Kenyera must have solicited their help. But that’s very strange! We’ve always traded with the Toubabous and bought weapons from them, but they’ve never participated directly in our wars. What has brought about this change?”

“What should we do now?” Zaiwulo asked. He had never looked as helpless as at that moment, and Kemeh-Brimah patted him on the shoulder to reassure him.

“We can’t return to Kankan in this state. Not as a defeated army. We must know who those men are and what they want. My brother would never forgive us if we returned empty-handed. We must confront them again.”

Kemeh-Brimah was hinting at the possibility of Zaiwulo leading the sofas to fight an army in possession of new destructive weapons.

“How can we fight an enemy with such weapons?” he said.

“We cannot fight them head-on,” Kemeh-Brimah said. “They will slaughter us if we do.”

“Yes, you are right, Uncle Kemeh-Brimah,” Zaiwulo said, thinking. “We isolate them and fight them in pockets. We need to be faster, more agile than they are. In a one-on-one fight, we stand a chance!”

9

The sofas had been trailing the white forces for some time now, and from what their scouts gathered, the enemy was heading toward Bamako, a small trading post along the Niger River. Now, they had caught up with them. The Toubabous stood out in their blue-and-white uniforms. The shape of their headgear—the shako—and the glinting weapons, especially the mysterious cannons, were unmistakable. There they were in the camp down the slope, on the other side of the River Woyowayanko. Zaiwulo and a few thousand sofas were lying pressed hard against the ground on the other side of the slope. The cavalry waited below them.

The village was named after the river, Woyowayanko, a tributary of the Niger. It was a tiny strip of water that would henceforth pour into an ocean of legends, for the Djeli Morifin-Djan Diabate, though absent at this event, would sing it into life, seasoning it with episodes of his own making, ignoring important details that did not fit his narrative.

Zaiwulo could see the men in the camp polishing their weapons. Some were drilling and others singing in a language as strange as their appearance. Their carefree laughter was borne by the winds toward the sofas. One of them, whom Zaiwulo would later learn was the French general Gustave Borgnis-Desbordes, was sitting under a tree away from the rest. He was tall, with a mustache, and his sun-scorched face was as red as the earth around him.

Borgnis-Desbordes paused from his task and stared in Zaiwulo's direction, aware of his presence.

"Tell me what you see, son," Kemeh-Brimah said.

The sofa general had come along despite his injured leg. Whenever he was tired of moving with crutches, the sofas would carry him on a wooden stretcher.

"I think they are settling down," Zaiwulo said.

"This is the right moment then."

Without leaving his seated position, Kemeh-Brimah gave the order to attack. "No one under any circumstances is to deviate from our plan of action," he said. "Remember, don't fight the Toubabous in large numbers, but in pockets."

The sofas, who were divided into units of a few dozen men, crept down the valley and forded the narrow river to the other side. They positioned themselves in such a way that each unit would attempt to separate the enemy from each other. However, as soon as Zaiwulo saw the cannons, he neglected Kemeh-Brimah's words.

"We need to seize those weapons by all means," he told his men.

He was barely done when the French unleashed their firepower. Stationed in front of his men, Zaiwulo escaped the onslaught but not the bulk of his men on the right and left flanks of his unit. Most were swept up and buried under the rubble of cannon fire. Those who remained standing, undeterred by the dead and wounded around them, raced towards the cannons before they were reloaded again.

Zaiwulo looked up and saw his men surrounding the cannons. He rushed forward, crawling on all fours to avoid being hit by bullets. On reaching the sofas, he found himself face to face with one of the protectors of the cannons, who was almost done loading.

Zaiwulo hauled himself at him. The Toubabou was not old, and as Zaiwulo gripped the man's waist and attempted to pin him down onto the cannon, he wondered if the man had a woman like Massah who worried about him. What was he doing in this part of the world? Those thoughts vanished when the man broke free and raced in the direction of the river. Zaiwulo pursued him. The two were separated from the rest now, and they pulled and tore at each other, throwing clumps of mud, grass, dirt, and anything within reach. They landed in that part of the river that was shallow, and Zaiwulo, who could not swim, led the fight back to the bank.

Zaiwulo grabbed the Toubabou below the shoulders and lifted him. He was about to fling him to the ground and finish him off when he felt a searing pain in his eyes that blinded him. But he did not panic or let go of the man. The fight seemed to be over, because, for a long time, the white man did not move. It felt as though he had succumbed to Zaiwulo's grip.

Meanwhile, the sofas had managed to secure the cannons.

Kemeh-Brimah, who had been closely watching the battle, saw his chance. Sensing victory, he ignored the pain of his injuries. "Help me onto a horse," he shouted to his men. With the French deprived of their cannons, he reasoned that they posed less danger. The sofa general directed the cavalry towards Gustave Borgnis-Desbordes to capture him.

But it was as if the French general had anticipated their move. As the sofas closed in, he directed his forces to form a block around him and deter their advance. The French general was able to sustain this for what seemed like forever until a shot fired by a keen sofa near the river hit him below his right shoulder.

Borgnis-Desbordes was immediately carried off on a wooden stretcher. The human cordon formed around him was so thick that every time a wedge was created by a sofa's shot or an arrow, another man filled it. This strategy frustrated the sofas, but Kemeh-Brimah's words echoing through hundreds of sofas across the battlefield kept them strong.

"Don't let them escape," he ordered.

Pockets of sofas went in pursuit of the retreating French, while the rest attended to the dead and wounded. By then the sun had set and silence descended on the battlefield.

The sofas met Zaiwulo and the Toubabou entangled in each other, their bodies covered with so much mud and blood that the sofas could hardly tell them apart.

"It's enough now, son," Kemeh-Brimah said. "The red ears have taken to their heels. We've won. The battle of Woyowayanko is over."

Zaiwulo let go of the man, and when he stood up, he realized his eyes were coated with a layer of mud and blood. He could not see. He rushed in panic in the direction of the river to wash his face, but he stumbled and fell in the mud. He thrashed about as if in search of his eyes or of something that would restore his sight.

"I can't see, Uncle," he cried. "I can't see!"

"We will treat your eyes with herbs. You are not blind. It's because of the mud and the blood. You will get better. Thanks to you and your sofas we were able to get hold of those dangerous cannons. We have two now. We will see how they work."

Zaiwulo paused, stricken by paralyzing fear. He felt enveloped in an absolute emptiness that impeded his movement, as if he had been thrown in a well with no end to his fall and with nothing to hold onto. He thought of Demba. Perhaps, the blind man has cursed me for longing for Massah, he told himself.

Kemeh-Brimah sat beside him. "In a matter of days, you will see, son."

All around him, Zaiwulo heard movements. He could not bring himself to accept his new reality. His whole body throbbed with the dread of the unknown. Yet Demba, deprived of sight all his life, had been able to not only amass knowledge but to love another human being with all his heart. He was greater than all of us, Zaiwulo thought.

Kemeh-Brimah patted Zaiwulo on the shoulder. "We've taken the white man and other Black fighters prisoner," he told him. "The Toubabous can hardly move, but we will nurse him back to health. He could be of use to us during our negotiations with the whites."

The white prisoner, according to the interpreter Al-Kamesah who had also been captured, was called Jean Durand. His father was stationed in Saint-Louis as one of the assistants to the governor of Senegal. Jean had grown up there. Through Al-Kamesah, Zaiwulo and the sofas learned that the Toubabous were French and that the Black soldiers were parts of The Tirailleurs Sénégalais, an army corps based in Senegal that consisted of people from different parts of Africa.

That night, the sofas led Zaiwulo to a makeshift tent of grass. One of them, a herbalist, applied a poultice of herbs onto his eyes and tied them with a piece of cloth.

"Don't take it off for a few days," the herbalist said.

Left alone, Zaiwulo was keenly aware of the sounds of mosquitoes and insects. His hearing was compensating for the loss of his sight. He felt around him and his hands touched the bed of grass, smooth now as a result of his body resting on it. Would he ever see daylight again, he wondered. The hope of regaining his sight and of seeing Massah was at one moment so overwhelming that he sat up and laughed out loud. I will look into her eyes for weeks on end, he told himself. I will never leave her side. I will help her become as successful as Sarankenyi, and I will take her to the forest to meet my people. But there were those moments when his spirit sagged because he was assailed by thoughts that he would remain blind forever. During those periods, he would pound his fists on the ground in frustration.

Alerted to the noise of Zaiwulo's fight with himself, Kemeh-Brimah interrupted Zaiwulo with a cough. The sofa general did not enter the tent.

"Son, we will leave early in the morning to conquer Bamako," he said.

Zaiwulo had heard of the trading post along the Niger which was populated by Mandé speaking people like him and the sofas. It would be an easy conquest. "How is the Toubabou doing?" he asked.

"He is still in critical condition. If we had not separated you two in time, he would have died," Kemeh-Brimah said. "Take the needed rest. We leave at dawn."

The people of Bamako welcomed the sofas like heroes and swore their allegiance to the Faama of all Faamas. Kemeh-Brimah decided to spend some time in the town to give Zaiwulo and the sofas enough time to recover before further conquests.

Every day, Zaiwulo would wake up with a severe headache. Blood churned in his head. Sunlight tormented him. Life tormented him. He was a wreck, his nerves frayed, he flared up at the slightest provocation, and so, everyone avoided him.

One morning, in the third week in Bamako, the interpreter Al-Kamesah came to see him. He had brought a guest with him, he told Zaiwulo. It was Jean, the Toubabou. The Frenchman had recovered enough that he could walk with crutches.

"He insisted that I bring him to you," Al-Kamesah said.

"I don't want to meet him," Zaiwulo growled. He felt searing flames dart across the darkness of his vision.

"He came to thank you for sparing his life," Al-Kamesah said.

"If he comes any closer, I will end that life," Zaiwulo said.

The two men went away.

That night, Zaiwulo's mother appeared in his dream. She came closer to him than ever before, her owl eyes so large that they almost engulfed him.

"You can heal yourself, namesake of my father," she said. "When someone washes your back, even if he's a white man, you must wash your chest."

Her voice was still resounding in his head when he woke up. He untied the binding, and like a child learning to walk for the first time, Zaiwulo attempted to open his eyes. A flood of light invaded his vision. A cry escaped him. The first thing he saw was a mouse nibbling at the crumbs lying in bed near him. He did not move for fear of disturbing it. When the animal sensed him, it scurried away. Zaiwulo left his chambers, a spacious one-room house where he had spent most of his time and walked into the sun.

The earth had never been so red-brown, the sun so bright, and the grass of the savannah so vividly green. He went about looking at his men. The various textures of their skin. The curved shapes of their lips. Their eyes, noses, and ears. They all looked so special and beautiful that he had the urge to embrace them all and tell them how much they meant to him.

One of the many people who came to see him that day was Jean.

"I've taught your men how to use the cannons," Jean told Zaiwulo through the interpreter Al-Kamesah.

Zaiwulo was sitting outside, staring in front of him, awash with a sense of well-being that seemed unreal, as if he was in a dream. Zaiwulo turned to the Frenchman. From up close, Jean's weary mustache, slender hands, and the carefree way he carried himself were at odds with his vocation as a soldier in this part of the world. He will not survive here for long, Zaiwulo thought.

"So we are weapons richer," Zaiwulo said.

When Al-Kamesah interpreted this, Jean's face took on a vague but perceptible smile. Zaiwulo turned to the interpreter. "You didn't bring him here to mock me, did you?" he said, and Al-Kamesah shook his head.

"Yes, but we have more cannons," Jean said through the interpreter.

"Tell him, Al-Kamesah, that we are making our weapons now. We are better equipped than ever before. They will never defeat us."

"You think so?' Jean said. "I recommend you visit Saint-Louis. You will be astounded by the power of France. What you've seen is child's play."

Zaiwulo could not explain the confidence that Jean seemed to portray. It bothered him. Why was the Toubabou so sure of himself?

"What is he talking about Al-Kamesah?" Zaiwulo asked.

"I don't know, Faama. These Toubabous!" Al-Kamesah said.

Zaiwulo could see from the interpreter's nervousness that he did know something.

"I want to write to our governor to suggest that we sign a treaty of understanding between us, because we are here to stay," Jean said.

"A treaty is a good idea, but I doubt you will stay here."

"One day all of these lands will be ours, my friend."

Zaiwulo laughed. "We, and our emperor, will never allow it."

"Then you and your emperor have got a problem."

"Why do you say that?"

"Because you spared my life, and I've come to regard you as a friend, Zaiwulo. I am being honest with you. We are here to stay."

The conversation haunted Zaiwulo. Why would Jean and his people want to take over their lands? What did that mean for his future?

Some weeks later, news reached Zaiwulo and the sofas in Bamako that the French had expressed the wish to sign a peace treaty with Samori at Kenyeraba-Koura.

Zaiwulo thought of Jean's letter.

The Frenchman came to see him again.

"The war between us will end with the treaty," he said.

10

Samori summoned the rulers of all the lands in his empire as well as all his advisors and envoys—including those in Freetown—to be present as he received the French.

On the morning of their arrival, Zaiwulo was lying in bed when he felt a presence beneath the birdsong that sounded in the trees around his house. He had been dreaming about Massah. She had a child strapped to her back, and a storm was heading their way, threatening to sweep them away. He hastened on horseback to save them, but he was hampered at every turn by the weight of a presence. The presence was the edge of a knife pressing hard against the nape of his neck. This is not a dream, he thought, and he heard a voice that sounded familiar.

"You thought you could escape from me," the voice said, "but here I am. I know you stole the Haidarah Manuscript. I came to get it back."

It was Osman, Talata's son.

"I don't have the Tareequ." Zaiwulo tried to move but the knife scratched his skin, and he began to bleed.

"Liar! You stole the manuscript," Osman said.

"Your father has the manuscript. He fled Koniyan together with Naminata and is now in Bopolu. He wrote me a letter."

"I've been to Bopolu. He's not there."

"I don't have it, Osman."

"I knew it the first time I saw you. You bring misfortune and sow chaos wherever you go. Tell me where the book is."

Zaiwulo had had enough. With a swift movement, he threw Osman off him and sprang to his feet. He sucked his teeth. "The manuscript is safe with your father, I say."

"I don't believe you. You took it."

They were interrupted by voices and footsteps in front of the house.

"Where are you, son of the forest?"

It was his old friend Kemoko-Bilali. Before Zaiwulo could respond, Kemoko-Bilali burst into the house. When he saw Osman, he frowned.

"What are you doing here, Haidarah? Visiting your brother?"

"He's not my brother! He stole the family treasure, Uncle, the Haidarah Manuscript. It has been in our family for hundreds of years. As the eldest of my father, I'm entitled to it."

The sofa general turned to Zaiwulo.

"Is this true, Zaiwulo?"

"Haidarah has the Tareequ, Uncle Kemoko. Osman refuses to believe me. I have a letter from Haidarah to prove it."

"Why doubt him, Haidarah?"

"Because he's a liar."

"Don't ever insult Zaiwulo again, do you hear me?" the sofa general said. "Forget about that manuscript. Your future is here. You've convinced the English to sign a peace treaty with us. As a result, they now supply us with better weapons. You've become, despite your youth, one of our Faama's most trusted advisers. Now the French will be here today to sign a peace treaty with us. Those red ears have all been pacified and everything you ever dreamed of will become yours, with or without the manuscript. You will become greater than your father. If he were here today, he would be very proud of you."

Somnolent light filtered through the door and the chinks between the roof and house. In the hazy light, Kemoko-Bilali looked like a giant out of a dream. His head almost touched the thatched ceiling. "Come, the Faama has a surprise for you, Zaiwulo. People are saying that you alone defeated the French, and I believe them."

The sofa general looked around the room.

"Why are you staying here?" he asked. "Kemeh-Brimah told me that he tried convincing you to join him at the palace but you refused. You have to learn to live."

Zaiwulo washed and came out of the house in a white tunic which one of the city's inhabitants had presented him but which he had not cared to wear. He joined Osman and Kemoko-Bilali on their way to the square where the French would be received. People threw lofty greetings at Zaiwulo, which did not escape Kemoko-Bilali.

"They all admire you," the sofa general said.

Zaiwulo smiled.

"We've conquered all of Koniyan, including Musadu," Kemoko-Bilali told Zaiwulo. "Parts of the forests and large swathes of lands which once fell within the English sphere of influence now belong to us. Gbanguno Saaye is dead. He was betrayed by one of his wives, who turned out to be in love with our Faama. She was the one who pointed out the weak spots in the walls around Gbanguno Mountain. After days of pursuit, Saaye and our Faama stood facing each other in a plain as green as a cassava field. They fought each other for four months, four days and four nights, neither willing to cede ground to the other, but our Faama gained the upper hand. One of the greatest warriors the world has ever known has been brought down by an equally great warrior. Now the enemies of our Faama claim that at the spot where Gbanguno Saaye was slain, a spring as clear as daylight has sprouted. All nonsense, of course. The man is dead and buried."

Zaiwulo approached the throne.

When Samori saw him, he stood up. Behind his throne sat some members of his household and those of his allies in Kenyera. Samori extended a hand and a scarlet gown appeared out of nowhere. It was handed over by a valet who had made himself insignificant and invisible in the emperor's presence.

Samori threw the gown over Zaiwulo.

"You've become a father to a beautiful child. I named her Sianeh, after your mother. The mother Massah is in good health. I slaughtered seven cows for the occasion."

Zaiwulo was stunned. How could this have happened? He could not remember ever sleeping with Massah. Or was the dream he had had about her not a dream at all? He was not sure now. Haidarah must be the father, he thought, but Talata had been away for so long. Who then was the father of a child named after his mother? The thought that someone else had fathered a child bearing his mother's name hurt him so much that to contain his rage, he threw himself in Samori's arms, vowing to one day force the truth out of Massah.

Thousands had gathered in the square that had been built by knocking down homes. The crowd was in an anticipatory mood. Murmurs rose as the French riders came clad in their blue-and-red uniforms. Cylindrical shakos adorned their heads. They wore long boots, as if they were immune to the heat. Their swords were drawn, their rifles rested on the flanks of their horses. Each carried a pistol in an exquisite holster. They slowed down as they approached the crowd.

Some sofas on polished horses, in fresh tunics and with loaded rifles rode to receive the French delegation. They flanked them, bellowed war cries, and pranced around to exhibit their mastery of horses, but the faces of the envoys remained placid. As each envoy dismounted, a sofa darted forward, encircled him, and broke into a war cry.

The head envoy was a sturdy man with a mottled face. He dismounted and edged briskly forward. His name was Peroz. He did not kneel but bowed before the emperor, and then he turned to Jean. Through the interpreter Al-Kamesah, Zaiwulo understood that Peroz wanted to know how Jean had been treated. Jean answered that he'd become friends with Zaiwulo.

Indeed, during their journey back to Kenyera, Jean had begun to teach Zaiwulo some French and Zaiwulo had taught the Toubabou some Mandé.

Peroz gazed at Zaiwulo and nodded his appreciation. "We come as friends," he said. "Young Jean tells me that you treated him like a human being. He suggested this treaty."

Samori was keen not to reveal his emotion before these white men. They were never to know how he truly felt, and so, he turned to Morifin-Djan Diabate.

"We are proud of our men," the Djeli said.

"We've heard that the English are your allies. I must warn you that they are not people of their word. They are after your throne."

"We know the English as traders," Morifin-Djan said, and he turned to Osman who stood on the right side of the podium. "We've never had a cause to worry about them, but you fought us and are still fighting us."

"Yes, that's because you attacked Kenyera which falls under our sphere of influence. We warned you not to do so."

"We received no such warning," the Djeli shook his head. "All we wanted were the Kabbas who sought refuge in Kenyera."

"So you are not working with the English?"

"We are here talking to you. If we were interested in the English, we would have been talking to them right now. So let's talk about the future."

"We've heard that the English, including Queen Victoria, have expressed their clear wish to be your allies, and that the English newspapers are talking about you, especially after the last confrontation with us. They are saying you are heroes."

"Those are mere rumors. We've discussed nothing with the English. What they think of us is not our concern. Why should it be?"

"We came to offer you the possibility of working together, of being our friends. We will agree to confine ourselves to the left banks of the Niger if you agree to confine yourself to the right. That's why we are here."

Morifin-Djan turned to Samori. Both men had reached a point in their lives when such peace was needed. They were both old and exhausted, but most importantly, there were territories on the right of the Niger that could still be conquered. With those lands secured, no power, not even the French and English combined, could defeat them.

Samori nodded to Morifin-Djan.

"We will think this over," the Djeli said. "Stay here for a while, relish our hospitality. In the course of your stay, we will answer you."

"We are here not only to sign this treaty," Peroz said, "but we also want to invite your heir, the crown prince, to our land. It would be a great honor if he were to meet our president. Jean will accompany him to Saint-Louis, from where he will board a ship to France. We are doing all of this to prove our friendship and honesty in our dealings with you."

The crowd burst into jubilation, but Samori did not twitch a muscle.

"Our Faama accepts his son, Jawulen-Karamoko's, invitation to visit your country," Morifin-Djan said. "He's ready to sign a treaty of understanding with you."

The Djeli stood up and faced the crowd.

"Let it be known to all, including our ancestors, that whosoever breaks this agreement will be regarded as an enemy to humanity. We are all witnesses," he said.

That same day, the Treaty of Kenyeraba-Kora was signed.

Part Four

THE REVOLTS

1890

1

From the blue window of his room in Saint-Louis, Senegal, Zaiwulo could see and hear the birds in trees similar to the ones in Kankan, Musadu, and Haindi. This reminded him that he was at a crossroads between his world and the unknown. He had been in the city for more than two years now, but he remembered his arrival as if it were yesterday. He and Jawulen-Karamoko had been taken to see the governor, a bulky man who sweated in the spacious office of his mansion, his mottled hand trembling as he held it out to touch Zaiwulo's.

"You will like it here," he said several times through the interpreter. "Yes, we will make sure of that.'

That same day, they had taken a tour of the coastal city with some French officials including Jean and his father and the interpreter Al-Kamesah. They visited the French school, the barracks, the armory, and various other institutions. It turned out that the Toubabous had a huge supply of cannons, far more than the mere two which the sofas had captured. That, however, was not what bothered Zaiwulo as he and Jawulen-Karamoko left each morning to take their French lessons from Jean's father, whom the governor had instructed to teach them the language. Everywhere he turned, Zaiwulo was struck by the permanent presence of the Toubabous. They seemed at ease in his part of the world.

Zaiwulo left the window and went out of his room, crossing a long corridor to the outhouse, which was the bathroom. The birdsong followed him as if he was still in Musadu or somewhere in the forest. Tomorrow, Jawulen-Karamoko would leave for France.

Zaiwulo wished that he could accompany him, but from the onset, Samori had made it clear that Jawulen-Karamoko, the heir to the Wasulu Empire, would be the one to sail to France to meet its president.

"You will go with your brother to Saint-Louis and help prepare him for the journey," Samori had told him.

He had then addressed Jawulen-Karamoko. "Karamoko, my son, you will be our eyes and ears in that land."

The emperor had accompanied them on horseback to bid them farewell at the end of the first day, but one day became four days and then a week, as though he was loath to part with them. "Learn the language, and by all means, acquire the knowledge necessary to know the white people. If we do, they will cease to surprise us," he had said.

Samori had turned his horse around and with his retinue, headed back to Kenyera.

Jawulen-Karamoko would not cease to remind Zaiwulo of his father's words. One day, during their midday meal, he asked Zaiwulo. "What if I fail in that land?"

"You will not fail, elder brother."

They were sitting outside on the verandah of the large white-washed house with enough rooms for a dozen people, which the governor of Senegal, eager to impress the heirs of France's greatest adversary, had allocated to them. On the table before them were dishes of spicy fish, chicken, rice and couscous—Thieboudienne—Zaiwulo's favorite, which the Senegalese cook had prepared.

"According to Jean, the treaty still holds," Zaiwulo said. "But I wonder about the state of affairs in the rest of the empire. Is peace reigning everywhere?"

"The distance makes it impossible for us to know," Jawulen-Karamoko said. "You have to help me prepare for the task ahead, little brother."

"I wish I could go with you," Zaiwulo said.

"Next time, you will go in my stead."

The two were resolved to master the French language. Their instructor, Monsieur Durand, was a restless and impatient man. Tall and scrawny, with a weary look on his face, Monsieur Durand walked with a cane, perhaps more out of habit or an appreciation for a culture he'd brought over from France than his reliance on the stick. His house could have offered a breathtaking view of the sea were it not for the trees that surrounded it.

On that first day, he received the two young men on his verandah, with the singing sea in the background. The Frenchman immediately set to work.

"I want to teach you the fairest of languages," he said through the interpreter.

Both Jawulen-Karamoko and Zaiwulo laughed.

"Our languages are the fairest of languages," Zaiwulo said.

When Al-Kamesah conveyed their words, the Frenchman's face clouded with irritation, and he turned to his son Jean, who said: "You don't know their languages, Father."

Monsieur Durand shook his head and went on teaching them. "It's a lost cause," he said after a while. "You will never master our language. I thought Jean had prepared you well."

"Be patient with them, Father," Jean said.

The old Durand grumbled.

But when Zaiwulo and Jawulen-Karamoko returned the next day and repeated the lesson with confidence and gusto, Monsieur Durand changed his mind. "Now we can begin."

Whenever the lesson was over, Zaiwulo, Jean, and Al-Kamesah would take long walks along the city streets and the sandy beach. His face wet with sea salt, Zaiwulo would return home to an angry Jawulen-Karamoko.

"Have you forgotten that we are here to learn?" Samori's son would say, for he regarded the walks as a waste of time. "You are approaching this so lightheartedly."

"I'm learning, elder brother," Zaiwulo would answer.

"Is spending your time roaming the streets what you call learning? My father tasked us with the responsibility of understanding the Toubabous. Your approach is not the way."

"But I am here to support you, elder brother."

"Then, behave like it. The future of the empire rests on our shoulders. This is not child's play. We have to do more than our best."

Zaiwulo didn't know what to say.

•×•

Now the day was almost upon them. The cook had prepared Maafé served with rice as a farewell gesture. The seasoned fish was so well done that when Zaiwulo took his first bite, the taste reminded him of the fresh fish which his mother often prepared. Jawulen-Karamoko was not with him. He was away attending a meeting with the governor.

"I should go with you," Zaiwulo insisted, but Jawulen-Karamoko shook his head.

"The governor asked to see me, little brother."

"I don't want the Toubabous to get to us, elder brother," he said.

"What are you talking about? I'm doing my best to influence them. What do you think we've been doing all this time? We are here to protect the empire."

Zaiwulo stood up and held Jawulen-Karamoko by the shoulders, and it was as if he was standing before Samori, for the resemblance was so uncanny. It calmed him.

"Our father decided to send the two of us here," he said. "We make decisions together. When we move, we move together. The Toubabous should always see us together."

"You worry too much! Whatever I do, it's in the interest of the empire."

Zaiwulo had hoped, as he had watched him leave, that it would be over soon and that he would return to a world in which he was not plagued with so much uncertainty regarding the Toubabous. He longed to see Massah and to resolve the issue regarding the child named after his mother. He longed for his slates, for the time to jot down his feelings and thoughts. After his meal, he sat in the dark waiting for Jawulen-Karamoko.

When Samori's son returned, Zaiwulo could hear his voice from the street. The excitement in his voice was unmistakable. He was every bit his father as he strolled up the steps to the verandah, his steps measured and unhurried, a younger version of Samori, the heir to the empire.

"I will show the French how dignified we are, little brother," Jawulen-Karamoko said when he reached him. "They will see that I am the true son of our father."

It filled Zaiwulo's heart with pride to hear him say that, and all his fears that Jawulen-Karamoko was not up to the task, were dispelled.

"The moment I arrive in France, my only goal will be to meet its president Jules Grévy and ensure that we sign a permanent treaty with his government."

"Don't be intimidated by what you see over there, elder brother."

"Doyoumeanthewomen?"Jawulen-Karamokolaughed.

"I mean everything, elder brother," Zaiwulo said.

"I promised our father not to go near their women, although every part of me longs to do otherwise. Have you noticed how they look at us here?'

The two hardly slept a wink. They fantasized about life in France all night. The first light of dawn met them in the same room, with Jawulen-Karamoko sitting on a chair, while Zaiwulo, stretched out on the bed, went on advising him to remember who he was at every turn in France. "You are there to learn how to protect us."

"I will make you all proud, little brother,' he said Jawulen-Karamoko.

Samori's son left to take a cold shower and to prepare himself for the future. An hour later, Zaiwulo sat with him in the coach with a driver sent to fetch them.

In the distance, as they approached the harbor, Zaiwulo could see Équateur Paris, the ship which was to take Jawulen-Karamoko to France. When he stepped off the coach and walked closer to the ship, Zaiwulo was fascinated by the large vessel and the well-dressed passengers—most of them French—who were standing in line to board it.

Zaiwulo hugged Jawulen-Karamoko.

"I will be back before you know it, little brother," Jawulen-Karamoko said. "Then we will return home and become great rulers. The world will remember us."

Zaiwulo nodded. As he watched Samori's son walk up the gangplank and merge with the crowd of passengers, a pang of sadness crept over him. He was left alone in Saint-Louis with only Jean and his father as company.

2

Jean met Zaiwulo sitting on a gray rock.

His bare feet was in the water which ebbed and flowed around him. Zaiwulo had taken to frequenting this side of the beach, not far from Monsieur Durand's home. After his French lessons, which he pursued with a singular purpose, Zaiwulo would take walks along the narrow sandy path to the sea where he could feel the pebbles giving way to the touch of his bare feet. He had no need for sandals or for the boots the French had supplied him with. He would walk into the water until it reached his waist. Taking a deep breath, he would spread his arms as if to swim the vast expanse and join Samori's son, on the other side.

With time, Zaiwulo developed an affinity with the water that brought him to the same spot every day. He almost always had a book and a dictionary with him, flipping through the pages or watching the sunset, determined to learn every word.

"Father told me that I would find you here," Jean said.

Zaiwulo looked up. His French was now good enough that he could understand Jean. Once in a while, the Frenchman would come to see him or share a meal with him. Sometimes, the two strolled the muddy streets while Zaiwulo, unabashed and unafraid of failure, tried to communicate with him in French.

"Jean, do you have any news from France?" he asked.

"Your brother is on his way," Jean said.

Zaiwulo stood up. "That is good news."

He led the way back to Monsieur Durand's house with the intention of walking home. There, he would spend the evening at the table, learning. Jean followed him. The Frenchman had been helpful in many ways. He always encouraged Zaiwulo and never mocked his attempts to speak the language, but Zaiwulo could not grasp Jean. He seemed a bit aloof, as if their friendship was dictated by laws that were not clear to Zaiwulo.

"Your father has broken the treaty," Jean said.

Zaiwulo stopped. From where they were standing, he could see Monsieur Durand watering his garden. This piece of news hit Zaiwulo like a slap in the face. The treaty was everything to the Faama. Why would he breach it?

"I don't believe it," Zaiwulo said. "The emperor is a man of his word."

"We have evidence that he's not held to the agreement."

"I will write to the Faama."

"If the treaty fails, you know what that means."

"What does that mean?" Zaiwulo snapped.

"You should write to your father," Jean said, stepping back.

Zaiwulo did not respond but waved to Monsieur Durand, and he took another path to avoid further interaction with Jean and his father.

That night, Zaiwulo wrote a letter to Samori.

To the Faama of all Faamas, ruler of the greatest empire since Sundiata, light of our world. Peace be upon you.

Greetings from your humble servant. All is well here in this city along the sea. My brother has been away for a while, and I await his return any moment now.

I've managed to learn the language of the Toubabous, and in some of their books, I've begun to find my way but still with much difficulty. But I am determined to go on until I succeed.

A message has reached me that fills my heart with worry. The Toubabous accuse us of breaking the treaty. Tell me whether this is true or whether it is a mere rumor.

I await your reply with much impatience.

Your dedicated son,
Zaiwulo

When he was finished with the letter, Zaiwulo was not sure how long it would take to reach Samori or whether he would receive it at all. The distance was too much. Nevertheless, he entrusted the letter to a group of traders traveling through Kayes to Kankan, and he spent the days with his head in books, putting his hopes elsewhere, waiting for a reply.

It did not come.

One morning, Jean told Zaiwulo that a ship had arrived from France. Jawulen-Karamoko had returned. Zaiwulo left immediately to meet him.

Samori's son was accompanied by five men walking behind him and carrying his luggage. Instead of the long gown and shawl with which he had left, Jawulen-Karamoko had on a gray suit. The ash color of the clothes emphasized the darkness of his skin.

Samori's son hugged Zaiwulo. "We leave for Kenyera at once, little brother. I need to talk to our father," Jawulen-

Karamoko said. There was excitement in his voice and a playful smile.

"First, tell me all about France," Zaiwulo said.

"I signed a treaty with the French government, a treaty much better than the one we signed at Kenyeraba Kora. The French president Jules Grévy, his ministers, and other officials, including the generals, were present at the ceremony. The Toubabous welcomed me like a true Faama!"

Jean and his father, together with other French officials, had also come to receive Jawulen-Karamoko. Zaiwulo noticed that Samori's son would keep turning to the men who carried his luggage, not sure of their intention.

"Those are the presents I brought," he said. "Some are for you, and some are for our father. I brought you one of the best pistols in the world and a good rifle."

Jean and his father had arranged for a coach which took them to the house which the two had once shared. On their way, Jawulen-Karamoko said, "I'm sure you want to know about the women." He nudged Zaiwulo. "Well, I met many. Some were very beautiful, some less so. They were all fascinating, but not very different from our women here. Don't worry, little brother, I kept my promise to our father, despite my inclinations."

"The French say we broke the treaty," Zaiwulo said. "I wrote the Faama about it."

Jawulen-Karamoko's face clouded with anger. "Father didn't do that." He was disappointed.

"I don't believe he did."

Jawulen-Karamoko was silent. "In that case, we leave tomorrow. I need to talk to Father."

For the rest of the drive, Samori's son was silent. The enthusiasm with which he had greeted Zaiwulo was replaced by a solemn look that did not leave his face even during the long journey back home. Jawulen-Karamoko seemed troubled beyond words.

On the day of their departure, Jawulen-Karamoko promised the governor of Senegal that he would make sure the emperor abided by the treaty signed in France. The French supplied them with horses. Jean and his father presented Zaiwulo with more than a dozen books, including the ones he had read during his stay.

"I hope to see you soon again, Zaiwulo," Jean said.

Zaiwulo nodded. "Thanks for the books. You are a true friend."

"You will hear from us soon," Jawulen-Karamoko said.

It was raining when the two left, accompanied by carriers hired by the French. Samori's son was wearing a French uniform, despite Zaiwulo's objections.

"Father will not mind. We are allies of France."

3

Zaiwulo and Jawulen-Karamoko were sitting, having their midday meals in an enclosure of the palace in Kenyera. Before them sat bowls of food. The sun was so fierce that not even the shade of the tree under which they sat could offer them solace. Zaiwulo had insisted that the food be seasoned with pepper of the spiciest kind. He and Jawulen-Karamoko dug into the food with their hands, their faces sweating, noses dripping.

Samori was not in Kenyera to receive them because he was embroiled in a war with Tieba of the city of Sikasso, a rival he originally thought he could pacify with a simple gesture of friendship. But his efforts had failed.

Zaiwulo and Jawulen-Karamoko washed their hands after the heavy meal and picked their teeth. Their eyes were becoming heavy when one of the palace guards rushed in with a message. "Faamas, a large crowd has gathered outside, and they are calling for you," the man said.

Zaiwulo and Jawulen-Karamoko came out and met an angry crowd.

"What has happened?" Zaiwulo asked.

A man answered that a local scholar and a sofa commander were holding more than ten men prisoners hostage and were about to cut off their hands for stealing millet. For more than three years now, the man said, hundreds of hands had been amputated. These men were punished for merely speaking to women who were not their spouses, and people were stoned to death for committing adultery.

The crowd led Zaiwulo and Jawulen-Karamoko to a square where a young scholar was reading out the charges. The prisoners' hands and feet had been tied up and they were lying bundled up on the ground, like cattle. Flies fed on the wounds sustained in prison. One of the prisoners had already been decapitated and his head stood on a pike.

"The hands which stole that which did not belong to them will be snatched off, for theft is a serious crime," the young scholar said, and no one dared contradict him. The scholar looked up and saw Jawulen-Karamoko and Zaiwulo. "Welcome, Faamas," he said. "Witness justice being meted out to people who rightly deserve it."

"Who are these people?" Zaiwulo asked.

"Thieves and adulterers, Faama."

"Do you know their names?" Jawulen-Karamoko asked.

"Their names, Faama? What does it matter?"

"Not only their names but their stations in life, their past, and how the theft or adultery was committed. What do you know of these things? The facts—tell me."

"Faama, these things don't matter. What matters is that they've broken the law."

"How can you exert the same punishment on everyone without knowing the real reasons for the offense?"

"The divine law is sacred, Faamas. I'm only an instrument that implements it."

"Until you tell me who those people are, their names, their occupations, the circumstances of their crimes, and the testimony of the witnesses, I say release them. I mean now," Jawulen-Karamoko said.

"You are the son of our Faama, I'm very much aware of that. But your father appointed me the judge in this part of the empire. He alone can tell me to stop."

"You will regret it if you don't release them."

"With what can you possibly threaten me? With torture? With death? Do you know that if I were to die today, heaven awaits me? A place where rivers of milk and honey flow, where fruit-laden branches bow at my behest, where virgins of all colors answer to me, virgins as white as milk, and as dark as the night? That's the place that awaits me, Faama."

Jawulen-Karamoko reached for his pistol and shot the scholar.

"No hands will be cut off again and no one will be stoned to death without any form of process," Jawulen-Karamoko told the crowd. "No one."

The jubilant crowd rushed to him, but Jawulen-Karamoko shoved them aside. He wanted to be alone with Zaiwulo. He instructed that the dead be buried, and the accused be offered a fair trial. After a thorough process, they were to be punished according to the old jurisdiction, if found guilty.

Jawulen-Karamoko sucked his teeth. "How could our father allow such cruelties to take place in his name? Has he lost complete control of the empire?"

They returned to the palace.

"There may be more to this than we think," Zaiwulo said. "I suggest we wait for the Faama to receive us. I will not hesitate to confront him with these questions. What bothers me most is that Karamo-Sidikie, my teacher's brother, could tolerate such things."

"I think it has to do with these so-called scholars who make laws that have nothing to do with our realities. They are silencing those moderate scholars who are calling for common sense. Even Karamo-Sidikie, even my father, can be influenced by them. It's pure insanity, little brother."

"I wonder how they treat the nonbelievers," Zaiwulo said.

"It's all about power. And power corrupts. Even my brother-in-law Karamo-Sidikie is not an exception. He can be corrupted. He is but human."

What would happen, Zaiwulo wondered, if it became known that the woman he claimed to be his wife was his teacher's? What would happen to Massah or to him? What would happen to the child? The only one who could answer those questions but whom Zaiwulo did not dare ask was Morifin-Djan Diabate. The Djeli had arrived from Sikasso where Samori was still waging war. He was accompanied by fifty sofas and his personal guards.

4

Morifin-Djan Diabate seemed hesitant in his every gesture. The Djeli was restless. This was the man who once exuded great self-confidence, serenity, and who was regarded by many as the wisest man in the empire. Seated across him on the mat in the main courtyard, Zaiwulo wondered what had transpired during the years to have brought about such a profound change.

Jawulen-Karamoko joined them in his French outfit.

The Djeli sucked his teeth. "Get rid of those clothes," he hissed. "That you would dare wear such filth in my presence is a grave insult to me."

Samori's son was stunned, but he bowed, left, and returned in a tunic. Without revealing his feelings, he took his place beside Zaiwulo.

"Tell me everything about the French," the Djeli said.

Jawulen-Karamoko burst into a stream of words, as if all the impressions, all the feelings he had stored up as he waited to see his father were eager to come out at once.

"You are behaving like a child," Morifin-Djan interrupted him. "Calm down and start again."

Jawulen-Karamoko swallowed hard. "They are invincible, Uncle!" he said. "They have weapons more powerful than the ones they used against us during the War of Woyowayanko. Their army is the most disciplined in the world. They are in their thousands. Their cities are so clean you would hesitate to walk on the street. They don't know nights, for their streets are lit at night. Their president resides in a palace twice the size of our Faama's. The French—"

Morifin-Djan jumped up as if bitten by a snake. "Were you instructed by those red ears to say this? I believe you were, for if you had listened to yourself, you would have noticed how ridiculous you sounded."

He turned to Zaiwulo. "You are the clever one. It was my mistake to have chosen this fool to go to France instead of you. Tell me what you saw in Saint-Louis."

Zaiwulo told Morifin-Djan about life in Saint-Louis, Senegal, which he believed was the same in France. "Uncle, in Saint-Louis, I learned that besides the French, other Toubabous like the Portuguese, the Germans, the Spanish, and the English were planning to divide the lands of the Black-skinned people amongst themselves. To stop them, we have to make sure that the treaties we signed hold. Or show them what we are capable of."

Morifin-Djan shook his head. "The French have violated the treaty, child. While we were fighting Tieba in Sikasso, they were supplying him with weapons."

"So they were lying to us," Zaiwulo said.

"Karamoko, son of Jawulen," the Djeli said. "I was the one who chose your mother for your father. I saw her for the first time washing clothes at a river near the village of my birth. In that little girl, I recognized the woman she would later become, an ideal partner for a Faama. Only one man besides me deserved such a treasure, a man I still regard as my other half, as my blood twin brother, no, as more than a brother, as my best friend. Out of that union, you were born. I, not your father, was the first to hold you. I whisper my prayers and hopes in your ears. Over the years, I've made sure you remained in your father's favor. I've fought Sarankenyi, who has plans for her son. Now, you've disappointed me. What am I to make of this?" Morifin-Djan left the enclosure.

"You should have told me this about the French, elder brother," Zaiwulo said.

"You would have stopped me from telling uncle Morifin-Djan or our father. They have to know the truth, little brother. We need the Toubabous for our empire to survive."

Zaiwulo could not believe his ears. "I warned you against this, elder brother. Don't let them get to you. You went to France to learn how to defeat the Toubabous not to be persuaded by them."

Jawulen-Karamoko shook his head.

Morifin-Djan Diabate returned. "Here's what we will do," he said. "You two will tell no one else about what you saw over there. I will do all the talking. No one is to know what you think of the Toubabous. If you disobey my order, you will cease to exist to me."

That same night, the Djeli woke Zaiwulo. "Get dressed and follow me."

Morifin-Djan had returned with Zaiwulo's horse Sundiata. Zaiwulo's union with the horse was the one positive event that made it possible for Zaiwulo to endure the Djeli's long silence. They rode all night. Dawn met them at the outskirts of a small village, far away from Kenyera.

"For more than two years, we've been fighting Tieba, the king of Kenedougou," the Djeli finally said. "He has confined himself within walls his enemies and subjects call the Tata, the unbreakable. But our Faama is determined to defeat him. Tieba is being aided by the French. More than the desire for conquest, this betrayal hurts our Faama so much that he is determined to fight on, despite the odds against him. Meanwhile, scholars who were once of no consequence have now taken over the empire for which we sofas fought so hard. Many are harsh in their interpretation of the laws. It has resulted in people revolting against us, against the Wasulu Empire."

In the first light of dawn, Zaiwulo noted that the folds around the Djeli's eyes were more pronounced. He was getting old.

"Your secret has been revealed, child," the Djeli said. "In Kankan, the scholars have spoken hard against your relationship with Massah. At first, I was angry until the girl told me her story. She told me that the marriage between her and Haidarah was never consummated and that she did not want the scholar, who also had no desire to have her. But you are a wanted person in the empire. Some people are even intent on killing you. Your friend Kemoko-Bilali and I decided to intervene. We brought the girl and the child to this village. Go with her to the forest, and don't ever return to this part of the world."

Zaiwulo could not believe his ears. Who were the people who wanted him dead?

"Does the Faama know about this?"

"No, he's busy with the war. But sooner or later, he will."

"And my teacher, Haidarah?"

"We've done everything to track down your teacher in the forest, but he's not in most of the known cities and villages. I'm afraid that your teacher wants to be left alone. Scholars do that sometimes. He doesn't want to be found," Morifin-Djan said.

"On which side does Karamo-Sidikie stand?" Zaiwulo said.

"He's but one scholar among thousands. We who were there to support him are fighting Tieba. Go to the forest. It's safe there."

The Djeli turned his horse around and rode off. Zaiwulo rode his horse into the village to meet Massah and the child. On dismounting, he stumbled, as if he'd lost the ability to walk.

5

The child was chasing a goat in an alley between two houses. The animal was heading toward Zaiwulo. The goat had probably stuck its muzzle into a mortar, he thought, for its mouth was full of cassava meal and its neck and parts of its flanks were white with flour. The goat darted past Zaiwulo, but the child stopped to glance at him. She looked like a bird, he thought, a butterfly actually, adorning the ochre earth. Her finely plaited hair was unbecoming of her, for it made her look older. Smiling, Zaiwulo knelt before her, his arms spread wide to receive her, and then, he heard Massah calling her. "Sianeh, Sianeh, where are you?"

Massah let out a cry when she saw him. She rushed forward but stopped halfway, as if she did not trust what she was seeing, as if it was not true. "When did you arrive?"

"Just now," he said.

The child joined her mother who drew her closer, as if she needed her daughter's proximity to be able to bear his presence. "You must be hungry. I was just about to prepare some breakfast," she said.

He followed her and tethered Sundiata to a tree behind the house. The house was dilapidated, miserable, too small for mother and daughter. Beside the house, Massah had cultivated a garden. She had been in that village much longer than he thought.

The child hid whenever Zaiwulo tried to glance her way.

"Where do you keep the cutlass?" he asked Massah.

She looked concerned. "The breakfast is almost done, wait until after you've had some food," she said, as if she had guessed his intentions.

Zaiwulo was adamant. When Massah fetched the cutlass, Zaiwulo hurried to the outskirts of the village. He gathered some grass, cut down some slender trees, and lopped off the branches. He bundled them all up with ropes from trees and carried them on his head to the house.

"Your breakfast is almost cold!" Massah said.

Zaiwulo ignored her and fetched water from a nearby well. Gathering a heap of dirt, he used his feet to mix the mud and grass. "I am going to break down parts of the wall of the house and build a bigger home for you and the child," he said.

He went on clearing the house of their meager belongings.

"You must eat, Zaiwulo, please!"

"I cannot bear seeing you living like this."

Massah burst into tears. "They came after us in Kankan," she said. "Were it not for sister Sarankenyi who hid us in the palace, we would have been killed. No one believed me when I said that Haidarah and I were never husband and wife. Your friend Kemoko-Bilali and the scholar Karamo-Sidikie rescued us. Why has the Faama not put a stop to this madness, Zaiwulo? Or is he part of it?"

"How long has this been going on?"

"For more than three years," she said. "People live in constant fear. Even sister Sarankenyi does not dare say what she thinks. There are spies everywhere, ready to report anyone who breaks the law. People are beaten for the slightest accusation, even stoned to death. When Karamo-

Sidikie intervened, they accused him of sympathizing with the nonbelievers."

"We will stay here until the madness blows over. If not, I will take you to the forest."

That night, Zaiwulo slept on the ground of the extension. From there, he could hear Massah's heavy breathing. "Zaiwulo!" her voice implored him.

Every fiber in his body craved her, but he held himself. He was up before Massah, and he fetched water from the nearby well. He was bathing when she woke up.

"You are bathing with cold water," she said.

"Yes, I didn't want to wake you up."

"Tell me about those white women. I was afraid that you would wed one of them and return here with her."

"I went to Saint-Louis where some Toubabous live, not to their land, Massah. I didn't have time for women. I was there to study and to make peace."

"So you are a Toubabous now."

"I'm not a Toubabous, but I admire their scholars. One of them reminded me of Haidarah. He said, *I think, therefore I am* which is more or less what Haidarah wrote in one of his early poems: *If you had not created the world, beloved, then our thoughts and our will would have done so according to our likeness. Therein lies mankind's greatness.* They are talking about the same thing, Massah, do you understand?"

Massah nodded. Haidarah's name cast a somber spell on the two, but a laughing Sianeh broke it as she came running toward her mother.

"Use the hot water for the child," Zaiwulo said.

"Her name is Sianeh." Massah expected Zaiwulo to broach the subject of the child, to confront her with their common past, but all he did was nod with uncertainty.

"I will be heading to the village to introduce myself. People have to know that I am here and that you are here with me," he said.

"They know about us," she said. "I told them you would come when the time was right. And you are here. They don't know about Haidarah."

They agreed to tell the village elders that the war between Samori and the Toubabous had led them to flee their homes.

When Zaiwulo presented himself at the village, an elder asked, "Why are the Toubabous fighting our Faama?"

"Because of land," Zaiwulo answered.

"But the Toubabous have their own land, right?"

"Clearly, it's not enough for them."

Sometimes, he would ride out with Sundiata. As the two of them covered long distances, he noticed that the horse had changed. Gone was its rebellious spirit. Meanwhile, Massah busied herself with plucking cassava or leaves in the garden. Sometimes, she planted new seeds. He would return and meet her at work.

One day, Zaiwulo recognized his mother in Sianeh's face. The resemblance unsettled him. He could not sleep that night. He rode out at dawn intending to never return. Was it possible that Sianeh was his daughter if he had not shared a bed with Massah? He thought of running away. He could escape deep into the forest, far away from it all, like his teacher had done. But at a certain point, struck by the longing for his mother and the child with her eyes, he saw himself turning around and racing back to Massah.

He belonged to them.

"Is Sianeh my daughter?" he asked.

"Stop it, Zaiwulo, stop it, now."

"But we were never together, Massah!"

"What about that night in Musadu when I came to you?"

He remembered the dream. It was not a dream.

"Now you are beginning to see, Faama Zaiwulo. We are not going anywhere without you. Do you hear me?"

"What we did was shameful, Massah!"

Though he was angry with her, Zaiwulo realized that being with her had been his deepest longing, the one thing he had desired since he first saw her, even while the blind man had been alive. If there was anyone who was at fault, he was the one. He had encouraged her.

"Yes, longing for your teacher's wife is a shameful act! You chose the wrong woman, Zaiwulo. This act will haunt you until your last days. You wanted to have some fun, well, you had it, Faama! Now comes the responsibility. My advice to you is to flee with me and your daughter to a safe place before you are caught and decapitated by those mad scholars."

Massah was right. There was no safe place for them in the Samorian empire. He would have to take them to a place where he would have a future with them, a place where he would teach his daughter the knowledge he had acquired, a place where they could be free: Haindi.

He would take them to his mother and sisters.

6

Zaiwulo learned that the only route to the forest which did not pass through Kankan or Koniyan was the one that went through distant Kong and other places he'd never heard of before. He was reluctant to take that route. He worried that the people in those parts might be hostile to him and his family or refuse them passage altogether. The safest option was to travel through Kankan and the cities in Koniyan. It was the heart of the madness.

A few days before their departure, Jawulen-Karamoko came riding to see them. He met Zaiwulo splitting firewood with an ax. "So you've been hiding out here with your wife and daughter?"

Samori's son greeted Massah. She was weaving baskets to sell at the local market. Jawulen-Karamoko dismounted, took a seat on the mat beside her. "Did he tell you about those white women, sister Massah?" he teased her. "One of them vowed to marry and accompany him."

But Massah did not take kindly to the teasing. "So that's what he's been hiding from me," she said. "I knew something must have happened over there."

Jawulen-Karamoko poured more oil on the fire.

"Yes, I had to remind him that you were waiting for him. The white women wouldn't let him be. I don't know what they saw in him. Perhaps it was because he spoke their language so fluently and talked about their scholars with great ease."

"There was no woman for me over there, Massah," Zaiwulo said.

"Go on denying it. How about that red-haired girl Sophie? Massah, she was our mentor, Monsieur Durand's daughter!" Jawulen-Karamoko was laughing now.

"The mentor did not have a daughter—only a son, Jean."

Jawulen-Karamoko scratched his head. "I see that you people are not in the mood for jokes. I give up, sister Massah," he said. "I must admit that I loved their women. I would walk the streets of Paris in my best clothes, ignoring offensive remarks from people who did not take to the color of my skin. I miss Paris, the opera, the grand receptions. Those Toubabous even delayed a whole show after I'd fallen ill, all in an effort to impress me. Over there, I was the true heir to my father! Over there I felt like a Faama of all Faamas."

"Why did you return then?" Massah said.

"I returned to free us from laws that forced you and my brother to hide out here in such a remote place. Why force a person to wed someone like we do here?"

Jawulen-Karamoko took Zaiwulo to the rear of the house where they sat beneath the shade of a tree. There, he confided in Zaiwulo. "Father is after me, little brother," he said. "His generals say they intercepted a letter to me from the French. In the letter, the French promised to make me emperor if I betrayed my father. They also accused me of inviting the French into the empire."

"Did you invite the French, elder brother?"

"No, I didn't. What if I did? In the eyes of many, I'm already a condemned man. My father is directing his frustrations at failing to defeat Tieba at me." Wringing his hands, Jawulen-Karamoko stood up. "I believe that the French are serious when they say that they will leave our father alone if he accepts their protection."

"But they are supplying Tieba with weapons."

"'Mere rumors. The fact is Tieba built impregnable walls. Our father thought he was invincible. Our Uncle Kemeh-Brimah, one of the best sofas in the empire, a man who never wavered before a challenge of whatever kind, fell in Sikasso."

"Uncle Kemeh-Brimah, the great sofa?" Zaiwulo fought to suppress his tears.

"They say Uncle Kemeh-Brimah managed, by some miracle, to break through the walls of Sikasso with a group of his personal army. He survived the rain of bullets, arrows, and spears pouring down on him and his men. They say that he even cut through the defenses within the walls. But in the end, face to face with the dreaded Tieba and his army, our uncle met his end. Yet our father continues to fight undeterred."

"Someone should talk to him," Zaiwulo said, throwing his hands in the air.

"He's ceased to listen to anyone. He lives in his own world," Jawulen-Karamoko said.

Zaiwulo heaved a weary sigh and stood up. "We were about to leave for the forest in a few days. If you want, you can go with us to my birthplace."

"I will go with you, little brother."

They shared the meal Massah had prepared. Later, they retired to the extension Zaiwulo had built for Massah and his daughter. The two went on talking for most of the night, with Jawulen-Karamoko expressing his wish to one day succeed his father and bring about the changes that were necessary for the survival of the empire.

"The harsh winter in France made me appreciate the beauty of our world," Jawulen-Karamoko said. "Over there, I became acutely aware of the transience of beauty and of the relativity of existence. Being over there made me long for the grass of the savannah, for the voices of our people. I learned to appreciate us more than ever before."

As Zaiwulo shared stories of his struggles with the French language in Saint-Louis and Samori's son voiced his various adventures in Paris, they were so taken by the power of their recollections that they did not hear hoofbeats until it was too late.

7

"Zaiwulo, come out and tell me what you really learned from the Toubabous," Samori's voice sounded through the night. "Since your return, your brother, who I know is with you, has done nothing else but spout nonsense. Come out and tell me everything."

Zaiwulo reached for his pistol, ready to fight to protect his family. But Jawulen-Karamoko said, "Don't, little brother, they are not here for you but for me."

The two walked out of the house. There were a few hundred sofas with torches spread out across the village like fireflies. A group of them fell on Jawulen-Karamoko like famished hyenas and vanished with him into the night.

"I want nothing to do with him," Samori said. "In Kankan, he will stand trial for his deeds."

Samori dismounted. "Son of the forest, you warned me about this madness which had been unleashed in my absence by people in whom I put my trust."

Samori moved toward Zaiwulo. "Come here, son," he said. "Tell Soko Kenneh's daughter to come out with your child. I mean you no harm. No one will do you any harm."

Though their embrace was tight, it was deprived of the warmth he had often, and perhaps mistakenly, associated with Samori. Or perhaps the Faama was simply troubled.

"We will not spend the night here," he said.

Zaiwulo helped Massah bundle up their belongings and get Sianeh ready.

The three of them sat on his horse and rode in a darkness through which flames from torches flashed like lightning. Every time Zaiwulo drew level with the emperor, he could feel the man's unease. A deeper issue than that of his son Jawulen-Karamoko or the experience in Sikasso bothered him. Zaiwulo didn't have to wait for long to find out what it was.

"I always thought that the scholars deserved our veneration because they were educated," Samori said. "But I was wrong. Instead of love, they preached hate. By listening to them, I committed some terrible deeds. One of them described hell to me with such vividness that I allowed two of my daughters to be stoned to death because they were supposed to have committed adultery. Yes, that's how deep I sank—I admit to my shame."

Samori was silent for so long that Zaiwulo thought he was about to succumb to the weight of his conscience. "I will never allow it again, never," he said.

"Where is my teacher?" Zaiwulo said.

"Somewhere in the forest. It's obvious that Haidarah doesn't want to work with me. I've done everything to get him here but in vain."

"What about Musadu?"

"Our alliance with the rulers of Musadu remains intact. I made sure that your teacher's manuscripts were transferred to Kankan."

Zaiwulo wanted to inquire about Osman, but he was not sure how Samori would react. So instead, he asked about the English.

"I sent Osman to England to sign a new treaty with the English. I don't know why he has taken so long to return.

The English are not playing straight with me, Zaiwulo. They are fighting me while pretending to be my friends at the same time. If you were not needed here, I would have sent you to Freetown."

If the English refused to work with the empire, Zaiwulo thought, where would Samori get better weapons? From Liberia perhaps?

After weeks on the road, the Samorian entourage arrived at the main gate of Kankan. The crowd that came out to receive them was much larger than the one that had gathered after the conquest of the city.

"The people have not abandoned me after all, Zaiwulo," Samori said.

Soon, he would discover how wrong he was.

•×•

Samori had always been aware of the fragility of his empire. Its cultures and people were so diverse. He had known that implementing uniform laws amongst animists who were the most loyal of his subjects would prove difficult, for they ascribed to different beliefs and traditions. He had directed the lawmakers to consider these people when interpreting the laws. But while Samori had been away fighting Tieba, animists were being forced to attend the mosque or risk being publicly tried, whipped, or killed. The laws with which successful empires had been governed—renowned empires such as those of Sundiata Keita, Mansa Kankou Musa, and Askia the Great—had, under his leadership, resulted in suppression and chaos.

Sarankenyi fell on the ground at the sight of her husband. She had not seen him in years. She was trembling as Samori dismounted, and he gathered her up in his arms.

"Is that you, beloved? Kabako—a wonder!" she said. "We were told that you and your brother were killed by Tieba of Sikasso, but you are alive!"

Only then did it dawn on Samori that the people of Kankan had come out in such large numbers not because they were enamored of him but to satisfy their curiosity, to see whether he was really alive. Rumors of his death must have triggered the insurrections, he thought.

Samori retired to his chambers. Sarankenyi had decorated it according to his taste. She laid out fresh, starched black and white tunics and bulbous trousers. In one corner was a jar of water from the best well in Kankan and a bowl of kola nuts from the forest. At the head of the bed were flasks of musk and other scents that her traders had purchased from Kano. When they were alone, she caressed his weary-looking face. Never before had she seen him more troubled, more absent in her presence.

Sarankenyi spread herself under him, ready to receive him, but Samori did not move. "Where are you, my Faama, my beloved!"

She accepted him as he was, as she had always accepted him, but this time, with a tenderness that crawled over him like shame. He could not stand it. He picked himself up and fled the chambers. Sarankenyi followed him. The silence in the courtyards hung heavy as if sensing the futility of his hopes and unfulfilled dreams of expanding his empire beyond those of Sundiata Keita and Alexander the Great. Samori fell to his knees and kissed the earth. Then, with a dagger in one hand, its sharp edge held tightly in the other, he pulled until blood trickled down and merged with the earth.

"With this blood," he said, "I vow to protect all those people who have sworn allegiance to the Wasulu Empire." Samori turned to Sarankenyi. "Send for your son."

Sarankenyi hurried away and returned with Sarankenyi-Mori.

"You've grown, son!' Samori said. "You've grown! How far have you gone with your education? Can you read and write now?"

Sarankenyi-Mori nodded.

"What about your command of horses?"

"I am one of the best horsemen in Kankan, Faama. I can shoot an arrow or hit a target with a rifle at full gallop," the boy said in a steady voice. "I've trained hard, Father."

"Show me then, Mori, son of Sarankenyi!"

Sarankenyi-Mori followed his father out of the enclosure and to the large square before the palace where a crowd, which still did not believe that Samori was alive, had gathered. Some sofas, including the Djeli Morifin-Djan Diabate, surrounded Samori. They all seemed concerned.

"What is it, my friend?" the Djeli whispered, leading his friend away from the crowd and other courtiers, afraid someone might overhear them.

"I've decided to do what's necessary," Samori answered.

"It's too soon. The child is not yet ready. Think about the people."

"I am not doing this because of him, Morifin-Djan. He will not be given power, but it must be made clear to all, including the Toubabous, that we are determined and resolved to fight on, that our empire will live on long after we've gone."

"What about your other wives? What about Jawulen-Karamoko?"

"I want to know first whether it is true that he conspired with the French. You know the loss we suffered in Sikasso. Thousands of our sofas fell during the siege because the French armed Tieba. You've seen the letter, my friend. Was his name not mentioned in the letter? Moreover, his behavior only seems to confirm our suspicions. I will wait until you've spoken to him. I will also ask Zaiwulo to speak to him. If he explains the letter, then I won't need to do what is expected of me."

Samori instructed the sofas to set up a target. Sarankenyi-Mori mounted his horse and rode across the square. His horse gathered speed as he approached the target. When he was so close that everyone thought he had passed the target, Sarankenyi-Mori took a shot that split the target in two.

"You did well, Mori," Samori said. "This proves that you are ready to become a sofa. From now on, you'll be your brother Zaiwulo's right-hand man. Learn from him. Observe what he does."

8

After he had taken his family to the Haidarah compound in Kankan, Zaiwulo joined Samori. He met the emperor sitting on a carpet under the shade of a tree. He was trying without success to radiate calmness. Samori was fretful, his eyes a contradiction of anger and bewilderment. Before Zaiwulo could take a seat, Samori said, "Talk to your brother. He refuses to disclose the nature of his relationship with the French. We have to know."

Samori handed him the letter which the French were supposed to have written to Jawulen-Karamoko. Zaiwulo saw that the letter was indeed addressed to Samori's son. The emperor then listed a series of charges against Jawulen-Karamoko, the steps he was believed to have taken to bring down the empire.

"He has to tell us what he knows," Samori said.

Jawulen-Karamoko was held within a tall, oblong wall with a tiny wedge at eye level, through which he could see and receive food. The space was so narrow that he could hardly sit or stretch his arms and legs. "I've been kept here for so long that I've ceased to count the days," he told Zaiwulo. "What is pain if you choose to ignore it? What is death if its inevitability ceases to worry you? I'm ready, little brother."

Zaiwulo could see only his face. A fine layer of dust had collected on Jawulen-Karamoko's nose, around his eyes, and especially on his lashes.

"Father sent me," Zaiwulo said.

"I should have stayed in Paris and gone to one of its centers of learning."

"Father wants you to know that it pains him to see you suffer. But even as we speak, Porokerrie is fighting the French. And the English, who claim to be in an alliance with us, seem to have changed their minds. They are fighting Uncle Kemoko-Bilali in the West. The Toubabous are all bent on destroying us."

"They want to conquer the most powerful empire in Africa. Then the rest will follow. That's their strategy, little brother."

"Yet you support the French."

"I don't support them. I'm being realistic," Jawulen-Karamoko said. "They have weapons that we don't have. If our empire was equipped with half of what they have, then no one, not even all the whites combined, would have stood in our way."

"And the letter then? It's directed to you."

"What would it matter if I were to tell you that the French didn't reach out to me or if I were to confess that they did? To me, it doesn't matter."

"Yes, it does matter, elder brother. The truth will spare you the fate that awaits all traitors. Tell me the truth."

"But I am already a traitor in the eyes of the empire."

"You are also charged with planning to defect to the French with thousands of our sofas. Those men trusted you, elder brother. Why?"

"There was no talk of defection. That's the truth. I wanted to negotiate with the French on our Father's behalf—on *our* behalf."

"So you did indeed cooperate with the French? You did take the initiative? Do you know what their plans are?" Zaiwulo cried.

"'Their plans? Nothing I say right now will make any difference. I heard that Father has already replaced me with a child."

"Elder brother, please tell me!"

Jawulen-Karamoko smiled. "I will miss the memories of our time in Saint-Louis and of my life in France. I will miss memories of our efforts to master French and the books we believed would bare the soul of the Toubabous to us. But most of all, I will miss your stories, young brother. Promise me that one day you will tell the world that what I did was out of love for our father, out of love for us, that I tried to save our empire."

However much Zaiwulo tried, Jawulen-Karamoko refused to say another word. Zaiwulo left and met Samori seated shoulder-to-shoulder with his friend Morifin-Djan, their backs leaning against the clay wall.

"So you failed to persuade him, Zaiwulo," the Djeli said. "That means that the Toubabous have gotten to him."

"That's what happens when one cares too much for a child. He begins to think he's like you and possesses the same power as yours," Samori said. "He begins to crave that power."

"I still cannot believe that he would betray us," Morifin-Djan said.

"You must talk to him, Morifin-Djan. He's yours as much as he's mine. Betrayal means death. We have to know what the French are planning against us. If he tells us the truth he will remain my heir."

The Djeli left but also returned empty-handed.

Samori decided to give it one more try. This time he was accompanied by his daughter Jawulen-N'nagbe, Jawulen-Karamoko's sister, the wife of the scholar Karamo-Sidikie.

She knelt before her brother.

"Ijo, ijo, Nkuro—please, please, elder brother, tell us what you planned with those white people. Don't let Wasulu fall."

"Listen to your sister, Karamoko," Samori hissed.

Jawulen-Karamoko remained silent.

"Leave us alone," Samori said, avoiding his daughter's eyes.

She threw herself on the ground before him.

"Please spare him—nfa—Father. He's foolish."

"You should talk to him, not to me, daughter of Jawulen. Ask him to tell us the truth. He has to tell us the truth. He must tell us what he knows."

Jawulen-N'nagbe pulled at the wall behind which her brother was imprisoned, but Jawulen-Karamoko did not react. He seemed to have retreated into his own world. She tore at her face, threatening to no longer regard him as a brother. "You've caused us sleepless nights. You've filled our hearts with grief, elder brother. Look at me. Tell us what you know."

Jawulen-Karamoko did not flinch. In the end, Jawulen-N'nagbe left, screaming that her brother was a traitor.

"Zaiwulo, go home to your family," Samori said.

The emperor approached the wall.

"I've asked that you be given enough food," he said. "The wall can be damp at night, so I brought you some blankets. If you need to pass water, or to rest outside the walls, just ask the guards. They will let you out. You don't have to suffer. Just tell us what you discussed with the French."

Jawulen-Karamoko remained silent.

As the hours wore on, Samori's tone changed. He couldn't afford to be the laughingstock of the empire. The mere thought of his own blood going against his wishes and collaborating with his enemies enraged and paralyzed him. My son, he thought. My own flesh and blood!

The day dragged on. Every passing moment felt like an eternity to the emperor, testing his patience to such an extreme that he burst into imprecations of every kind, into pleas that made his heart ache.

"If you remain stubborn," he shouted, "I will let you rot away inside that wall!"

9

The dust that rose to meet Zaiwulo smelled of pounded dry pepper. He sneezed. The city should have been built on a hill, he thought, not on such a flat surface that exposed it to the elements.

Night was falling on Kankan and on his way out of the palace, Zaiwulo saw a spot of flame moving in his direction. It was Sarankenyi-Mori with an oil lamp. The boy was a replica of his father: fine chiseled face, glinting eyes, and an impressive height. His brother Jawulen-Karamoko's misfortune had suddenly elevated him to the position of heir apparent. His display of marksmanship and skill with horses had helped cement his right to the throne of the Wasulu Empire.

"Elder brother, you've returned. I want to hear everything about *faragbelah*—the land of the white-skinned people," he said and hugged Zaiwulo.

"I met many Toubabous but did not go to their land. How is Mother doing?"

"She wants to see you."

Sarankenyi was sitting in an empty courtyard surrounded by oil lamps which glowed like a halo around her. "My son returns and makes no effort to see me."

Zaiwulo knelt on the mat and hugged her, sniffing that mixture of musk, soap, and her natural scent that he missed so much. In the intimacy of her embrace, he felt at home.

"Mother, I was attending to business concerning the empire. Father asked me to talk to elder brother Jawulen-Karamoko."

"I don't understand why he still refuses to talk after all his father has done for him, for his mother, relatives, and people."

She turned to her son. "Listen to me, Mori, I can tolerate anything from you, but not when you betray your father. If you ever do that, I will sever all ties with you. Do you hear me?"

"Mother, he will never do that," Zaiwulo said. "I will make sure of it."

"Will you promise me? The way to the throne is long and littered with pitfalls. To get there, he will need you more than anybody else."

"He will be joining my sofas," Zaiwulo said.

"Take care of him. Protect him if necessary. Be to him what Morifin-Djan Diabate is to my husband."

"I will, Mother," Zaiwulo said.

"I told your father that with the rumors of his death still circulating, it would be better if he gathered all the rulers of the empire to pledge allegiance to him again. This time, instead of the symbolic degue, I suggested that the rulers let drops of their blood pour on the earth. It will take place in Bissandougou, but I will not be there with you."

"Why is that, Mother?"

"Your father needs capital to finance his campaigns. He needs my money, and I have to stay here to earn more with trade. Your brother will go with you. You two must never part again."

Zaiwulo returned to the Haidarah compound and met his daughter sitting on Karamo-Sidikie's lap outside of his study. Sianeh tore herself away and raced to her father who lifted her and swung her around. He held her as he took a seat on the mat across from the scholar.

"Welcome again," the scholar said. "You must have learned a lot in that land."

Zaiwulo told him a detailed story of life in Saint-Louis.

"The Faama told me that he arranged for your brother's manuscripts to be moved from Musadu to Kankan," Zaiwulo said.

"Yes, they are safe here."

"Any news of my teacher?"

"According to the latest news, he's not in Bopolu."

"Who is heading the Haidarah-household in Musadu?"

"Ma-Sona heads the family now."

"I will go to see her after things have calmed down."

"Like my brother, who escaped it in time, I'm not a man of war, son of the forest. Like him, I hate all fights in the name of religion. This madness has crippled me."

"The Faama will put a stop to it," Zaiwulo said.

"I hope he does."

•×•

At dawn the next morning, Zaiwulo went to see Samori. He found him seated in the same position he had left him the previous night. The ruler was still pleading with his son, still trying to get him to talk. The sunlight captured the emperor's face. The folds around his eyes were prominent, revealing the extent of his exhaustion. He seemed older than his years.

"He still has not said a word, Zaiwulo," Samori said.

"Nkuro—elder brother—are you there?" Zaiwulo said.

There was no answer. Jawulen-Karamoko had turned his back to the world, he stood erect, his bare back clothed in dust.

"We are left with no other choice." Samori turned to the guards. "Do with him as you please."

Samori left that part of the palace with Zaiwulo.

"The Toubabous will come," he said. "I must leave for Bissandougou to protect the capital and bring all the rulers together to pledge allegiance to the empire. You and other generals will make sure that the borders of the empire are protected."

"The borders will be defended, Faama," Zaiwulo said.

"Good. I leave this week."

10

On the day of departure, the Liberian Benjamin Anderson visited Samori. The emperor had heard of the Liberian during his days as a trader. The fact that there was a country inhabited by a people who, except for the color of their skin, were in many aspects white, had always intrigued him. Over the years he had maintained trade links with a few Liberians. The arms and other goods that he purchased from the country were often of high quality but were not enough to make the trade profitable, which was why he had turned his attention to the English in Freetown.

Since his last visit to Musadu and his failed attempt to reach Buré, Anderson had turned to some Liberians and Americans financiers to fund his next expedition. They were all impressed by his stories about the riches of the savannah and the gold mines of Buré.

On his way to Musadu with Talata's son, Karamo, accompanying him, he had learned that Buré now belonged to Samori. When Anderson was announced, Zaiwulo told Samori that he had met the man in Musadu.

"What does he want?" Samori asked.

"He wants to visit Buré."

"We will see," Samori said.

Samori received the Liberian in one of the smaller courtyards of the palace. Zaiwulo was with him. Anderson seemed not to have aged a day. His forehead glowed with youth, Zaiwulo noted, and he seemed calm, unperturbed by Samori. Karamo, on the other hand, looked preoccupied, as if everything around him affected him in terrible ways.

"What brings you to Kankan?" Samori said.

"In my country, there are talks about your ambitions and your wars with the white people," Anderson said. "We are worried."

"Worried? What about?" Samori asked.

"We are worried that your wars with the whites might pose a danger to our country. We are very small and vulnerable."

"But your country is already in danger. The Toubabous will not give you the opportunity to make your country stable."

"You could stop the wars."

Samori laughed. "I'm not the one waging the wars. I'm being attacked on all sides. Didn't you know that? The French bribed my son into betraying me. And the English have probably taken your brother Osman hostage, Haidarah," Samori said, nodding toward Karamo.

Anderson realized then that he was dealing with a man with two faces. The gracious ruler who strove to meet the needs of his people, and the ruthless one who, according to rumors, had slaughtered so many people during the siege of a city, that there was no ground left to walk on. Perhaps the journey had been a mistake, he thought.

"I need your friendship," Samori said. "We black people must unite against a common enemy, against a common danger."

"If you allow me access to the gold fields of Buré, I will make sure that the Liberian government helps you against the whites," Anderson said.

Samori smiled as he remembered that Buré was not as he had expected. Its gold was not enough to finance his ambitions. After the conquest of Kankan and his complete control over the mines, Samori discovered that Buré was a myth that fed the fantasies of people. The gold fields had been exhausted. The profits from Sarankenyi's trade alone fetched much more than the gold of Buré.

"Buré is not the way it was, my friend," he told the Liberian. "The stories about the place are exaggerated, but I will make sure that you leave with some gold if you assure me that I will get the support of your president. I will allow you full access to the gold fields of Buré if your government supplies me with arms."

"My goal here is to visit Buré, Faama."

"You don't have time. We are preparing for fresh campaigns. I will give you gold, and you must leave. The faster I get the weapons, the better."

Anderson was confused. If he failed to reach Buré, what would he tell his financiers? In this matter, it seemed he had no choice.

"Tomorrow, we leave for Bissandougou," Samori said. "You will accompany us. From there, we will help you reach the coast safely."

Samori stood up to indicate the end to his audience. He asked Zaiwulo to arrange lodgings for Anderson.

"Haidarah, I want to have a word with you alone," Samori told Karamo and they waited until everyone left. "Liberia is our only means to procure weapons now. Your single goal will be to make sure that its rulers supply us with weapons. Tell them money is not an issue. Tell them that when we win the war against the Toubabous, we will make sure their country is one of the richest in the world. Don't disappoint me, Haidarah."

"I will do my best, Faama," Karamo said.

"Your father decided not to work with me. I don't blame him. Sometimes, violence is required in the absence of peace. Most of my conquests took place without violence. I wanted to tell him this, but he didn't give me the chance to explain. I feel that I failed him in that aspect."

Samori left the courtyard and gave instructions for Anderson to be supplied with some gold. He also asked for fresh horses to be prepared for the journey to Liberia.

Zaiwulo was more interested in what Karamo had to say than in what had brought him and Anderson to Kankan. He took Karamo to his home within the palace and sat on a mat across from him. "Tell me about your life in Liberia," Zaiwulo said.

"I am now a representative of the government to the indigenous people. I try to look after their interests. I married a mulatto whose parents disapprove of me. They felt their daughter should have married a man of their standing, but we love each other."

"I saw many mulattos in Saint-Louis."

"Were you in France?"

"No, but I studied French and met many French people in that city."

"You've come a long way, Zaiwulo, but be careful of Samori. A man who kills his own son is not to be trusted."

"Jawulen-Karamoko betrayed him."

"But he was his own son, his own blood."

"Yes, he was, but he betrayed him."

Karamo shook his head and changed the subject. "I met my father in a tiny village deep in the forest. He talked about you and hoped that you would return to Musadu. That's why I was surprised to see you here. I'm restless like my brother Osman but you are not, Zaiwulo. My father believes that only you can keep the family together, and I think that he's right."

"Is he thinking of returning to Musadu?"

"I don't know. He's afraid of Samori and the king of Musadu. He is afraid of everything that's happening here. He wants peace; he wants to rest."

"One day, I will return to Musadu. These are precarious times. Many rulers, including the king of Musadu, have revolted against the Faama. We have to maintain order."

"I might return to Musadu to take my father's place and to help my mother. Whenever I'm here, I don't want to leave, but after a while life begins to become stifling, then I long for life in Liberia, for my wife, and my books. Once there, I'm fed up with some aspects of life there."

"I know that feeling. Sometimes, I long for the moments to sit and write down my thoughts and experiences, but tell me more about your father."

"He's not alone in the village. Naminata is with him. Whoever thought that she could persuade my father to accept her as wife? Naminata has grown in status. She's like a blanket that protects my father. Anyone who seeks my father for advice must first consult Naminata. Yes, she's achieved her goal."

Zaiwulo was glad to hear this news.

"I want you to take Massah and my daughter to my parents in Haindi until the wars with the English and the French are over."

"So, she chose you," Karamo said. "I liked her, you know. All of us did, but I couldn't imagine a life for myself in Musadu. I had to go to Liberia. I will take Massah and your daughter to your parents."

"Thank you, Karamo."

"Where are your daughter and her mother?"

"They are here in Kankan."

"What are your plans?"

"I will stay here to defend the empire."

The two hugged each other.

"Take good care of my family."

"I will, Zaiwulo."

11

Zaiwulo was lying in a trench, ready to put a halt to the advance of the French army. Sweat dripped down his temples and forehead, stinging his eyes, but he did not move from his position. The trenches were scattered along the route believed to be followed by the Toubabous. Zaiwulo and his men were spread out along the flanks of the trenches. Beside him was Sarankenyi-Mori. They had been waiting all morning.

A buzzard alighted on a nearby tree. Others soon followed, and a fight ensued among the birds over where they could perch on the branches and watch the battle unfold. When a cannonball landed in one of the trenches and filled it with bodies, the buzzards began to flap their wings in agitation.

Zaiwulo jumped to his feet. "Sarankenyi-Mori, stay with me!" he shouted.

Convinced that the Toubabous who were strangers to that landscape would not deviate from the main road, Zaiwulo led some of his men out of the trenches, out of the chaos of cannon fire and onto the road. The sofas took positions at the rear of the long but tight French column and unleashed their firepower. There was a lull in the battle, as if the enemy, surprised by the maneuver, was about to flee. But once again the earth opened up to salvos of cannon and rifle shots. The anthills scattered their contents of termites and ants.

Something hit Zaiwulo in the face. As he wiped it, he found his palm red like the cow blood shepherds sometimes fried and ate. It was one of his sofa's blood.

As Zaiwulo struggled to cut through the French column using a strategy that had worked before. He heard the sound of a weapon different from that of the cannon and other rifles. It sounded like the crack of wood in a blazing fire. The French had introduced a new weapon in the war, and it was wreaking havoc and death. He would learn later that it was the Lebel rifle.

Zaiwulo scattered his men along the French column. From these positions which afforded them great agility, his men launched counter attacks. Pockets of sofas would fall on the French column, quickly withdraw and then charge again. But the French held on. Zaiwulo and the sofas were forced to retreat behind a hill where they waited until night fell. Meanwhile, the Toubabous had settled behind another hill.

Zaiwulo was intent on fighting them. The sofas lit torches of dry twigs and followed him. His whole body was wracked with exhaustion, his ears whizzed with a shrill sound that grated on his nerves. He kept hearing the sounds of cannon shots long after they had died down, but he pressed on in silence with his men.

The sofas came to a halt below the hill beyond which the French were camping out for the night. Curious, Zaiwulo scaled the hill alone, grabbing with each step the tall grasses for balance. In the light of the campfire around which some of the French were gathered, he saw that they looked vulnerable and at his mercy. If we had enough horses and weapons, Zaiwulo thought, we would have put a permanent end to their ambition in this part of the world.

Zaiwulo returned to his men.

"We will not leave them alone. We attack now," he said and no one protested. "The Djelis will sing your names, and you will be remembered forever. We will drive the Toubabous out tonight."

The ascent was difficult with no torches to guide them. The sofas held onto each other, each the guide of the other, and they descended the hill on the other side in complete silence.

When the French saw them, they were so surprised that they broke into a run. Zaiwulo and his men pursued. The panic resulted in the split of a small force from the main French column. Or perhaps, Zaiwulo thought, the split was part of the French strategy. It seemed no small coincidence that this small force, armed with cannons and Lebel rifles, had managed to escape in the cover of darkness. Unfortunately, Zaiwulo and his men had realized this only after a French prisoner revealed that the small force was on its way to Kankan.

"We must get there before they do," Zaiwulo told his men.

The French were at an advantage, but their heavy weaponry was sure to slow their progress, Zaiwulo reasoned. The sofas pursued the enemy on foot. Some succumbed out of sheer fatigue. Others, including Sarankenyi-Mori, begged Zaiwulo to stop, but he refused.

"If Kankan falls, the empire falls," he said.

•×•

For days, the sofas slogged through grass and mud, the wounded among them slowing down their advance. On reaching Kankan, they met a deserted city, parts of which were burning. There were large holes in the city walls, most of which had crashed. Corpses littered the grounds. Buzzards feasted on the corpses left unburied. Mice ran amok in celebration.

Zaiwulo applied all his persuasive powers to get his men to follow him to Bissandougou, the capital of the empire. "It is up to us to protect what is left of Wasulu. We are the last hope of the empire. We will fight until our last breath to defeat the Toubabous," he said.

But the sight of Bissandougou rendered him speechless. Thousands of people were scattered across the plains outside the city walls. Some were clearing bushes to erect impromptu shacks and others were racing to and fro, carrying huge loads of goods on their heads. It was as if the whole population of Kankan and all the towns and cities around it had descended on Bissandougou. The capital was too small to hold such a large number.

Zaiwulo realized that any French attack would be calamitous. But he wondered where those red ears were.

12

Samori was standing on a battlement, a tall edifice that was attached to the twin baobab trees in the heart of the city. He was thinking about ways to protect the remains of the empire. The French advance had been so rapid that he had not had time to ponder his next course of action. Every eye was on him, searching for a speck of fear or hesitation, or for some leadership.

I must not disappoint them, he thought. They need me more now than ever before.

From the depth of his despair and the abyss of defeat, there came to him the most effective way to crush the enemy in a plan that was as clear as daylight. Samori smiled, certain of the fate that awaited the Toubabous, but as he thought it over, a dust of sadness settled over him. The damage that would be inflicted upon the empire would be severe.

It was this sadness that Zaiwulo caught in Samori's eyes when he climbed the wooden, ladder-like stairs to meet him. He thought that the emperor was about to surrender. His heart ached. "The Toubabous are using my son's death as an excuse to fight me, as if they were not the ones who incited him against me," Samori said. "My son, my own blood!"

The sofas below the stairs broke into a song of defiance, but Zaiwulo noted a slight hesitation in their reaction, they were not sure of their emperor's state of mind, or his next move.

Samori had suppressed the rebellion triggered by rumors of his death. He had punished rebellious kings and those scholars who preached hate. He had even killed some of them—including the king of Musadu—who was accused of sowing discord in the empire. But the death of his son at his own hands had left many wondering about the future of the empire, for Jawulen-Karamoko was to many a far better choice as heir than Sarankenyi-Mori.

"Where's Sarankenyi-Mori?" Samori said.

Zaiwulo beckoned to the boy who was standing at the bottom of the stairs. Sarankenyi-Mori climbed up the ladder to reach his father.

"He fought bravely, Faama," Zaiwulo said.

"I knew you would do right by him. Tell me what happened," he said.

Zaiwulo recounted his encounter with the French.

Samori shook his head. "Then we are left with no other choice but to do something never done before in our history. It's the only way, Zaiwulo."

"What is that way, Faama?"

"I will tell you later."

Samori climbed down the stairs, and Sarankenyi-Mori and Zaiwulo followed him. He turned to his Djeli. "Has everyone arrived for the meeting?"

"All the rulers of Wasulu and all the sofa generals will be here before sunset. Most are already here, Faama," Morifin-Djan answered.

"I want to address the people now. We need to assure them that we will not abandon them, that they are safe here." Samori's courtiers followed him, but Zaiwulo left to see Sarankenyi. He wanted to know whether Karamo had left with Massah and his daughter for the forest as planned.

He met her in a crowded part of the palace.

Sarankenyi was overseeing the men and women loading her goods in sacks alongside bundles of clothes. Beads of sweat had collected on her fine nose, on the space between her brows. Worries about the fate of the empire had taught her to use her powers in the most meaningful and effective ways. She looked effervescent, her bristling energy affecting all around her.

"Yes, Massah left with Karamo for the forest. We should be heading for the forest, too," she said.

"It has not yet come to that, Mother."

"You think so?" Sarankenyi wiped the sweat off her face with one end of her wrapper. "The English and the French are fighting us east and west. It's time we made for the forest and from there fight to reclaim the empire."

"We are still fighting them, Mother!"

"I saw what they did in Kankan."

Zaiwulo shook his head. "But fleeing would mean giving up the empire."

"Your father never gives up," Sarankenyi said. "He will fight those Toubabous to the end, but we are vulnerable here with so many people concentrated in such a small place. One cannon shot could kill hundreds—*hundreds*, my son."

She was right, Zaiwulo thought.

That afternoon, Samori's meeting with his court progressed along the same lines but for a few exceptions, which came from the Djeli Morifin-Djan.

"We should send half of the people back to Kankan. Karamo-Sidikie and your daughter could lead them. The people will listen to them," said the Djeli Morifin-Djan..

"My daughter has not forgiven me for the death of her brother. She says he was young and stupid, and I should have forgiven him."

"She will work with her husband, Faama."

Samori turned to Karamo-Sidikie. "You are admired and respected, even by our enemies, Haidarah. No one will harm you. Do you want to return to Kankan with the people?"

Karamo-Sidikie seemed frail and very ill. He coughed, cleared his throat. "I will return with those who are willing."

"What do we do now, Morifin-Djan Diabate?" Samori asked.

"We head for the forest, Faama."

Samori turned to Zaiwulo who sat across from him in that circle of confidantes. He shook his head. "No, my mother's people might find it difficult to cope with this population. No place in the forest is large enough to contain us all. My mother's people might accept me because they cannot refuse me anything, but I might end up losing their respect."

"Then let's head in the direction of Kong, the crossroads between the Ashanti Empire, the Gyaman kingdom, the Baules and the Mandé kingdoms of Dabakala and Bobo-Dioulasso."

"That's a very long distance, Morifin-Djan!"

"If we want to save lives, Faama, it's the only way."

Samori leaned back on the wall of the enclosure. He was silent for a while. "But this would mean abandoning the empire we've struggled to build for over forty years. This would mean leaving behind Koniyan. Would our ancestors forgive us?"

"There's nothing to forgive," the Djeli said. "We've made our ancestors proud. It's been a long time since our people have meant something. We rose from nothing to the height of Sundiata Keita and Mansa Musa. Even Alexander the Great would have respected us. We conquered lands and brought together people who had been fighting each other for ages. We founded the Faamaya Empire which the world will forever remember."

The Djeli's words touched Samori so much that he left the gathering and the palace. When the thousands who were crowded around the palace saw him, they cheered him. "Admired One, we are with you," they shouted.

The crowd was hungry, confused, and were relying solely on Samori's leadership. How would they react if he were to ask them to follow him to an unknown world? Would they survive the long trek? But if he abandoned them, they would become English or French subjects. This he could not allow.

He returned to the gathering.

"If that's the case," he said, "then let's begin preparing for the journey at once. We will show the Toubabous that they cannot just take over the lands of our ancestors. We will show them how hard we can be. The Faamaya Empire will never give up."

13

A sofa stood in front of Samori's palace in Bissandougou. In his hand was a burning branch. He glanced at the rooftops, at the polished walls of the enclosures, and at the numerous homes. With all its occupants gone, including the horses, and with all the rooms cleared of everything that once adorned them, an eerie silence reigned over the palace. Despite the crumbs of grain that littered the grounds and the clay rainwater holders that stood before its every enclosure, it was as if the place had never been inhabited.

The granaries had been cleared and the food stored away by sofas who had ridden out ahead, along the route Samori had set out for his people. With measured steps, the sofa approached a building that had once housed his fellow sofas. He erected a ladder against the building's wall, climbed it, and threw the burning branch at the roof's summit. The reeds hissed and the fire flared up in flames. Soon, tongues of flames were lapping up the roof, the flames descended on the building itself, curling around rusted arrows, spears, and gray walls against which sofas had once propped their backs and dreamed of more glories and conquests.

Samori's chambers were next.

The sofa thought he would have no problem setting them ablaze until he drew closer to them. Stripped of everything that once made it home, the chambers were a collection of mud houses that revealed nothing about their occupants. Recently, he had sat in one of the enclosures, and gazed at those chambers and where he had rubbed shoulders with their occupants. Why erase such an invaluable history? Would people ever recall that in that place, which he was about to reduce to ashes, lived a man who once ruled a swathe of empire so large that its boundaries were never clear-cut? The sofa turned his back to the enclosures in a bid to let them be, but, squashing all emotion, he turned around and set fire to all the houses and buildings. As he left the palace, the flames jumped in excitement.

That sofa was Zaiwulo.

He and his men had been entrusted with the task of burning down the whole capital. Bissandougou was on fire. The fire burned the ground of the city, which cracked open, releasing insects and worms that singed upon encountering the flames. The trees of Bissandougou burned, including the giant twin baobab trees under which Samori had sat and supervised the quelling of the rebellion in his empire. The smoke from the flames merged with the clouds, turning the skies dark.

Outside the city, the yellowish-green grass of the savannah burned. Trees cracked as they fell, and the burning grass exuded liquids as though they were shedding tears. It was a desolate landscape of charred grass and uprooted trees, of caked and scorched earth which stretched beyond the gaze of the sofa arsonists. Hills, tree stumps, and anthills looked like dark statues of abandoned gods, still aflame after the animals, ants, and termites that once populated their realms had burned.

The instruction had been clear. “Leave nothing behind for the enemy,” Samori had told his sofas. “Nothing for the

Toubabous to conquer. No human beings, no animals, no trees, not even grass—nothing."

But the Toubabous, aided by many of Samori's enemies, braved the burning landscape. Their unmistakable shakos and uniforms, their glinting bayonets, and their drums were soon heard and seen as they negotiated one obstacle after another. The deep trenches, the burning bushes that crashed on them out of nowhere, the poisonous arrows that rained on them, all claiming many lives and leaving many paralyzed. They encountered wells—those lifelines scattered across the savannah—now laced with poison. Those in the enemy's army who survived were received with open arms in some of the villages, only to fall prey at night to arrows, spears, and knives.

It was Zaiwulo's task to distract the enemy from the main population heading toward Kong. Thousands of people, the greatest exodus in the history of that part of the world, journeyed with Samori. The sun that day, like the days before, was fierce, for it was the end of the dry season. Zaiwulo, with close to four thousand men under his command, led them away from the forest and Liberia and to the south, away from the route the emperor and his people had taken, and in the direction of Sierra Leone. The heat only magnified the stench of burned bushes.

From his scouts, which included Sarankenyi-Mori, Zaiwulo had learned that the French column that had set out to fight him and his army was led by Archinard, the same man who had conquered Kankan. Samori's son had insisted that he be part of that group of scouts. The boy had managed, to Zaiwulo's surprise, to survive the fierce encounter with the Toubabous. His stamina had endeared him to many sofas, including those who, at first, had opposed him.

The sofas prepared their rifles and tried to calm the horses which sweated and foamed at the mouth because of fear and excitement for the battle. Zaiwulo was brushing down his horse Sundiata when Sarankenyi-Mori approached him.

"I know how to bring down the leader of the Toubabous, elder brother," Sarankenyi-Mori said. He stood on the other side of the horse, helping brush the horse with his bare hands.

"You are still a child," Zaiwulo said.

"A single rifle shot is all that is needed. If we want to stop the Toubabous, we must aim for their commander. If he falls, they all fall," the boy said.

There was a determination in his voice that compelled Zaiwulo to pause with caressing the horse. He stared hard at the boy. When he detected no fear in the boy, he thought of the promise he had made to Sarankenyi to protect her child by all means.

"This is what we will do," Zaiwulo said. "You will be part of the unit that will give me cover as I go for Archinard. You will clear the way to him and I will bring him down."

Sarankenyi-Mori agreed. From the hilltop, Zaiwulo sat on his horse Sundiata. The horse was calm, and Zaiwulo, all courage and determination, gazed around him. With his men surrounding him, including Samori's son, Zaiwulo raced down towards the French army to confront the French commander and end the war.

There he was now, the notorious and feared Archinard. He was the bulky Toubabous on a gray horse, at the head of the column of his men.

While his men cleared the way before him, all defiant in the face of cannon shots and Libel fire, Zaiwulo raised his rifle and aimed it at the shako of the French commander.

He was about to fire when his horse stumbled. As Zaiwulo struggled to steady the horse, Sarankenyi-Mori, intent on carrying out his own plan, released the trigger. The boy was not sure whether he had hit Archinard but he thought he saw him fall off his horse.

Sofa war cries rose in his wake. The French began to retreat.

This time, Zaiwulo did not pursue them. By now he had learned that overconfidence was dangerous and could cost lives. His goal was to frustrate the French advance, so he and his men took over the hill from where they watched the movements of the French.

The sofas surrounded Samori's son.

"You are truly your father's son," one of them said.

Sarankenyi-Mori smiled.

Zaiwulo patted him on the shoulders. "You will lead our scouts toward Sierra Leone, where Uncle Kemoko-Bilali is fighting the English, little brother," he said. "See how far we are from the border. When you return, we will decide our next course of action."

"Thank you so much, elder brother," the boy said.

The next day, Sarankenyi-Mori left with three other sofas. Meanwhile, Zaiwulo and his men began to prepare for the next encounter with the enemy. There was enough food and ammunition, and the losses were limited.

"The Toubabous will return," he told his men. "We will lead them toward Sierra Leone, to Uncle Kemoko-Bilali. Together, we will defeat them."

•×•

A few days later, Sarankenyi-Mori and the scouts returned with the news that the sofa general Kemoko-Bilali had driven the English across the river bordering between the Samorian empire and the English sphere of influence.

"Uncle Kemoko is waiting for us," Sarankenyi-Mori said.

"Now, we can face the Toubabous," Zaiwulo said.

Zaiwulo led his men across the scorched earth to a valley where the enemy had camped out. He thought that the fight would be over before the day was out. However, later that afternoon, he and his sofas saw a figure looming large above the French column. It was Archinard.

The sofas were stunned. How would they fight a man who had risen from the dead? Did the Toubabous possess the secret to eternal life?

"The Toubabous commander was not dead," Zaiwulo said. "He was merely wounded. We will lead the enemy to Uncle Kemoko-Bilali. I have a plan."

The landscape was an undulating spectacle of corpses. Hundreds of them had been pecked clean by vultures, kites, and buzzards. The skulls, severed off the bodies, were scattered along earth like river stones, turned dark by fire and soggy by early rain.

In a village at the farthest reaches of the empire, a foul stench led Zaiwulo and his sofas to a heap of bodies that were piled up as high as the walls. Whatever battle had taken place had left no survivors. The homes, the roads, and the entire village reeked of the dead.

It dawned on Zaiwulo that the carnage must have been the result of a confrontation between Kemoko-Bilali, his sofas, and the English and their allies.

•×•

More than four months after leaving Bissandougou, Zaiwulo finally met the sofa general. Kemoko-Bilali had aged. His tufts of hair had turned gray and his eyes, once threatening and lethal, were now glazed over with exhaustion. Only his body, which had resisted injuries and survived the piercing tips of arrows and spears as well as the ravages of rifles and bayonets, was still as firm as the body of his youth.

Zaiwulo and his men were soaked by rain that had not let up for days. Inside the thatched hut, the two men embraced.

"I thought you were dead," the sofa general said.

"No, Uncle Kemoko-Bilali, I survived the madness. The Faama himself came to my rescue."

"Where's Massah and the child?"

"With my family in the forest."

Zaiwulo told Kemoko-Bilali about Samori's exodus.

"I have a plan of attack against the French," he said.

"Tell me, son."

"Where are the English now?"

"They are on the other side of the river that divides us."

"When night falls, we will lead the French to the river and from there shoot at the English and the French at the same time. Each camp will mistake the other for our forces. Then we will sit back and watch our enemies finish off each other. What do you think, Uncle?"

"Let's put the plan into action," Kemoko-Bilali said. "Zaiwulo, you will wait with the rest of the sofas beyond that hill while I and a handful of sofas engage the French and the English." He pointed to a hill beyond them. "If our efforts fail, you will intervene."

The sofa general set out with less than fifty men until they reached the river, which was not large. On the other side, they could see the English and their allies.

"We should move closer to the river," the sofa general said, and his words were relayed to other sofas. Behind them, the French approached. "Now we wait."

The sofas waited until it was dark and the French were very close, and then they began to shoot at the English. Quickly they turned and opened fire on the French. Each army of the the Toubabous thinking that it was being attacked by the Samorian forces, responded by furiously shooting at each other. To a sign from Kemoko-Bilali, the sofas began to retreat sideways along the river, but not without losses.

In the crossfire, the sofa general was wounded.

The sofas rushed with their leader to the point beyond the hill where Zaiwulo and his men awaited them. The wound was fatal. Kemoko-Bilali was dying but did not show it.

"Bury me here, son," he told Zaiwulo. "Tell our Faama that we managed to bring the English and the French to war against each other."

14

In the empty villages and towns swept clean of food by Samori and the people, Zaiwulo and his men would stop for a few days or weeks. They would dig the grounds with hoes and bayonets in search of edible roots and worms, or forage in the bush for insects like grasshoppers and termites. Sometimes, for lack of fire and the essentials required to prepare a proper meal, they ate the food raw, which caused diarrhea and spells of dizziness that impeded their progress. At other times, as he gathered with his men around the meager food they managed to salvage, Zaiwulo would detect a pent-up rage in them. He feared mutiny and thought of deviating from the route and heading to the forest, to his people, but the distance was so great that he soon abandoned the idea.

They were all held captive by the utter desolation, the countless corpses littering the roads, and the inconsolable emptiness around them. The stench of death tampered with their resolve. Where was this all leading? To a new empire? To a new beginning? Zaiwulo had ceased to care. He was certain that sooner or later, one of his men, driven by despair and the madness of hunger, would draw a knife across his throat and end it all.

In the first few weeks, every time one of them was unwell, the sofas would tend to him with care uncommon to them. They would cover long distances in search of food or herbs to cure the ailing party, but soon, as the number of the sick increased, the men were forced to abandon them on the roadside or in the villages so that the rest could survive. Still, there was no sign of Samori and his mobile empire. Sarankenyi-Mori and his scouts would be gone for days only to return with no news regarding where the emperor had decided to settle down.

The sofas had exhausted their strength. Whenever they paused in an empty town, charred and burned down to make it impossible for the Toubabous to catch up with them, each sofa would seek refuge alone, under a tree that had survived the scourge, in the shadow of a standing wall, or farther away from everyone. Groups were formed and abandoned. Fights ensued which Zaiwulo quelled by threatening to cut down the one who initiated it. He did not dare look into the faces of his men every time he addressed them for fear of gazing at death in their eyes. His singular goal was to move on.

For a while now he had stopped counting the dead among his men, or the ones who simply deserted, taking different paths to the unknown. There were also those who, when they arrived in a village, were unable to stand on their feet and asked the rest to go on without them.

They trudged this way for months until one day, Sarankenyi-Mori and his scouts returned with the news that Samori had settled in Dabakala, the capital of his new empire. The roads gasped under the deluge of constant rain as Zaiwulo and his men crawled their way toward the new capital. It was an endless expanse of villages, hamlets, farms, and bushes. Zaiwulo left his men on the outskirts to meet Samori and arrange food and accommodation for them.

The roofs of the homes in the outskirts were so low, the clay walls so thin, that Zaiwulo wondered whether they were inhabited by human beings at all.

A man was working in front of one of the houses, his legs and arms smeared with mud. He was building a shack smaller than its adjacent one, singing an old sofa war song in a deep voice.

"You there," Zaiwulo called. "Where can I find the Faama?"

The man turned, and then he smiled and bowed.

"Faama, I didn't recognize you at first," the man said before he moved close to Zaiwulo and laughed. "You look so skinny. Hunger must have reduced you to this state. It must have been the kind of hunger that drives a man to consider whether to eat his own kind. I know that hunger."

"Tell me where the Faama is or I will cut off those ears."

"Forgive me, Faama," the man said and turned toward the shack. "Sinkarie, come out here and see the sorry state my sofa brothers are in! And you thought we had a rough time on our way here!"

Zaiwulo rushed toward him, about to slap him for making light of his situation.

"Please, Faama," the man said, stepping back. "I was only concerned about you and what you must have gone through. I lost family members during the exodus. We lost everything along the way."

A woman came out with a suckling child clamped to her breast. She ignored her husband and turned her attention to Zaiwulo.

"Sister, please ask the women around here to take care of my men while I go in search of the Faama," Zaiwulo said.

The woman did not respond.

"Our Faama will compensate you," Zaiwulo said.

"Compensate us?" she said, sucking her teeth. "Your Faama led us to a land we were told was richer than our lost homes. Where is that wealth?"

Zaiwulo did not know what to say.

"Perhaps we should have stayed home and accepted the Toubabous after all," said the woman. "Perhaps they would have made us all rich. Yes, that would have been much better."

"Shut up, Sinkarie," her husband snapped. "How dare you say such things before the prince!"

"Even if he was the Faama himself I wouldn't have hesitated to speak my mind." Turning to Zaiwulo, she continued, "What my husband is afraid to tell you is that we lost our children during the journey. Your Faama's decision to move such a large population was a mistake. What we witnessed on our way here is indescribable! The misery, the dead, the countless dead." She stifled a wail, then gathered herself. "Your Faama is not my Faama," she spat.

"Sister, what you are saying is a result of your suffering and loss. I understand, but please help my men. They are hungry."

The woman hesitated before disappearing behind the shack. Zaiwulo could hear her calling out to other women in the neighborhood.

"Where is the Faama?" Zaiwulo asked again.

"I will lead you to him," the man said. He washed his hands and face and threw on a dry but dirty tunic. "The Faama is receiving the king of gold today. They say the king sleeps on a bed of gold, wears golden cloth, and sprinkles his food with gold dust like we sprinkle our food with salt."

"The king of gold, you say?"

"The Ashantihene, king of the Ashanti people. They say that eating gold makes you live for hundreds of years,

Faama, which means that we the poor are really done for. But on the other hand, you the Faamas with all the gold at your disposal will live on forever, isn't it?"

Zaiwulo ignored his comment.

A crowd that had gathered to see the king of gold formed a huge block around the main square where the reception would take place. The Ashantihene appeared, not on horseback as Zaiwulo had expected, but on a beautifully decorated chair borne by four men. His name was Prempeh the First. He was flanked by his entourage who waved huge colorful parasols. Behind them, others carried sacks of gold.

The Ashantihene wore a golden crown. He had gold bracelets on his arms and ankles as ornaments. On his fingers were gold rings designed like human heads. Another ring had two birds and a porcupine. For footwear, he had a pair of leather sandals with talismans of carved wood covered with gold leaves. The Ashantihene was young. His dark skin was glossy. His nose and mouth were identical to those of the deceased Jawulen-Karamoko, Zaiwulo thought. This resemblance and Samori's reaction would later trigger persistent rumors that he had fathered the young king.

The moment he saw the Ashantihene, Samori, whom few had seen cry, burst into tears and hastened down the platform to meet him. He threw his arms around the youth and led him to a seat beside him.

If the Ashantihene was taken aback by this display of emotion, he did not show it. Instead, he gestured to his men with the sacks of gold. The men edged forward and set the sacks below the throne. One of them opened a sack, grabbed a handful of gold dust, and let it stream through his fingers.

The Ashantihene spoke through an interpreter.

"These presents are a gesture of our willingness to ally ourselves with you, Faama," he said and turned to Samori who nodded.

"The English are threatening my existence and that of my people," the Ashantihene went on. "They've already conquered parts of my kingdom. I heard of your heroic deeds against the English and the French. I heard that you routed the English army in a recent encounter close to my kingdom. You are notorious. They say that even their queen, that old woman, fears you!"

"Thank you for your presents, Your Majesty," Samori spoke, not through his Djeli Morifin-Djan as was his habit. He looked at the Ashantihene as he spoke, his voice almost tender. "Who would have thought that I would have found an ally here such as you?"

"All the gold of the Ashanti people is at your disposal, Faama. Together, we will drive the whites out of our lands. Together, we stand a chance."

Samori turned to his son Sarankenyi-Mori who sat beside the Ashantihene, and he was struck by the resemblance between the two. Now he nodded to his Djeli Morifin-Djan.

"We will send sofas to train your army," the Djeli said. "We are new here, Your Majesty. But from today onward, consider us as your family."

The Ashantihene nodded.

"Stay with us for a while," Samori suggested.

Later, the two rulers walked hand in hand to the palace which Samori had taken over and expanded to accommodate his huge number of courtiers. He was aware that by publicly displaying his emotions, he was doing away with the myth he had cultivated as a hard and unflinching ruler. But ever since abandoning parts of his empire to the English and the French and the horrible exodus that followed, he had softened his attitude towards protocol.

Samori showed the Ashantihene to his chambers. "Your Majesty, rest here and we will meet later," he said.

Samori went to see Sarankenyi. "We will succeed here, Saran," he said.

Two women were plaiting Sarankenyi's hair and embedding leaves of gold crafted into talisman shapes. Seated between the two women, she looked imperial. Around them were other women, some who were from Wasulu Empire and others from parts of the kingdom of Kabadougou, once ruled by two brothers, but which now belonged to her husband. Sarankenyi wanted to show the people of the new empire that she was one of them.

Samori sat beside her. "If only I had had as much gold before as I've been promised here, Saran. If only Buré yielded as much gold, then I would have bought all the weapons of choice and we wouldn't be here. With the king of gold as an ally, I will give the Liberian government so much gold that they will have no choice but to supply me with weapons. Then, it will be over."

Sarankenyi dismissed the women by waving hands decorated with henna. She looked radiant despite the hardship of the exodus. It struck Samori how quickly she had adapted to this new life.

"The child came with so much gold, Saran," Samori said. "You should see him. He's a replica of me! He looks like Jawulen-Karamoko!"

It pained Sarankenyi to hear this. Since the death of his favorite son, Samori had not been the same, which troubled her. She knew she had to share in his joy, lest she lose her place in his heart. Sarankenyi smiled. "I want to meet this young king, beloved."

"Yes, you will. With his help, we will defeat the Toubabous."

Sarankenyi did not contradict him, but his confidence troubled her and brought back memories of all the misery of the previous wars. She was exhausted.

"From here, we will expand our new empire to enable us to regain the old one," Samori said. "One day, you will return to Koniyan, Saran."

"Koniyan, you say, Beloved? It sounds so remote, almost like a dream. I cannot wait for the moment to sit on its soil once again."

15

The roofs of the homes in the palace in the new capital were flat, unlike the conical ones of the lost empire. The walls were clay-red and the tall trees and bushes scattered through the new capital suggested proximity to the forest. The palace language of Dabakala was a variation of the Mandé languages, which the newcomers picked up easily. In one of the four sections of the palace, Samori, his Djeli Morifin-Djan, his wife, and son Sarankenyi-Mori sat listening to Zaiwulo recount the encounter with the English and the French.

"Your friend Kemoko-Bilali has passed on, Faama," he finally said.

Samori stood up and strolled up to the wall that separated him from the chambers occupied by the Ashantihene. From there, he could hear Morifin-Djan mourning the fallen sofa.

"Life is but a wink of an eye, and it's over. Where is Alexander the Great? Where is Soumangourou, the man who subjected our people to his rule? Where is Sundiata Keita, who freed us and built an empire that rivaled Alexander's? I ask, where's Kemoko-Bilali, that man among men? Where are all those who once subjected the earth to their whims and thought themselves invincible? They are all gone. That should be a lesson for the arrogant amongst us. Listen, people of Dabakala, Kemoko-Bilali is no more."

The Djeli's voice brought the palace to a standstill.

Samori realized that time was tightening its grip on him. He joined the others.

"A great man has departed," he said.

"He was the pillar of Wasulu," Morifin-Djan Diabate said. "The *Mali*—hippopotamus—of the Niger. A giant tree has fallen."

"What now, my friend?"

"The French and the English are fighting each other. We couldn't have wished for a better outcome. Kong, the center of trade in this part of the world, is ours, despite the French attempt to wrest it away from us. We now rule over Bobo-Dioulassso, Bona, and Waa, kingdoms with envious pasts. But the crown to them all is Bondoukou, the capital of Gyaman, which awaits you. When your son Sarankenyi-Mori and I entered it for the first time, it was as if I was coming home. You've done in less than two years what took us years to achieve in our lost empire. Once again, the ancestors have deemed it appropriate to favor you with greatness. But be careful how you dispense that power. It is time to make peace and return home. My bones ache to be buried on a hilltop overlooking my town of birth."

"What do you plan to do with the Ashanti gold, Faama?" Zaiwulo asked for he was thinking of the forest, of home, of Massah, and his daughter.

"Porokerrie will carry the gold to Liberia to persuade its rulers to sell us weapons. The forest is nearby. We need those weapons just in case the Toubabous attack us again. But where is Osman? I'm beginning to distrust him. What is he still doing in England?"

"Perhaps he's gotten used to life there, Beloved," Sarankenyi said.

Zaiwulo did not want to discuss Osman. He was convinced that Talata's son had betrayed Samori. "I could go to Liberia, Faama."

"No, you will stay here to rule this kingdom. I've decided not to concentrate power in one place. If Dabakala falls, we could move the capital to Bondoukou. We have to be ready at all times."

"You are making a real Faama of my son, beloved," Sarankenyi said. "His brother, our son Sarankenyi-Mori, can stay with him."

"Despite his courage, your son still has much to learn, just like his brother Zaiwulo did, Saran. He needs to fight many battles to achieve that."

"But he has been with his brother all this time. He has proven himself, beloved. Let him stay here in Dabakala," Sarankenyi said.

Morifin-Djan interrupted them, shifting the discussion to another subject.

"We should dispatch envoys to all the Toubabous and declare our intention to make peace with them. We must ensure our survival," he said.

"We will do that this very week. I'm even thinking of offering the hand of friendship to Tieba of Sikasso and Agibou of the Toucouleur kingdom."

"Kabako—a wonder," Sarankenyi said. "The man who killed your brother Kemeh-Brimah and allied himself with the Toubabous?"

"We need his alliance, Saran. Moreover, I've heard that his brother Babemba is wiser. We will focus on Babemba. If we don't, the Toubabous might end up persuading him to take up arms against us."

"The Faama has spoken, Ma-Saran," the Djeli said.

Samori glanced at Zaiwulo. "Where are your men now?" he asked.

"At the city's outskirts, Faama."

"Ask them to join their brothers in the quarters allocated to them outside the main city walls," said Samori. "Sarankenyi, please ask the women to prepare food for them. We have to build them new homes."

"We should invite the Ashantihene to accompany us to Bondoukou," the Djeli suggested, and Samori agreed.

They all went to see the Ashantihene.

They found him mounted on a horse, receiving riding lessons from a sofa. The ruler of the Ashanti people had exchanged the gold finery with a simple yellow cloth wrapped around his shoulders. It covered his body from shoulders to ankles. "I don't want to return home without at least learning how to ride a horse. Your reputation as great horsemen precedes you," he said.

"You will ride sooner than you think," Samori said. "I want to invite you to accompany us to Bondoukou. They say it's beautiful."

"Yes, it is. Your sofas' presence there led me to you. I will go with you. There are very few horses in my kingdom."

"Then I will present you with some of the finest horses in my empire, including my own, Your Majesty."

"Thank you, Faama."

"We will leave a week from now," Samori said.

"A week from now I will be a horseman. My mother will be surprised."

"She must be proud of her son," Sarankenyi said.

"To be a ruler in my country is decided through the matriarchal line. My mother was a sister to the last king, and I was her firstborn."

"So women decide who is king?" Sarankenyi exclaimed.

"Yes, Mother! What my mother says goes."

"I wish I was an Ashanti. I cannot wait to meet your mother."

The Ashantihene turned to Zaiwulo. "I heard that you interacted with the white people, right?"

Zaiwulo nodded.

"Tell me more about it later today," he said.

They left the Ashantihene still on his horse. Sarankenyi asked Zaiwulo to go with her to her chambers. She wanted to talk to him. "I missed you so much, my son," she said when they were alone. "During the long trek, I thought that I would never see you again."

"We survived the journey, Mother, and my brother Mori was very brave. But there are no words to describe the hardship we went through."

"But both of you are here now, and I am very glad. Your father insists that your brother lead his own army. If my son is hurt in any way, I will never forgive him. Do you hear me? I will fight him to death."

"Don't worry, I will talk to the Faama to let my brother stay here with me. Together we will protect Dabakala."

"You are a gift to us," she said.

Just before dusk, the Ashantihene summoned Zaiwulo.

Zaiwulo met the young ruler with his interpreter. The excitement from horse riding was still visible in his eyes. His handshake and embrace were cordial. He inquired about Zaiwulo's interaction with the French. Zaiwulo told him about his experience in Saint-Louis and his wars with the English and the French.

"Tell me then in all honesty whether we can win this war against the whites. Can we chase them back to the sea?"

"That depends not only on you but, also, on your people. Will they continue to fight as we've been doing? Or will they give up?"

"My people will never give up. That would mean the end of us. I will never give up." The Ashantihene pointed to his chair. "You see that chair? It's my throne. My seat of power. It's not man-made. It descended from heaven, sent by our ancestors. I must fight on."

"In that case, our Faama will assist you."

"The English will be surprised by our alliance. We will chase them out of our lands."

16

Bedbugs fed on Zaiwulo as he slept on a sheet of cloth laid out on the grass. A shack made of reed and wood protected him from the elements. It was one of many flimsy shelters in a camp he shared with thousands of his men. When he woke, he sat up, and the bugs trembled and fell off his body. Ignoring them, he left his shelter. Every time it rained, the camp's ground turned to slush and the shack became damp. It usually smelt of stale grass and mud. It was one of many times in more than two years since he had traded the palace for the camp.

After a week or two in the palace, when he had begun to get used to its comfort as well as the attention and admiration he received. He wondered whether he was becoming someone else, perhaps a strange version of himself who was gradually being corrupted by power. When that happened, he would flee back to the camp.

News regularly reached him of alliances Samori had forged with large and small kingdoms, with Ouagadougou and the Toucouleurs, with the Moussi, with the Dangombas, with the Emir of Sokoto and Kano, and with the Akhan people. Tieba of Sikasso and his brother Babemba had responded to Samori's gestures with the promise never to turn to the Toubabous again. The Ashantihene sent more than a dozen sacks of gold with which to purchase weapons from Liberia. But the Sofa General Porokerrie, who had traveled to Liberia, was yet to return. Rumors spread across the empire that the sofa general and his men had been eaten by cannibals in the forest.

Zaiwulo took a quick bath behind the shack. It was a ritual that invigorated and readied him to take on the task of ruling that part of the empire. Refreshed, he threw on a tunic that smelled of the herbal soap that had been used to wash it. With a Dutch pistol and a Wasulu rifle resting on his lap, he sat on a chair outside to preside over the affairs of Dabakala.

Sarankenyi-Mori came to see him. Zaiwulo had been with him since Samori retired to Bondoukou together with his court. Several times a week, Zaiwulo rode out with Sarankenyi-Mori to visit remote places in the kingdom of Dabakala to solidify their hold on the populace.

"There's an Englishman with Haidarah's son at the main gate, elder brother. They want to see the Faama, to see you," Sarankenyi-Mori said.

Zaiwulo immediately thought of Osman. Haidarah's son had succeeded, not only in traveling to England but also, in returning with an Englishman. He went to meet them with Sarankenyi-Mori.

The Englishman was being carried in a hammock, while Osman walked in front. They were followed by carriers with large cases and bags on their heads. Zaiwulo thought that perhaps the cases and bags contained weapons. Skipping greetings, which was an insult in itself, Osman blurted out, "So you are alive? I thought you were killed by those crazy scholars."

So it was Osman who revealed the secret of his relationship with Massah to the world, Zaiwulo thought. Why would he go to such lengths? Would there ever come a time when Talata's son would cease to hate him, or would they fight until death? Zaiwulo opted not to respond, for he was looking at his teacher in Osman's face. That was the only thing that kept him from slapping or locking him up. Instead, he led the guests to the palace and asked a courtier to fetch a good herbalist for the Toubabous.

"The Englishman is called George Garrett," Osman said. "As you can see, he's in poor condition. We came by boat from Freetown to the coast of the Ashanti kingdom. The Ashantihene told us that he was an ally of the Faama, and he arranged escorts to accompany us here. I must speak to the Faama right now."

"I am the Faama here," Zaiwulo said.

Osman laughed.

"What did the French teach you? Nothing, I guess. In the world of tomorrow, the French will not count. That world will be ruled by the English and English speakers. The Faama made a mistake by appointing you to this position. I will make him see that when I meet him."

"Go ahead, Osman. But while at it, you will do what I say or you will see how difficult I can be. Why is the Englishman here?"

"I will tell you when I see the Faama."

"I am the Faama here now. You must learn to deal with it."

Zaiwulo went to see the Englishman and met him lying on a mat while the herbalist fed him a concoction. He tried speaking to the man in French, but the herbalist did not respond.

"Will he make it?" Zaiwulo asked.

"Yes, he will, but it will take a long time," the herbalist said.

Zaiwulo returned to his chambers. The presence of Osman transformed the palace into a small space not big enough to hold them both. He knew that he could not constantly keep evading Osman, but what he feared was that his irritating presence and ability to bring out the worst in him might influence his function as ruler of Dabakala.

That evening, during dinner, Osman said, "I know where the Faama is. When Garrett recovers, I will go to Bondoukou to meet him."

"You cannot leave Dabakala without my permission. No sofa will dare go against my will. My command is that you don't leave the palace. When the Englishman is well, I will let the Faama know. As for the rest, I want little to do with you, Osman. Don't test my patience."

"So you are keeping me prisoner here?"

"If you refuse to work with me, why should I care about you? I have better things to do than participate in your childish games. I have a kingdom to rule."

"You will pay for this, Zaiwulo."

Zaiwulo ignored him.

A few days later, while he was meeting with some elders and sofa generals to discuss affairs of the empire, a sofa rushed into the courtyard. "A French column led by Monteil has been spotted heading toward Dabakala," the sofa said.

According to Zaiwulo's scouts, the French commander was well equipped and determined to destroy everything in his path. The French had been supporting and fighting alongside smaller kingdoms bordering Kabadougou, the heart of the new Samorian empire, to weaken him. They had laid waste to entire towns and villages.

"Dabakala will not be another Kankan," Zaiwulo said.

With Sarankenyi-Mori, he went to see Osman and the Englishman.

"The French are here. Are you going with us?"

"I will stay here with Garrett to care for him. Go and stop the French."

Zaiwulo was astounded by the fear he caught in Osman's eyes. Why was he not willing to fight for Samori? What did that mean? Zaiwulo went to the stables. On seeing him, his horse Sundiata withdrew to the shadows.

"Sundiata," said Zaiwulo, "I need you now like never before."

The ties between horse and rider had slackened because of Zaiwulo's long absence. Although Zaiwulo was constantly at odds with the horse, Sundiata allowed himself to be led out of the stable. The horse stood still, a pillar of muscle and strength as Zaiwulo mounted it. The animal seemed not to have lost its vigor, which surprised Zaiwulo. He felt blood surging through the horse's body, arousing a fighting spirit in him.

Zaiwulo rode out to meet his sofas who, spread across the plains, were waiting for him. "We cannot afford to lose this campaign, sofas," he said.

"O, Admired One, we follow you," his men shouted. "Wherever you go, we go. Whatever you do, we do, till death."

The sofas marched out to meet the French Tirailleurs Sénégalais. The enemy was so close that Zaiwulo could see the shapes of the insignias on their uniforms. When he issued his order, the sofas fell on the French.

Monteil, the French commander, had received a direct order from Paris to finish off Samori once and for all. But as the battle raged, he was astounded to see his men breaking ranks due to the fierceness of the Samorian forces. Using cannon and rifle shots, Monteil tried to wedge a passage through the throng of sofas. It was a suicidal attempt, he was well aware, but he had the artillery and the latest rifles whereas the sofas could only boast of spears and simple rifles produced somewhere in their empire.

However, the sofas seemed immune to bullets. They would rush forward, and as those in front fell, those behind would surge forward, breaking through the French defenses and falling on them with spears, rifles, and bare hands.

Zaiwulo saw Jean in the distance, and his heart lurched. He stood still for a while, shocked at the sight of a person he had known and interacted with but who now stood on the other side of the war as his enemy bent on destroying him. He thought of Jean's loyalty to France and to everything it stood for. Did he choose France simply because he happened to be French? Could Zaiwulo say the same thing about himself? Why the war? Why could the differences not be resolved through a set of agreements? Perhaps, it was not that simple, Zaiwulo thought, for it involved two powers with opposing visions: one with the confidence that made it possible to wage a colonial war far away from its shores, and the other with the ambition to build the greatest empire in Africa. It was about life and death. Zaiwulo, who wanted life, rushed forward with Sundiata, intent on reaching Jean. But the distance between them was covered by a wall of his men, and Jean was enclosed in that wall. Stupefied, Zaiwulo watched as the sofas fell on Jean, trampled over him, and headed towards the next target. To them, he was just an enemy with a history none of them cared about.

Zaiwulo fought on but without the passion that characterized him. Before him, and all around him, his men were overwhelming the French forces. A sofa bullet grazed the French commander's neck but Monteil ignored it until he felt a gust of wind sweep through his body, a light wind, so merciful, so soft like the snow of his country or the caress of a woman's hand. At first, he welcomed it until his feet buckled and he descended into a void. His men gathered around him and carried him to the back of the line.

Monteil and his men had been dealt a crushing blow.

•×•

News of the defeat of the Toubabous spread like wildfire and reached Samori who left Bondoukou to personally congratulate Zaiwulo.

The road to the largest square in the city, where Zaiwulo would be received, was adorned with colorful clothes upon which he was supposed to walk. Ten black and white horses loaded with presents of gold, silver, clothes, and perfume awaited him.

Zaiwulo was sitting in his chamber in the palace. He hoped that he would never have to fight another war that would pit him against anybody, whether he knew that person or not. He was fed up with war. Every part of him longed to be left alone, but dozens of women who stood outside his chambers looked forward to seeing him, including Sarankenyi who was resplendent in her yellow tunic and wrappers. Her hair was plaited with scarlet threads that held gold coins at each end.

The voice of the Djeli Morifin-Djan Diabate, who had come with Samori, rose and burst over the crowd. "It was meant to be," he said. "A child will rise from the forest, from the line of your mother! When you meet him, you will recognize in him the mother for whom you traded your freedom to purchase her own. The child will unite what was bound to be united from the very beginning. The Toubabous will forever remember this day, the day we defeated them, not by using arms, but by relying on courage and courage alone, that most effective of all weapons. The child is the reincarnation of your mother, Masoronah. The child is you."

As she waited, Sarankenyi envisioned a future in which Zaiwulo would take over from her husband. In that future, her son would be by his side and later become an emperor. Whichever way the Samorian story played out, she would emerge a winner. She broke into song, and the women picked it up. *We thought we abandoned fortune on the roadside in Wasulu, but behold, it is here, it is here*, they sang.

The crowd took up the song when Zaiwulo came out.

He rode on his horse toward the square where he dismounted, walked up to the platform, and paused before the emperor.

Samori stood up.

"Come down and meet your son," the Djeli Morifin-Djan said. "A mother's bond is stronger than a father's. We know that. We've always known that, so by celebrating your son, we are actually celebrating your mother, Faama."

Samori came down and hugged Zaiwulo.

"If anything happens to me," he whispered, "you will head this empire, you will be its Faama. You will carry on what we started. You must promise me that."

"I will never let you down, Faama," Zaiwulo said with a heavy heart.

"Say it again. You will fight to unite all the lands of the Black-skinned people. You will carry on our dream."

"I will carry on our dream, Faama."

"The torch rests with you now. From now on, every encounter with the Toubabous, every attempt at expanding the empire and my hope of returning home will be headed and supervised by you. The affairs of the empire will rest in your hands from now on, my son."

The crowd burst into the square and surrounded Zaiwulo. Standing beside Samori, enveloped in the crowd's adulation, Zaiwulo felt it was all a dream and that sooner or later he would wake up to reality.

17

Samori gave the Englishman George Garrett more time to recover before meeting him.

A few weeks later, the Englishman was not only able to walk, but he had the habit of wandering around the city followed by a group of children singing: *Here comes the Toubabous bearing a rifle on his shoulders*. Sometimes, he would turn around to the children and glare at them with his steel-blue eyes, and the children would scatter in fear. Unsure of his reaction, they would watch him from a distance. He did not carry a gun. And when he inquired from Osman what the song meant, Osman answered, "The first guns here were sold by white people, hence the song."

Garrett had not yet fully recovered when Samori decided to meet him.

"What brings you to our empire?" he asked him.

Garrett had met Osman in London during a conference of Black intellectuals who wanted to fight colonialism and promote African unity. "Osman told me about you," Garrett said. "The stories about you in the British newspapers and your image as a freedom fighter and resistance leader led me to you. I came formally as our ambassador, but in secret, I want to do business with you."

"I need arms and ammunition," Samori said. "But tell me, does my mother Queen Victoria support your decision to help me?"

The Englishman laughed.

"No, the old queen and the English government do not know about this plan of mine. What I am doing is risky, but I want to help you."

Samori turned to Osman. "Haidarah, what did you discuss with the English?" he asked in Mandé.

"The English assure us that they will do everything to keep a good relationship with us. We could wait to see how that plays out. We don't need to do business with this man yet."

Zaiwulo, who sat on Samori's right, could not understand why Osman was distancing himself from Garrett. He wondered if Osman doubted Garrett's honesty.

"If you don't trust him, why did you bring him here?" Samori asked.

"He can be trusted, Faama, but his offer can wait. If the English were to find out that we bought weapons behind their back from a man who's trading for himself, it could jeopardize everything," Osman said.

"But if we let this chance pass and the English attack us, then we are left empty handed," Zaiwulo said. "Faama, I suggest we work with Garrett. We don't have to wait for the English who violated our trust before."

Aware of the rivalry between Zaiwulo and Osman, Samori considered his choice. If Osman was right—and he was inclined to believe him, wouldn't it be prudent not to provoke the English? So as not to hurt either of the two young men, he decided to postpone his response. He would send Zaiwulo to Bondoukou to rest, and, in his absence, make a decision.

"Osman, tell our guest that he's welcome, and we thank him for his presents. Before he's fully recovered, we will give him our answer."

In the days that followed, Samori often met with Garrett and Osman. Talata's son drew a remarkable picture of England and its people. "We could learn a lot from them."

But Zaiwulo doubted Osman's intentions. Had he really met the queen and her government? Was he not a traitor and had he not come to some arrangement with the English, as Jawulen-Karamoko had done with the French? Was he plotting to undermine the Faama?

"You look tense, Zaiwulo," Samori told him a few days later. "Go to Bondoukou. You can rest there."

"But Faama," Zaiwulo protested, "I think that Osman—"

"Don't worry about him," Samori said. "I know him. Go to Bondoukou."

Realizing that further protestations were useless, Zaiwulo relented and agreed to follow the Faama's advice.

18

Zaiwulo rode into Bondoukou with Sarankenyi-Mori beside him.

From the distance, the city appeared to him like a secret shrouded in a green mantle. The walls of its homes were smooth and whitewashed. The cylindrical rooftops and narrow passages reminded him of Kankan. He dismounted, gathered a handful of dust in his hands and Koniyan rose like a mirage before him. The scent of the nearby forest, the trees and bushes were achingly similar to those of Haindi. Zaiwulo rode on toward the palace where servants who were anticipating their arrival had prepared their chambers.

"Sarankenyi-Mori, I want to take a nap," he said.

Samori's son nodded.

Zaiwulo retired to a room whose walls were covered with white cloth. Its floor was carpeted in scarlet, and its bed was large and comfortable, however, his exhaustion was so vast he paid little attention to the interior. Instead, he went straight to bed and slept long and deep.

He woke up to Massah's voice arguing with his daughter over her bath. "Come here, Sianeh, or the water will get cold. Come now or I will call your father..." But there was no Massah or Sianeh, only his longing for them. This fact upset him but not enough to rid him of the exhaustion. Zaiwulo stayed in bed for most of that day and days afterward, shedding off the fatigue of his long and arduous campaigns.

One day, Zaiwulo left the palace to wander in the forest. He would pause at a stream or a creek, clear the surface of fallen leaves, gather the water in his hands and drink before he would rest in the shade of trees. They were august and majestic like rulers of bygone eras. In their terrifying silence, the trees seemed to be listening to his innermost thoughts, to the questions that still plagued him. Would the wars ever stop? Would he ever lead a normal marital life or raise his daughter as a father ought to?

When night came, Zaiwulo cleared the leaves from a hollow at the base of a large tree, crept into it, and fell asleep. The animals—squirrels and lizards—which burrowed into the space around his feet and arms did so silently as if they understood his good intentions.

The next morning, Zaiwulo faced the rising sun as he bathed in a nearby river. Beads of water gathered on his face like nuggets of silver in a world of extraordinary beauty. He returned to the forest almost every day to delight himself in its deep silences, in the animal or bird calls, and its profound mysteries.

Zaiwulo would sit at riverbanks and listen to the flow of the water. At other times, he would watch the birds and animals drink while wishing that his family could share in those precious moments. Whenever he returned from his long walks with his body and soul replenished, the palace cooks would place before him a plethora of delicacies he had denied himself for so long. They prepared toe and rice served with sauces that consisted of meat and greens, varied and rare fish, baked ripe and green plantains, seasoned yams, and a host of other foods that were new to him.

One day, more than a year and half into this habit, when he had become so used to idling away his time in the forest and to sleeping with little or no care in the world, Zaiwulo returned from one of his walks to meet an agitated Sarankenyi-Mori in the palace.

"A sofa has arrived from Dabakala, elder brother," he said. "We've been searching for you all day. The French have conquered Dabakala, and father has fled to an unknown destination."

"We will go in search of the Faama," Zaiwulo said. With more than fifty sofas under his command, Zaiwulo rode in the direction of Dabakala, hoping to find answers as to the whereabouts of the emperor. They had not ridden for half a day when they encountered the French in a small village. Zaiwulo chose not to confront them, but from then on, at every turn he and his men took, the French seemed to be everywhere.

Zaiwulo and his men decided to return to Bondoukou to defend the city. To their dismay, they were told that the French had taken it.

"Sofas," Zaiwulo addressed his men. "We will head for the forest of my birth and wait for the Faama. If he's alive, he's bound to follow us there."

"It could mean the end of us," Sarankenyi-Mori said. "Remember what happened to Uncle Porokerrie. The cannibals."

"If we continue roaming about, we are bound to be caught," Zaiwulo said.

"We could surrender," one of his men said. "They say that the French are lenient to sofas who have deserted our Faama."

"Out of the question," Zaiwulo said. "We are going to the forest."

They were barely halfway there when Zaiwulo and his men realized that they were not prepared for such a long journey. After a while, they traded their horses for provisions. Even Sundiata was not spared.

"I hope you will be kind to my horse," Zaiwulo told the new owner.

The man nodded.

Zaiwulo caressed his horse. "You were special to me, Sundiata," he said. "I will remember you forever, and I hope to reunite with you one day."

In a nearby village, they acquired clothes—scarlet tunics, caps, and bulbous trousers accompanied by the scent of strong perfumes that was the hallmark of the traders who came down from Kano, Sokoto, and other kingdoms—to disguise themselves as traders. Zaiwulo and his men avoided the main roads for fear of stumbling into the French and journeyed on until they arrived at the last outpost to the deep forest. They scoured the village for traces of the French. After finding none, they decided to rest for the night.

The enemy must have had spies in the village for, the next day, the French entered it, cordoned it off and began to comb it for sofas.

They were methodical, choosing to search all the inhabitants for the effects of wind, sand, and thorns on faces. That was how sofas were easily recognized. They also examined ankles for smoothness, for many sofas were known to ride horses without footwear. In no time, Zaiwulo and his men were identified, arrested, and put in shackles.

The French commander was a young man who reminded Zaiwulo of Jean. He approached the chained sofas with a rifle in hand. "Where is your leader?" he asked through an interpreter. Zaiwulo noted his eagerness to make his mark and to impress his superiors. "Where is he, tell me?" he roared, but the sofas were silent.

The commander sat on a chair, legs spread apart, now and then wiping sweat off his face with his hand. "If you tell us where Samori is, we will reward you all with gold. We will make you all chiefs in your villages, towns, or cities."

The sofas did not even acknowledge him with a glance. It grated on his nerves. He cursed and swore in French, and Zaiwulo thought that his ambition made him capricious and lethal. They had to be careful.

"Where are the sofas about whom I had heard so much in France? Where's your valor? Your indifference to death? Do you know that your wars with France resulted in the downfall of our government?"

Zaiwulo and his men did not respond.

"The one who tells us where your leader is will never be poor again. His children will grow up speaking our language. You realize that everything here and all the lands that once belonged to your chief now belong to us?" The French commander jumped to his feet.

"We will dig holes and bury you all alive," he said. "We will cut off your heads and place them on pikes and then parade them across the conquered territories." He cursed, swore, and kicked the ground, raising dust that landed on the sofas. "Allez, we will take them with us," he told his men. "They are bound to break sooner or later."

They left the village and proceeded to the French headquarters in Ivory Coast. When it began to rain, they stopped at a ramshackle camp where the men who guarded Zaiwulo and his men tied their chains to a tree and rushed for shelter.

One of the sofas managed to break his shackles with a stone lying close to him. "Faama," he called out to Zaiwulo and ran to help him. As the sofa tried to break the shackles off Zaiwulo's ankle, the stone hit his commander's leg. Zaiwulo forced himself to forget the pain when he was finally free and saw that he could walk.

Zaiwulo and the sofa had work to do. They went on freeing the other sofas and were almost done when they saw the French commander approaching them. Zaiwulo and the sofa hauled themselves at the commander. The man fired. The bullet hit Zaiwulo in his leg, but the sofa fell on the commander, breaking his neck with the ease of a man breaking a kola nut.

The sofas escaped.

Despite the pain in his leg, Zaiwulo walked on while fighting hard to ignore the blinding agony. His leg began to swell, but he had no time to pause and attend to it. They went on until it became impossible for him to move. Zaiwulo's men took turns bearing him for days on end.

One late afternoon, around dusk, Zaiwulo and his men saw a colossal chain of walls that were taller and thicker than any they had ever seen before.

The sofas stared at the citadel as though they were dreaming.

19

"I am building a wall around a city that will be home to all my people, the ultimate line of defense against the Toubabous. I will call it Bori-Bana—no more retreat," Samori told Zaiwulo.

They were sitting outside the walls of the city, overseeing its construction. "We will stay in Bori-Bana until the Toubabous have exhausted all their resources in their fight against us and decide to leave. The walls will be stronger than any built in *Farafina*, the lands of the Black-skinned people. It will be a thousand times better than the Tata of Tieba in Sikasso. It will be like the walls Alexander the Great constructed to prevent Gog and Magog from invading the earth and putting an end to humanity. When it is finished, Bori-Bana will hold more than a million people. From within its walls, we will fight and drive the Toubabous out of our lands."

A flame shimmered in Samori's eyes which Zaiwulo took to mean hope.

Samori bristled with energy. He could afford to smile again for the work on the walls had not ceased since the idea occurred to him. Before the fall of Dabakala, Samori had secretly led more than half of his people out of the city and beyond the borders of his new empire, to Worodougou, the land of kola nuts. He moved farther to a site at the fringes of the forest, where he began to build the walls and the city that would house his people.

The ever-prudent Samori had posted his sofas along every route that led to it with the explicit order to stall all movements toward Bori-Bana. The place had to remain secret as long as possible. The site was exactly as he had imagined it—a plain that stretched beyond the eyes, crossroads between the lost new empire and the forest of his mother's country.

Zaiwulo's wound had almost healed thanks to an herbalist who once a week wrapped a poultice of herbs in leaves and placed it around the wound to prevent it from festering. Now the spot was dry. The dead skin had peeled off, leaving a pale surface and slight indentation in his ankle that sometimes itched. He could walk now without the aid of a cane.

The sun was at its zenith, implacable in the distant sky, a sign that the dry season was about to end. The walls of the edifice had to be completed before another rainfall.

"The English did not keep their promise, Zaiwulo," Samori said. "They are fighting me, as are the French. They've betrayed me. Or should I say that Osman betrayed me? Did he become in England what my son Jawulen-Karamoko became in France? That's why I've sent Morifin-Djan to the French and the English to suggest a new treaty that will make it possible for us to return to Wasulu. It is all meant for us to gain more time."

"It's a good move, Faama."

"If Morifin-Djan works out a truce with them, even if it is for just a year, it will enable us to complete the walls. Take a ride around the walls on my horse and see for yourself."

When he mounted the horse—the first time he had done so in months — Zaiwulo felt like that child in Musadu who, so many years ago, rode a horse for the first time and who was hesitant and vulnerable but gradually overcame his fear. With a slight movement of his legs, the horse took off and Zaiwulo closed his eyes to feel the wind sweeping over him. Would he ever return to Koniyan or to the forests, he wondered? Would he ever sit in the shade of the flame tree he had planted and teach hundreds of students? What if Morifin-Djan failed to sign a new treaty with the Toubabous, would the incomplete walls protect them?

At every section of the walls, Zaiwulo found more than a thousand workers adding one stone to another, pushing one huge tree against the other, spreading a mixture of sand, grass, and dirt over stone bricks. They toiled day and night without respite, one shift replacing the other. The people worked as if in a trance, now and then bursting into songs that swelled and faded away into the nearby forest.

Zaiwulo rode closer to the walls and greeted the women who were mixing mud, stones, and grass with their feet. The women reminded him of Massah and his daughter. Had Massah managed to reach the town of his birth, Haindi? Were they safe, Zaiwulo wondered.

Meanwhile, Samori had retired to one of many villages the sofas had built to house his mobile empire. It was located a distance from Bori-Bana so that the sofas would have enough time to protect the walls if the French or the English attacked them before their completion.

Zaiwulo reached the village around dusk. On his way to the palace, he met Sarankenyi. She wanted to see him.

"I will be with you after I've taken the horse to the stable, Mother," he said. He fed Samori's horse some grass and whispered his hopes to it. "The walls will be finished in no time and our people will be safe behind them. You and the Faama will head a victorious army, and we will reclaim our lost empire as well as every piece of grass and speck in it."

Sarankenyi was standing outside her chambers under the full moon.

"Follow me," she said. She led Zaiwulo outside of the palace walls, as though the walls had ears eager to listen in on her. Now and then, she would slap her plump arms to drive mosquitoes away.

Sarankenyi stopped and turned to face him in the moonlight. "I see you are on your feet again, my son," she said. "We need your strength during these difficult times. Your father is old now. He depends on you, on your brother, on his children and advisers. Now that you are well, you will oversee the building of the walls, won't you?"

"The walls will be finished before the Toubabous discover this site, Mother."

She reached out to touch his shoulder. "When you take over from your father, be kind to your brother! Don't let him make stupid mistakes."

"Yes, Mother."

"Where is that brother of yours?"

"He's out inspecting the sofas along the route leading up to this place. We need to always be on guard."

"He's a child of his father," she said.

"He's a capable young man, Mother."

Sarankenyi began to walk toward the palace. Zaiwulo followed her. "Will you come to see me every day after work?" she asked. "Your father is preoccupied with Bori-Bana. His mind is not on me. Gone is the man I knew in Koniyan. Now, he's all weariness. I want my husband back."

"Things are difficult for him. You could talk to Morifin-Djan."

"That man hates me as much as he hates the Toubabous, but I hope with all my heart that he succeeds, my son. I miss Koniyan."

"You will see Koniyan again, Mother."

He left her and retired to his chambers.

20

Morifin-Djan Diabate returned with a piece of news that he was reluctant to share with Samori. Instead, he decided to meet Samori's brothers and sons, the sofa generals, and the entire court first. The men gathered at dawn in an abandoned shed outside of the town. Burning twigs lit the shed.

The Djeli was solemn as he spoke. "Brothers," he said, "the French in both Ivory Coast and Senegal have rejected our peace offer. And the English accused us of aiding our ally the young Ashantihene, the king of gold. As a result, they've conquered his capital Kumasi and they think it's futile to sign a new treaty with us. The French want our Faama to surrender unconditionally."

Then Morifin-Djan revealed the secret which was the real cause of his concern. It sounded so terrible that the sofas advised him not to tell Samori.

"It would kill him," one of them said.

"Wait until the right moment to tell the emperor," said another.

"By then it would already be too late," the Djeli responded. "Secrets have a way of revealing themselves. Let me tell him now."

One of the generals, the youngest in the gathering, said, "If you want a dead man on your hands, Uncle Morifin-

Djan, then go ahead and tell him. While you are at it, I will prepare to surrender to the French."

"Surrender, Keletigui?" an elderly sofa general said. "Shame on you! We will never surrender. Death is better than surrender."

"If we allow Uncle Morifin-Djan to go ahead, then we will have no leader to get us out of this predicament," Keletigui said. "What is a tree without its roots? What is Wasulu without its emperor?"

"Our Faama has faced many calamities before and he has survived them all, we shouldn't forget that," another sofa said.

"But nothing as grave as this one," Keletigui said.

While the elders, the family, and commanders debated, Morifin-Djan stood up and moved toward the road. Keletigui blocked his way. "Over my dead body, Uncle Morifin-Djan" he said. "I will never allow you to tell the Faama, for you know as well as I do that after telling him, you will have no valor to recount. You will cease to exist."

"Move aside, Keletigui, I have a duty to carry out."

"You are a messenger of death, Uncle Morifin-Djan!"

"If you are so bent on killing me, why don't you come with me and wait until I've told the Faama and then shoot me."

"I will do it, I swear," Keletigui said.

Keletigui followed the Djeli to Samori. The two men waited until Samori had emerged from his chambers. The emperor pointed at Keletigui. "What is he doing here, Morifin-Djan?"

"He's sworn to end my life right now if I tell you what I came to tell you, Faama. You know your sofas."

"I am more than curious as to what has compelled one of my men to take such a decision. I hope it's worth it,

Morifin-Djan," Samori said. "Keletigui, put down that rifle. Have you gone mad?"

Keletigui burst into tears and fell on the ground before his emperor. "Don't listen to your Djeli—your blood—Faama," he said.

"What is the meaning of this strange behavior?" Samori said. "Speak, I say! Hold nothing back, Morifin-Djan."

"Sikasso has fallen to the French, Faama," the Djeli said. "And Babemba has committed suicide to avoid being captured."

Samori stared at his friend for so long that Morifin-Djan thought he would keel over at any moment and crash on the ground. "You are saying that the Tata of Sikasso has been destroyed? Is that what you are telling me?"

"The French blasted it away with their cannons. It seems they have developed better and more destructive cannons which even the walls of Bori-Bana cannot withstand. We've given it our all, my friend."

Samori was silent for a long while. Finally, he spoke, "You've been my friend since childhood. We've built and lost empires together. What do we do now, Morifin-Djan Diabate?"

"It is time that we turned to our allies, Faama. Your mother's people will protect us. They will never deny us anything. They will go hungry to feed us. They will die to protect us. We must head for the forest," he said.

"Go tell it to the people, Morifin-Djan. I don't have the strength to speak anymore. I am tired. Very tired."

21

The Samorian empire was on the move again, this time, toward a forest only a few people had ever traversed. Thousands filed out in columns that stretched out a day's distance on horse. The exodus was uneventful at first, but gradually, the landscape began to alter, from a sparsely grown forest to dense, impenetrable woodland. The skies would burst open with a deluge that would not let up for days.

First, the horses died. All of them. Tsetse flies and insects never heard of or seen before fed on their blood. The deep morasses through which they were forced to transport people and goods sapped their strength. The huge expanse of the forest with its colossal trees drove them into madness. Occasionally, for no apparent reason, a horse would break into a gallop and plunge with rider and all into a deep morass. One after the other, the horses succumbed to fatigue, despair, and madness, and the ones that survived refused to stir, even after the sofas, afraid of losing them, whipped them to stand up. Their neighing cries tore through the fetid swamps like bullets through a silent forest and lodged into the hearts of the wearied sofas. Though trained to withstand the most horrid situations, the sofas could not muster the strength to bury their horses. So they were abandoned. When the sofas had grown tired of combing the streams, the soggy ground and the trees for food, hunger compelled them to slaughter the remaining horses for the masses, with the most tenacious of them taking up the task. They ate the meat with funereal solemnity and swallowed it as though it were human flesh. Some outrightly refused the meat and others threw up moments after the meal.

The horses were soon forgotten when the swamps and the rain became their singular concern. The downpour continued unabated for weeks on end. The skies turned dark during the day and the day merged with the night, making it impossible for the sofas and the commanders to find their way, let alone the thousands who followed them.

Instead of skirting the forest bordering the savannah, a thin line that passed along Sanankoro, Bissandougou, Beyla, Jacodu, Musadu and the places he once called home. Instead of retreating through the lost empires, which would have meant surrender or certain death, Samori had chosen the route through the Dan Forest which was the thickest and most impenetrable of all the forests he had ever seen.

Now Samori and his men were stuck.

The earth became a stagnant swamp, a vortex that swallowed everything within reach, a carnivore that fed on feet first, then waists, arms, and necks. Stretching so innocently before them, covered with dead leaves, were swamps which took hold of a woman or a child, a father or a son, and then gobbled them up without leaving a trace.

For hours, the sofas would try to move a dozen people out of thousands, it was a forlorn enterprise, but one to which they stubbornly stuck because there were no other alternatives. The rifles, soaked by rain and mud, were rendered useless. Everything of worth—the gold and the silver accumulated during the last campaigns, the priceless cotton clothes, the cowries, and metal currencies—were abandoned at one point or the other. The forest had become the new enemy and was more potent and lethal than the Toubabous.

Zaiwulo carried only a sword with him. Due to the insect bites, he had developed a terrible itch. He could not sleep and tried to hide his condition by sometimes isolating himself. Once hidden, he would attack his body. He would scratch so hard that dark patches began to form around the spots where his body itched the most. The patches sat around his eyes, his arms, his neck, his knees, legs, and back, which he would scratch with a stick.

Rumors spread that the cannibals who inhabited that part of the forest had begun to feed on the refugees. This caused further panic. Through it all, Samori tried to maintain some form of inner peace while staring at failure in the eyes. He would wake up before dawn and sit outside an impromptu shed built for him. There, he would meditate and recall aspects of his childhood. Those early periods of his life came to him now like a dream. He could not reconcile the image of the child who craved food and fought his brothers over crumbs of boiled cassava with the image of a man who once ruled over a huge populace.

This habit of waking up before dawn effected a shift in his mood for he began to appreciate the majesty of the forest, to see how his mother's people regarded the forest as a source of refuge, as a means to connect with the ancestors. Samori understood now why the forest was venerated and worshiped. Soon, he began to see his mother in the light that fell through the trees, in the shades of those trees, and on the ground around him. In the cracking of a branch of the tree under which he sat, he heard his mother's reassuring voice, "What you regard as failure is no failure, my son. Be calm, you are not lost."

In the wake of his mother's words, Samori finally realized that the forest was not their enemy. There were no cannibals. There was only their fear.

"We will set up camp here and wait out the rain," he told his men. "If the Toubabous catch up with us here, so be it," he said.

So they waited.

One morning when Samori was sitting outside his shed, listening to the women who were preparing edible roots scavenged from the forest and molding clay collected at the edges of the hills to be consumed as food, he heard skirmishes behind him.

He did not move or twitch a muscle as the French surrounded him.

Sarankenyi-Mori, who happened to be in the vicinity, rushed toward his father with a sword, but the emperor raised his hand.

"It is all right, my son. The fighting is over."

Part Five

THE HAIDARAH MANUSCRIPT

1900

1

Zaiwulo was disguised as a beggar. He was part of the crowd that waited at the harbor in Saint-Louis for Samori to board the ship anchored off the coast. He had been waiting all morning.

Late in the afternoon, the crowd stirred and protests broke out as Samori was led to the ship accompanied by his best friend and Djeli Morifin-Djan Diabate. His wife Sarankenyi and son Sarankenyi-Mori followed. There were other members of his household too, his sons, daughters, and a few brothers, all of whom Zaiwulo knew and had once interacted with.

To show the world that his empire had indeed fallen, Samori had been paraded for months through Musadu, Sanankoro, Kerewanie, Kankan, Kenyera, Kayes, Dabakala, and Bobo-Dioulassso. They had taken him through Kong, Bamako, and Bondoukou; through cities and towns in the Ivory Coast, through Dakar in Senegal, parts of the Ashanti kingdom, Freetown, and all the land that was now occupied by the French and the English.

Samori was being led to the ship bound for another world which Zaiwulo had learned was called Gabon. Such a peculiar name, this Gabon, he thought. It evoked raging seas, high mountains, and deep mysteries. Why Gabon, he wondered.

On arriving in Saint-Louis, following the trail of the French who held Samori and some members of his court prisoner, Zaiwulo had found that Samori was held in a separate place. The others, including his wife and his Djeli, were in a prison overlooking the sea. As he moved around the city, mulling over means to deliver a message to Samori or his Djeli, or to try to free them if possible, Zaiwulo would think about Jean's death which still haunted him and about their walk through the streets of that city. Was Monsieur Durand, Jean's father, aware that his student was now roaming around disguised as someone else? Was he celebrating the fall of Samori? Zaiwulo thought of the decisions that led to his being a fugitive on the run from people with whom he had once interacted with. Was his choice to side with Samori the right one? Was resisting the French and the English the only option open to him? Were there other ways? If so, what were those ways?

Zaiwulo had observed that the house in which Samori was held was guarded by one person at a time. He had searched and found a wedge in the fence that separated the compound from the street.

One night, he forced his way through the fence and into the compound. The guard was sitting on a chair in front of the house Samori was kept at. Zaiwulo approached him from behind and fell on him, pressing his head to the ground until he ceased to move. He then broke the lock to the door in which Samori was held and entered. "Faama, it's me," he said, but there was silence. Groping in the dark, he found Samori lying on the floor unconscious. Zaiwulo felt his pulse. The emperor had attempted to end his life.

But he was still alive. Zaiwulo knew that his priority was to keep the Faama alive. He could not free him while he was in such a grave condition, so he went out and shouted for help. When he heard the French approach, Zaiwulo had escaped through the wedge.

Now he was standing at the harbor disguised as a beggar, just a face among many in the crowd. Sarankenyi and her son walked past him without recognizing him.

Then there was the Djeli Morifin-Djan Diabate:

Who says it is over, Faama? he sang,
Lift up those shoulders high, look straight ahead of you–
no, not that way, my friend, yes, walk straight like a pole.
Look down on those who think they are your equal.
They are not your equal. They will never be.
One day you will return to rule the lands of your ancestors.
You will walk on water if necessary, you will fly if need be,
but you will return, Faama.

As Samori approached the ship and drew level with Zaiwulo, he turned. It was the briefest of movements, but the gesture was affirmative, almost grateful. A silent goodbye. That was all.

•×•

On his way back to the forest to reunite with Massah and his daughter, Zaiwulo noted with consternation the speed with which the English and the French had conquered his part of the world. It was as if Samori had never existed. Those who talked about him did so in hushed voices, within the walls of their homes. Rumors persisted that he had not boarded a ship to Gabon and instead, he was hiding out somewhere in his lost empire, waiting for the right moment to rise again and deal the Toubabous the ultimate blow. Samori lived.

Many people were in awe of the ambitious plans the Toubabous had to build railroads, schools, and headquarters for the governors and officials of the new empire. To achieve these goals, Zaiwulo noted, people were forced to work at the railroads for free, taxes were levied on homes, and the populace jailed if they refused to pay them. He decided to go to Musadu first and, once again, visit his tree and the Haidarah compound. He owed it to himself and to the memories of the place that had formed him. Alone and in disguise, he posed no danger to the colonial authorities.

Zaiwulo arrived in Musadu at night after months on the road. The walls of the city had disintegrated. The city itself seemed to have shrunk. The remnants of what were once formidable walls were now an assault to the eye. There were no sentinels at the gate, no one to welcome him. Out of prudence, however, Zaiwulo avoided the main gate and climbed the remains of the back wall that once protected the Haidarah compound.

The Haidarah household was asleep. The three hearths were still in the main courtyard and wooden writing slates rested against the stones that formed circles around them. The hearths were burning. So there were still students in the house, he thought. So life still went on in the Haidarah home. He wondered who the teachers or the new leaders of the once-bristling compound were. Zaiwulo walked to the flame tree. Its branches were thick and long, adorned with fiery orange-red leaves. The scent wafted to him. He plucked one of the leaves and brought it to his nose.

"I'm here," he whispered. "You are part of this world now, as much as I am."

Though the desire to wake the household and reunite with new and old faces was great, he suppressed the urge. The time was not right. Zaiwulo walked back to the crumbling wall, climbed it, and was on the road again heading to the forest of his childhood.

2

On the outskirts of Haindi, at the point where the farms and gardens took over, Zaiwulo paused, rattled by doubts. What was he doing in Haindi? Why was he not raising an army as he had promised Samori? What if the answers he had come to seek turned out to be unbearable? If Osman had spoken out of malice all those years ago, and his claim that he was a slave turned out to be false, then what was the truth? Who was he? He sat on a bed of grass on the roadside, under an orange tree, vacillating with each passing moment between letting go of the past and clinging to it as if his entire existence depended on it.

Zaiwulo was overcome by a longing to be with his daughter and Massah. He stood up and plucked an orange, dug his thumbs into it, and ate it with the avarice of a child.

Further down the road, he met a group of women hoeing a farm, old women with bent backs, sagging breasts, and gnarled fingers. Zaiwulo threw a string of greetings at them in a language he thought he had forgotten. The women, catching a whiff of hesitation in his voice, turned around and answered him. One of them asked, "Whose son are you?"

His answer was met with ululations. "Koh, koh, koh—a miracle," one of them said. "Don't you recognize your aunt Kiabeh?"

It was his aunt Kiabeh who headed the old women as they left the farm to lead him to town. "Kollie's son is back. Yes, he's here," she told anyone who asked. "Yes, the child who left us. Yes, the child we lost. He's back!"

By the time they arrived at Zaiwulo's home, a crowd had merged with the old women. They all followed him. People pelted him with questions, some of which landed in the dust unanswered. An old man appeared before Zaiwulo, his face wrinkled with weariness, crow's feet holding the regions around his eyes prisoner. Zaiwulo recognized his father. Once upon a time, he had trembled before this man who now carried a walking stick, his back bent, a shadow of his former self.

Zaiwulo's father searched his eyes, perhaps for signs of recriminations, for signs of the trouble to come. He found none. The two embraced awkwardly, the old man holding onto him a bit longer than was comfortable.

"He's become a man," his father said. "Look at him. He's so big!"

"Kollie, take hold of yourself," Aunt Kiabeh said.

"Just look at him, sister-in-law," the old man went on. "Who could have thought that my child would turn out to be so huge?"

The road was ochre red, hewn by trodden feet out of what must have once been a hill, but in Zaiwulo's memory, the road had been sandy. Haindi was like a tiny splatter of dust across a huge canvas of forest. The compound where he had played with his sisters was an insult to the image and memory of the opulent home onto which he had held for years.

The constant frown on his father's face, which had once troubled him, was replaced by an avuncular smile, the fire extinguished by the caprices of time or by the cruelty of existence.

What had time done to his mother?

There she is, he thought, as a woman came racing toward him. She threw herself at him.

"You are home, elder brother," she said.

It was his youngest sister Juah, the one he doted on. Before he could recover from her sudden embrace, his other sister joined them. "He's become as old as you, father, just look at the gray in his hair."

Only then did he notice the reason he had come to Haindi. Massah was leaning against the mud wall of a house. Beside her stood a young woman, his daughter Sianeh.

"She came to us with my granddaughter," his father said. "You made us proud, son of Kollie," he said.

In his daughter, he recognized the Massah of his childhood.

"Greet your father, Sianeh," Massah said.

Sianeh held out a hesitant hand, her gaze lowered, in awe of the legend he had become. He embraced her. The fluttering butterfly had matured and was ready to take wings. Then he moved to Massah. He embraced her so hard that the crowd burst into laughter. The joy he detected in her eyes seemed like that of someone at peace with herself, as if the waiting had been worth it. He had come as promised.

Massah sat beside him under the flame tree, a sister to the kind he had planted in the Haidarah compound in Musadu. For the first time, he felt at ease with Massah.

They were, at last, a couple.

Zaiwulo turned to the people gathered around them. The many cousins, uncles, and aunts, including the elders and the king, seemed familiar but at the same time strangers to him. His nervousness heightened their unease. The years stood like a wall between them, insolent and unforgiving. Zaiwulo heaved a sigh of relief when Sianeh brought him a calabash of water and set it before him. What must he do to bridge the years between them so that his daughter could learn to know and understand him better?

Someone brought a beautifully carved wooden chair for his father who now approached, humming a tune. He danced before the crowd, swung around, and came to a halt. "My son is back! Now I can join the ancestors in peace," he said. "From now on, there will be someone here who will take over this home, who will be its head. I will retire in the shade of the trees of my home and pluck the fruit of the labor that's my son."

"You sound as if you will never do a day's job again," Aunt Kiabeh said and the crowd laughed. "Look at you!"

"Do a day's job, Kiabeh?" he said. "But Massah relieved me of that burden long ago. You all know that thanks to her, I sleep in a bed she bought from those wigis in Monrovia who came from across the sea. She made me a wealthy man long before my son's arrival."

"Yes, she did," Aunt Kiabeh said.

"Your hair is all gray, my son," Zaiwulo's father said. "What worries do you carry in your head? Tell me."

Zaiwulo took a long swig of water. It was sweet, like the scent of stone and wood, like the scent of the flame tree under which he sat. "I will tell you in good time, Father, but where is Mother?"

His father hesitated for a while.

"Your mother died a week after you and I left for Musadu," he said. "When you told me how she rescued you from drowning in the Jon River, I did not go to see your teacher Talata, because I knew you were telling me the truth. Your mother reached out from the ancestral world to save you."

Tears glazed Zaiwulo's vision. He had come so close to finding the truth only to have it snatched away from him. More than anyone else in Haindi, his mother was the one person he could rely on to tell him the truth.

Zaiwulo fell silent. He would not talk. Soon, the crowd petered out.

Many had expected Zaiwulo to share his heroic exploits, to confirm the stories they had heard about him single-handedly wiping out battalions of French and English armies. They wanted him to say that he spoke the white people's language perfectly and had been to their countries. They waited to confirm that he was a great scholar, a Karamo, like his teacher Talata.

Night met him still sitting under the flame tree.

3

Massah waited in bed for Zaiwulo. She had taken a bath and rubbed her body with oil sprinkled with musk. Earlier that evening, she had asked her daughter to leave the house. "From now on, your father and I will sleep here," she had said. Sianeh had obeyed.

Alone, Massah had regarded her body in the light of the hurricane lamp. She looked at her arms, her stomach, her legs and wondered if she was capable of bearing his weight? Would her arms sustain him and her breasts withstand the pressure of his body? Somewhere along the path life had carved out for her, she had lost her youth and some of her looks, but her hunger for Zaiwulo was soon to be sated. The thought of having him every night for the rest of her life made her press her waist-cloth between her thighs so hard that she moaned. Massah turned in bed over and over again, waiting to hear his footsteps approaching the house, waiting for certainty.

"Daughter, your husband refuses to retire to bed," she heard her father-in-law Kollie say. "You two can put up in my house. It is bigger."

Massah sat up, wondering what troubled Zaiwulo. She had thought that their ordeal was finally over. She was in a daze when he held her in his arms, this man who was once a boy, then a young man with authority, and now a hero to so many. Her Zaiwulo.

Massah left the house with the hurricane lamp she had bought in Monrovia, where she traded with the Liberians. More than twenty people were in her employment, farming for her, hawking her goods in villages and towns along the route to the coast. She bought teak wood, palm oil, tapped rubber, and other goods which she sold in Monrovia to Liberians and white traders who frequented the coast. She had rebuilt her father-in-law's house and bought him a king-size bed when he had begun to complain of backache. She had found her place in the forest amongst its people. "I will talk to him, Father," she said.

The old man reached out with his hand and touched her. "You are truly my son's wife, a daughter to be proud of," he said.

Massah walked to the flame tree under which Zaiwulo sat. "Your father tells me that you don't want to go to sleep, but you must be exhausted after such a long journey. Come to bed."

Zaiwulo did not respond.

"Your daughter is attending the school which the white missionaries have opened here, the first of its kind in the forest. I insisted on it, for I've seen the world around me change. I've seen you change."

Only then did Zaiwulo clear his throat to acknowledge her. He had dreamed of educating his daughter himself. He would teach her everything he knew. He would teach her to write her own stories and those of her people, both in the savannah and the forest. His absence in her life had nagged at him.

"You've taken good care of her, Massah," he said. "Had the wars not separated us for so long, I would have taught her myself."

"She has your eyes, Zaiwulo. Those eyes," she said, laughing now, moving closer to him. "Every time I looked at her, I saw you in her."

"But she has your face, your beauty. She looks like you!"

"Come to bed."

"My beginning is here, Massah, but I know nothing about it. I know nothing about the circumstance of my birth and why I was sent to Musadu."

"You've only just arrived. Give the old man some time and he will tell you everything you need to know. There's no haste."

"I need to know now. I've waited all my life for this moment."

"Listen, Zaiwulo. When I came here, your people accepted me as one of them. I could have joined sister Sona who's in a village here in the forest. Haidarah is buried there. Yes, your teacher has passed on."

"When did this happen?"

"I don't know exactly. People flock to his shrine with wishes and hopes which they believe come true. He's regarded as a holy man."

"So my teacher is gone," Zaiwulo said and fell silent for a while. He then stood up and strolled to Massah. "I will visit his grave as soon as possible."

"What I am trying to say is that I waited for you so we could be husband and wife. Don't do anything to separate us again."

Massah did not go to her father-in-law's house, despite his insistence. Instead, she chose the one she had shared with his daughter. She was restless. She turned around in bed. If he fails to come, I will leave him, I swear it, she told herself.

Soon, Massah heard his footsteps.

She held her breath as he entered. It was dark in the house. Her heart lurched when she heard his clothes fall to the floor. Then she felt him bend over her, his hard breath on her. His touch sent a tremor through her, a powerful shudder that rushed from her toes up to her head. She trembled. "Zaiwulo," she whispered, "what's happening to me?"

Zaiwulo held Massah tight to calm her, to wait for her body to rest, to prepare to receive him. But her body was still in the throes of his first touch when, all of a sudden, she felt as if she was being lifted off her feet and flung into oblivion. Fear of losing control of her bladder gripped her, but all her attempts at bringing some kind of mastery over herself failed. She never thought it possible that she could be at the mercy of a force beyond her control. As she ascended improbable heights and plunged into deep abysses, she searched for something to hold onto and found his back, around which she wrapped her legs and arms. She sank her fingernails in his back in an attempt to draw him into her world. She found that she could rise to his every effort, that she could compensate his every move with the singular need to be one with him. She would not let go of him even after he had rested his head on her chest, spent.

She held him tighter and tighter.

4

Massah slept deeply and peacefully. Her soft breath rose and fell against his neck. Zaiwulo marveled at the hunger with which they had fed on each other. The fact that a woman he had longed for so long was now with him—her head resting on his chest, a human being with a history and a bond that went beyond mere physical need, excited and terrified him. He felt the shape of her body against his own, her feet, her toes close to his own, sending a titillating sensation through him every time she moved. It would have made everything inconsequential but for the reason that he had returned to Haindi. He had to know.

Gingerly, so as not to awaken her, Zaiwulo slipped out of Massah's arms. He threw on his garment and left the house to see his father. In the early dawn of light, he could see his father sitting under the flame tree, munching a kola nut.

"I couldn't sleep," old Kollie said.

"I couldn't either, Father. Something troubles me."

"You've just arrived. We have enough time to talk, but not now. I'm overwhelmed by joy. Let's talk about your conquests, about your life in those lands."

"I've waited for too long. I need to know, Father."

"What if it were to hurt you and me? I made mistakes that still haunt me. Be wise and wait for the appropriate time for me to explain."

"Your pain is not as terrible as that of an abandoned child."

"I thought you were wise, my son."

"Why did you leave me alone in Musadu?"

"Do you realize what you are doing?"

"Why did you sell me into slavery?"

"Sell you into slavery? That disgusting word? You dare utter that horrible word in my presence? You dare accuse me of such an act?"

The old man's distressed voice awoke Massah. She realized that Zaiwulo was not with her. But what was her father-in-law so upset about? And where was Zaiwulo?

"No, you will not stay in this house," she heard the old man say. "You will leave immediately, Zaiwulo. How dare you humiliate me?"

Massah sat up in bed.

"Me, your father, sell you into slavery? Who do you think I am?"

Massah rushed out of the house, upset with Zaiwulo for being the cause of the old man's sorrow. She would never forgive him for disturbing her peace of mind. She would leave him and take their daughter along with her. Perhaps, he did not deserve her love. If he did, he wouldn't have angered his father. He would have listened to her.

By then the compound had awoken. Family members gathered around the old man. Kollie was saying that he had been dishonored by a son he'd hoped to see one day. "There's a stranger in my house, people of Haindi. I don't know him. Make him leave. He does not belong to us. He is not a Kpelle. He's not part of this family. He's not my blood!"

"Don't say that Kollie. He's speaking as a child," Aunt Kiabeh said.

"Why is he still sitting under my tree, in my house, laughing at me?" Kollie turned to Aunt Kiabeh. "You say he's a child but look at the gray in his hair. He returned to disgrace me."

The old man tore away from Kiabeh who tried to restrain him.

"No, not even a child would ask such a question. I wish his mother was alive to answer that question. I never expected my blood to ask such a question? I, Kollie, sell my son into slavery?"

"Sell him into slavery! Did he say that?" Aunt Kiabeh wailed.

"Yes, that's what he said," Kollie said.

"Then he's completely lost his mind," Aunt Kiabeh said. "If that's what he thinks of us, then he should leave Haindi. Yes, let him leave. He's not one of us. Leave, Zaiwulo. We don't trade in people like others do, and you accuse your father of such a crime?"

She flung herself at Zaiwulo who stood morbid, not responding to the blows and the anger of the women pouring down on him. Though the accusation that he had been sold into slavery had hurt his father, Zaiwulo felt there was something more to his father's rage. Perhaps the unease with the past had triggered it, and his father's inability to deal with it had inflamed the anger.

Zaiwulo had not reckoned on Massah's reaction. She fell on the ground and rolled in the dust. "No, Aunt Kiabeh. Before he leaves, I will leave him first."

A group of women gathered around Massah, trying to calm her. Another group focused on Kollie. "He did not mean it, Kollie," they said. "All those wars must have affected him. He's not himself. You have to forgive him, be glad that he's here. He will set things right. You don't need to worry. We will lay him out in the dust, before the people of Haindi, and we will ask you to give him fifty lashes. What are we saying? A hundred lashes. If you don't have the heart to do so because he's your son, then we will do it, because, by insulting you, he insulted us all, we the people of Haindi and the whole Kpelleland. It doesn't matter that he's a great warrior, that he fought the white wigis and defeated them. We don't care if he's educated in the ways of the white wigis or that he's a scholar, a Karamo. To us, he remains a child, our child who has dared to spit in our faces. He must be punished."

Massah rushed back to the house to prepare for her departure. "We are leaving, Sianeh. We don't belong here." Massah fetched some of her clothes piled up in a wooden valise in a corner of the room. "If your father stops being a child, then he knows where to find us."

Sianeh, who stood at the door, did not move. "We have to stay and help him, Mother."

"Help him with what?" Massah stared at her daughter.

"The wars must have affected him."

"Pack your things, I say. We are leaving right now for Musadu," Massah said.

"I want to stay with my father," Sianeh answered.

"Your father? Since when did he become your father? He was never a father to you, Sianeh. He's a stranger who's yet to learn how to be a father."

Outside, Zaiwulo managed to tear away from the women and approach his father. At first, the old man was reluctant to receive him.

"I was wrong, Father," Zaiwulo said. "Please forgive me. I will never doubt your intentions again. I don't want to talk about the past anymore."

"Listen, we can talk about the past. But for a long time, I'd given up the hope of ever seeing you again. I was not prepared for your arrival or your questions. One day, I will tell you everything."

"That's what I want. Thank you."

"We don't trade in humans here, my son, that's why your accusation pained me so much. That's why your words hurt me. We parents always try to spare our children pain and suffering by not telling them everything. I thought that you were too young to know about my decision to take you to Musadu. Perhaps, I should have told you everything."

Falling to his knees before his father, his hands touching his father's feet, Zaiwulo begged the elderly man. Kollie was touched by the sight of his son curled at his feet, and he touched his head to forgive him, to bless him.

"Stand up, child," he said. "Go to your wife. Don't let her leave."

Zaiwulo ran to Massah who was surrounded by women trying to stop her from leaving. They made space for him. She was covered in dust.

"I will never hurt you again, Massah," he said.

Massah stood her ground. It was time for him to fight for her.

"We will stretch him out in the dust," one of the aunts said. "Yes, we will punish him for angering a good woman."

"Lie down, child, get rid of those clothes," Aunt Kiabeh said.

Zaiwulo threw off his tunic, and the women burst into laughter.

"This is no laughing matter, people. Lie down, I say." Aunt Kiabeh said.

Zaiwulo knelt before Massah, touching her feet. He stretched out in the dust before her. One of the aunts gave her a cane. “Beat him, daughter,” she insisted. “Beat him.”

The crowd was laughing so hard that some people grabbed their stomachs to get hold of themselves. It infuriated Massah.

“Shut up, all of you,” Aunt Kiabeh said. “If you offend our daughter, Zaiwulo, you get a beating. Now, daughter of Haindi, here’s your chance. Whip him and teach him a lesson. Yes, he will learn.”

Massah was so upset that she snatched the cane from Aunt Kiabeh and lifted it with the intention of hauling it at Zaiwulo. But when she gazed at him, he looked so vulnerable, lying in the dust and at her mercy. She knew that she could not beat or leave a man with whom her past and future were so entwined.

Massah dropped the cane.

Haindi heaved a sigh of relief.

5

The villagers asked Zaiwulo and his family to wait at the gate for a proper reception. The three had come to visit Talata's tomb. "You are Haidarah's student," the chief said. "He talked about you all the time. You are no stranger to us. No, we will receive you like one of our own."

Massah and Sianeh sat on a fallen tree trunk. Behind them, a river covered in a canopy of tree branches. Its presence detected only by the whispers of its coursing water.

Mother and daughter watched Zaiwulo move around, inspecting the village walls. Curiosity had become a habit to him, acquired from his sofa years. But, to Massah, Zaiwulo seemed a different man as he went on searching the walls, poking his fingers into parts of the wood. Moving to and fro along the walls, he was so intent on his goal that her fears returned.

She had gotten used to his presence around her, to his leadership in Haindi, and to his helping their daughter with her lessons. The routine that crept into every relationship had soon set in, and she had welcomed it, for it made what the two of them shared normal in the eyes of others. Now, once again, she was seeing the man whose outlandish exploits, whose war stories and victories reached her, even in the forest.

The architecture of the wall fascinated Zaiwulo, and the tall giant trunks closely knitted together were impressive. The wall looked formidable from the distance. It was meant to deter the enemy but not a Samorian sofa out to conquer, who would have found those soft spots in the wood, broken through them, and descended on the village. The chaos that would have ensued at the sight of him on a warhorse would have resulted in victory.

"We are going to wash and prepare for the reception," Massah said, causing Zaiwulo to snap out of his reverie. "Don't come around until we are done."

Zaiwulo turned to her with a smile.

He is back, Massah thought.

The atavistic silence of the forest reminded Zaiwulo of the recent conversation he'd had with his father regarding his origins.

One evening, his father sat him down under the flame tree. "Your mother and I did what we thought was best for you," said his father. "But the decision to send you to Musadu hurt her much more. Our land had heard of this great miracle worker, a man to whom kings bowed, your teacher Haidarah. We asked for his help to protect us against our enemies. We had sacrificed everything to be at peace with our neighbors, but it was in vain. So, we turned to him. He came and our king asked me to lodge him on behalf of our people. Your mother cooked and cared for him. She was so anxious to have a child that she was up at cockcrow to warm his bath. She laughed at his jokes, preferred his words to mine, and was at his beck and call. She was convinced that he was capable of giving us a child by the power of his prayers. Jealousy began to eat away at my peace of mind. I was often in the dark regarding the two of them. Indeed, Haidarah seemed to confirm my suspicions by consulting her on many issues concerning us. So when your mother's stomach began to swell with a child, with you, my son, on the day he was about to leave, I promised the scholar, that if the child was a boy, he would be his student. In truth, I was getting rid of you to spite your mother whom I suspected of betraying me. Of course, she was opposed to it. We kept putting off the promise, but fear of the consequences of breaking a promise to a man with your teacher's reputation forced us to act. We were afraid that he would turn against us as our enemies had done before he intervened. It was only when we arrived in Musadu that doubts began to assail me. Perhaps, I was being too hard on your mother, too hard on you. I shouldn't have taken you to a place so far away, but by then, it was too late."

Zaiwulo's father would say no more.

His explanation was inadequate, many questions remained unanswered, and though Zaiwulo needed his mother to fill in the gaps, he had been grateful for his father.

Now Zaiwulo waited. After Massah and Sianeh had washed in the river, Zaiwulo took a quick ablution and joined them. Soon he could hear the villagers dancing and singing to drumbeats and the rattling sound of gourds and drumbeats. One of the dancers faced the drummer, his gaze locked with him, daring him to catch the rhythm in the swift movements of his feet. The drummer burst into a frenzied beat which rose and fell to the prancing of the dancer. The dancer shook his head, mourning a lost youth when those arms and limbs drove a drummer mad with their skills.

Several women with tiny bells around their limbs pounded the ground with their feet. They swung around and came to a sudden halt. They parted into two groups, making way for one of them. This woman edged forward, her steps calculated while the drum throbbed to her every move. When she lifted her head and faced him, Zaiwulo's heart skipped a beat. It was Naminata. He rushed toward her and threw his arms around her. She held his hand tight.

"I will never let you out of my sight again, Zaiwulo," she said.

Followed by the villagers, Naminata walked hand in hand with him to Talata's tomb. The tomb was covered with white sand. A slender tree draped in luscious greenery towered above it. Other trees in the vicinity stood as tall as a sofa after a victory.

Zaiwulo knelt, scooped up a handful of sand, and rubbed it on his face. He whispered a prayer, stood up, and turned to the crowd. He saw Sona, Talata's widow, wearing a benevolent smile, despite the solemnity of the moment. Time seemed to have spared her, her forehead was still smooth.

Zaiwulo walked up to her. "Ma-Sona, you made it. I thought that I would never see you again. It was Massah who told me about you."

"The news that Haidarah has passed on and that people were going on a pilgrimage to his shrine reached us not so long ago, Zaiwulo. I decided to leave with some women and girls for the forest. I met Naminata here. We all thought that she was mad but look at what she's become. She has more authority and respect than all of us. She's the key to the tomb."

Massah embraced Sona who held her tight, as if to make up for past wrongs. Exile had strengthened their bond. The past seemed forgotten.

"I was with Haidarah when he died, Zaiwulo," Naminata said. "After the attack on Musadu, I fled and found your teacher in Beyla, where he was hiding. With the Tareequ, I followed him to the forest. I stayed with Talata as his wife until he passed on. I did live, Zaiwulo. After his death, I asked the villagers to build a roof over his home to protect his work. You will see."

The villagers had indeed put up a roof over Talata's compound which consisted of two large houses covered with thick palm thatches. Beside the main house where Talata had slept and worked, there was a larger house that heaved under the weight of hundreds of manuscripts.

Talata had turned everything within reach into writing material: the walls of the house, the palm thatches, the pieces of cloth, the huge leaves which grew on the surface and alongside rivers, the hundreds of wooden slates. Even the mat before the door to his study was covered with writing. Zaiwulo paused before the door, leaned forward and lifted the mat. Even though it was covered in dust, he could read the writing.

"Whoever enters this house will be changed forever," it read.

Without hesitation, Zaiwulo stepped into the study. He sat cross-legged on the well-swept mat, beside a pile of manuscripts. On opening one of the books, he found that Talata had written about the village. After escaping Samori and the king of Bopolu who had become a thorn in his flesh, he thought that it was an ideal place.

Here, I've found the peace that has been denied me all my life, he wrote, *a place where no one, besides Naminata, knows me. A place where my status does not count, where my knowledge is secret to all. Here I will work on my legacy, on my manuscripts, until the end.*

The next manuscript was about Talata's children. The scholar wrote about their births and detailed their childhood, and he mentioned a rare moment when Osman saved Karamo from drowning in the Jon. According to Talata, Karamo was neglecting his gifts.

In Karamo, Talata wrote,

> *I see a reflection of my fears, the fear of the singular desire to be myself, not the person the world wants me to be. The fear of breaking away with everything, of ceasing to be a scholar, a husband, a father, the fear of being what I want to be, a bird free to take off and perch on the tree of its choice—those impossible cravings, more potent and alive in my son than in me, might end up destroying him. Perhaps, like me, he might not have the courage to escape them. Perhaps, he might end up confused and in limbo.*
>
> *Osman, on the other hand, knows no fear. Where others hesitate, stumble or fall, he presses on. He's very ambitious and knows what he wants, a unique characteristic in a human being. A hundred years after these words have been written, his descendants will still be prosperous.*

Talata's study was separated by a large curtain that was as dark as the one in his study in Musadu. Zaiwulo stood and drew the curtain aside.

Not knowing what awaited him, he was hesitant.

He froze when he saw the Haidarah Manuscript lying before him. It was neither hidden or covered up by other manuscripts nor was it adorned with gold or silver. Instead, it was bound in leather, as if it was a work of little importance.

Talata had simply left it lying on a mat in plain sight.

Zaiwulo sat crossed-legged before the manuscript. With great care, he flipped open the first page. It was brittle and almost falling apart. What he saw confounded him. The page was filled with numbers, not words. He turned to another page, and it was the same. There were numbers written in red, blue, brown, and yellow ink, but not with words. Everywhere he looked, there were only numbers and more numbers. Zaiwulo regretted now not having learned the art of transforming words into numbers and the other way round. He decided to browse through all the pages, including the recent ones which were written on cloth and leaves.

On one of the pages, Zaiwulo found a clue: his teacher had explained how to transform words into numbers and vice versa.

Zaiwulo went to work, and a new world began to open up before him.

On deciphering the content of the Haidarah Manuscript, a cry escaped him. The most recent page of the manuscript began as follows:

Zaiwulo came from the forest to Musadu carrying a fiery red tree.

He was silent for a long while, stunned, flabbergasted. Nothing had prepared him for this revelation. Parts of the Haidarah Manuscript were about his life. This was what made the book so precious.

In the Haidarah Manuscript, one came face to face with one's past and future as imagined by the custodian of the manuscript, who, in doing so, was displaying the power of words. As Zaiwulo read on, he realized then that he was the custodian of the Haidarah Manuscript. Events such as his fights with Osman and his attempts to reconcile Sona with

Talata were drawn vividly on the pages, even those events done in secret. Talata had written about him as if Zaiwulo the reader and the Zaiwulo of the manuscript were the same person, which, in fact, they were.

Talata had composed a mirror to his life. Except for some inner conflicts, which he had struggled with first as a child in Musadu and then as scholar and sofa, and other minute details about battles won or lost, the work was accurate. Even those aspects of his life as a Samorian sofa were not excluded. He read about his love for Massah and about the child that was the result of that love, his Sianeh. As he went on deciphering the pages, Zaiwulo could only conclude that his teacher was either a great seer or a gifted storyteller, or both. If the written word could be a mirror to life, what was his teacher trying to tell him? That he had the choice to escape his life as written in the manuscript and was able to make other choices, or that he could not escape that world, no matter how much he tried?

Zaiwulo went on reading about a future in which he set out for Monrovia, the Liberian capital, after raising an army of more than twenty thousand men.

The decision to raise an army came about when Zaiwulo heard that the French, the English, and the Liberians were dividing the lands that once belonged to the Samorian Empire, Talata wrote.

> *Zaiwulo goes to the new boundaries. There, he meets Osman. He is one of the few Black officials in a group of white French and Englishmen and nearly a hundred black soldiers. Osman wears a khaki uniform with an English insignia.*
>
> *"So, we meet again," Osman says.*

"You lied to the Faama," Zaiwulo answers. "You convinced him to refuse Garrett's help. What did the English promise you?"

Osman laughs. "Garrett was a hopeless case. He thought, like Samori, that he could bring down the biggest empire in the world with money earned within that empire. I learned in England that life was a game in which only those who knew how to play it well had any chance of survival."

The two are in a town whose oldest man refuses to budge to the French, English, and Liberian surveyors. And when the French and English soldiers threaten to arrest him, he climbs a tree and says: "Take your land and replace it with the land of my ancestors. That's the land I want to live on. That's the land to which I belong." The soldiers laugh, but the old man insists, "You claim that this land is yours, then give me back my land. I will remain in the tree until you bring back my land."

Zaiwulo can do nothing, for he's without an army. His anger turns to helpless frustration as he watches the old man being carted off and thrown in a house that serves as a prison and is guarded by ten armed men.

"Do you want to be like that stupid old man?" Osman says. "If you don't accept the new reality, you will end up just like him."

"Why are you siding with them, Osman?"

Osman answers without hesitation. "I am trying to play the game. You should do the same. I always knew that I would emerge the winner in the end. I was the one who revealed your secret. When I told everyone about you and Massah, I thought it would be the end of you. I thought Samori would hunt you down and cut you into pieces, but

I was wrong. The emperor had changed. He had grown mellow with age. No wonder he believed me instead of you regarding Garrett. The Englishman really wanted to help him. Do you know that he was arrested and accused of betraying England? That's what happens if you don't play the game or if you don't know the rules, Zaiwulo. While you were fighting, I was studying in England. They are a gullible people. Once you show them how passionate you are about their culture, they become as meek as lambs. The French are even worse. They begin to regard you as French. I won their trust by always appearing to please them. All I need right now to make me emperor of all the lands Samori once ruled and more is the Haidarah Manuscript. Then everyone will bow to me."

"You will never lay hands on that manuscript because you don't deserve it, Osman. You never deserved it," Zaiwulo says.

"Who can stop me? In a few years, the borders will be permanent and those who will matter in the new world will be people like me. How will you confront me then? Tell me, with spears, arrows, and brute force?"

"I will raise an army mightier than any Samori ever assembled, and when we confront each other, Osman, I will not hesitate to cut you down."

When Zaiwulo leaves Osman, he is determined to translate his words into action. It takes a while to assemble a much larger army, and then he leaves for Monrovia to convince the president of Liberia to join him in the fight. He stays with Karamo and Benjamin Anderson, who share the same compound.

Monrovia is a small city, and unlike the clay or mud homes of the savannah, the houses here are of wood. The streets and the roads are dusty and the houses stand far apart with a bunch of them clustered in some places. There are also some cresting hilltops to escape the morass below. The wood out of which the houses are constructed is old and dilapidated, but some of the wood is as hard as stone.

Karamo's wife, Rachel, attends to Zaiwulo as if he's a relative, a lost brother who's returned. She's so light in color, she could pass as white. She's worried that her husband might leave her. "I gave him everything," she says, "I turned my back on my family to be with him, but he doesn't want to fit in. He wants to return to Musadu. Please advise him otherwise."

Zaiwulo talks to Karamo who insists that he has to return to Musadu to run what has remained of the Haidarah household.

"It's time to go home, Zaiwulo," he says.

Zaiwulo shares his plans with him and Anderson.

Anderson shakes his head.

"Liberia simply doesn't have the power to fight the whites."

After a long stint in the government, Benjamin J. K. Anderson spends his time carpentering in a shed attached to the compound or teaching math at Liberia College. On his part, Karamo meets representatives of the different people living in the forest and along the coast. The people come to him seeking clarifications regarding their status within the new Liberia, and sometimes, he intervenes in disputes between the natives and settlers, or between themselves. The work occupies him day and night.

"Why don't you return to Massah and Sianeh?" Karamo says.

"I will return to them after this is over."

"But this will never be over," Karamo says.

Zaiwulo is adamant.

"Then I will take you to see President Barclay," Anderson says. "He's my friend, and I am his mentor. I taught him once at Liberia College."

The woodwork of the office of the president reminds Zaiwulo of the ancestral wood carvings in Haindi. Through the large windows drifts a sea-scented breeze and behind the president sits his whole cabinet, all of whom had heard of Zaiwulo's exploits against the French and the English.

The president, Arthur Barclay, is a tall, slender and soft-spoken man. He exudes an air of stability. In a land plagued by a fragile history whose narrative thread is so delicate that a mere push is bound to set her off course, he has managed to elevate himself into an envious position.

Zaiwulo speaks in halting English which he had learned to prepare for this moment, but there's no hesitation in his voice.

He begins with his years in Musadu and how he came to serve Samori. Then he detailed his sojourn in Saint-Louis, among the French. He quotes writers and philosophers to illustrate his decision to fight for freedom. "We have to fight together," he tells the president. "You cannot continue to appease the English and the French. One day, things are bound to change."

President Barclay realizes that he's dealing with a rare specimen, with a man who, like him, knows exactly what he wants from life.

"It is because we are vulnerable that we need to be shrewd," he says. "We cannot defeat those two powers. And you alone cannot fight them."

"Thousands of people from the forest and the savannah want to fight alongside me," Zaiwulo says. "Do you know how the English and the French treat our people? They force them to work day and night without pay and charge our people taxes on their homes in exchange for nothing. With your help, it will be possible to defeat them. All we need are weapons. I know your land was founded on the principle of freedom. That's why I'm here."

"Times have changed," the president says.

He comes from behind the table and walks up to Zaiwulo.

"Those people you say are devoted to the cause now belong to Liberia, England, and France. The boundaries have been drawn."

"But I don't recognize those boundaries."

Benjamin Anderson joins in. "Your Excellency, as you know, the French don't believe I ever visited Musadu and other cities in Koniyan, not to mention Kankan. I was against the drawing up of the boundaries in the first place. I did everything to persuade your predecessors to work together with Samori, but in vain."

"My dear Benjamin, my mentor, you are a worthy citizen of this country. Do you expect us to fight the French and English over boundaries?"

"So you will not help us," Zaiwulo says.

"Even if I had the means, I wouldn't do it. It's time to stop fighting and accept the inevitable. We are surrounded by the English and the French. Samori has surrendered to the French, even though rumors have reached us that he

was not even captured, that he's waiting somewhere in the forest for the right moment to reappear. It's in the papers—Samori died in the French Gabon. He's no more. So it's time to stop."

"I gave Samori my word to fight on."

"Join us to build this country. You are an intelligent man," the president says. He turns to Karamo. "Talk to him, Karamo, you've known him since childhood. Persuade him to join us."

"I've already tried, Your Excellency."

"If I leave Monrovia, Mr. President," Zaiwulo says,"'it will be to lead my men across the savannah."

The amicable Barclay turns to his cabinet, and his voice is sharp now. "I warn you not to endanger Liberia. If the French and the English were to complain about you, I will be forced to take their side."

"So be it, Mr. President," Zaiwulo says.

Zaiwulo leaves the president's office. That same day he returns to the forest. Some months later, on a sultry, dry seasonal day, Zaiwulo marches out with his army toward the savannah. They arrive at a point where the forest begins to peter out into a verdant green of low savannah grass.

In the distance, Zaiwulo and his men see a man astride a horse.

The horseman is Samori.

Zaiwulo closed the Haidarah Manuscript. He didn't want to go on reading or to peer deeper into the future. He didn't want to know. He thought of his wife and daughter who were now waiting for him outside, hoping he would emerge unscathed and lead a predictable life with them. He thought of Sona and Naminata. He thought of his sisters and his father. He could not imagine a life without them, and because he could not envision a future in which his people, including Massah and Sianeh, were not free, Zaiwulo found himself at a crossroads, torn between two equally important choices, each pulling hard at him. He put down the Haidarah Manuscript and left the house.

About the author

Vamba Sherif is a novelist, essayist, speaker, book and film critic. He's a lecturer in African Literature at Leiden University. His work has appeared in many languages, including Dutch, English, French, German, Spanish, Polish, and the Indian Malayalam. He has also published essays, stories, film reviews, columns and opinion pieces in *The New York Times*, the German *Kulturaustausch*, *African Writing*, *Trouw*, *Volkskrant*, *NRC* and *ZAM-Magazine*, among many others. With Ebissé Rouw, he compiled *Black: Afro-European literature in the Netherlands and Belgium*, a unique anthology of Afro-European experience in the Low Countries. About his work the German newspaper Berliner Zeitung wrote: 'Vamba Sherif creates whirlpools of Shakespearean intensity.'